Aberjay Rising

A Tale of Courage

Joseph Michael Lamb

Zero Bubble Press

Contact the author at josephmichaellamb.com

Zero Bubble Press
Alpharetta, GA 30004

First Zero Bubble Press edition: August 2023

ISBN: 978-1-961354-01-2 (Paperback Edition)

ISBN: 978-1-961354-00-5 (Ebook Edition)

ISBN: 978-1-961354-02-9 (Hardback Edition)

Editor: Bob Cooper (Bob-Cooper.com)

Cover Art by: MIBLart.com

This book is dedicated to my sister Ashleigh Lamb and all Asian-Americans who face each day with courage.

Chapter 1

THE WALL

Leena dug her hands deep into the topsoil. It was a deep black charcoal color. She loved to feel the dirt between her fingers, even when she was wearing gloves. The color came from the fertilizer. It was not available to residents in this zone, requiring her to make her own. She used a recipe her family developed decades ago. The fragrance was evidence of manure as a chief component. This added ingredient was the reason the garden grew some of the best produce in the area.

The wind was cold and blew against her cheek. The moist air froze instantly, and Leena wiped her face with her arm. The rooftop garden was a solitary place to grow food, but the height certainly made it more difficult in the winter. She was thankful for the damp conditions though. Gardens don't grow without water.

She had tended this garden almost every day of her life, as far back as she could remember. Her surviving family, just her and her mother, had lived in this building for more than twenty years. Tending the garden, as well as working at the family's fabric store, was a family tradition when she was growing up. Now it was her only means of survival since the store was gone.

Feeling confident the soil was well-mixed and ready for planting, Leena moved to a small bench. She knocked the fertilizer off her boots and shuffled some germinating pots around to make a little more room. She felt ownership of the garden because she spent so much time there.

She caught a scent of snow in the air, which made her pause and gaze at the distant clouds. Her eyes were drawn north of her building as she removed her gloves, slowly rubbing her fingers—first to bring feeling back, as they were numb from the cold, and second to rub clear remnants of dirt that had penetrated her porous gloves. She knew the fertilizer contained manure, and she didn't want to carry it around on her hands for the rest of the day.

The garden was on the top of her building, eight floors up. The rooftop location provided a view of the north wall. Her building was only a few blocks inside the wall that separated her zone from the Aberjay. The wall was strong and unwavering, made from cold steel and rough stone. Even though the wall was constructed before she was born, she had seen it being repaired enough times to know its components. Towering about sixty feet high, it was taller than most buildings in that part of the city. The city once had towering skyscrapers and was the largest of the southern cities, but war had destroyed them some time ago. It used to have a name, but no one used it anymore. This was Zone 6.

Leena moved to the table and grabbed a basket and a cutting tool. It was *first frost*—time to harvest some leafy greens. She learned to garden from her mother, who taught her not only the planting schedules of each vegetable but the scent that each one put out when they were ready to be harvested. She could sense the collards most of all, she thought. Or maybe that was just because those were her favorite.

The garden spanned the entire rooftop and was community-managed. Each tenant had their own area. Most tenants were good at managing their section, but when they were lax or unable to manage it, Leena always stepped in to help. She found solace in the garden as it distracted her from her mother's health.

The building was communal, so they lived as a group, agreeing to share resources. This was how the Miniyar survived. The garden atop the building provided food to eat, and when there was a surplus, a product to sell at the market. The market was always open if there were people to manage the booths, but food was not always available for sale. Traders imported food from other areas. The consistency of deliveries to the zone was unpredictable. A shipment into the market could be every few days, but often, especially during the winter, the market could be empty for weeks at a time. Proper food planning was essential.

Leena began hacking at the base of the greens. Collard greens were her favorite, but there were also mustard greens, chard, some cabbages, and kale to retrieve. The garden was a year-round effort as it was the primary means of food for the building. Once the basket was full, she grabbed another and continued. It was quiet on the roof. She thought that maybe this was why she enjoyed the work so much. Or maybe it was a distraction from her worries.

Leena's mother Mei was born out west after the last Great War in the late twenty-first century. She migrated to the east coast in her teens after the rising temperatures in the west and the lack of water made living practically impossible. The Chinese renamed the area the Federated States of China shortly after the U.S. signed the peace treaty. It included California, Oregon, Washington, Nevada, and parts of Arizona.

Mei contracted an infection that destroyed her kidneys about eight years ago at thirty-eight. Leena was only eleven at the time, but she remembered her mother winning a medical lottery that allowed her to have a transplant. She was grateful for the transplant, but years of sacrificing meals for her children and drinking contaminated water had put her back into the position of needing a new kidney. Leena hated thinking about what would come next. No one wins the transplant lottery twice.

Leena took the greens she had harvested to the wash station. Water was so scarce; she did not wash them anymore. The only water source was rainwater collection, but it didn't rain enough to waste it. For now, they had to settle for a small, hard, bristled brush to sweep the dirt from the leaves. She placed each leaf carefully on the table, brushing away the dirt without damaging the leaf. She finished one basket and then grabbed the other.

As she stacked the big green leaves, she thought about what her life might be like once her mother was gone. She had Diego, but he was aging himself and would not be around for that many more years. The weight of it was daunting.

Leena cried at the thought of losing her mother. Her mom figured there wasn't much left to do and had given up. Leena felt her mom's emotional battle in her stomach. A sick feeling of dread that brought physical nausea. But what could she do? She had no credit to buy medication even if she could get her hands on some. Knowing that the medication her mother needed to live was right on the other side of that wall made her angry. She clenched her fists and grew sick thinking of how unfair it was that someone so gentle and innocent had to die because the world had deemed her not worth saving.

The door to the roof swung fast and struck the wall behind it, making a loud noise that startled Leena. It was Claire coming to tend her part of the garden. Claire also lived in the building and managed her part of the garden with a precision and order that made Leena believe she may have had military training. She liked Claire, but her heavy-handedness always kept people on edge around her. And if she caught you in the stairwell, you were likely to be there for a while. Claire loved to talk.

Leena moved back to mixing the topsoil, this time choosing a hoe rather than getting her hands soiled again. A dark cloud had rolled in, but no rain was in sight. Diego was already at the market with some vegetables she had picked the previous day, so she completed her task and hurried off the roof with a basket in each hand. She moved swiftly down the stairs, in part because she was in a hurry to get to the market to see Diego but also because she feared Claire might be on her heels and stop her for some long-winded conversation.

Leena stopped on the third floor and pushed open the door to her apartment. There was a scant odor of breakfast she had cooked earlier. Leena thought the smells were important. Living in such a drab place could be depressing, so she always tried to have something that brought a fragrance to counter the sight of the dwelling. Flowers, dried mushrooms, or perfumes if she could find them were always a hit in her mind. Plus, she figured that mom never left the room, so she needed variety.

"Hi Mom," she said in the most positive tone she could muster as she lay the baskets on the ground by the door.

Mei replied, "How's the harvest?"

Their apartment was once a nice place to live, with two bedrooms, a single bathroom, a large living area, and a kitchen. The original building was a luxurious apartment, but war had left the structure practically uninhabitable. The stability of the building was questionable, but the residents faced greater challenges to their survival. It differed from the modern buildings that were designed for the masses with their micro-apartments and communal areas. Because they were more than a century old, the rooms were large, as were the hallways and stairwells. That was where the luxury ended, however; lack of proper care had taken its toll. The walls were peeling, and many of the stairs were cracked or missing altogether. Caution tape, duct tape, or rope had replaced handrails in many areas.

"The harvest is good today. I am going to head to the market to meet Diego but wanted to stop by on my way and make sure you have everything you need," Leena said to her mother as she moved closer to her bedside and positioned a pillow behind her head to make her more comfortable.

The bed she lay in used to be in a hospital, and the head section inclined to help with positioning. The buttons had ceased to function, and the metal components were full of rust. The bed sat by the window in the living room. Leena and her mother no longer use the bedrooms as water had crept in and softened the walls over the years. Somehow, the rain made it to this little apartment on the third floor and missed the five floors above it. It was a mystery that they had yet to figure out as building maintenance professionals were nearly extinct in this zone.

Mei acknowledged Leena's good news and thanked her without words for moving her pillow, then closed her eyes to continue resting. Her breathing was shallow, and her face was pale.

Leena carefully cut up several of the carrots and celery stalks from a previous harvest, smeared a plate with a little peanut butter, and placed it next to Mei's bed so she could easily reach it when she woke later. She gently shook her mom's water bottle to ensure she would have enough water to get down the plate of veggies. Grabbing the baskets of harvested goods, she continued out the door and down the stairs.

Her building was ten blocks from the market. She hurried along the streets, always mindful of her surroundings. While the streets at one time in the past were clear, that was no longer the case. Barriers of stacked vehicles were common—a remnant of a previous conflict. These boundaries made it difficult to use the sidewalk without cutting through abandoned stores or burned-out buildings.

Leena ducked under one stack of cars and turned a corner before having to take several steps up to walk a makeshift path that was just a wide board placed between two stacks of cars. She made it safely to the other side, and after a quick turn to avoid some debris, she was back on the straight path toward the market.

Her neighborhood was mostly safe. Colors signified the safety ratings of each area to keep people out of dangerous zones. Green zones were the safest. All of the Aberjay zones were green zones. The blue zones were next, then orange, yellow, and red. Leena's neighborhood, because of its proximity to the massive gate that separated her zone from Zone 7, was an orange area.

Leena passed several groups of homeless living in makeshift alley homes. She wondered how they stayed warm at night. It made her thankful for her apartment, even though she couldn't use all the rooms.

While Citizen Protection Units (CPU) kept crime low in the Aberjay zones, they rarely entered the Miniyar areas. There was enough of a presence near the gates though to keep crime far away from Leena's neighborhood. She was grateful for that but never felt that the CPU were present for her benefit. While their mantra implied the protection of all citizens, the CPU were more interested in protecting the Aberjay *from* the less desirable citizens than protecting everyone.

The streets were empty. It was cold, and the precipitation was just a haze. It was not really raining, just a light drizzle. Weather that makes you long for a bowl of hot soup. Most people stayed home on days like this. More than half the population was out of work, so they saved more money by staying at home. There had been no jobs since the creation of the MIRO program.

The Mechanically Intelligent Robotic Operators (MIRO) program created a fleet of artificial intelligence machines that could do any job a human could do. The idea was to give everyone the ability to use a MIRO to perform their job function and thus free up their time for loftier pursuits such as art, music, or working on scientific innovations. But the MIRO were expensive. Only the wealthy could afford them. As they put the MIRO to work in the factories, they realized that they no longer needed as many human workers. With every software update, they grew smarter and more capable. Most factories were now void of humans except for some ancillary positions that the MIRO had yet to master.

Leena walked by a boarded-up store and stopped for a moment, looking through the boards. She stopped to look every day. This was their old store. She worked there as a child, helping Mom turn fabric. When she behaved, mom would let her use the scissors to cut some of the scrap patterns into clothes for her dolls. For a moment, she thought that maybe that was the beginning of her keen fashion sense. Then she chuckled to herself as she stepped back and looked at herself in the mirror of the store window.

She wore old brown boots coated in fertilizer, baggy pants with holes in both knees, and a belt replete with staples. It was long and wrapped around her several times. Was it crafted for a horse? Her once-white cotton shirt was tight around her chest, way too short to cover her belly, and was no longer any color that resembled white. Her coat was an old brown leather bomber jacket that she believed once belonged to her dad. The only color she wore was a blue scarf she wrapped tight around her neck to keep it warm. Her hat was a well-worn leather pilot cap she found, used by Chinese flyers during the last Great War according to Diego. She had the goggles that went with the cap somewhere; she just could not remember where she left them. Her eyes turned to the reflection of baskets full of vegetables on the ground beside her. She grabbed the veggies and made her way toward the market.

The market lined one long street and filled one big open area, with booths fashioned out of whatever objects were available. Some were solid, but others looked like twine, and duct tape held them together. The weather had caused the traders' booths to dull and peel their bright colors of red, yellow, green, and blue.

Each seller was responsible for their own, so they used what they had on hand or what they could find in one of the many rummage piles in the neighborhood. There were more than a hundred booths, and it was not uncommon to see neighbors sell car parts, soap, or other non-food items. Bartering was quite common.

A volunteer group of neighbors kept the market secure. The small force was in sharp contrast to the heavy military presence of the CPU that roamed the Aberjay zone. Leena once considered volunteering for the market security detail but assumed they would prefer men, so she abandoned the idea. Her stature was small, and she didn't see herself as big, tough, or violent. She once found an enormous spider in their house and escorted it out with a magazine rather than end its life. She wrestled with the idea of dying. Making something else die just didn't seem right.

She had to walk past many booths before she could get to her friend Diego, who had already been there for a few hours. She had helped him make the booth of mostly old lumber retrieved from a section of dilapidated residential homes in the western part of the zone. She remembers the day they went to get them. Diego had borrowed a motor cart with a flatbed. They spent two hours pulling salvageable lumber out of burned-out homes in several of the scary abandoned neighborhoods. Although they built it together, the booth was there for the residents of her entire building to use when they chose.

Leena turned the corner and could see Diego completing a transaction. She smelled the stoves and campfires that were alight, helping people to stay warm. She caught a scent of fried okra that she loved. Occasionally, the wind would shift, and the stench of garbage or sewage would almost knock you over, but she didn't care. She loved the market with all its eccentricities.

Diego was short. Hispanic, she believed. His age was a mystery, but she guessed he was in his seventies. He was always full of stories from the distant past, so he must have been alive for a long time. He walked with a slight limp, and his back was no longer straight. He was already short, but the curve in his back made him hunch forward, reducing his stature to match Leena's, who was only five feet tall. His beard was short and gray, like his hair. He smelled of elderberry. It must have been the throat lozenges he always seemed to carry in his front right pocket. He would often offer one to Leena, but she always declined. She did not care for the taste.

She thought about her affection for Diego as she approached. He had been a father to her. She never knew her dad, so it was nice to have someone she knew she could count on. Diego lived in the same building, but he didn't need to. He was the father of Fernando Martinez, a city leader and advocate for Zone 6, responsible for the health and welfare of the zone. Diego could certainly live with his son, but he lived in our humble building. Leena was not sure why.

Leena slipped in quietly behind Diego and gave him a wink as she rounded the corner, conscious of the transaction he was involved in while gently unloading her vegetables onto the table and placing the baskets under the counter. The booth had skirting around the front that Leena had made with fabric scraps years ago. This gave them storage that was out of sight of those who would pass by and provided a space for Leena to take a nap on days when they were there for long hours.

Selma Jorgenson waved to Leena from the other side of the market. Selma was a kind woman with six children. She was always at the market. Rain or shine, she would be there. She sold a collection of items. Sometimes walnuts, while other times it was hand woven blankets or socks. With so many children to feed, she did whatever she could to make money. Leena politely waved back at her as she turned to wrangle one of her smaller children.

Leena thought back to her childhood in the market as Diego finished his conversation with a customer. She loved to read growing up and would often climb under the table and read for hours as her mom and Diego would sell vegetables. She didn't think about where their food and clothing came from in those days. Now that she was caring for her mother, the weight of the challenge felt surreal. She had to ensure they had food on their shelves, sold enough at the market to pay the bills, and that her mother had someone looking after her around the clock.

Diego completed his transaction and turned to Leena. "How is my Turnip today?" He called her Turnip because when she was a baby, Diego would give her pieces of turnip to chew on, and although bitter, she seemed to enjoy it. She didn't remember those treats but her mother was fond of telling the story.

"I am good," Leena responded. "I left lunch for Mom, so I can stay for a little while if you need to go do something else."

Diego walked slowly to a chair that was waiting for him. He turned and carefully sat down while making a small grunt that expressed the difficulty of the operation. Diego did not respond to the comment she made about him doing something else. Leena assumed he didn't have anything pressing. Diego rubbed his face and beard like a man attempting to wake up after a long nap and then stared at Leena for what seemed like several minutes.

"You are sad, Turnip. I can tell by your eyes. They give you away every time. Is it your mom?"

"No," Leena replied, then thought for a moment and said, "Yes, I mean, I think so." She composed herself, shifting her shirt that had become twisted by carrying the baskets. "I am sad about everything. Why does life have to be so hard? Why does mom have to be sick? Why can't I find a job? What is the point of it all?"

"Wow, that is a lot of questions," said Diego, trying hard not to answer them. He was sure she was not done yet.

Leena continued a little louder and with more anger. "Why doesn't it rain enough for people to live where they want? Why are there no clothing stores or grocery stores, or hardware stores here like there are in the other zones? Why is life not like the books I read? Why can't I find a job?" She paused for just a moment, realizing she said that already.

She took a small bite out of her lower lip and wiped her nose with her sleeve. Taking a breath, she continued in a quieter voice, "I don't know why life is so hard." Then she took a long pause, looking at the ground, and kicked at the broken pavement. "Why do people have to die?" She cried a little but tried to hold it in.

Diego waited to respond, giving her time to complete her thoughts. Then he motioned for her, as it would be too great a feat for him to stand and make his way to her side of the booth before she broke down. She responded quickly and ran into his arms, bending awkwardly as he sat in the chair. He held her as she wept into his chest so that no one would hear her. Diego ran his hand across the back of her head, soothing her.

"Your life is a gift, Leena," he said, purposely using her real name to show the seriousness of the conversation. "You must make the best of what you are given. As for your mom, we don't know how much time she has on this Earth, but we know the comfort and love we give her will make the time she has left more tolerable."

Leena wept on Diego's chest for a few minutes and then stood up and composed herself, walking back to her side of the booth. She looked up at the sky as if expecting to see answers to her questions or something that might take her away from all of it.

Diego stopped as a short Hispanic woman walked over to the table. Leena popped up quickly and held out the terminal to withdraw her funds. The customer swiped their bracelet across the terminal, and it rang out loudly in three high-pitched tones to announce the completion of the transaction. "Thank you," Leena said as she hurried off with a bunch of collard greens.

Leena heard a sound in the distance. It sounded like something exploded. She thought maybe it was a store being firebombed. The kids did that for fun. Within seconds, another sound emerged in the distance, as if slowly rising out of a fog. They were trucks. It was unusual to see vehicles in this part of town because of the old blockades that cut up the neighborhood like boulders in a stream. As they grew closer, she recognized the sound. They were CPU trucks.

Leena looked around and saw many of the street vendors closing their shops by pulling down barriers that allowed them to lock their humble huts when they went home at night. The CPU were rarely in the zone, so this incursion was evidence of trouble. She knew the trucks were close because she could hear their gears change as they navigated the barriers at the end of the street.

As she strained to hear the approaching vehicles, three shadowy figures came running past the booth. Two she did not recognize, but the other was an old schoolmate named Liv Zolenski. They were classmates in the ninth and tenth grades, but Liv was absent the following two years. The rumor was that she needed to care for her parents and work because her dad had broken his back falling from a building. Leena had lost touch with her during those years. They were never close as Liv was always very abrasive. She was crass and had a temper, so it was easier to avoid her than to befriend her.

She didn't look much different, although Leena had not seen her in years. Liv was tall and dressed in army fatigues that were mostly green with patches of brown. It was in stark contrast to her short, bright blonde hair. She had a thick black belt and some sort of knife or weapon in a holster. Her boots were black leather and worn, indicative of their secondhand nature. Liv's family was poor. Probably everything she ever had was from secondhand stores. Leena had never really thought about her ancestry but believed her to be Ukrainian.

Liv made momentary eye contact as she ran past. Leena was not sure if she recognized her, but one thing was for certain. If the CPU was chasing Liv, she was in serious trouble. She wondered what kind of life Liv must have to run from the authorities. And what would compel a person to risk their life in such a way? The CPU was strict on crime. Minor infractions could land you in prison for life.

Just after Liv and the others ran past the booth, the trucks turned the corner and stopped. She was accurate in her prediction. Two CPU trucks full of soldiers stopped just fifty feet from her position, and the men filed out of the trucks.

They were all dressed identically except for one, who looked like a supervisor. Dark-navy jumpsuits with wide, black utility belts held their weaponry. Their rifles and helmets were also black and glossy, which reflected the sun like a well-polished sword. Darkly-tinted visors covered their eyes. Leena knew from a field trip she once took to Zone 7 that the helmets contained technology that allowed the CPU soldiers to speak to one another, view health statistics, and keep track of their ammunition.

The soldiers left a couple of their numbers behind and ran past the booth in the direction that Liv traversed with her comrades only seconds earlier. Diego sat still and motioned for Leena to get down. He knew it was better not to engage.

The supervisor wore similar clothing but had a nicer helmet and four red stripes on his left arm. He moved toward their side of the street, peering into each booth to ensure no one was hiding. As he drew closer, Leena could read a nametag on his upper left chest that read *Sgt. McBride*.

He was a towering man with a clean-shaven face, strong features, and an expression that announced to the world that he was in a bad mood. He stepped right up to the front of the booth where Leena was crouched and leaned over the counter.

"Anyone hiding in here?" McBride asked with a sneer. Leena remained quiet and unconsciously stopped breathing. Diego spoke up and said, "It's just the two of us here, sir." McBride looked side to side in case he had missed something the first time and then turned to walk to the next booth.

Leena waited until he was about four booths away before she exhaled and began to breathe again. "Wow, that guy was scary,"

Leena said to Diego as he leaned over to look down the street to ensure he was gone.

"I don't know what he was after, but I am sure glad we did not have it," Diego said, making a joke.

Leena was too frightened to acknowledge the joke with laughter, so she just sat back down and began staring at the soldiers by the trucks, hoping they would stay where they were. She watched several neighbors who had closed their booths hurry by with their baskets of fruits and other wares. She could tell their pace was driven by fear as they pushed by her on bicycles, pedal carts, and anything that would get them out of the area fast.

Leena could see Sgt. McBride making his way from booth to booth. As he neared Selma's booth he stopped and leaned inside, much as he did in her own booth just moments before. Leena could not make out the dialogue, but voices were raised. Selma was pushing back on the intrusion and waving her arms around. Sgt. McBride lost any patience he might have had and reached inside to grab Selma with one hand, pulling her across the small table that separated them. He pulled her about ten feet while her feet dragged along the ground, struggling to make firm contact with the street so she could regain her footing. McBride let go of her and she fell to the ground. He placed a boot on her neck and bent over to shout in her face. Leena thought she could hear him taunting her and calling her names but could not quite make out the words. Moments later he walked away as if a sudden boredom overtook him.

Selma sat up, watching him walk away. She repositioned her flowered dress that had become twisted in the altercation and slowly rose to her feet and ran back to her children to comfort them. Leena wanted to run and help her, but she knew there was little she could do. The CPU did as they pleased, and any opposition was dealt with severely.

Within a few minutes, things seemed to de-escalate. The drizzle that was present all morning had waned, and the sun was peeking through the clouds. It was still cold, but Leena could feel the day beginning to warm and looked forward to drying out a little.

"Psst!" came a sound from behind her.

Leena looked around to her left and her right, but in her position, could not turn her head all the way around. She thought maybe she was hearing things.

"Psst!" The sound played again.

That time she knew it was not in her head, and she swung her body around to see Liv crouching behind her booth with her head poked slightly inside the two curtains that hung in the back to provide some privacy in the booth.

Leena looked at her, stunned, wondering what she could want from her. She knew the soldiers had been looking for her and her friends, but the gravity of what might happen to her if the CPU found her with Liv escaped her attention. Diego had yet to notice her or hear the snake sounds she made to get Leena's attention.

Liv mouthed something to Leena, but she could not make out what she said. She moved toward Liv to get closer, but Liv put up her hands, clearly expressing her desire that Leena stop so she wouldn't inadvertently give away her position. Liv put her hands over her head and made a gesture. Leena tried to interpret the gesture, but she looked like she was covering herself with an imaginary blanket. What could that mean?

Leena turned to the street and caught a strong odor of diesel fuel as the weight of her situation began to set in. She immediately knew what Liv needed and crouched low, out of sight of the two soldiers guarding the trucks. She sauntered to the back of the booth and grabbed Liv by the hand. Without eye contact, she dragged her toward the front.

Liv pulled back with great strength, almost yanking Leena off her feet as she had not expected it. Leena looked up from the ground and made the covering gesture that Liv had made earlier while mouthing the words, "I am trying to hide you." Liv then understood and helped her to her feet. She walked slowly to the front in a crouched position with Leena, staying under the radar.

Diego quickly understood the activity taking place behind him and in a hushed tone said, "Leena, no!"

Leena pushed Liv under the table at the front of the booth and pulled the fabric coverings she had made tightly together to shield her from view. She looked at Liv and put her finger to her lips to signal her to be quiet, but Liv was way ahead of her and knew what was at stake.

Leena sat back in her chair and began to sweat. She knew if the CPU caught them aiding a criminal, she would suffer severe consequences. She did not know why she was taking this risk. She always wanted to be liked in school. Maybe she was trying to undo some of the exclusion she felt in high school by this girl and a hundred others. Then she gained her faculties and determined the risk was too great. As she bent down to reveal the criminal and break the news, she heard the soldiers making their way back to her position.

Lenna closed the makeshift curtain and glanced at the soldiers to ensure they could not see Liv in her hiding place, then made her way back to her stool and crouched a bit in her chair to avoid suspicion. She heard the soldiers' approach and their radios beeping and clicking as other soldiers on the other end relayed their position and the status of their search. The soldiers marched past her booth, but just as she thought they were free from suspicion, Sgt. McBride popped his head into her booth a mere two feet from her face. Without saying a word and with a terrible grimace, he scanned the booth and then fixed his eyes straight on Leena. Her heart pounded in her chest. Her entire body felt warm as if she was wearing too many clothes. Sweat beads began forming on her brow. She tried desperately to hide her anxiety. Diego was also quiet, knowing they were in dire straits if the CPU discovered their ruse.

"What is your name, girl?" Sgt. McBride asked in a low, calming but insidious tone.

"Leena Zhen, sir," she replied.

"Are you a resident of Zone 6, Leena Zhen?" he continued.

"Yes sir," Leena said with barely enough air to get the words to leave her lips. She thought for sure that he knew she was hiding something. Why would he single her out? Why is he not asking Diego or someone at one of the other countless booths on this street?

Sgt. McBride looked away for a moment and then his eyes came back to Leena. "Did you see three young people come running through here? They are wanted for serious crimes."

Leena began to speak but then took a deep breath to ensure what she was going to say would not reveal her guilt. "I saw three people run by a few minutes ago. They were running from where the trucks are parked to the east side of the market."

"Did you see them come back?" McBride asked in a tone that made it clear he was getting agitated.

"No sir." Leena stopped short of any further comment, assuming that any more words she used would only aid in revealing her nervousness.

Just then a soldier came running up to McBride and said, "Team Four has spotted them in Sector Two, sir. They believe they are hiding in a warehouse." McBride shot another ominous look toward Leena and then Diego and turned and walked back to the truck, signaling his men to prepare to leave.

Within moments, the trucks sped away, and Leena breathed deeply, attempting to extricate the stress from her body. She was shivering. Diego moved closer and offered comfort, whispering, "You did good, Turnip. It's all over."

Liv crawled out from under the table, cautiously scanning all around to ensure no one could see her. "Thanks, kid," Liv said. "That was a close one."

Leena responded angrily but quietly in a hushed tone, "You had no right to put us in danger like that!" She worried that her boldness would set off some violent tendency within Liv that she had heard about through many stories at school, but Liv just shrugged it off like it was nothing.

"It's okay, kid, nothing happened. You made it through." She paused for a few moments and then, seeing that her exit was clear, looked back at Leena one last time and said, "Let me make it up to you. Come to my house tomorrow." And then she was gone as quickly as she had appeared.

The event had shaken Leena. The adrenaline coursing through her body made it challenging for her to calm down. She wondered what would happen to her mother if the CPU had arrested her. She just could not allow that to happen. She thought through the scenario and imagined Diego trying to take care of Mei or possibly Jordan, or some residents of her building, and quickly surmised that it would be disastrous if she were not around. She also wondered, *Why on Earth would Liv invite me to her house? And why did she call me "kid?" We're the same age.*

Leena knew she did not have the time to think through this anymore. She was certain she would never go to Liv's house; she had many more important things to do. Leena gave Diego a quick hug and said, "I am going to meet Vincent to get Mom some dinner. I will see you later."

Diego nodded in affirmation and replied, "Be careful. You know that area can be dangerous." Leena nodded back and grabbed her backpack from under the counter where Liv had been hiding.

Leena loved her backpack. If there were things in life that define who you are as a person, for her, it was the love of bags. All kinds of different bags: purses, knapsacks, duffel bags. She preferred canvas to leather, and her backpack was a gift from Diego many years ago. It was made of green canvas with some leather accents and tight black stitching. The bag had the faint opaqueness of a red cross on the outside, leading Leena to believe the army used it for medical purposes. It had several zippers that divided the compartments and allowed Leena to keep her electronics (the few that she had) as well as her books and pens for writing her stories, which she would often do to pass the time.

Leena exited the booth, put both arms into her backpack, and slung it on her back, then headed toward the Aberjay zone. She hoped today's excitement was over and the area would be clear. She needed no more attention from the CPU.

Chapter 2

CARE PACKAGE

L eena hustled through the streets toward the wall as she knew it would be dark soon. The rain had subsided, but there was still a dampness in the air. She was about three blocks from the main entrance but knew she could not go that way because the CPU would stop and question her. She headed east about six blocks to an area in her town that was less friendly to outsiders than her own. She knew several of the residents, so she felt the risk was low.

She passed the Simmons Street crossing and the far-too-familiar CPU sign designating the area as *yellow*. Leena had never felt this area was any less safe than her own. Most of the crimes were robberies of some sort. Poverty brings out the worst in folks. But she also felt that it could bring people together. Just like it did in her building. They were communal, shared food, shared credits, shared supplies—almost everything. Everyone had what they needed because they shared.

She also knew that circumstances tested the model, and when residents were tight on food or supplies, the charity among neighbors broke down. She preferred to believe that people were inherently good and that given the opportunity, they would usually do the right thing. Not that there were no evil people in the world who were more concerned with themselves than with others. That was a given. But she chose to stay the optimist, believing that while some would do harm to others if it benefited them, most people didn't behave that way.

Leena tried to put those thoughts out of her head and concentrate on the task at hand. She needed to get to Zone 7 and retrieve the package before nightfall so she could get back safely. She hurried along the sidewalk, ducking into an abandoned store briefly as it was the only way to get around the barricade of concrete that blocked the street. She popped up a block later, emerging from the dark abandoned store. She brushed off the cobwebs she encountered going through the cave that she believed used to be a sandwich shop. Her thoughts went back to her own parents' fabric store as she passed store after store.

A few stores in her neighborhood were still open, but only about twenty percent of the storefronts had working businesses. She enjoyed going to the noodle shop when they had the funds. They served a delightful ramen dish and, on some occasions, even had fresh eggs for a small surcharge. Meat was rarely available to the Miniyar. Mainly because of its cost. Leena had grown up eating mostly vegan, but she enjoyed a piece of salty pork or some red meat on special occasions when the neighbors would have a celebration. It was a special treat for sure. Unfortunately, there had not been much to celebrate lately.

Leena walked into a small park that separated the row of buildings from the wall. It was about one hundred yards from the entrance of the park to the wall. She looked up, and from the entrance of the park, she could see the towering structure. The lights on top indicated that the Security Alert Profile (SAP) was green. The lights would turn red when there was an alert to warn citizens to return to their homes. It didn't happen often, but when it did, gunfire and explosions often accompanied the event. Major conflict among the zones ended more than twenty years ago, but pockets of resistance still popped up from time to time.

She always loved Banyan Park. She played there as a child. It held special memories for her. She used to spend her day playing on the swing set, chasing after the squirrels, and climbing the trees. Her mom would hold her hand as they strolled the brick path that wound through the park. It formed a circle. But when she was young, she thought they had walked for miles and miles when they had never left the park. She passed the swing sets, now old and rusty. Children no longer played there. It was mostly a hangout for teenagers and criminals now.

She finally reached the end of the park. The wall was enormous from this vantage point. Making a sharp right turn, she traced the boundary, dragging her hand behind her, slightly touching the wall as if it helped her stay on track. She ran her fingers over the wall, feeling the rough texture of the giant stones and the gritty mortar. It was rough against her fingers as she walked, trying to ensure she did not let go. This was a game she played when she made these trips.

She came upon a large tree growing within an arm's length of the stone. Its stature matched the height of the wall, and its branches extended over it. The branches were trimmed from time to time as it was an obvious security risk for one who might choose to climb the tree and gain access to the zone, but no one had done it lately.

Leena took off her backpack and put her arms through the straps in front of her so that it rode on her chest. She put her back to the tree and her legs on the wall. Using her legs to power her ascent, she slowly crawled up the side of the tree. Leena had a secret. The wall was old. Not only did it have many cracks and weak points due to countless rebel incursions, but the weather had also taken a toll. The Aberjay valued their wall, but funding its maintenance was not a high priority.

Leena knew the wall had a hole about halfway up the tree. The park hid it on one side, and its height obscured it on the other, so you could walk right by it and not know it was there. Additionally, the shadow of the hole and the darkness of the stone on that side of the wall created an illusion that kept it hidden without careful observation.

Leena reached midway up the tree, revealing her secret hole. She had used this hole for many years and had rigged this side of the wall with some old climbing gear she found that allowed her to attach a short length of rope, about three feet long, to the top of the hole on the inside. This hole might have been a drone staging area at one time. The Aberjay used drones for surveillance, citizen tracking, and sometimes assassinations. The Federal Government's Drone Elimination Act made drones illegal, but many of the staging areas in the wall remained.

Once she was at the proper height, she could reach above her head and grab hold of a tree branch while flipping the end of the rope out of the hole with her foot. Then, in one clean motion, she would grab the rope and fall against the wall, then gently pull herself into the hole. It hurt, but she learned that if she landed just right, her backpack would take the brunt of the trauma.

She completed the motion flawlessly and pulled herself safely into the hole. This took a tremendous amount of practice, she thought, beaming with pride, although no one was around to notice. She swung her backpack around to rest on her back once again and then rested for a minute or two. The wall was about eight feet thick, so she had to crawl to the center of the wall and then wriggle her body through the metal rebar that was only wide enough for her small frame. She told no one of her discovery because she knew no one who would fit through the hole.

Once she was on the other side of the rebar, she took another breath, for a moment thinking that the hole might be getting smaller. She justified this as nonsense by realizing that she had likely put on a few pounds since high school. She wondered if there would come a day when she wouldn't fit anymore.

Leena lay flat on her belly and wobbled out of the hole, feet hanging in the air. There was a tree to climb on one side of this great wall, but on the other, she had to climb down the stone. She had spent some time chiseling out footholds to make it easier, but she was no expert, so it still presented quite a challenge. The hardest part was just getting out of the hole, she thought, as she slowly lowered half her body, bent like an L-bracket, legs searching for those homemade ledges. As she found them, she reached up to another rope she had affixed in her initial construction, which helped her move the rest of her body out of the hole and provided some relief while she found rocks her hands could grasp before the next step, the vertical shimmy.

Leena was never afraid of heights. She didn't know why so many people were. Maybe all the climbing she did as a kid helped prevent that fear from taking hold. As she lay flat against the rock wall, drifting down, she would look over both shoulders to ensure there were no bystanders and no CPU. She knew someone in a house could probably see her through one of their windows if they happened to be looking, but she had done this enough times to believe it was not a high risk. Even if someone did see her, there were good odds they would not report it. Most of the Aberjay kept to themselves unless something or someone threatened their security. A short Chinese girl climbing down the wall probably did not meet that criterion.

Homes of freshly-painted blues and greens faced the wall on this side. Each home had its own distinct look and a driveway for residents to enter their garage. At the base of the wall was a private street, more of an alley, which was there only to provide access to each home's garage. This thoroughfare was noticeably quiet, which is probably why the CPU had never discovered the hole.

Leena hit the ground, swinging her body around and crouching for a moment. She was stunned at how different the Aberjay zone looked compared to hers. They had clean streets, pristine lawns, and fresh paint. They drove new cars and motorbikes. They had streetlights on every street to light them up at night, while the Miniyar lived in darkness like rats scurrying about. The difference probably lay in the jobs. Most of the Aberjay either had a job that paid well or a MIRO that did the work for them.

Leena followed the wall for a short time and then cut between two blocks of houses to reach another immaculately pristine street. She looked down at her clothes as she walked and realized they would give away her origins if anyone were to question her presence. And if her clothes did not reveal the truth, being Chinese certainly did. There were few Chinese in Zone 7. After years of war with China, the Aberjay failed to see the distinction between Chinese-Americans and their Chinese enemy. That thought made her pick up the pace. The sun began setting, which probably helped her stealth, but she had to face it—she stood out.

She walked for another few blocks before entering the Aberjay version of Banyan Park. It was a single park before the CPU built the wall, The Aberjay side was much smaller than hers though, as the housing needs of the Zone were more important than the park and much of the original park was eradicated to make room for new homes.

In some ways, it made her feel the Aberjay and Miniyar had this in common. How many days were there Aberjay lounging in the park while just on the other side of the wall, the Miniyar were eating their lunches, playing on the swings, or taking naps? Both sides did not look the same, however. On her side, the swings were rusty, the streetlights shed no light, and there were no concession stands to provide cool drinks on hot days.

She crossed two streets and noticed several electric-powered vehicles pass her. She barely heard their buzzy little motors and hoped they were driving fast enough not to notice her attire. She looked down at her clothes as she entered the park and realized they were dusty from the journey through the wall. She patted herself down with force to beat the dust out of her clothes. The dust made her cough. She removed her pilot hat and placed it in her backpack, then took a moment to bend over and shake out her hair to give it a fluff. She was meeting Vincent by the swings and wanted to look her best.

Leena reached the swing set and sat in the swing closest to the path in case she had to make a quick getaway. It had never been necessary before. The CPU were spread so thin it was unlikely to run into them in the park, but the afternoon's events still had her on edge, and she preferred not to have any more interactions with them today.

Leena had a plan if the CPU were to find her. She would run to the hole and get through it before they could get to the gate and find her exit on the other side. In her mind, if she had a direct line to the hole in the wall, she was safe. Many things could go wrong with this plan, but she had done the trip so many times that getting caught and punished for being a Miniyar crossing the Zone 7 border without permission seemed very unlikely.

There was no one in that area of the park, but she could see families on blankets in the distance and a few couples having a picnic at a table far to her left. She could not hear their words but occasionally heard their laughter rise above the sound of the wind. She could see them pouring wine that looked clear. She wondered what it tasted like as she had never had any alcohol. She imagined it was sweet, like a fresh peach. Or what she imagined a fresh peach tasted like as she had never had one of those either.

Leena waited for Vincent and used the time to review her day. She wondered how a day could start so well and go wrong so quickly. She shook from the afternoon's events. If she never saw the CPU guards again, especially that McBride fellow, it would be too soon. She debated in her mind whether she should tell Vincent what happened when he arrived. He wasn't really her boyfriend, so maybe not. But she had no one else to confide in about the event. She posited he would be supportive but was unsure if she wanted to test the theory.

She scanned the horizon for Vincent. She knew she didn't have much time. It was 5:08 p.m., and he was supposed to meet her there after his shift. Vincent worked for his dad, who owned a restaurant in town. It was not far, and she knew Vincent had a bicycle, so she wondered what was keeping him.

She met Vincent on a field trip when she was fourteen. Her class had ventured into the Aberjay zone to tour the CPU headquarters. They saw jail cells, courtrooms, and some very fancy homes along the way. Vincent was also on a field trip with his class, and although their teachers had tried to keep them separate, he had noticed her in the crowd of students and kept an eye on her all day. They eventually met up by a tree in the park outside the courthouse during a lunch break and exchanged phone numbers to keep in touch. They were the same age, although that is where their commonalities probably ended.

Leena communicated with him via the phone for some time. Then she had to give up her phone. They didn't speak for years after that, but once she found the hole in the wall, she hunted him down. They met here weekly, and Vincent always brought a care package for Leena and her family. She always thought about kissing him but had never gathered the courage. *What would he think? Does he even feel the same way? Why hasn't he made a move yet? Am I misreading the entire relationship?* Her mind often debated these questions. She had never really had a boyfriend, so she didn't know what was normal.

Vincent rounded the corner, riding his bike down the same path Leena had walked moments before. She knew it was him because his hair was dark and neat, trimmed short like he was in the military. His clothes were bright and clean. He wore an oversized shirt of thick maroon and orange horizontal stripes and tight, short jeans that showed his maroon socks above his bright white tennis shoes. Leena thought he had a great sense of style and wondered if he knew the socks matched his shirt, or was it accidental? Or maybe his MIRO chose his clothes each day. That was more likely.

Leena heard his electric bike whiz as he came to a stop and leaned the bike against the pole of the swing set. She jumped to her feet, excited to see him, but he failed to make eye contact.

"Hey," he said as he turned to retrieve the package from his bike, which was strapped on the back with bungee cords. He removed the bag and unceremoniously handed it to Leena. He made eye contact for the first time, but then his eyes quickly darted away. He was nervous.

"Thank you, Vincent. What did you bring me today?" Leena said, trying hard to hold down her enthusiasm for the meeting. She reasoned he liked her, or he would not continue to show up for these meetings, but she was unsure why he had so many problems expressing how he felt. *The boys were so one-dimensional.*

"The same as last week, I'm afraid," Vincent stated, "but I got some face creams and nail polish you might like. I also found some aspirin that might help your mom." Vincent listed the items as if he had been scavenging some blown-up mini-mart, but Leena knew the items he usually brought were probably swiped from his mother's bathroom.

She wondered for a moment if she should inform him that patients with kidney failure could not take aspirin, but she thought better of it. She didn't want to hurt his feelings after he had made such a gesture. It wasn't likely that he could get in trouble for delivering these care packages, but he risked his reputation associating with a Miniyar, and she didn't want to give him any reason to stop coming. Although she could live without nail polish, as she had never worn nail polish in her life, they needed the food more than she wanted him to know.

"I always appreciate anything you bring me," Leena said, trying not to blush. She looked in the bag and saw the face cream, nail polish, and aspirin he had mentioned, along with a quart of what looked like miso, a container of grilled vegetarian moo shu, and another container filled with fried rice. Vincent's dad's restaurant was American but had several Chinese items on the menu, and he knew this was her mom's favorite.

"How is your mom doing?" Vincent asked in a formal tone that lacked empathy.

"She is okay today," Leena replied, "but she has good days and bad days. She really needs medicine. I believe it is called Xithraxin. Any chance your mom has *that* in her bathroom?" She turned away quickly, realizing she had just unintentionally called him out on the source of his treasure box.

Vincent sat on the swing next to her and stiffened a bit. "No, probably not. You know I would love to help, but I don't have access to drugs. Even if I did they are probably expensive."

"I know," Leena said, sounding a little defeated. "I just don't know what I'm supposed to do."

"Maybe it's time you accept that there may not be a solution to this problem, Leena," Vincent said with even less empathy than before.

Leena grew angry and retorted, "What if it was your mom? Wouldn't you do anything you can to extend her life?"

"Well, my mother would have the money to..." Vincent said, knowing he had stepped over the line. He put up his hands to block the certain verbal blow that was incoming and quickly tried to save himself. "What I mean is, sometimes you need to just accept the way things are."

Leena cried but turned her face so he would not see. After composing herself a little, she stood up and turned to Vincent, raising a forefinger. Knowing that this was probably not the best posture, she slowly lowered the finger and took a breath before continuing. "I don't believe that we should abandon people just because they were born poor. And certainly not my mother, who has done nothing in this world but be a good citizen, teach me about life, and keep me safe from harm."

"Maybe not," Vincent quickly parried. "Life isn't fair sometimes."

"What does that have to do with it?" Leena shouted. "Just because life isn't fair doesn't mean we have to resign ourselves to fate. We can improve our lives." Leena was not sure if she had upset Vincent, and at that moment cared little whether she did.

"I don't want to fight with you. I think everything happens for a reason. Not that your mom deserves to be sick. You just never know what it will lead to... I mean..." Vincent trailed off with a small grin as if he had won the prize at the fair. "Let's stop talking about this. I am sorry I upset you. I don't want anything to happen to your mom. You know I would help if I could, but there is nothing I can do."

Vincent then walked to her slowly, not yet understanding her level of fury, and began rubbing her arms to provide comfort. Because she did not resist, he moved in closer and hugged her.

"I have some good news," Vincent said attempting to change the subject. "I have been accepted to a prestigious program in the capital. I am going to be an aid to one of the senators. It's an internship."

"You are going to be a politician?" Leena asked.

"I don't know, maybe, it is a prestigious program." He stammered, realizing he had already said that. "It could lead to a great job in the capital."

"I really need to get back," Leena said. "I have been here too long already." Leena was glad she did not share her tumultuous afternoon event with him. An event that could have led to her imprisonment or even her death. He would not have understood. She would process this conversation later a hundred times over, but at this moment, she struggled to see why she had feelings for him. They were so different. She quickly recoiled from his grasp, creating distance.

"Okay, Leena, same time next week," Vincent replied, trying desperately to change the tone of the conversation so he wouldn't feel like the bad guy.

"Yes, thank you," said Leena as she grabbed the bag and headed for the park exit. She was still upset and felt Vincent needed a good thrashing, but she would contain her indignation until she had time to do it properly. She knew he was wrong. She didn't have a brilliant answer for him, but she knew that his parents and the school he attended jaded his viewpoint. Leena tried to shake it off and hurried toward the multicolored houses, trying to get her mind reconciled to her task of exiting the Zone as the sun started to set and cast an orange hue across the sky.

Leena made her way back to the hole in the wall and scaled the wall in record time. She shuffled through the wall's interior and was able to slide down the other side. She had done this trip so often that the bark on the tree she used for support as she went up and down had broken off, leaving a finely sanded surface that felt crafted for her form. It was her own little elevator.

She hit the ground on her side and made her way quickly through the park. She noticed some shadowy figures lurking by the old rusty swing set as she approached, so she took a detour around it so as not to attract unwanted attention. It was probably just teenagers blowing off steam or drinking, but she did not want to find out.

Making her way past the entrance to the park unscathed by strangers, she took the same path back to her apartment that she had originally taken, avoiding the front gates of Zone 7. It was dark now, and her movement was a little slower than during the day. She had to be more careful. She recalled her mother's words: "Darkness is always a magnet for mischief."

When she rounded the street where her building entrance was accessible, she noticed Diego sitting on the stairs out front. He would make some excuse for why he was out there, but she knew he was waiting for her. He knew she did these runs and was always terrified that something would go wrong.

"Well, it's about time you came home, Turnip!" Diego said sarcastically.

"I would send you on these runs if I could, but you won't fit through the hole," Leena responded in kind. And then she noticed his facial expression change. It became somber and pale like he was about to be the messenger of bad news.

"Turnip, your mom had a spell. The doctor is in with her now. She is stable, but she is very weak right now, so please try to stay calm for her sake." Diego was ready for a big hug, but Leena blew past him with her package and ran up the stairs to the third floor.

Leena burst into the room to see Dr. Singh adjusting an IV bag full of fluid. There was a bag of blood next to the IV bag that was in use as well. She knew it was her mom's blood. Mom had these transfusions regularly as dialysis to clean out her blood. Her blood went through a machine that removed any toxins and then sent it back to her bloodstream. It was a good thing that Dr. Singh made house calls. She had no money for hospitals.

"What happened?" Leena whispered to Dr. Singh. She tried not to look her mother in the eyes. She was too worried she would break down in tears and upset her. She was not sure if she was conscious but didn't want to take the risk.

"Leena Zhen!" exclaimed the doctor. "It is good to see you! Have you been taking care of yourself?"

"Of course, doctor, but how is my mother?" Leena replied with a tinge of frustration in her tone. She never understood why Dr. Singh would always start with small talk. He was a peculiar fellow. He was short like Leena and about as narrow as a young pine tree. He wore thick glasses and the hair that was left on his head was gray with age.

As she moved closer to the bed to demand the doctor's attention, her mom touched her hand. Leena looked up and saw her mother's loving eyes piercing her soul. The tears flowed, but she choked them back as best she could.

Mei used all her strength to remove the oxygen mask and say, "Hello darling, did you have a good day?" Leena could not hold back the tears anymore and let them flow. Mei was disturbed but not surprised by her daughter's reaction, and she shed a few tears of her own. They gazed at each other momentarily as if speaking a secret code that only their eyes understood.

"Leena, let's step outside a moment and let your mother rest. There is no need for all of that crying." Dr. Singh moved toward the door and motioned for her to follow. "Mei, we will be right back," he said with a big smile as he left the room.

Leena followed him into the hall and began wiping the tears from her face. Her mother's selflessness to ask about her day as she lay there in such a diminished state spoke volumes to her about who her mother really was, and it only reinforced how unfair it was that she was losing this battle. Leena wanted to run. She wanted to hide from this, but she knew she was just avoiding the inevitable and that her mother would want her to be strong. It was always her mother's voice in her head that brought stability and sanity to her world.

Dr. Singh walked down the hallway a few steps and then turned to wait for Leena to catch up. "Leena, your mother is in kidney failure, and there isn't much we can do about it at this point but make her comfortable. I think the hospital is the best place for her right now, but I know she would not allow it. I am afraid she is no longer responding to the dialysis."

"What does that mean?" Leena asked, grasping for any amount of truth that would help her mother's fate.

"It means that your mother is not responding to the only treatment we have at our disposal. She is okay right now and is not in any pain, but she will grow weaker in the coming weeks."

"Is there not medicine that might help? Is there nothing else?" Leena asked, searching for an answer to this catastrophe.

"We can continue treatments, Leena, but it is no longer helping as much as I would like. Her body just cannot keep going this way much longer," the doctor finished. After patting Leena on the shoulder, he began to walk away.

"How much time, Dr. Singh?" Leena asked with tears in her eyes and a crackling in her throat. She felt a sadness that overwhelmed her. The confusion she was feeling was so intense that it took over her senses and rendered her speechless. She could not process what she was hearing.

"It is difficult to predict these things, Leena, but a month, maybe two, is my best guess. But in these situations, the body has a way of making its own schedule. Just try to be present. She needs your love and support right now. I will stop by again tomorrow." The doctor went back into their apartment to finish the treatment, leaving Leena to break down in the hallway.

Leena saw Diego at the top of the stairs. She had not noticed him before, but he was most likely there all along, knowing she would need him. She ran to him, and he received her gladly. She sobbed for at least ten minutes. She was so distraught; she did not even notice the doctor walk by and make his way down the stairs.

Diego said, "Let's go sit with your mom. Maybe she will eat some miso." This reminded Leena that she had soup. Diego must have smelled it in the bag she brought. She entered the apartment and retrieved the soup from the bag, pouring it into a white bowl from the cupboard. She grabbed a spoon and went to her mother's bedside to get her to eat.

A nightmare startled Leena out of her slumber. She couldn't remember what it was about, and she didn't even remember falling asleep. It was dark in the room, and all she could hear was the whizzing noise of her mom's oxygen machine. It was about nine p.m. With Mei sleeping, she used the opportunity to take a shower.

She shed her dirty clothes and stepped into the shower, but the steam was no match for the tears that began as soon as the water hit her eyes. She loved taking showers. Electricity wasn't free, and water was in high demand, so one per week was the limit. Something about the water hitting her face and wiping away the dirt made her break down. She knew she had an emotional day, and this was all of it, just spilling out into the river that ran between her feet. She looked down at the muddy river of brown and black, the result of her climbing. She secretly wished her pain would follow the water down the drain.

She didn't know how to receive Dr. Singh's pronouncement. She was trying to wrap her head around it but felt there had to be a way to save her mother. She knew there were treatments; they were just out of reach. She hated that money was the divider—the one thing that determined if her mom would live or die. She just could not accept it. She *would* not accept it.

She dried off after scrubbing her shoulder-length hair and gently rubbing some conditioner into it. She dressed in red-and-white pajamas and then returned to the living room to check on her mother. She didn't know how she would save her, but she knew in her gut she was not ready to relinquish her resolve. She would find a way.

She replayed the events of her day in her head, mainly trying to process what had happened to her. Her run-in with Sgt. McBride was enough to give her posttraumatic stress disorder. Her mind kept going over it and over it. What am I missing? None of this has to do with Mom. *Why does my mind keep bringing me back?*

And then it came to her: *Liv invited me to her house! Maybe Liv can help get the medication we need! But where does she live? Can I even remember?* She pondered these questions until she fell into a deep sleep.

Chapter 3

NEW FRIENDS

Leena woke to the sun beaming through the apartment window and the whirl of Mom's oxygen machine. She was not sure what woke her but felt certain it was later than normal. She felt well rested. She had her bed in the living room so that she could easily observe her mother while she slept. On most mornings, she would pop up and begin breakfast. She was a morning person. But today was different. Something hung in the air that made it different. Maybe it was the events of the previous day, the stress she endured hearing the doctor's diagnosis, or the realization that her world was about to change dramatically.

She looked at her mother, still sleeping, straining to breathe, appearing unmoved from the previous night's position in the bed. She knew she should get up and get moving, but she lingered just a little longer in bed. She stared at the ceiling, listening to her own breathing, thinking about what she would do without her mother. Then her thoughts turned to Diego. He was not a young man, and she had noticed his mobility declining in the last year. Leena knew he would not live forever, but until now she had not visualized her life without these two people she loved so dearly in her life. What would her future be like? Who would she talk to about her day? It all seemed so meaningless. Living just to die.

After pondering these troubling life questions for a few more minutes and hearing her mother stir, she jumped up from her mattress on the floor and went into the bathroom. She ran a brush through her hair and put it in a ponytail. She could not wear her favorite pilot hat with it in a pony, but she did not have the strength to fashion it any other way this morning. She washed her face and brushed her teeth, and then made her way to the kitchen to fry up some greens and beans. This was one of her favorites. The greens were turnips or collards. Mixed with pinto beans it made a hearty breakfast. The greens had always seemed like the healthiest vegetables to her. She was not sure if it was true, but knowing she was doing something good for her body added to her affection for the meal. She always added homemade hot sauce made with peppers from the garden. It gave it a kick that she felt started her day off right.

She filled a small bowl for her mother and spent some time trying to get her to eat it, but it was clear that Mei had little appetite. Few words were spoken between the two. Mei looked resigned to her fate while Leena was angry about the situation. Even after a good night's sleep, she was not ready to let her mom go without a fight.

"Mom," Leena said quietly, "I am going to go visit a friend this morning who I think might help you." She avoided telling her the complexity of the task because she did not know where Liv lived these days and she had yet to hatch a workable plan. She also knew if her mother knew of the events of the previous day, she would certainly forbid her to go, even if her protest would only be ceremonial.

Her mother did not respond verbally but just looked at her and gave a slight shake of the head to signal her protest. Leena did not need to hear the words; she knew it was a gesture of defeat. If her mom were to speak, it would be to tell her she was wasting her time, that there was nothing left that could be done, and that she would prefer to just spend time with her daughter until the end came.

Leena had already weighed the decision of trying to find a solution versus spending time with Mom and accepting the inevitable. She reasoned that if there was a chance of helping her mother, she had to try. She did not even know what success looked like outside of a rich benefactor whisking her away to the Aberjay zone and paying all her medical bills to restore her back to health, but she knew she had to try. She was not sure if the action she wanted to take was to appease her conscience or to ultimately free her mother from her fate. But it was not in her to lay down and concede.

A knock at the door signaled to Leena that her expected guest had arrived.

"Diego is going to sit with you today while I try to work some things out, okay?" she stated as a question, knowing she was going to do it even if her mom protested.

Mei reached over and gave her three taps on the hand, which was their secret sign of love and admiration. Leena received the message clearly, tapped back on Mei's hand three times, and then leaned in and kissed her forehead.

Leena opened the door for Diego and began collecting her things. Diego refrained from asking about Mei's condition. He knew her state was not likely to improve. Leena issued a few last-minute instructions to Diego. He listened intently, but they both knew he had been taking care of her for the last year and was well-qualified for the task. With no knowledge of her destination, Leena said her goodbyes and ran to the stairs.

While most folks started their day with coffee, Leena loved tea. She had no clue where Liv might live but knew where the coffee shop was located. She thought she would head in that direction and get a cup of tea, figuring that the caffeine and nutrients in the hot beverage would help her plan the day.

Sitting down with her fresh cup of tea, she positioned herself next to the window. There was an overabundance of people in the shop this morning. It had grown busier since the other shop down the street closed. She sipped her tea while looking out the window. A small blue bird was hopping around on the sill. Every few minutes, he would jump up and peck at the glass and then fall back down to his previous position. Over and over, he would peck and then fall. Leena wondered if he was trying to get inside because he sensed the warmth coming from the store window, or possibly he was looking for a mate and thought he found his perfect match in the reflection. She giggled a little watching the tiny bird. She wondered why the bird could not learn that he could not get through the glass.

How do I find Liv? she thought. *It seemed sort of rude for her to invite me to her home and not tell me where it is. Maybe she thought I already knew? If that were the case, then maybe I should know.* She tried hard to remember if she ever visited her house when they were in school together but could only remember avoiding her as much as possible.

The bell attached to the door rang out as someone familiar walked in. A nice-looking Hispanic man dressed in a clean blue suit with pinstripes commanded the attention of the room. His shoes were shiny and black and coated with fresh polish. His tie was black and gold, with hints of blue that matched his suit. He even had a gold pendant attached to his tie that looked like some sort of tree.

She immediately recognized him. Fernando Martinez was the Zone Advocate and Diego's son. He represented the Miniyar zone to the Aberjay officials. A congressional council governed the state; a group of business leaders elected to represent the people. None of the twelve senators on the council were residents of Zone 6, but they often negotiated with the Zone Advocate when decisions they were making affected the Miniyar. Leena was not sure what he did from day to day, but knew his work was important. He spent a lot of time in meetings to better the lives of the Miniyar. Because he was Diego's father, they had spent time together, usually around the holidays when he would visit Diego at the building. And sometimes when she was little, she accompanied Diego to the Zone Advocates' residence, which was near her building.

Fernando ordered a coffee drink and recognizing her, dashed to her table. He didn't take a seat but placed his hand on the back of the chair and looked down at Leena.

"Hello, Leena, how are you today?" he asked gracefully.

Leena looking up at him from her seat. She mustered a smile and said, "*I* am doing okay," clearly emphasizing the *I* part of the phrase.

"I was very sad to hear of your mother's battle, Leena. I hope she heals quickly," Fernando said, oblivious to the change in her status.

"I am not sure that is possible, Mr. Martinez. She is in the late stages of her illness now. There is not much left we can do," Leena said plainly. She realized that this was the first time she had said that out loud. She had heard "hope she is doing well" or "sorry to hear she is sick" for years but had never once had to respond with such dire news. She wondered if it was too much. Was she begging for help, strangely cloaked in cordiality? Could he see through the bluff if that were the case?

"I am very sorry to hear that," Fernando continued. "If there is anything I can do, please don't hesitate to call my office and make an appointment."

Make an appointment she thought to herself. What a strange thing to say. Leena knew they were not close, but she thought she was a few levels above *make an appointment*. She realized he was saying he wanted to help only to be polite, not to offer true assistance.

And then the idea popped into her head to ask about Liv. She hesitated for a moment as Fernando went back to the counter to retrieve his order. She wondered if he would be supportive of Liv's rebellious nature toward the Aberjay or if he even knew her at all. She fought her best advice and decided she had nothing to lose if he said no.

"Mr. Martinez," Leena said as she raised a finger in the air. "Do you know Liv Zolenski?" She wasn't even sure if she had the last name right.

"Yes, I have met Ms. Zolenski," he replied in a tone that made it clear the rendezvous had not been positive. "Why do you ask?"

"I am trying to find her home. Any idea where she lives?" Leena felt clever using the term *find her home* rather than *find her* to clarify whatever it was about her that Fernando did not seem to like would not be surreptitiously applied to her.

"I am sure someone as bright and friendly as yourself can find better folks to associate with, Leena."

"We are not friends. I just need to ask her something." Leena said sadly, hoping to garner some information in response based on pity.

"I believe Ms. Zolenski lives in a warehouse community in Cabbagetown," Fernando said while heading for the door. "Try the Owens Warehouse Consortium." With that helpful tip delivered, he headed out the door. Leena was glad he was gone or else he would have seen the beam of joy coming from her face. She had left her home with a half-baked plan and no information but now had what she needed to rally the troops and lead them to victory—although she had no troops and still wasn't sure what victory would look like.

As she was reeling from this good fortune, she thought about Cabbagetown. She knew it was a yellow zone. Unlike where she was the previous day, she knew the area to be dangerous. She thought she might need a partner in this venture, and her mind turned to Jordan. She quickly finished her tea and, now possessing a purpose, grabbed her backpack and headed out the door.

Leena exited the coffee shop and found the first street heading west toward Jordan's side of town. She knew Jordan would help as they had been good friends for many years. She had not seen him much in the last year. Jordan Lin was lucky. He didn't have much but won a job lottery during his high school senior year and obtained one of the few jobs available to the Miniyar. He worked in a plant in the Aberjay zone.

While most jobs available in the Aberjay factories went to people who lived in Zone 7, they offered a quota of jobs each year to graduating seniors in the Miniyar zone. It was some sort of charitable offering to the underprivileged because most of the jobs were in the Aberjay zone. As she thought about it, she believed that Mr. Martinez was involved in the development of that program.

Leena was on a heavily trafficked street heading west. She knew she had a long way to go. Jordan lived in a nicer neighborhood on the northwest side of the zone. The homes were not large there, but the people who owned them worked hard to keep them in good shape. The streets weren't as nicely kept as the Aberjay districts, but it was the most manicured part of Zone 6.

Leena stayed on the sidewalk as cars were quite common on these streets. She passed rows of homes and then a more industrialized area where the traffic subsided a little. She crossed several train tracks and remembered that the last time she crossed these tracks, there were many empty cars in the rail yard, which was just a short distance from the crossing she was traversing. She noticed there were very few cars in the rail yard on this trip and pondered why that would be. She was good at noticing things that were out of place.

Leaving the rail yard, she walked for another mile or so as the scenery turned residential once again. The homes she passed were small and incredibly old, but in each driveway was a car or motorbike of some sort. These were working-class people. Their homes were probably no bigger inside than Leena's, but she gathered that they likely had use of the entire floor plan and did not deal with leaky ceilings and broken windows like she did in her building.

Leena's stomach grumbled a little as she looked down, walking the sidewalk block after block. Eventually, she sat on the curb to tie her shoe and took just a moment to wonder what it would be like to live there. It was really a step up from where she had lived her whole life. She banished the thought as unattainable and headed toward Jordan's house. And then a terrible thought crossed her mind. *What if he was at work?* Because it was Sunday, she hoped it would be his day off. Most people who worked in the Aberjay zone worked six days a week. In her mind, she began rebuilding her plan based on the possibility that he wouldn't be home.

As she reached the next block, she knew she was close. She had been here many times, just not recently. She kept walking and finally spotted the house. It was a white home with black-trimmed windows. Rocking chairs were on the porch, which leaned a little to one side. She noticed a motorbike in the driveway and was fairly sure it was Jordan's. She ascended the creaky stairs leading to the front door and knocked lightly.

The door opened to a good-looking young man with short curly hair and a dark complexion. "Leena!" he shouted with great excitement. "What are you doing here?"

Leena was pleased to see Jordan and opened her arms wide for a hug, walking directly across his home's threshold and into his arms. "Hi, Jordan," she said as she hugged him tight. He was taller, so his hugs always felt like bear hugs. She loved his scent. She inhaled deeply, hoping he would not notice. She wasn't sure if it was cologne or just what men smell like, but it was intoxicating.

"Come in and sit with me," he said as he escorted her to the living area. No one else seemed to be home, or at least in that area of the house. A TV on the wall was playing some sort of sports game that she didn't recognize. His family was not rich, but they had a few more luxuries than Leena, who didn't own a TV. "Can I get you anything?" he asked politely.

"Do you have any water?" she whispered, realizing it was a dumb question once it left her mouth because everyone has water in their house. "It was a long walk from my house," she added, justifying the request.

Jordan bounded into the kitchen and came back shortly with a large glass of water. Leena put it to her lips and drank the entire glass, secretly hoping that her gulping was not as loud as it was in her head.

"So, what are you doing here, Leena? I mean, it is great to see you, don't get me wrong, but it is not often that you just pop up in my neighborhood. I hope everything is okay." Jordan waited patiently for an answer with his eyes fixed on hers, showing genuine concern.

"I need your help, Jordan," Leena began, hoping that she would not have to persuade him too much. "I need to go see someone in Cabbagetown. Can you go with me? I know I could probably make the trip myself, but that area is scary, and I would feel better if I had some company. I know it isn't that close to this area." She then remembered he had a motorbike outside. "We could walk or take the bike, but I really need to find someone."

Leena stopped to review what she just said, hoping it made sense, and watched closely for his reaction.

"Of course I will help, Leena," Jordan said. "Who is it you are looking for?"

Leena thought to herself for a moment, debating whether it would help or hurt her case to tell him. Knowing she kept very few secrets from Jordan, she said, "Liv Zolenski—do you remember her from school?"

"Liv Zolenski? Why would you want to mess around with her? She is bad news. Yes, I remember her. She used to threaten to beat me up until I grew taller than her. She was always a bit of a ruffian. I thought she got arrested for blowing up a truck or something." Jordan got up and, still talking, began collecting things he needed for the trip.

"It isn't important why, Jordan. I just need to talk to her," Leena said, a little more reserved.

She watched as Jordan removed his shirt, revealing a well-formed chest and abs. Leena blushed and turned away, thinking that maybe it was wrong to stare too long. She never thought about Jordan that way and realized that to this day, she had never seen him shirtless. Jordan went to a fresh pile of laundry in the corner of the room and pulled out a gray, long-sleeve thermal T-shirt and a black, long-sleeve button-up flannel shirt. He pulled the T-shirt on and unbuttoned his pants briefly to tuck it in. He then put on the flannel but only buttoned the bottom two buttons.

"Are you ready to go?" Jordan asked Leena, snapping her out of her doe-eyed gaze.

A little surprised at his willingness to help with such sparse information, Leena awkwardly stood up and headed out the door. Jordan grabbed an extra helmet from behind the door and followed her out to the bike. She had never ridden on a motorbike before but thought this was probably not the right time to tell him.

Jordan strapped on his helmet. Handing the extra helmet to Leena, he swung his leg over the bike and took it off the kickstand. She assumed he was waiting for her to get on. Knowing her ponytail would not fit in a motorbike helmet, she removed her hair tie and dug in her bag for her pilot hat. The pilot hat was just a piece of leather fashioned into a covering for her head. She thought it would make a good separator between the helmet and her hair, which she had freshly washed and wouldn't do so again for another six days.

Placing the pilot hat on her head and then the bike helmet, she fiddled with the tie strap but could not figure it out. Jordan gestured for her to come forward because he was holding up the bike and could not turn around. She stepped to him, and he quickly tied the helmet for her. Stepping up to the back of the bike, she noticed the peg and assumed that was where her foot should go. With her backpack securely strapped on, she placed her left foot on the peg and swung her other leg to the other side.

"Are you ready?" Jordan shouted from within the confines of his helmet.

Leena gave a thumbs-up with her hands and then returned them to his hips as that was the only leverage keeping her on the back of the bike.

The bike launched forward, and within seconds they were on the street heading toward the first intersection. A battery powered the bike, so it made little noise as it traveled. It was super thin, and the seat felt like it was not big enough for a human posterior. Jordan was an expert at driving it through these streets. He easily zipped around barricades and through alleys to get to his destination. Often, he would have to stop at traffic lights, but Leena could tell he took many shortcuts to avoid having to stop. Every time he engaged the accelerator, she would squeeze him tight so as not to fall off the back. At one point, she felt as if he were doing it intentionally, and that made her smile.

Leena loved the wind in her hair. She had seen people ride these things for years, but never really understood that there was a draw outside of cheap transportation. Now she understood. There was something freeing about speeding through the city streets with nothing to protect you from the pavement except momentum. The danger of it, along with the freedom it allowed, was exhilarating. She could feel her body meshed with Jordan's, and they became one in the way they swayed from side to side as he navigated the bike around obstacles. It was cold, but holding on tightly to her friend who she had known for so long comforted her and warmed her body.

Jordan pulled up to the Owens Warehouse Consortium building and stopped short of the entrance. He kicked the kickstand down and motioned for Leena to dismount. She carefully got off the motorbike by swinging her right leg off and then hopping down. She struggled with the helmet again, but Jordan politely reached over and unstrapped it. She removed her helmet and looked around to get her bearings.

The area they were in was filled with trash. Groups of homeless were spread about in the alleys, on the sidewalks and in many of the abandoned stores. Many residents called them Tent cities. Large groups of people that had no where to live. They would construct homes made from trash, old boxes, wood pallets or anything that would suffice to keep the weather off of them. Strung together for warmth and safety, the residents created small cities. There were some near Leena's area, but they kept out of sight, usually located in the depths of an alley or in an abandoned warehouse. The Tent cities in Cabbagetown were not hidden but overflowed from the alleys to the streets and sometimes blocked the intersections.

Houses in Cabbagetown were once as nice as those in Jordan's neighborhood, but over time, the lack of attention ruined them and left many abandoned. The warehouses that were built to replace the buildings ruined by the wars had not fared much better as time went on. For housing, the consortium was cheaper and more efficient than building homes. They were communal, like Leena's building, but instead of large apartments, they contained micro-apartments of less than one hundred square feet each. The kitchens and bathrooms were part of the common areas.

Leena realized suddenly that she did not know her next step. She thought Liv might be here, but if so, how would she explain that she brought a guest? She knew Liv was very paranoid and would not interpret it well. Conversely, she did not want to walk into the building without her 'bodyguard.' After quick deliberation, she decided it was worth the risk of venturing alone.

"Jordan, I need to go in by myself. Liv is not expecting you and may not take it well. You know how she can be."

Jordan looked hurt for just a moment and then became the polite guy she knew and loved. "Sure, I understand. I will just

hang out in the coffee shop right over there until you are done."
He pointed to a coffee shop across the street. Both Jordan and
Leena were concerned about leaving the motorbike unattended
so he pushed it to the other side of the street near the coffee shop
so he could keep it close.

Leena turned and headed toward the entrance with no idea
how she would find Liv. She entered the two frosted glass doors.
The lobby was tiny, and the walls were red brick, echoing the
sound of her footsteps on the gray stone floor. A reception desk
made of black-painted cinderblock gave her hope that she might
ask where Liv's unit was or look her up in a directory, but as Leena
reached the desk, there was no one there. No sign indicated that
someone would return, and it didn't look like anyone had been
there recently. She thought that surely if someone had stepped
away, there would be a steaming cup of coffee or an open book.
It looked too tidy.

Figuring there was no help to be found here, she went past the
reception desk to another pair of frosted glass doors. She opened
them and peered down the long hallway. The apartment doors
were spaced evenly on both sides of the hallway. Obviously, these
were the apartments, but *how do I know which one?* she thought.

She made her way down the hall and noticed nameplates on
each numbered door. Unfortunately, the nameplates were not
in use as each one was blank or missing entirely. As she moved
closer to the end of the hallway, she could hear what sounded like
gym activity. She heard people talking loudly and weights being
dropped with loud clangs. As she reached the end of the hallway,
she found herself in a large, open part of the warehouse. To
the left was a living area with couches and an antique television
affixed to the brick wall. In front was a large kitchen with a giant

island for communal meals. The chairs surrounding the island created an ideal spot for gathering, and the picnic table next to the counters was just like the one where Leena had sat in Banyan Park the day before. To her right was a small gym full of weights and workout equipment. Mats covered the stone floor that cushioned it from the drop of some of the heavier weights.

Three people were in the gym, including the target of her search, Liv Zolenski. Leena made her way inside, but she had yet to be noticed. Walking past the first set of machines, she put herself into Liv's line of sight as she was just finishing a bench press. Liv pulled herself up from the bench and fixed her eyes on Leena.

"Look what the cat dragged in," Liv said. In a flash, Leena was taken back to her days in high school and a recollection of one of the sharp remarks Liv would make to put down some student who hadn't done anything wrong. "How did you even find me?"

"I can be resourceful when I need to be," Leena replied, attempting to embellish her scrappiness a bit to match the company.

"Leena, this is Julian," she said, pointing to the young man behind her, "and that is Zoe," she finished without gesturing in Zoe's direction. "They're friends of mine."

Julian's build was solid but not overly large. He wore shorts, a black armless T-shirt that was a little too large on him, and a red bandana. He was unusually white for a Miniyar and had perfect teeth. Zoe was a tall African-American woman with skintight red pants and a matching top. They both wore fingerless gloves that were old and worn. The shape of their bodies showed their commitment to the gym, and their attitude seemed to be one of suspicion.

"Nice to meet you," Leena said, lifting a hand to shake before promptly deciding against it. A quick nod to each person would have to do.

Aluminum foil covered their identity bracelets, the devices used to track citizens and give them access to their digital currency. She thought that maybe this was a fashion statement, but these three were probably not pioneers of the latest trends.

Liv noticed that Leena's eyes were fixed on Julian's ID bracelet and said, "The foil disrupts the signal so they can't track you. We don't do it for long. Any more than a day or so and they come looking for you to ensure you haven't removed it. We just like to keep them guessing."

She continued, "I wanted to thank you for what you did yesterday, Leena. Those guys were right on our tail, and we thought we were done. Julian and Zoe were able to lose them on the back streets of the market, but I caught one of the guard's eyes when I rounded the corner and knew that if I continued with Julian and Zoe, we would all be caught." Liv laid back and began another set of bench presses as she continued with a slight grunt in her voice each time she lifted the barbell. "You handled it well, kid. Have you ever thought of expanding your skills to become a little more engaged in the war?"

"What war?" Leena slowly moved toward a small chair next to a mini-fridge where she could sit out of the way of Julian and Zoe as they began setting up another machine to continue their workout.

"What war?" Liv parroted her. "What world are you living in, girl? The war against oppression. The war against tyranny. The war to end slavery. Don't you watch the news?"

Leena wanted to sound like she was more knowledgeable, but after a second of searching her brain, she really did not know what Liv was talking about. She decided it was best to play it safe. "I don't have a TV. We had to sell it a couple of years ago."

"You, of all people, should be pissed. You are Chinese! Aren't you tired of people treating you with disrespect, living on next to nothing while the Aberjay feast on meat and wine every night?" Liv finished her reps and sat up slowly, unzipping her gloves and removing them.

"I guess I never really thought about it. My life is what my life is. We have never really had much. And then Mom got sick..." She tried to continue, but Liv cut her off, standing up with her legs on both sides of the bench.

"Why do you think your life is that way? It is *them*, girl! They decide what you eat, what you drink, where you go, what you learn. They are always keeping us down. They don't want us learning or succeeding because we are a threat to their way of life."

"I don't know about all that," Leena said, discomfort in her voice. "I am just not very political, I guess."

"The time for sitting on the sidelines is gone, kid. You need to decide which side you are on. You may not know it, but we are in a war for our lives." Liv noticed Leena's unease with the conversation and backed off.

"Anyway, thanks for the help the other day." Liv unlocked the mini-fridge next to Leena. Reaching in, she handed her four bottles of water, about a liter each. "Take these."

Leena took the bottles and placed them in her backpack. This was a gift indeed. Water was hard to find. Rainwater was one thing, but these bottles contained distilled water. Leena could tell by the seal. It required a good bit of equipment to make large quantities of this stuff. She wondered where Liv would have retrieved such a treasure because the fridge looked full of them, but thought it was better not to ask.

"I appreciate the water, but I wanted to ask for your help with something."

"What do you need, kid?" Liv asked while wiping her body down with a towel.

"My mom is sick. She needs a drug called Xithraxin, but the pharmacies here don't have any." Leena knew she was telling a little lie as she had not even checked the inventory of the local pharmacies because she knew she would not be able to afford it even if they had it. She figured it would help persuade Liv to offer assistance if it was not just a lack of money but a matter of oppression that she seemed so fond of discussing.

"Why don't you ask Jordan? Doesn't he work for the Aberjay?" she said sarcastically. "I am sure he is over there all the time."

Leena glanced out the window toward the coffee shop where she knew Jordan was waiting for her and for a moment thought that Liv had figured out that she came with Jordan. She was still unsure how Liv would accept that if she knew.

"Well, it isn't just about finding it," Lenna continued. "The meds are expensive. If I don't get some quickly, my mom is certain to die."

Liv looked back at Julian and then at Zoe, who both gave a silent nod, indicating they had no connection to make that happen. Liv walked over and sat on an old green leather couch that seemed out of place in the workout area. The couch was full of holes and marks from an attempted patch-up with tape. She put both arms up on the couch, and said, "If we could help you with these meds, it would take longer than a few days to set up. And the person we would get to retrieve them for you would want payment. My guess is that payment would also be out of reach for you. No?" She looked intently at Leena to gauge her response to see if maybe she had more resources than she was admitting. Leena shook her head to show it wasn't a negotiation because she had nothing with which to negotiate. She had nothing someone else might want apart from vegetables.

Leena watched Liv's face as she thought through it. She hoped she was devising a sophisticated plan to help her. Then she watched her face change from deep thought to resolution as she jumped up off the couch and said, "Why don't you just get it yourself?"

Leena was confused. "I already said I don't have the money to…"

Liv cut her off again. "Just steal it, kid. They have pharmacies on every block in Zone 7. Just wait till dark and sneak through that hole of yours and break in and take it."

Leena was a little surprised to hear that Liv was aware of her secret hole. *I guess I am not the only one who uses it or the only one who knows of its existence,* she thought. She briefly sized up all three of them to determine which one she thought might fit through the hole but then shook her head and brought her mind back to the conversation.

"I don't know. I don't really know how to steal things. It seems way too dangerous. What if I get caught? There are serious penalties for stealing." She was certain she was not that type of person.

Liv moved from the couch to kneel in front of her. She bent down and looked her straight in the eye. "Kid, you will get nothing in this world by wishing for it. You must take what you need. The world is unfair, and you have been shortchanged. If you don't correct this balance of power, people will walk all over you until you are dead. If it were my mom, I would tear that whole place to the ground if I knew they had the cure."

Leena had never been one prone to mischief. But sitting there, looking directly at Liv, fighting back a tear that Liv would certainly interpret as weakness, it was difficult to argue. Liv was making sense. This was her mom's fate she was talking about. Why shouldn't she be able to save her?

"Okay," Leena said, only half-believing herself, "I will do it."

Leena ran down the long hallway toward the exit. She found new energy. She found hope. Bursting through the doors, she scanned the street for Jordan so they could get on their way but didn't see him. She began walking back to the motorbike and remembered he was in the café. She crossed the street and headed for the café, only to see Jordan coming out at the same time. He must have seen her. She thought about how long she had been there and considered whether she would need to apologize. An hour was not too bad, she thought.

They met up in the middle of the street, and Leena pivoted on her heels and headed toward the bike.

"I assume you found Liv?" Jordan said.

"Yes, I found her."

Jordan handed her the extra helmet as he threw his leg over his steed, motioning once more for her to jump on the back.

They rode back to Leena's house in silence. Her head was spinning, and she felt intense guilt even though she had not yet developed a plan to steal, much less act on it. Shivers rippled down her body as she thought about what she was going to do. *This isn't who I am*, she thought. *I don't steal.* Then she thought about her mom dying in her apartment, and her resolve grew. She thought about Liv and wondered if she had read her wrong from the beginning. *Maybe there is some truth to the war Liv talked about. Is my life controlled by the Aberjay?* Her mind raced through her life as she thought about things that she once thought were the result of poor luck or dire circumstances and slowly came to realize there was another explanation. The answers were not plain, but she was slowly realizing that the life she thought she understood may not be as clear as she once thought.

Jordan raced past burned-out buildings and stores enroute to her home on the north side, and thoughts flooded Leena's mind. She thought about how nice the Aberjay neighborhoods looked from her perch inside her hole. She thought about the smell of fresh-cut grass and honeysuckle that she would sometimes take in as she walked by the homes belonging to the Aberjay. She had never really put together the idea that one set of people ruled over another set. She didn't feel oppressed. But maybe concrete and bars are not the only way to keep someone in bondage. Then her thoughts turned to the wall as Jordan turned onto her street. She tilted her head up and from within her mask could see the towering structure way down on the other end of the road. For the first time in her life, she saw the giant wall in a different way. She always knew she lived outside the wall, but for the first time, she saw herself as the danger the wall was seeking to keep out.

Leena grew nervous as they approached her building. She knew what came next. Not only would she have to reveal the extent of her mother's illness, but she would also have to ask for help. And this was going to be a big ask. She was unsure of how Jordan would accept it, or even if she should tell him at all, but reason dictated that she must have help with this operation. She could not do it alone.

Jordan and Leena walked up the stairs to the third floor. Leena had convinced Jordan to stick around so they could talk. She did not look forward to it.

"Jordan, can you wait for me in the garden? I want to check on Mom, and then I will be up." Jordan nodded and kept walking up the stairs.

Jordan was quite familiar with the garden as he had been there multiple times. Before starting his job in the Aberjay factory, he'd helped Leena with gardening and selling their vegetables at the market. Leena and Diego felt the impact of him getting a job and not being around much. Fortunately, Diego and some other neighbors were able to pick up the slack.

Upon entering the apartment, Leena saw Diego feeding her mother some lunch. Leftover broth was on the menu, along with beans. She came close to Diego as he lifted a spoon of broth to her mother's lips. She restrained herself from asking how she was doing but gave a subtle squeeze of Diego's arm to communicate her gratitude that he was there. Leena threw her backpack on her bed and informed Diego of her date waiting for her on the roof.

Leena headed up the stairs feeling a sag in her step, knowing the conversation was going to be a tough one. She found Jordan looking through the garden, pruning plants, and pulling off the dead leaves. He had done this enough in the past that he was just as adept at tending the garden as Leena.

Leena stopped at the door for just a moment, knowing that if she let it go, the door would slam and he would turn to look her way. She needed another moment. She watched as he ran his hands along the stalk of a large okra plant looking for weaknesses or dead growth he could remove. She thought about how together he was as a person. She had never really pictured them as a couple. As she gazed upon his dark-skinned arms and thick head of hair, she could not remember why. He was available, and they were compatible. Then her mind pictured Vincent and her weekly rendezvous, which she quickly erased as irrelevant.

She let the door slam and as expected, gave up her advantage. He looked in her direction and immediately began to apologize for fiddling with her greens, but Leena waved her hand to indicate it was not a problem.

"Can we have a chat, Jordan?"

Jordan followed her to a bench they could share. They both sat down and after a pregnant pause, Leena broke the silence.

"I need your help, Jordan. My mom is sick. Really sick. The doctor says she may not make it much longer. I want you to help me break into a pharmacy and steal the medicine she needs to live."

Leena finished and could see the shock in his eyes. She knew this was as contrary to his soul as it was to hers. She waited for what seemed like an eternity. And then she took his hands and communicated with her eyes. She could see him processing what she had said but could not determine how he might rule on the matter.

Jordan kept her gaze and returned the squeeze of her hand. Looking deep into her eyes, he uttered just one word.

"Okay."

Leena burst with happiness. She expected it would require a long discussion to convince him. She knew what she was asking. If Jordan was caught, he'd be out of a job, have his work permit revoked, have no more income, and could be in jail for quite a while. She felt the weight of this as she thought through the risks and costs of this agenda. She wondered if his willingness to help was because he thought it was the right thing to do or because he secretly had a crush on her. She was not sure which one she preferred.

"How" was the next word out of Jordan's mouth.

"Well, I was hoping we could figure that out together. We should go in at night when the store is closed and find one close to the wall, so if something goes wrong, we can make a quick getaway." She heard herself talking like a gangster and could barely believe this was coming from her mouth as if something had possessed her. She also realized by studying Jordan's expression that he had just realized she wanted to steal from an *Aberjay* pharmacy.

"Wait, are you saying you want to sneak into Zone 7, break into a pharmacy, steal a bunch of drugs, and then escape to the other side of the wall?" Jordan began breathing heavily. "And all without being caught on camera or running into a CPU patrol?"

"Yeah, that is the gist of it," Leena said casually. "But it's not like we're drug dealers. We are trying to save a life. That makes it okay right?"

"Whoa, let me think about this for a minute."

"Take all the time you need. But we should probably go tonight," Leena said while raising her shoulders and squinting, waiting for the blow.

"Tonight?!" Jordan gasped, standing up from the bench. Seeing that Leena was prepared for his explosion, he then decided to lower his energy.

"Leena, this is a big deal. This isn't stealing pies from someone's window. The Aberjay see everything. They have cameras everywhere. The CPU patrols are routine. They have fences around fences and locks on their locks. They are not fooling around."

"But that works in our favor, doesn't it?" Leena said, grasping for anything to make this plan seem a little less mad. "If they are routine, we can observe and have the confidence of knowing when the best time is to get in and get out."

"That makes sense," Jordan said as he scratched his shadow of a beard and continued to mull over the idea.

"There is a pharmacy close to the factory where I work. It has an alley behind it that might be a good place to sit and wait for the opportune moment. But the back of the pharmacy likely has cameras, so we will need to mask ourselves somehow. We also have this problem," he said, pointing to the bracelet on his wrist. "We need to find a way to cover the signal for a little while."

"I have heard that foil will disrupt the signal, but I don't know how well," Leena said, thinking back to earlier in the day when she had met Liv and her friends.

"Okay, so we have somewhat of a plan then. I need to be at work in a couple of hours. I will be done at midnight. Meet me at Banyan Park at about 12:30 a.m. I will have my bike so we can leave it there and then make our way to the pharmacy and check it out. If we don't like the look of things, we are out of there. I am not spending my life in jail for this." Jordan seemed to be sweating even though the air was quite cold. "If we think we can do it safely, we can break in through the back door, grab what we need, and make our way back to the park. I will then go out through the gate like normal, and you can take the meds up through the hole in the wall. Does that sound good?"

Leena responded with a nod to show she was in, but she was terrified at the prospect of doing all that the plan entailed. She had become quite good at getting into the zone, but that was for soup and always during daylight. She did not know what the zone looked like at night or how many patrols there were. She began thinking of all the things that could go wrong and began shaking. Assuming she was cold, Jordan wrapped his arms around her.

"Let's get off the roof," he said as he guided her to the door. "We have a big night ahead of us."

Chapter 4

ESPIONAGE

I t was dark. Very dark. Leena could not remember the last time she was out past midnight. Maybe as a teenager, she would roam the streets with friends and stay out past curfew, but it was not often. She thought about how simple life was then as she zipped up her bomber jacket to shield her from the wintry winds. Her pace was faster than usual, mostly due to adrenaline, as she made her way through the streets to her side of the wall. She could see a few barrel fires still lit from earlier street gatherings that evening, but the streets were eerily quiet now. Most residents did not welcome a curfew violation. Although normally it was just a fine, repeat offenders got jail time. And because the CPU didn't really play by the rules, it was best not to tempt their better nature.

It was nearly midnight when she reached her side of the park. She had been in the park at night, usually when coming back to her zone after hours, but she had never seen it this dark. It was difficult to see the path through the woods that led to the swings. A fog had taken residence in the park. She had a small solar-powered light she had retrieved from her backpack and, after turning it on, clipped it to the front of her jacket to provide some light. Still, her surroundings played tricks on her eyes. She would walk a few steps forward then stop frequently at the sight of something she could barely make out in the darkness that she was certain was a zombie or some other childhood fear, only to realize it was an illusion.

Leena reached the wall and, as usual, made her way down its edge to her tree. Reaching the tree, she nearly collapsed from the tension caused by the walk through the woods. The night was alive. She could hear more sounds of chirping and rustling bushes and cracking than she had ever heard before. She wondered if the sounds were there during the day, and perhaps she had just never noticed them. *Every sound sounds like a predator*, she thought, as she strapped her backpack over her chest and made her way up the tree. In the darkness, she could not see the hole in the wall that was her destination, nor, as she gained some elevation, could she see the ground. She hoped with all her might that the hole would still be there, but something in her told her it was taking too long to reach.

She closed her eyes and quickly inched her way higher and higher until, like a pool of water in a scorching desert, the hole appeared just as she remembered it. She flipped the rope to her hands and pulled herself into the hole. A family of doves flew at her face the moment she entered. They flew everywhere, screaming loudly as Leena struggled to hold onto the rope and pull herself in. A slight error in balance could send her plummeting to the bottom of the wall.

Leena composed herself once inside and desperately wanted to scream, but she knew it was not the best idea. Slithering across the hole and through the rebar, she gained a view of the Aberjay zone. The fog was thick, cloaking the night in a blanket of darkness. Streetlights and home security devices lit up the neighborhood, but the mist that hung in the air made it difficult for the light to travel. At first, this frustrated her, but as she thought more about her view, she realized this benefited her. *Limited visibility will keep me from being seen as I walk through the streets*, she thought.

Once at the bottom of the wall, she took the usual crouching stance to look around and get her bearings. The Aberjay had a similar curfew, and they took it seriously. The streets were empty. She heard nary a sound. Not even the sound of insects and their harmonious symphony. An eerie silence without a single cricket chirping. The transition from the loudness of her side to the tranquil quietness of the zone of the privileged was jarring.

While she normally would take the first main road and make her way down the well-manicured sidewalk, she thought better of it this evening. Sticking to the wall, she walked west toward the park. Just as she had many times before, she placed her left hand on the wall as she walked to ensure she stayed on track and to anchor her in case the fog caused her to lose sight of her destination. She could feel her heart race. She knew she had been here before, so this should not be any different, but this time, the stakes were higher. She knew that getting caught in this zone after curfew carried at least two different charges that were sure to land her in the CPU detainment center.

As she walked along the wall that bordered the back of several houses, she noticed that a car had turned onto the alleyway and would soon overtake her position. She picked up the pace and tried to outrun the car's destination, but it was clear she would not make it. Having nothing else to do, she threw herself to the ground at the base of the wall and put her hands over her head as if to blend into the ground. As the car came around the bend, it turned into a driveway, and the headlights illuminated the wall above Leena's head ever so briefly. She lay silent as the resident exited the vehicle and walked to the back door of their garage.

The stranger paused, then turned, and walked to the end of the driveway. Standing only about thirty feet away, Leena could hear them breathing, and out of the corner of her eye, she could see their warm breath contacting the brisk night. She thought there was little chance they didn't see her lying there. She prepared to run. As quickly as they made it to the end of the driveway, however, the shadow turned and walked back to the door to the garage. Once inside, the light in the garage was extinguished, and Leena felt safe to continue on her path.

As she rounded the next bend, her feet tired as she strode over the uneven ground, she saw the familiar park she had visited so many times before, usually to see Vincent. She felt relieved as she made her way from the dirt and rocks and onto the nicely manicured grass. Large oak trees filled the park, providing significant cover. Walking between them made her feel safe, and she began to relax just a little.

Once at the meeting point, a concession stand in the center of the park, she crouched behind the fabricated wood walls and retrieved a water bottle from her backpack. After drinking heavily from it, she returned it and scanned vigorously for Jordan. Checking her watch, it was now about twenty minutes past midnight. She wondered how far away Jordan's factory was and how long it might take him to travel the distance. Surveying her surroundings, it was clear she was alone. The fog was dense through the park, and it was dark, but the moonlight on this side of the wall provided more reflected light than on her side, providing better visibility.

As she waited for Jordan, her mind wandered to the concession stand that was serving as her hiding place. *What did they sell here?* She could not remember. *Was it ice cream? Soda? Maybe popcorn?* She vaguely remembered going past it with Vincent on one of their many walks but could not recall the primary product that was peddled there.

Leena went into her bag and pulled out several pieces of crinkled aluminum foil she had taken from her kitchen a few hours before. She wrapped them carefully around her bracelet to ward off those who might use technology to locate her. Liv told her plainly that this would disrupt the signal, but she did not know to what extent. The CPU had the ability to call up any citizen and see their location and their history, but the law forbade them from using it as evidence in criminal proceedings as they could easily be hacked.

Leena did not know how to do so, but she had schoolmates who were certain they could change the name and ID information broadcast by the bracelet with a few lines of code. The real value of the locator bracelet to the CPU was real-time visualizations. They could use their tools to see who was in a specific area at a specific time.

Did the aluminum foil cause the signal to show weak, or disappear altogether? Was there software that scanned the streets for bracelets after hours? It would be easy enough if that were the case to send CPU guards to any area where people might be after curfew to hand out citations. These realizations concerned Leena, and she felt further rumination was probably not wise. She was already on her way. No point in second-guessing now.

Suddenly, she could hear the whiz of an electric motorbike. She was certain it would be Jordan as it would be unlikely that anyone else would be out this late. The only people allowed out after curfew were CPU and residents with work permits. She quickly came up with a plan just in case it was not Jordan. Run. Yes, running would have to be the plan as she had little time to devise anything else. Fortunately, as the motorbike came into view through the fog, it was Jordan wearing his familiar helmet and work clothes.

Jordan pulled up next to Leena and, in one motion, sprung off the motorbike while guiding it to a stop. Without any greeting, Jordan began, "We can store the bike right here and head out. The streets are just about empty, so we should be able to make our way to the pharmacy. I drove by there on the way over, and it was quiet."

Leena handed Jordan some strips of aluminum foil for his bracelet, and he quickly covered it. He then grabbed her hand and, with a slight pull, guided her away from the concession stand and into the darkness. She welcomed his guidance as her knees shook with fear of what might become of them if this endeavor failed.

As they approached the pharmacy, Leena grew warm. She unzipped her bomber jacket to allow some air flow as she could feel sweat beads forming under her arms and down her backside. It was still winter, and the temperature was low, so it was not the weather causing her perspiration.

Still holding her hand, Jordan led her to a small alcove connected to the alley. A foul-smelling dumpster provided some cover, although the stench was so off-putting that it forced them to cover their noses and breathe through their mouths. They crouched together, and Jordan pointed toward the back door of the pharmacy, which was within sight about fifty feet away. They were both shielded from view from both sides of the alley. A fence that was quite tall lined one side, and the rear walls of several businesses were on the opposite side.

They sat and listened for activity but heard nothing short of what they assumed were trash trucks moving about several streets away. They took turns staring at the back door of the pharmacy. Leena assumed Jordan was concocting a plan of action.

"I see there is a camera back there," Jordan said, pointing to the door. "But I think if we wear masks and do this quickly, it won't matter."

Jordan reached into his bag and pulled out a crowbar. It was short, only about the size of a hammer. He then gave Leena a ski mask while he put on a spooky mask of a zombie, complete with rotting flesh and exposed teeth, that he'd worn on past Halloween nights. Leena giggled a little, and he cut his eyes at her to remind her that this was not a time for humor.

Leena thought back to her trip through the park in the dark and thought to herself that if Jordan had ridden up to her wearing that mask in the park, she would have died right there. She loved zombie movies and books, but never wanted to meet one in real life.

"Let's go," Jordan said as they made their way to the door.

Jordan wedged his crowbar into the door but could not find enough space to get the leverage necessary to pry it open. He searched and searched for a strategic place to insert the tool but failed to locate one.

"What are you doing?" Leena asked a little louder than she intended.

"I am doing the best I can here," Jordan retorted. "I can't find a place to pry open the door."

"I figured you knew how to do this," Leena said, more nervous about the situation than critical of Jordan.

"Give me a minute; I need to think!"

As they stood with masks on in the glow of the security camera lights, trying to figure out how to proceed, the sound of a large truck startled them. This one was closer than several blocks away.

"Run!" Jordan said as they scurried back to the safety of their dumpster.

As they came near to the dumpster Jodan inadvertently dropped the crowbar causing a loud sound to ring out. Leena bent down and retrieved it and continued to safety. Crouching behind the dumpster, they could hear the truck getting closer. The smell of diesel fuel and putrid trash gave them hope that this was just a trash truck.

"Just stay right here," Jordan said to comfort Leena, who was clearly not okay. "Hopefully, it will just drive past us."

The sound of the truck came closer and closer until it felt like it was on top of them. Then a new sound was clear, and a colossal bang came from the dumpster they were hiding behind. Without warning, the dumpster floated off the ground as if suspended by invisible strings. The bright lights of the truck once shielded by the dumpster were now glaring at them, and they had no choice but to run or surrender.

Jordan and Leena put their hands up as if they had been caught and were resigned to their fate, watching as the truck released the large dumpster into the back of the truck and then lowered it back down to the ground. Leena reached back and dropped the crowbar that was still in her hand into a small opening in her backpack. She felt that holding a weapon in her hand may be considered a threat.

As the dumpster hit the ground and the truck backed up, they both realized they were safe but were only hindering the driver from doing his job. They turned to look at one another, and taking off their masks, they laughed. What started as nervous laughter turned to a roar as they saw the truck turn away from them to continue its way down the alley.

The laughter abruptly stopped when the bright lights of the truck revealed a new shape that emerged from the darkness. It was a CPU vehicle, which had stopped just behind where the truck had just revealed their position. It was small and electric, so it hadn't made a sound. It pulled forward a little and turned to cast its headlights onto the two laughing young people.

"Now we run," Jordan said as he grabbed Leena's hand and took off, running past the garbage truck and into an adjoining alley.

"Stop!" shouted the CPU guards as they realized what had just happened.

The garbage truck eased their getaway as the CPU vehicle could not pass it in the alley. This slight delay gave Jordan and Leena a head start as they ran faster and faster down the alley. As they sprinted, their hands separated, and they reached full speed. They crossed a major street and darted into another alley before turning to the left and making their way toward the park, where they thought they might hide.

Another CPU vehicle, likely alerted to their presence in that section of the zone, came around the corner as they reached the end of the alley just outside the park entrance. These were small vehicles that only fit two guards, but they were silent and fast and allowed the CPU to cast a large net over an area via radio communications between the cars.

Turning to head in the other direction, they were not sure what they could do next. Leena ran until she felt a sharp pain in her side, and her breathing became difficult. Huddling together in a back alley, they tried to gather their strength to continue.

"What are we going to do, Jordan?" Leena whispered.

"I don't know. I think we lost them for now, but they will have the entire guard out here before long. We need to find a place to hide off the streets."

They both breathed heavily for several minutes, trying to come up with the next plan of action. Leena became emotional thinking about how she had failed but choked back the tears. She wondered how she could have been so stupid. Why did she think this plan would work? *What am I, a master thief?*

Then it came to her. Like good news from afar. She began looking around and said, "I know where I am. I know where we can go!"

This time, taking Jordan's hand, she ran to the east without another word.

Leena ran through the east side of Zone 7 as if she lived there. She crossed street after street, leaving Jordan more than a few yards behind her. Enormous trees lined both sides of the residential area, divided by four wide lanes of road. The center median was decorative more than a traffic deterrent, but the trees that grew in the center provided a canopy that almost covered the entire road.

Walking briskly down this street while trying to regain her breath, Leena counted, knowing she had been here several times. It was three houses past the roundabout, she remembered. When she reached her destination, she turned around to meet Jordan's gaze, fully prepared for his first question.

"Jordan, I have a friend who lives here. He will help us."

Jordan stopped to rest, looking up and down the roadway to ensure they were not being followed. He glanced up at the house that was probably five times the size of his own and meticulously maintained, with stately white columns and black exterior shutters that looked as if the homeowner had painted them yesterday.

"Who do you know that lives in Zone 7, Leena?" Jordan asked with a tinge of judgment.

"His name is Vincent Ryder. We are..." Leena paused as she realized she was not sure what they were. They had never really discussed it. They held hands, and they took long walks. They kissed. But the *define the relationship* conversation had never really taken place. "Friends," she eventually added to the end of that sentence.

Jordan looked at her inquisitively with eyes that held shock, disbelief, and a little hurt. Shock because he didn't think she knew anyone in the zone. Disbelief because this was serendipitous that she just had a friend living nearby. And hurt because he had just learned that the object of his affection for years could have a boyfriend.

"Leena, it's 1:45 in the morning. How are you going to get his attention? I assume this is his parents' house, right?"

"Yes, this is his parents' house, but he lives in a guesthouse out back. It should be easy to wake him," Leena said, half-believing what she had said. "This way," she continued as she motioned for Jordan to follow her through a gate at the side of the house.

As they came around the house, Jordan's facial expression communicated that he could not believe what he was seeing. Glass covered the entire back of the house. While dark inside, the pool that it looked out on was brightly lit with underwater lights and light pillars all around the area. Large flagstones covered the deck to provide a smooth surface, and directly across from the home, on the other side of the pool, was a small house about the size of Jordan's own home.

"This is amazing, Leena. Did you say you've been here before?"

"Yes, Vincent had me over several times to hang out and study and go to a couple of pool parties."

"Who are you?" Jordan said under his breath, honestly wondering who this person was he had been spending time with for the last five years. He felt a little hurt that he did not know about this part of her life and decided not to speculate on why she had kept it a secret.

Leena walked to the window next to the door to the guesthouse and began lightly tapping on it. Within a few minutes, a light came on in the guesthouse and a barely-dressed young man came to the door and opened it. He stepped out, half-asleep and wondering if this was a dream.

"Leena? Is that you?" the young man asked.

Leena approached Vincent to hug him, hesitating for just a moment as she thought through what this might look like to Jordan, and then proceeded with the intimate gesture. "Thank you for getting up, Vincent. We need your help."

"We?" said Vincent, looking around and then fixing his eyes on Jordan, who was standing about ten feet from the front door where Leena and Vincent were now trading pleasantries.

Jordan moved in and offered a handshake. "Hi, I'm Jordan."

"Uh, hi," Vincent said, still half-asleep and trying to process what was happening.

"Can we come in, Vincent?" Leena asked in a soft voice.

"Sure, get in here," Vincent replied as he gestured for her to enter and then turned, following her in. Jordan slowly followed but could not decipher the body language between the two.

Vincent went to turn on a light, but Leena suddenly stopped him. "No, let's not." The living room had a long pit sofa for seating and a big wall TV. The only light in the room was coming from Vincent's bedroom. Jordan glanced into the bedroom as he passed, moving from the door to the living area, and quietly wondered as he looked in if Leena had spent much time there.

"Vincent, I'm in trouble... I mean, *we* are in trouble. We tried to break into a pharmacy over on K Street earlier and were spotted by a couple of CPU guards. They chased us. We were able to lose them. We need to hide out here for a bit."

Vincent, now fully awakened by this news, ran to the windows and rushed around the room. "You did *what?* Are they still following you? Why did you come here? Are you crazy?" He looked out each window, expecting to see an army of guards ready to raid the house.

Leena put up her hands in a gesture that was common to Jordan. "Vincent, sit down. Don't make a big deal out of this."

"A big deal? You say you broke the law and want to hide out in my house? Do you know how much trouble I will get in if you are found here? My entire future could be at stake. My parents will short-circuit."

Vincent sat but clearly in protest. He just looked at each of them and continued to breathe heavily. All three of them sat quietly for a spell before Jordan broke the silence.

"Leena, I must get back to the park and get my bike. If I can make it to the park, I can exit through the gate and head back home."

"No, they will suspect you!" Leena shouted.

"No, they won't. I have a permit, and I often work late. The CPU have no reason to believe I was not at work. It is more suspicious if I don't go back home like normal," Jordan reasoned.

"Wait a few more minutes for any patrols to die down. If you get caught before making it to the park, you could be in for it," Leena said.

"Why did you try to break into a pharmacy?" Vincent began, but then he quickly nodded his affirmation as he realized she was after the medication she had spoken to him about earlier in the week. "Well, you are both welcome to stay here if you are sure the CPU did not follow you. In a few hours, they should give up the search, and we can get you back where you belong."

Leena thought his tone was less than kind. And what did *where we belong* mean? She realized at that moment that she had never really seen this side of him before. Scared. Paranoid. Unwilling to show even a hint of compassion for what she was going through. She figured it was his half-woken state that was the culprit and lay down on the couch to rest her eyes for a bit.

Leena woke to find light streaming across her face from the sun shining through the window. She was still on the couch. She heard who she assumed was Vincent in the kitchen cooking. She sat up and rubbed her eyes, allowing her brain to adjust to her surroundings as she had not intended to fall asleep the night before.

As she was about to call out to Vincent, he emerged from the kitchen with two plates of food. He placed one plate in front of Leena as she grabbed a nearby fork and consumed the fried potatoes, some beans, and a slab of pork that was more meat than she had eaten in the last few months.

"Wow, you were hungry," said Vincent while sitting down and salting his meal briefly before beginning to pick at his food. "I am glad you got some sleep. You must have been worn out last night."

"How long was I asleep?" Leena asked between bites.

"About six hours, I think."

"When did Jordan leave?" she asked.

"He left about an hour after you fell asleep. He was very anxious. I hope he made it home okay."

Leena looked at him to see if she could detect sarcasm in his empathy for Jordan. "I will check on him later. First, I need to get out of here. Do you think, now that it's light, that you can drive me to the park so I can make my way back home?" Leena finished the last of her beans after cleaning her plate and sat back on the couch.

"Sure," Vincent replied, "let me just get cleaned up. Are you sure you know what you are doing? I am worried about you. I know you want to save your mom but this rebellion will ruin your future. You know that don't you?"

Leena just stared at him. She realized at that moment how different they were. She didn't have any hope of a future. She never did because of where she was born. His view of the world was quite different to hers, filled with opportunities. There was no way she could get him to see through her eyes so she decided not to try.

"I have to do what I can to help my mom Vincent. Now go get ready."

As she digested the meal she had practically inhaled, her eyes drifted to something irritating her arm. It was a strip of aluminum foil. Her bracelet had come free from the foil somehow, most likely while she was sleeping. Her mind began racing to remember whether it was like that before she went to sleep. *Did it fall off during the chase?* She just couldn't remember. *Is it possible they could have tracked her?*

The answer to her question came all too soon when, seconds later, the front door exploded, sending slivers of wood into the air as smoke and the smell of sulfur from the explosives filled the air. Leena jumped up and tried to run, but the CPU quickly captured her as an army of CPU soldiers stormed the small room. After they threw her to the ground, the soldiers handcuffed her and then jerked her into a standing position. Leena coughed from the smoke that filled the room. As she was being escorted from the small home, she thought she heard a soldier say, "Thank you, Mr. Ryder" as they rushed her into a CPU truck and placed a black fabric bag over her head.

The CPU had caught her. She didn't know what to say, or whether to cry out for help or keep silent. She could not see but heard the loud truck churn and whine as it changed gears and tossed her small frame from left to right, making many turns on the way to its destination.

She could feel the warmth of another body next to hers and for a moment thought it might be Jordan. She tried to lift her head to see through the black fabric but was punched in the gut by what felt like the stock of a rifle. Her seatmate was a CPU soldier. The sound of the trucks and the aggression of her travel mate caused her to realize it was best to keep her mouth shut. Maybe they would just take her to the other side of the wall and let her go?

Leena's hopes of a quick release were dashed when they removed her head covering and revealed they were entering the CPU detainment complex she had visited so many years before on a student field trip. In all her musings at the time, she never thought she would return as a criminal. Shame enveloped her as they brought her through a covered passage and then into an open area that was fenced on all sides. CPU soldiers dragged Leena from the vehicle and marched her into a building through steel doors at least ten feet tall.

A guard led Leena to a holding cell. When the guard removed her handcuffs, dark red marks were visible just above her hands where the cuffs were over-tightened on her small wrists. She rubbed the wounds with her hands to increase blood flow as she could see they were already bruising. Her cell was cramped, with a toilet and tiny sink in the corner, and there was a smell of stale air. She made her way to the back of the cell and sat on the cold steel bench affixed to the wall. Emotion overcame her, and she wept, first for her stupidity and then for her guilt at failing her mother.

There was no sleeping in this cell. It was not nearly quiet enough. The sounds of cell doors opening and closing, the screams of inmates, and the constant changes in temperature as the main doors opened and closed made sleep impossible. She lay on that steel bench, wondering what was going to happen next. She did not know the time, but it had to be midday as she had been there with no new information for many hours.

"On your feet, little lady," a loud voice rang out.

Leena turned to look and saw a large balding white man with a shockingly ugly brown suit and even uglier gray tennis shoes that did not match his outfit. She sat up but stayed seated. "Who are you?"

"I am your nu...nu...knight in shining armor, little lu...lu...lu...lady. Gil Vernon is the name. I am your lu...lu...lu...lawyer."

"I have a lawyer?" Leena asked with a sneer.

"You do when you don't have any muh...muh...muh...money. I am appointed by the court to represent you."

As Leena was about to reply, a guard moved past the oddly dressed attorney with the severe stutter and opened the cell to let him enter, and then closed the door behind him.

"Let's see," said Gil, looking through a stack of papers he was carrying. "Oh yes, here it is. You are charged with tu...tu...trespassing, cu...cu...cu...curfew violation, breaking and entering, and e...e...e...evading arrest. Does that sound about right?"

Leena just looked at him as if there was no suitable answer to his inquiry. Why did his speech sound so strange? She'd never encountered anyone with a stutter.

"Sorry, I have a spee...spee...spee... sometimes I stutter. Well, I suggest you plead guilty and hope the judge will give you...you...you...a lenient sentence. You have not been in trouble before, right?"

Again, Leena just looked at him, wondering when he was going to be helpful.

"Do you have anything to say for yourself? I am not the enemy here, lit...lit...lit...little girl. I am trying to help you."

Leena could barely believe she was in this position. She thought about how she had failed her mother. How she ended up in this place. Things she could have done differently. After a minute and a stray tear, she looked up at her attorney. "It was for my mother."

"I'm sorry, what did you say? It was for your mother?"

"I need medicine for my mother. She is dying. I was trying to get medicine from the pharmacy." Leena looked down at the ground, now crying quietly.

"Well, didn't you realize the pharmacy was cl...cl...closed?" Gil said, clearly indicating how little he understood of her situation. "You will need to go to an arraignment tomorrow morning.

I will be there, but you will need to say you are innocent or gil...gil...guilty. If you plead innocent, they will want to know why you...you...you...think you are innocent, and we can make a case. If you plead gil...guilty, they will give you the maximum sentence unless you allow me to arrange for a plea bargain for you ahead of time. I can probably get the breaking and entering thrown out as you never actually entered the place, but you will not get out of the tre...tre...tre...trespassing or curfew violation since you were clearly caught in a zone you don't live in and were caught on camera out after cur...cur...curfew."

Gil thought for a moment and then continued. "Yes, you need to plea bargain this thing. I can probably get you tuh...tuh...two years if you let me."

Leena thought about spending the next two years in prison. Her life was suddenly over. Two years would mean never seeing her mom again. It might mean never seeing Diego again. She would lose her loved ones, her apartment, her garden on the roof. The CPU would certainly ban her from any future school, and she would never get a work permit. Her mind raced to find a solution as she felt she would not survive in prison for two years.

"Fernando," Leena said without thinking.

"What was that you said?" Gil asked, acting as if he was only half listening.

"Fernando Martinez," Leena continued. He is a friend of the family. He is the zone advocate.

"Yes, I am aware of who he is, little girl, but just wuh...wuh...wuh...what do you think he can do for you?"

"He is a friend, well, he is a family friend. I know his dad." Leena's high hopes drifted downward as she thought about what he had told her in the coffee shop. He told her not to get involved with Liv, and now she was sitting in jail. *How would he see this? Would he even come to help?*

"Well, I will try to puh...puh...post a note to the zone advocates' office, but I would not put too much hope in that. I think you would be buh...buh...better off dealing with the issue at hand, young lady." Gil was now getting a bit irritated. "I'll tell you what. I will just let you decide what you want to do. I will be back tuh...tuh...tomorrow, and we can discuss which way you want to go before we go to court."

Her court-appointed attorney packed his stacks of paper and signaled for the guard to release him. Leena watched as he strode down the hallway to freedom, secretly wishing she could have hidden in the pocket of his ugly suit so he could take her out of this place.

Leena curled up on the cold, hard steel bench once more and got lost in her feelings of loss and despair. As she tried to warm herself by rubbing her arms, her mind transported her back to her arrest. Something was not right. As traumatizing as it was, something was out of place. Something was not sitting well with her soul. Then she remembered. "Thank you, Mr. Ryder," she heard the soldier say. And then it hit her.

"That son of a bitch turned me in!"

Leena slept little that night in the small holding cell. The bench was cold, and the prison was noisy. Her mind raced as she tried to come up with a solution to her life-altering dilemma. She knew little of the law and wished more than anything that her mom could come to tell her what to do. When she was young, all she wanted to do was grow up and be an adult. Now she just wanted to go back to her childhood and have others care for her. She wanted someone to rescue her.

She tried to wash her face in the tiny sink and waited as long as she could to use the toilet as it was out in the open with no walls or barriers to block those passing by her cell from seeing. At one point, a guard slid a tray into her cell: a slice of bread, lukewarm tea, and what can only be described as mush. She took a few bites of the bread and drank the tea but was hesitant to try the mush.

Several hours later, Gil arrived. Following the same procedure as before, the guard let him into the cell, and Gil fumbled once again for the right file. "Okay, Leena," he began, "what do you want to duh...duh...do about these charges?"

Leena felt fortunate that he had used her name. That was some progress, she reasoned. She had thought about what she was going to do all night but had little insight to guide her to the right decision, nor did she know if there was even such a thing in this scenario. It seemed to her she could say she was guilty and take the two years or say she was innocent and try to make her case. But did she have a case to make? As Gil had pointed out, she figured she might get out of the breaking and entering because she never got into the building, but the trespassing and curfew violations would be impossible to overcome. Nor could evading the CPU be successfully argued.

"I think it is best at this point to plead guilty to all but the breaking and entering charge, Mr. Vernon," she answered him.

"Okay, let me talk to the other attorney and see if we can get a p...p...plea deal in place before court. We are due upstairs in about two hours." Gil rose from the bench and, clutching precariously to his stacks of paper, motioned to the guard to let him out.

"I will see you soon, Leena," he said as he left.

The guard on duty handcuffed Leena and escorted her to a small room where she was asked to change clothes. A bright, yellow one-piece jumpsuit was provided. She took off her clothes and put on the small canary suit before being marched upstairs. After being escorted into a small empty courtroom, she was asked to sit in a barely human-sized glass box that contained one chair. A microphone in the box allowed her to speak so that she could be heard outside the glass. After sitting alone for a few minutes, several people filed into the court, including Gil Vernon looking disheveled.

Gil sat a few feet away from her at a big brown table, sorting through his papers. At another table was a well-dressed woman—apparently another attorney. A few others came in to fill the seats in the gallery of spectators. She didn't recognize anyone except Gil. She had hoped that maybe someone she knew would come to her rescue. Once the courtroom became quiet, a large African-American woman in a guard's outfit stood and declared, "All rise, this honorable court is now in session, Judge Waylan Hastings presiding!"

A door next to the judge's empty chair opened and a tall man with long white hair entered. He wore thin glasses on his long nose as well as floor-length black robes. After getting settled in his chair, he said, "You may be seated."

The expressionless, overweight guard then stated, "Zone 7 magistrate versus Leena Zhen, your honor" while handing the judge an electronic tablet.

"Very well," the judge replied. "Would the defendant please stand?"

Gil Vernon looked over and motioned for Leena to rise, which she did without hesitation, not wanting to show any disrespect for the formality of the proceedings.

The judge looked at Leena and then to Gil Vernon and said, "Your client has been charged with trespassing into Zone 7, breaking and entering, violating curfew, and evading arrest. How does she plead?"

Gil began fumbling through his files. "Just one muh...muh...moment your honor," he said as he flipped through file after file. He looked as though he had lost something.

Leena wondered why it was so difficult for him to remember a conversation they just had a couple of hours ago. *What is it that he is looking for,* she wondered.

"I am waiting, Mr. Vernon," the judge stated, irritated at having his time wasted.

"It seems, your honor, that I have fuh...fuh...fuh...forgotten an important file that is re...re...relevant to this case, and if giv...giv...given the opportunity, I would be most appre...appre...appreciative if you could see fit to let me retrieve it from my office..."

"Request denied, counselor," the judge snapped. "How does your client plead?"

"Well, it seems," Gil began as if continuing down the same path while still fumbling for files, "that my client does nuh...nuh...nuh...not believe there exists a cu...cu...cu...cause for charges to be brought against her in the mah...mah...mah...matter of breaking and entering and fuh...fuh...fuh...further believes that the other chu...chu...charges are a matter that causes me to recommend to this court..."

"Counselor, it seems you are not ready to have this candidate arraigned. Maybe it is in the best interest of this defendant if we postpone these proceedings until you are better prepared."

"Yes, your honor, I gu...gu...gu..." Gil replied in resignation.

"Case postponed for thirty days. Please remand the defendant to processing until a proper arraignment can be completed." The judge slammed his gavel and then demanded the bailiff call the next case.

"What does that mean?" Leena said into the microphone, hoping her attorney could hear her.

Gil just put up his hands as if to calm her. A guard motioned for Leena to stand and follow her as she led her out of the courtroom and returned her to the small brick cell where she had now been for more than twenty-four hours.

Leena had no idea what had just happened in the courtroom except that it was clear she would be in custody for at least another month. This was not good news but certainly not the worst. Within hours of being led back to her cell, a pair of guards came to retrieve her again.

"Where are you taking me now?" Leena demanded.

"You are being relocated to the prison," a guard said in a monotone voice.

Chapter 5

PRISON

Not once in her life did Leena think she would ever be in prison. She was a good girl. The one who finished her breakfast and always completed her homework. She understood right from wrong. Her mother had instilled a strong sense of ethics and community in her. Aside from a few rebellious years growing up, she had always done the right thing. Certainly, her incarceration was a mistake.

The guard outside the detainment building directed Leena to a waiting bus. It was green with bars on the windows and cages inside. She saw that there were a few other prisoners in the back of the bus. Once she was seated near the front, the bus made its way through the city streets to a highway heading north. She was not sure where the prison was located but knew her home was south. The bus made a clicking sound as it traveled, marking off the miles. Tick, tick, tick. With every tick, she knew she was farther from home. The sights soon turned from city streets and homes to trees and farmland.

The prison was an imposing building made of cinder blocks and separated into what looked like a shamrock of structures. It was surrounded by high fences and razor wire everywhere she looked. The lofty towers were populated by guards with rifles. As the bus drew closer to the facility and then made its way inside the fences, Leena grew more anxious.

As the bus passed an enormous field sectioned by more fenced boundaries, she noticed that all the inmates were wearing the same canary-yellow jumpsuits. She looked down as if to confirm she was now one of them, but she already knew the truth. She was hoping it was a dream rather than the nightmare she was experiencing. The prisoners in the yard milled about in the dirt that flew up when the wind blew. The yard was empty of chairs or any type of equipment that might shield them from the wind. They seemed to huddle together like rodents, forming small groups for warmth and security.

The bus came to a stop outside a small alcove with two steel doors like the detainment center she had just left. As directed, she stepped off the bus and walked through the doors. Once inside, the guard removed her handcuffs and put her in a line of prisoners who were marched to a large room where they were asked to take a seat and await processing. She looked around and realized that these were her bus mates. She had ridden with them from the detainment center to the prison, but she hadn't paid any attention to them. She was too worried about her own fate.

Shortly after arriving, the prisoners were processed one by one. As they were guided away from the room by guards, each one would disappear and then reappear a few minutes later with a handful of what looked like linens and toiletries. Leena began to panic. *This is really happening*, she thought. *There is no escape.* Then it was her turn.

Leena followed the female guards, conscious of the guard behind her as well. She entered a small room where she removed her clothing. She was embarrassed and tried to cover her private parts as the guard directed her to a small, tiled area that looked like a shower. The guards shone an ultraviolet light brightly on her body as she washed herself. After several uncomfortable minutes, she dried her body and once again donned the yellow jumpsuit.

A guard directed her to a window where a stack of goods was waiting. She could now see that the items included an extra jumpsuit, bed linens, a pillow, a tiny toothbrush, and a tube of toothpaste along with a bar of soap, shower shoes, and a roll of toilet paper.

After processing, another guard led her down a long hall with several doors that had to be unlocked electronically, which relocked behind her as she passed through them. She saw signs for A block, B block, and C block, and assumed these were the clover-like structures she had observed from the outside. Upon entering C block, she could see prisoners on the ground floor, some sitting in circles or playing cards at steel tables. The tables were bolted to the floor so that they could not be used as weapons.

Leena's new home had six levels with the cells on each level facing the open area in the middle. Stairs flanked both sides of the prison, and prisoners were allowed to mingle on these stairways. A cage prevented prisoners from jumping from their tier to the floor below. She wondered if those were installed due to the number of inmates that had jumped to their death after being in this place for a lengthy period of time.

The sound coming from the residents resembled a large ocean wave, almost deafening. As the guards led her and her fellow new arrivals inside the structure, the sound subsided a little as the existing occupants stopped to examine their new neighbors.

Walking up the stairs, Leena tried to keep her head low. All of the inmates were women. Women of all sizes and types. They were large, small, black, Hispanic, Asian, fat, or skinny, and wore short hair, long hair, or no hair. She felt their stares as she climbed higher, finally directed to turn down a hallway on the fifth floor.

"Zhen, you are in here," one guard said, pointing to a room marked C508.

Leena entered a small cell and could tell that half of the room was home to some other poor soul. The bed was made, and toiletries rested on a small shelf. Everything in the room was steel or aluminum, and probably once shined brightly, but after years of abuse had become dim, matching the demeanor of the occupants. Each side had a bed that was low to the ground. In the middle was a tiny sink and toilet that matched the one she had in her holding cell, along with a faux mirror made of aluminum that cast a faded reflection.

Leena was nervous about her missing roommate and needed to occupy her mind, so she began placing her toiletries on the small shelf, trying to match the layout of the other. She slipped her bath shoes under her bed and unrolled her bed sheets to make the bed. She looked at the other bed and wondered if the occupant had been in the military as she had never seen sheets tucked so tightly. Attempting to do the same, she tucked and tucked and ultimately decided it was easier to hide her handiwork with the blanket.

She was not sure what would happen next. The guards had moved on without further instruction, and the door was open. Prisoners seemed to go in and out of their cells at their leisure, and for a moment, she thought about going out to have a look around but thought better of it when she heard shouting that sounded like the beginning of a fight. She would soon learn that this happened often, though the chaos would typically subside as quickly as it started. As Leena sat on her bed, her mind was filled with so many thoughts she could not decipher them.

Leena spent the next hour crying, feeling sorry for herself and regretting many of the choices that landed her in prison. As she peered up at the ceiling, filled with chipped and peeling paint, her heart wrestled with a gamut of emotions. Fear for her new life in prison. Anxiety about what might become of her. Anger at Vincent for turning her in. Regret for getting Jordan into trouble.

She was not sure what happened to Jordan. She wondered if he might be somewhere in one of these prison blocks, just on the other side of this wall or that. She hoped not. She felt the connection she had with him had grown deeper. Even though she did not know of his fate, she still felt a strengthened bond because of the experience they shared. She knew in the back of her mind that he could be dead or imprisoned like her, but she chose to believe he eluded authorities and made it out of the zone.

From the doorway of the cell came a voice: "Hey, New Blood."

Standing tall in the doorway was a slender athletic girl, probably in her mid-twenties. Her hair was black and shaved short. She looked Asian but most likely Filipino rather than Chinese, which would be unusual in this part of the country. She wore the same canary-yellow jumpsuit but had ripped the sleeves off to reveal well-defined arms that spoke volumes about her workout regimen. Leena looked at her but did not respond.

"Don't you know when someone is talking to you? Are you deaf?"

"I am just not sure how I am supposed to respond to that. Is *New Blood* my new name?" Leena said matter-of-factly, trying to act tougher than she knew herself to be.

"It will be for a while. New blood gets a lot of focus around here. But before you know it, there will be more new blood to capture the attention of the masses." The girl walked to the bed across from Leena and sat with her legs crossed. "I'm Clover. Clover Reyes. What's your name?"

"Leena Zhen."

"What did you do? Curfew violation?" Clover asked with obvious sarcasm. "You don't look too dangerous."

"I prefer not to talk about it," Leena said, although that was probably the furthest thing from the truth.

"Alright, New Blood, no problem. I get it. You need to adjust." Clover repositioned herself on the bed to lay back and look at the ceiling. "But you need friends in here. You better decide quickly who your friends are, or this place will eat you alive."

Leena did not love the prospect of having to make friends in this place. Nor did she know how. She had never been good at making friends. Pity overcame her for a little while as she sat in silence with her new roommate. But then she decided she had to make the best of her situation if she ever wanted to change it. Leena sat up and faced the other side of the room and thought she would start her rehabilitation with Clover.

"I'm sorry. It's nice—well, I guess it isn't nice, but, um—to meet you, I mean. My name is Leena. I know I already said that. Sorry, I'm nervous. I have never..."

"Been in prison before," Clover finished her thought. "It's okay. I have been here for a bit. I will walk you through it."

"I would appreciate the help," Leena said, grasping for the next topic of conversation in this awkward exchange. "Maybe you could tell me a little about this place and how it works."

Clover sat up on her bed and turned to face Leena. She looked at the open cell door as if she was waiting for someone to enter. She reached over to her sink shelf and grabbed what looked like a small toothbrush and began picking at her teeth.

"It's simple. Make friends, but don't trust anyone. Mind your own business and try not to insult anyone or piss anyone off. Keep your eyes open at all times. If you need anything, let me know, and I can help you find the right person to get it for you."

Leena asked, "Can you help me get out of here?"

"No can-do, New Blood," Clover said emphatically. "The system has got you now. You may never go home."

Leena knew she said it sarcastically, but it still hit her hard. She did not want to give up and was resolved to find a way out.

Clover continued her thought with more helpful information. "We eat breakfast at seven a.m. and dinner at five p.m. The food sucks, but it will keep you alive. We can take showers once a week and are limited to five minutes. Don't forget your shoes and your soap; there isn't any extra in there. The guards will watch you shower, so you must get used to that. There are cameras everywhere, so they don't mess with us much. And most of the guards are women, so that helps. We go outside every morning at eleven for one hour. Other than that, we are just killing time in here."

"When do they close this door?" Leena asked, pointing to the cell door.

"At night about nine p.m. But that is a good thing, trust me. If they didn't, people would wake up with their cellmates' throats slit every morning. It opens back up around 6:30 a.m."

"Do we get visitors?" Leena asked, trying to pry as much information as she could before Clover's generosity expired.

"If you are lucky enough to have visitors, the guards will come get you and take you to them. You are not allowed to touch, and they can't give you anything, but they can add credits to your commissary if they want. Just like outside, everything is controlled right here," Clover finished, pointing to her bracelet.

Leena tried to process the information. As she did, she noticed the small window at the top of her cell. She had not really noticed it before as it was just below the ceiling. Clover noticed her investigating the window and offered some clarity.

"You won't get out that way. Even if you could break the glass, remove the bars, and get through that small hole, it is a straight drop to the ground. You would not survive it. It is nice to have a window and some proper light in here, though. Many cells don't have one. See there, your luck has turned already. You got premium accommodation. Let me go arrange for your spa treatment." Clover got up and left the room, but as she was leaving, she said, "I will come get you for dinner. Welcome to hell, little one."

The time in prison ticked away slowly. As if time was standing still. There's a reason they call it *doing time,* Leena thought. There's plenty of time to think about your failures. Those you hurt. Those you put in danger. You struggle to come up with a justification for your crimes, but there are rarely any that satisfy you. The time for dinner came, and Clover popped back into the room.

"Let's go, New Blood," Clover said in a less cordial voice than before.

Leena got out of bed and rubbed her eyes. She was not sure if she had napped, but the stress of the day was taking a toll on her energy level. She was hungry and thought about her garden. She hoped the food was better than at the detainment center.

Leena followed Clover to the dining hall along with about two hundred other prisoners. The hall was one big room with a line of food carts on one side and workers dishing out the food onto metal trays. In the middle was metal benching for prisoners to sit as they consumed their meals. The room filled up quickly, and she made her way through the line. She tried to follow Clover's lead and grabbed a tray and a set of plastic utensils. Working through the line, she would stick out her tray to each worker, who would slop the food onto the tray. The first looked like creamed corn, while the second looked like more mush. The third was a slice of burned bread, and the last was, once again, a cup of lukewarm tea in a plastic cup.

Leena followed Clover and sat down next to her. She could feel eyes on her and figured it was New Blood Syndrome. She ate what was on her plate, even though it had little taste. She yearned for her greens and beans, or maybe a bowl of soy okra—a combination of fried okra and salted soybeans. She decided in that moment that she would never take food for granted again. What she was eating was neither tasty nor nutritious. She remembered Clover saying that you could survive on it, and in her mind, she thought that if that were true, it was just barely true.

Leena met several inmates at the table. Claudia was in for murdering her neighbor over a disagreement about a television show. She didn't seem completely sane, and Leena made a mental note to avoid her. Maggie was a sweet one, a short Korean girl imprisoned for stealing food. She looked more afraid than Leena, but a large girl named Maxine kept her close and looked after her. Maxine was a truck driver. She was busted for running guns for the Resistance. It was a motley crew indeed. Leena was not positive she fit in with this bunch.

"Hey, New Blood!" Leena heard a voice ring out from behind her. She turned her head just in time to see the tray come at her like a bullet, smashing into her face. She fell back across the table and felt someone on top of her punching her in the stomach and chest. The room erupted in shouting as prisoners gathered around to see the new girl receive her welcome.

As she braced herself for another blow, she could see Clover through the eye that was not filled with blood. Her cellmate jumped the perpetrator and pulled them off and onto the floor. Clover began punching her in the face until the floor, her fist, and the victim's face shared the same red color.

Guards were on top of Clover and her victim within seconds and pulled them apart. It took two guards per prisoner to drag them from the room. Leena tried to wipe away the blood from her eye, which was gushing from the cut on her forehead. She was lying on the dining table and knew she needed to get up, but her stomach muscles were failing to provide enough strength. She inched her body slowly to the edge until she fell, first onto a chair and then onto the cement floor. Blood seemed to be everywhere, some of which was hers, but the majority belonged to the girl who jumped her.

Feeling embarrassed and unsure of what to do next, Leena pulled herself up to the table and sat on the bench, still feeling stunned while the entire room seemed to snap back into meal mode. Everyone looked back at their trays and began normal conversation as if nothing happened. Leena felt blood flowing down one side of her face and clasped her side as her ribs felt bruised.

A guard returning from wherever they took Clover coldly asked, "You okay?"

"I think so," Leena responded without really thinking about the question, responding more out of instinct than reason.

The guard handed her a handful of napkins for the blood and went back to her post.

Leena was sure she had done nothing to provoke this outburst but was certain she did not want to repeat it. She thought once again about *New Blood Syndrome* and wondered if it was some sort of initiation. She could think of no other explanation.

Leena returned to her cell by following the crowd. Clover was not there when she returned, nor did she show up that evening. Shortly after 9 p.m., a loud buzzer sounded, and the cell door closed automatically, as Clover had said it would. The swelling in Leena's face had subsided, and she cleaned the cut over her eye as best she could with sink water and some leftover napkins. She hurt all over. Once again, tears swelled up as she thought about her situation. She didn't think she would make it.

Her cell was dark. She could see through her little window that night had descended in the outside world. Her tiny home reciprocated as the four lights in the ceiling shut down simultaneously. The only light streamed in from the main courtyard, casting shadows on the wall behind her—a reminder of her captivity. She lay on her bed looking at the ceiling, writhing in pain and too afraid to sleep.

She thought about the slit throat comments Clover made earlier and wondered, if she were to sleep, would the perpetrators be able to get in? Maybe these night slayers had master keys? What if these ghouls were just waiting for the opportune moment to pounce? She reasoned that further internal debate about the possibility would only prevent her from getting sleep, which she would need to get through the next day. Closing her eyes, she tried to put the thoughts of what might happen out of her mind and focused on getting some rest for her worn body.

She could hear the prison settling down now. Leena heard only a few sounds, most of which she could not decipher. The movement of the residents had subsided, and all that was left was a ringing in her ears and the pounding of her heart in her chest. *What will tomorrow bring? Where is Clover? And what if she doesn't return before breakfast?*

Leena woke to the sound of the buzzer that signaled the opening of her cell door. She looked around in a daze and she was still alone. She was disoriented and sluggish, her body still tingling from the peaceful slumber she had been in, yet her injuries reminded her of the previous day. She crawled out of bed with an anxious eye on the cell door, quietly wishing any monsters away.

Grabbing her toothbrush, she began her morning routine. Going through the same tasks that she checked off every other day of her life, but now being in this horrible place, was surreal. It was like she stepped into someone else's body and began living their life. She looked at herself in the aluminum mirror, but the reflection was poor. Her left side was quite bruised from the beating she took the day before, and the swelling above her left eye had subsided, but the cut was still highly visible, and the pain she felt all over her body was still screaming for attention.

Clover entered the cell as swiftly as she had the day before. She did not speak as she entered but headed toward the sink to begin her morning tasks, starting with her toothbrush, just as Leena had.

Leena was not sure what to say. She looked fine, so her tussle with Leena's attacker did not seem to leave her beaten and bruised. Leena mustered the courage to speak first. "Are you okay?"

"I'm fine, kid," she replied, trying to mask any emotional hurt she might have suffered. "You really took a beating, didn't you?" Clover moved toward Leena, now sitting on the bed, eyeing her injuries. "Do you think you broke anything?"

"I don't think so, but it hurts pretty bad."

"I bet it does. You will want to take it easy for the next couple of days."

"What happened, Clover?" Leena asked, trying to understand what she did to invoke the wrath of her fellow inmate.

"Nothing, kid, they just saw new blood and wanted to make sure you knew not to mess with them. It happens a lot. Stasha is the girl who jumped you. She is an angry one. She is the muscle for Tina, who sells a lot of goods in here."

Leena considered inquiring about the merchandise but quickly assumed what it was and decided she didn't need to know the details.

"Next time that happens, fight back."

"Next time?" Leena asked loudly.

"Yeah, once they see they can get to you, they will keep coming. They are like bullies in high school. You have to show them you will fight back, or they will keep hitting on you again and again."

"I guess I am just not built that way," Leena said, quietly realizing that her small stature and lack of killer instincts were deficiencies in this place. She continued, "How did you fight off Stasha? She's twice your size. And you don't have a scratch on you."

"Well, I surprised her, for one." Clover boasted with a smirk. "But if you know a few good defensive moves, size is not really relevant."

This piqued Leena's interest. She had always been very self-conscious of her size, feeling less than others. She had been called little girl, shrimp, bonbon, half-pint, and other less-than-kind names over the years. At that very moment, it just dawned on her why everyone called her "kid." It always bothered her. Liv was not the only one. And now Clover seemed to have taken to the practice. She knew she had to learn this magic that Clover seemed to wield against oversized predators.

"Can you teach me some?"

Clover sat on her bed across from her, just staring for what seemed like minutes. Leena's face was one of desperation, attempting to break through Clover's rough exterior.

"It's called kali. It's a martial art. My whole family practices it. Are you sure you want to learn it? I can give you some basics, but I am no teacher."

"Yes, please. I took some karate classes growing up, but I was very young and I am not sure I remember any of it." Leena said.

"Okay, stand up. I want you to hit me."

Leena stood slowly but failed to attack. She lifted her hand above her head as if she was knocking on a door.

"No, not like that, kid, punch like this!" Clover demonstrated the exact motion of throwing a powerful punch while guiding Leena's fist until it made contact with her open hand. "Great, try it again. Hit harder. Now harder. Good. Now I am going to show you a defensive move. Hit me again."

Leena threw her punch a little faster than her previous attempts and, in a flash, was on the floor. Clover had taken her arm and, after a successful block, used her opponent's weight to throw her to the ground. Leena lay on the ground a little out of breath from the fall. Clover helped her to her feet.

"Great, now you do it."

They repeated the same moves with their positions reversed. Leena didn't really get it at first, but after a few tries, she was putting her opponent on the ground with little effort.

"This is amazing!" Leena said. "I don't even know how I am doing it."

"You are just using your attacker's weight against them. It's all physics."

Leena and Clover worked on different defensive moves until breakfast and then returned to their cell to spend the rest of the day and several days after that training. Clover taught her the ability to move her body to her best advantage when defending herself and quickly moved on to some basic hand-to-hand combat moves. They used toilet paper rolls to simulate knives in their simulations, giving Leena an education in not only hand-to-hand combat but some weapons training as well. The focus was always on defense.

Leena went to bed each night exhausted from the day's workout. They trained in the cell and outside in the yard. They even practiced at mealtime without leaving their steel bench. Leena learned about kali and some meditative techniques to calm her mind.

The training renewed Leena's spirit. She had never been an aggressive person but felt the techniques she was learning were beyond necessary to survive. It provided a self-respect she had never experienced before. She felt more capable in this world. Able to defend herself against anything, whether violent or otherwise. She also grew close to Clover, feeling like she was family. Leena hoped Clover felt the same about her. She had very few female friends and was more of a loner in school. This was her first authentic female friend since elementary school, and although she was still desperate to find a way out of the prison and back to her mother, she felt fortunate to have someone looking out for her that she could call a friend.

Chapter 6

VISITORS

L eena walked down the bright corridor with several other inmates wrapped in towels. She looked forward to the weekly shower. It was only five minutes, but it felt like the hot water washed away the painful regret of choices that landed her here. The shame, the guilt, the anger. It all seemed to wash away on shower day.

She followed several others back to her block, clutching her soap and towel tightly as it was not uncommon to have a fight break out in this hall over something as silly as soap. Not everyone was lucky enough to have funds in their commissary account, and soap was not free. Taking from someone else was the only option for that unfortunate bunch. Leena didn't have much, but they allowed her to transfer a few thousand credits from her bracelet when she first arrived. She did not know how she would refill it after those funds were gone.

Leena walked into her cell to find Clover getting dressed after her shower. She crossed the room to retrieve a comb and began running it through her hair. Leena didn't enjoy having to wash her hair with soap. It left her hair dry and brittle. It didn't seem to lie right. She could purchase shampoo with commissary funds, but she didn't want to waste the money and felt she could make the sacrifice. She really didn't know how long she would be there.

"Clover, you never told me what you did to get put in this place."

"No, I didn't," Clover said with an edge that showed it was sensitive territory.

"Come on, I told you my story. What is your deal?"

Clover grabbed the comb out of Leena's hand and made a quick jab at her to test her reflexes. Leena parried the strike and hit her attacker softly in the ribcage. This playacting was commonplace now that she was in training. Satisfied with the result of the impromptu exercise, Clover moved backward and sat on the bed.

"I am in here because I deserve to be here," she said, quietly composing her story.

"I live on the west side of the city near the wall like you," she said, motioning to Leena. "The CPU needed to make space to extend the wall and create some barracks or something on the other side of the wall. They showed up and said we had to move. They were going to take our house from us. Eminent domain, I think they call it. They told us they would tear it down along with several others on that street to make space for their project." Clover paused, getting a little choked up.

"I have eleven brothers and sisters. We all lived in that home with our parents, grandparents, and a few cousins."

"Wow, that is a lot of people in one house. It must have been huge," Leena said.

"No, not really. We slept six in each room and shared a bathroom. But we were together. That was all that mattered to us."

"So, that does not really answer the..." Leena started before being interrupted.

"I am getting to that. The CPU had started construction of a building that was to run right through my house. My family, along with a few friends, decided we would blow it up."

"Really?!" Leena asked. "That is insane."

"What else could we do? They were taking our house. No payment, no relocation. They just said to get out or we will bury you in it." Clover stood and began boxing at thin air to counter the powerful feelings she was having while telling her story.

"We knew it would not stop them, but we thought it might slow down the project long enough for us to figure out where we could go. We scored some explosives from a friend. My grandfather was in the army, so he knew how to set it up. We snuck over at night and placed the charges, but when we tried to set them off, they failed. We figured the detonator was bad, or possibly our friend had sold us faulty materials. We feared getting close to it in the dark and waited until morning when we might see breaks in the line or something. By morning, workers had shown up to continue construction, and the wall exploded without warning. The blast killed three workers and a CPU guard." Clover's expression revealed regret, and she dropped her chin. She then lifted her head and continued angrily. "I found out later they gave our homes away for some deal that was made with the Aberjay to increase work permits or something. It is just so stupid. We got put out of our homes so a few high school kids could get a job in a factory."

"That is awful, Clover. I am sorry you went through that," Leena said as she moved to comfort her.

"It's fine. Old news. But now I am stuck in this place."

Leena wanted to ask about the length of her sentence but figured the loss of life was probably enough to get her a severe sentence, and she did not want to hurt her anymore with the conversation. It was also unclear what happened to her family members. She assumed Clover would share the rest of the story in time.

"Hey, it's time for *yard*. You coming?" Clover asked as she headed toward the door.

Leena followed close behind, sympathetic to her friend but also thinking about her own fate. She wondered if she would also get a life sentence and be forced to live the rest of her days in this tiny cell. The thought sickened her.

The yard was large, about one hundred yards square. There was little to do, so the inmates just created small groups, tried to stretch, and get some exercise. Some would just lay in the dirt, as there was no grass, and stare at the sky. Some groups had exercise routines they would do in unison, while others practiced tai chi. Leena and Clover usually met with several other Filipino inmates by the fence on the west side and practiced martial arts. There was an ownership code that was honored in the yard. Each group laid claim to their own space and stayed in that area. When they strayed from that code of honor, fights would break out.

Leena always felt strange hanging out with Clover's friends as she was not Filipino, and there was a group of Chinese who would leer at her occasionally as if to say, *you belong over here.* But she didn't really know any of them and was only half-Chinese, so she stayed put. The Filipino group welcomed her. She was not sure if it was because she was close with Clover or because she practiced kali and showed great respect for their traditions. Either way, she was fine with the protection, and she learned just as much from some of them as she had learned from Clover.

Leena put her back to the fence and breathed deeply as Clover had taught her in meditation lessons. She contemplated her situation and recounted the things she was thankful for despite her incarceration. She would often close her eyes when she meditated, but she had learned it was not good to keep them shut for long as you never knew what could happen in the yard. Everyone was monitoring a rival group, mostly Hispanics, who were also next to the fence. They were next to Leena's group but down about thirty feet. They had been horsing around with one another, and their circle grew a little too wide, bleeding over into Filipino territory.

As is common in the yard, a few of the larger Filipinas stood tall and crossed their arms, looking directly at the offenders to remind them of their mistake. This started a shouting match, as it always did. One thing led to another, and the one group started migrating to the conflict and, like a couple of ships at sea floating toward one another, the two groups converged, and the shouting turned to fists.

Leena took cover behind Clover, but the enemy soon surrounded her. She watched carefully to ensure she could defend herself. As she turned to look behind her, a woman about twice her size was coming in throwing a punch. With no thought, her instinct took over, and she put the woman on the ground, giving her a quick kick to the face, more to stun her than injure her. As soon as she let go, two more were on her. All three then assumed a fighting stance as Leena waited for their strike. The first one moved in, trying to kick her, but she easily blocked the kick and thrust her fist into the attacker's side then swung her around to land her on the ground. The second lunged at her with a small homemade knife. Leena blocked with both of her arms, but the blade caught the side of her left arm before she could get a good hold on her attacker, leaving a long cut that bled. Grabbing the hand with the knife, Leena twisted it until that attacker was on the ground, crying out in pain. Another strike to her shoulder while she was still holding her hand caused the young woman to drop the knife, and a kick to the face rendered her unconscious.

The prison guards rushed in and began pulling people apart, carrying some who were wounded off the field of battle and into the cell block. Leena knew the guards would move the injured to the infirmary. She was shaking. She had been training for several weeks but did not know she could apply her skills in a real fight. The way she had defended herself was unreal. It was like she was watching it happen in a movie.

One of her friends handed her a small towel to wipe the blood from her arm. It hurt badly, but after inspection, it was only a shallow cut. After a few minutes of pressure, the bleeding stopped. The cut was long and ugly but would likely heal without scarring.

Clover had taken a couple of blows but overall, the Hispanic group did minimal damage to this well-trained group. Of the twelve Hispanic inmates, only four were still standing, and Leena's group took no losses. Her group rallied around her and cheered her victory. They had all spent some time with her over the last few weeks training her, so they were beyond proud of her accomplishment. Leena smiled. She had never felt a part of a group like this before. She cried a little, but they were tears of joy—of belonging.

As the dust settled and the cheers subsided, the guards sorted out the conflict and determined the Filipinas were defending themselves, so they issued no punishment. Most of the Hispanic inmates were now in the infirmary, so the guards figured they had got their due already.

As Leena took her place on the fence once again with a smile stuck on her face, she heard a guard call for her from the cell-block entrance. "Zhen, Leena, this way."

What might have changed the guard's mind? "All I did was defend myself," she said out loud as she headed toward the guard. Leena immediately grew angry at the prospect of being singled out for this tussle in the yard.

"What is it?" she said to the guard, ready to fight again if the answer was unwelcome.

"You have a visitor," the guard said.

Leena relaxed, opened her fists, and let her anger slowly fade as the guard escorted her to the visitor area.

She stood patiently, waiting for the green light above the door that would signal it was okay for her to enter and greet her visitor. No one had visited since she had been there, so she was not sure who it could be. Maybe it was the lawyer coming to prepare her for court the next day. Or maybe Jordan had finally come to tell her he had escaped. Or it could be Vincent, although if it were, she was prepared to verbally beat him for his betrayal.

As the light turned green, a buzzer sounded, and the guard motioned for her to enter. She slowly pushed the door open to see an empty room full of steel benches. Sitting in the middle of the room was Diego.

"Diego!" she cried.

Diego stood to meet her as he had done so many times throughout her life, but Leena knew she could not touch him, so she stopped short and sat in front of him, motioning for him to do the same. Glancing around, he immediately understood the silent instruction and sat down.

"I am sorry it took so long for me to visit. When you didn't come home, I had no idea what happened. We were so worried. I tried hard to find out what happened but couldn't get any news. How are you, Turnip?" Diego began.

"I am doing great!" Leena said, still high from her recent battle. "I mean, good—as good as you can be in a place like this." She forced herself to tamp down her emotion so she would not give Diego the impression she was enjoying her stay. She was bursting with pride to tell him how she defended herself but knew he would not understand the accomplishment.

"How is mom?"

Diego cleared his throat. "Your mom is not well. She asks about you every day, and I am not sure what to tell her. What are you doing here, Leena?"

"I got caught breaking into a pharmacy," she whispered. The judge had not declared Leena guilty of the offense yet, and she did not want to make it known that she was guilty, even though the room was empty.

"That is unfortunate, Leena. We must get you out of here."

Leena noticed the 'we' in that statement and once again felt like he was treating her like a daughter. This warmed her heart, but she did not want Diego involved if it might cause him trouble.

"I am not sure what we can do, Diego."

"I have spoken to my son; he is going to see if he can put in a word for you. I really don't know what he might do as he has little power on this side of the wall, but I figured it couldn't hurt." Diego finished, and a tear formed in his right eye. He quickly wiped it away. Leena had never seen him this way before. He was always positive and always ready to provide a solution to a problem. To see him speechless was unfamiliar territory.

"Have you heard from Jordan?" Leena asked inquisitively.

"Yes, he is the one who told me the CPU arrested you. Was he with you that night?"

"It is probably best if we don't talk about that, Diego. I have a hearing tomorrow. I need to plead my guilt or innocence. I am not sure what to do, but I will probably receive a sentence of two years or more."

"I am sorry, Leena. I wish I could do more."

"Go take care of mom. I will see what I can do to shorten my sentence. Maybe good behavior or something will get me out of here sooner," she said, only half believing it would be in time to see her mom again.

She wanted to cry but held back the tears for Diego's sake. They spent a few more minutes talking about her experience in jail. She tried to only speak of the positives: the people she had met, the Filipino culture, her martial arts training.

"Time's up, inmate," a guard called from the corner.

"I don't know if you can go to the hearing tomorrow, but if you can..." she started before Diego cut her off.

"I will be there."

Leena walked the long halls toward her cell in sadness, but seeing Diego reminded her of her life outside the walls and inspired her to find a solution to get home quickly.

Yard time had ended while she was with Diego. Inmates were making their way back to the cell block. Leena entered the block and strode straight into the common area, almost devoid of fear. Her recent combat had given her self-confidence. She knew she could not take on the entire prison population, but she felt as though she could. She made her way to a table in the center of the courtyard and boldly sat down. In time, others joined her, and she met a few new people who congratulated her on her successful defense earlier in the yard.

As the inmates hovered around her, she thought about how much she had grown just in the last few weeks. Tomorrow she would face her judgment. She shuddered at the thought of two years in this place. But if that is what the court decided, she felt she was ready to face it.

She looked up and saw Clover on the fifth floor, looking down at them from just outside her cell. She seemed to nod her approval as Leena sat for the first time without an escort in the center of the zoo. Prison life was tough, but she felt at home there. She worried about what she would leave behind if the courts released her. Clover. Friends. Her feeling of acceptance. Her new prison mates had become family.

After a few hours of socialization, Leena made her way back to her cell to get ready for the dinner call. She had found a few books Clover kept under her bed and read voraciously when she was not engaged in training. Her latest read was a classic: *Victors of Pride*. The book was written about fifty years earlier about a young girl who triumphed over her circumstances during the war in California. She admired the main character, Lin Loo, very much and saw a lot of her own struggle in the plot.

She had never been much of a reader but enjoyed it when she had time. She just didn't have much time growing up. She would go straight from school to the garden or to the market on most days. Before the store closed, she spent time there as well. Survival was more important than her education. Her mother would say over and over that *the size of the ship does not matter if there are holes in it*. She never really understood the saying but knew it meant working for the family was more important than school.

After reading through a few chapters, a guard entered the cell. "Zhen, you have another visitor."

Leena followed the guard back to the visitors' area. She delighted in having two visitors in one day as she had not had a single visitor since she arrived.

Upon entering the visiting area, she saw several inmates in their canary-yellow jumpsuits siting with family or friends. Scanning the room, she looked for who might have come to visit her. The site of Gil Vernon, the defense attorney, dashed her hope of a friend or family member coming to her rescue.

Leena made her way to the table and sat down.

"Hello, Ms. Zhen," Gil said as he pulled out several files and began shuffling once again for the right one. "I have some good news for you...you...you. The district attorney has decided to duh...duh...drop the breaking and entering charges against you. Unfortunately, the other chu…chu…chu…charges of curfew violation, trespassing, and evading arrest still stand.”

Leena tried to force a smile because Gil thought it was good news.

“What's the matter, girl? This is gu…gu…good for you. The maximum sentence for these crimes is five years tu…tu…total. And I have negotiated it down to two years for you. You just need to plead gu…gu…guilty to these charges, and we will have you home in no time.”

“Thank you for the help, Mr. Vernon, but spending two years in this place does not seem like good news.” Leena pleaded her case to Gil. “My mother is sick and dying. If I don't get out of here in the next few weeks, I am unlikely to ever see her again.”

“I am sorry to hear that, little lady, but gu…gu…going home is just not pu…pu…possible. Zone 7 is extremely strict on crime. I wish I could do more, but this is the best it is going to get.”

Summoning a new strength and calm, she stood and said, “I will see you tomorrow, Mr. Vernon.”

Gil Vernon collected his many files and stuffed them back into his attaché, giving Leena a quick wave as she disappeared through the door back to Cell Block C.

Sleep eluded her. She tried all night to fall into one of those deep comas that provided so much strength, but she could not find that place of peace. Her mind raced with thoughts of what might happen the next day. She felt out of control. She wanted desperately to just jump through that tiny window in her cell and fly away like a bird. The four walls around her emanated a deep cold that made her shiver and cling tightly to her blanket.

The sounds of the prison block were eerie that night. It was normal to hear snoring or prisoners occasionally crying out in misery during a nightmare. Often a skirmish could be heard but would then fade. But tonight, there was nothing. It was unusually quiet.

Leena woke like most mornings to the sound of the cell door opening. She looked over to see Clover stirring in her bed. She didn't sleep much and felt like she should stay in bed, but she also knew they could come to get her any moment for her transfer back to the detainment center. Although she could probably sleep for another hour, she pulled herself up and began her morning routine.

She could hear the prison coming alive. All the doors opened at the same time. She had healed of the injuries she received on day one, but she would occasionally get a tinge of pain in her side. She wondered if she might have broken a rib or injured some internal organ. The healthcare in prison was lacking, so she had pressed through the pain and hoped her body would heal itself.

A guard entered shortly after the breakfast call and announced they would need her immediately after mealtime, so Leena quickly finished dressing and made her way to the dining hall. She was one of the first to arrive, so she hurried through the line and sat to eat quickly. She was ready for the day to be over. She knew the verdict was likely not a good one, and although she was ready to face it, the time leading up to the pronouncement was eating at her.

She never put her back toward the prisoners anymore. She sat against the wall so she could keep an eye out for threats. From time to time, she saw Stasha, the woman who attacked her on that first day in the prison. Stasha was aware of how Leena handled herself in the yard as it had become part of the prison gossip, so she kept her distance. Leena was glad. Stasha was at least twice her size, and although she was confident in her new skills, she did not want to test them beyond their limits.

"Today is the day," Clover said with a smile.

"Yes, I am supposed to be transferred to the detainment center right after breakfast."

"I hope they will dismiss your case due to a lack of evidence and free you right there on the spot."

"I don't think that is likely," Leena responded.

"You never know; these courts are crazy. Never know what they are going to do."

"You are sad that I might leave you, aren't you," Leena said, trying to evoke some sentiment.

"Don't be silly. I want more room in the cell for myself. All your shit just clutters up the place."

"I love you too, Reyes." Leena used her last name to soften the sentiment because they had not really said that to each other yet. "I will probably be back in your bedroom by nightfall."

"Well, if you get your shot, girl, you take it. No one wants to stay here. *You* get out, you hear me? You get out."

A guard motioned for Leena, and she knew it was time to go. She took her tray to the cleaning area and handed it off to the workers through a cloud of steam generated by the dishwashers.

She then walked back past the table where she was sitting and wrapped her arms around Clover from behind, giving her a big hug and kiss on the cheek before making her way to the door.

Leena heard, "you get out" faintly as the guard closed the door behind her.

The bus guard handcuffed Leena and directed her to sit in the front. The same green bus on which she had arrived was in the rotation that day. She took a seat while the guard chained her to metal clamps that were bolted to the floor. This limited movement throughout the bus. She was alone for this ride today. She reasoned that there were a lot more people making their way to the prison than those making their way back to court.

She was calmer this time aboard this bus. She was cognizant of her breathing to control her heart rate and enjoyed the scenery as the bus went past farms and through wooded areas. She spent little time in the woods growing up. She was a city girl but always wondered what it would be like to go camping. She imagined foraging for berries, making campfires, singing songs, and other amusements. She had never fished either but wanted to try it. Now it seemed she would have to sacrifice all those opportunities, at least for a little while.

Leena had resigned herself to her fate. Prison was not pleasant, but within those walls she found some dignity, some self-confidence, a tribe she could call her own, and a level of acceptance she had never felt. Her mind struggled with leaving Diego and her mother behind, but she was also apprehensive of what it would mean to leave the confines of the jail she had called home for the last month. Her life was still waiting for her outside: her mother's declining health, her constant grind for survival, and the uncertainty of her future.

The farms and woods quickly became city streets and the multicolored homes of the Aberjay, along with their streetlights and manicured lawns. She wondered as she rode that smelly bus why things were so different between them and the Miniyar. They were all just people trying to survive, trying to make a life for themselves and their families. What was the actual difference between them? Money? That was the biggest distinction, but was it the only one? Certainly, she reasoned, if money was the only difference, there was hope for reconciliation. Why were the walls even necessary? It just seemed so ridiculous.

The bus pulled into the familiar parking lot and the gated area where the detainment center took in all the new arrivals. She was uncuffed from the floor and guided off the bus by a guard who had just entered it. He was much rougher with her than those who knew her in prison. The guard informed her she would wait for her courtroom appointment as he led her to the holding cell.

She sat again on the bench and thought about how she felt the last time she was there. It was such a contrast. She thought about how much a person can change in such a short time. She listened as other inmates were called in for their cases and guards were sent to retrieve them. Each took their turn and then was escorted back to their cell to await the smelly transport that would take them to their next stop. For many of them, it would be their final destination.

While waiting patiently, there were several other prisoners, all women, who were placed in her cell. Several of them were bloody from a fight, and a couple were clearly high on some type of substance. Leena attempted to avoid them but was unafraid. She knew she could defend herself if necessary.

The drugged-out transients provided some comical entertainment. Leena was watching them as she heard the door to the hallway buzz open one more time. Through its gate walked the same guard who had brought her in earlier with his hands on a familiar face. It was Liv!

The guard removed her handcuffs and led her into the holding cell. Liv looked at Leena as if she was having trouble focusing or was not sure what she was seeing.

"Liv, what are you doing here?" Leena asked, rushing to her side to grasp her arm.

"Hey, kid, I could ask you the same question."

"I am here for my court date."

Liv walked to the back of the cell and surveyed her fellow inmates. Rubbing her wrists, she said sarcastically, "What did you do, run over a bunny?"

"I cannot really talk about that right now," Leena said, looking around the outside of the cell to see who might be listening.

"Shut up! I am trying to sleep!" said one of the drugged-out inmates.

"Ignore her," Leena continued. "She has been shouting for hours. What about you Liv? Did you hit a bunny?" Leena was trying to be funny, but the joke did not land as well.

"I ran into McBride and smarted off to him. He brought me in on some trumped-up charge. They got nothing on me. I will be out of here later."

Liv didn't seem worried in the least. She had either been in this cell many times before or wanted Leena to think she had been there before.

"I'm glad it's not serious. My crimes may land me in jail for some time," Leena said.

"No shit! You lawbreaker. Look at you," Liv said in a congratulatory tone.

The loud inmate stood up from the bench where she was sleeping and rushed at Leena, yelling, "I said shut up!"

Leena called on her training once again and, in one quick move, stepped out of the line of impact and, grabbing an arm, flipped the attacker to the floor face down. Blood spattered on the floor as her head impacted it, most likely from a broken nose. Sensing that any danger had passed, she dropped the woman's arm. Her attacker passed out moments later, snoring in her own blood.

"Wow, when did you become a killer, kid?" Liv gasped with a stunned look on her face.

"I picked up a few things in jail," Leena said proudly.

"I would say you did."

Liv, still a bit shocked, giggled as if she had seen a mouse dance on the pin of a needle. She could not get over the change in Leena. After a good laugh, she continued.

"When you get out of here, come find me. I want to introduce you to some of my friends."

"Friends?" Leena asked in a tone that made clear she did not believe they were just friends. Leena knew Liv's associates were rebels, a gang, some sort of organization committed to revolution, but not likely friends.

"Well, it's more like a club. Some of them are friends. You will like these people. Common values. Similar desires and all that."

"*If* I get out of here, I will do that."

Leena was not sure what Liv was talking about but knew if being a killer was the prerequisite, she was not sure it was a club she wanted to join. Although she enjoyed being *called* a killer. She had never felt that way about herself, nor had anyone referred to her that way.

"Zolenski, you're up," the guard said as he escorted her from the cell and through the door. Leena sat back down to wait, and several inmates moved out of her way. *It's comical,* she thought, *being so small, yet people are getting out of my way now.*

Leena watched the blood of the fallen inmate create a pool and then eventually stop. She would have called for help if she felt it necessary, but a broken nose would not kill this woman, and sleeping off the drug was probably the best medicine.

"Zhen, it's your turn," a guard called out just moments after Liv's departure, and Leena went to the cell door and made her way upstairs.

Liv had been led in one direction, while this guard guided Zhen through the door to the courtroom.

"Bye, Liv, good luck!" Leena shouted before the guard pushed her through the door.

Chapter 7

JUDGMENT

Leena walked up the stairs and into the familiar glass box with the microphone. The courtroom was full. She investigated each face and spotted Diego in the second to last row. He looked tired. Worn, like her bomber jacket. Or maybe it was the lighting. She hoped she was not the reason for his disposition. She could not stand the thought of disappointing him.

She also located Gil Vernon at the table in front of her booth. But there were no others who she recognized. She was hoping Fernando Martinez had shown up and might somehow get her out of this situation, but her heart sank when she saw that he wasn't there.

In a familiar voice, the bailiff called out the case, and the judge, noticing Gil in the courtroom, addressed the court to ensure the attorneys were present and ready to do their work.

"The case against Leena Zhen is ready to proceed," the judge said. "Please rise and enter your plea."

Gil turned toward Leena and motioned for her to rise.

"In the case of Zone 7 magistrate versus Leena Zhen. You are being charged with violation of curfew, trespassing, breaking and entering, and evading arrest. How do you plead?"

"Your honor, we have reached a duh...duh...deal with the magistrate regarding this case." Gil Vernon spoke more clearly than he had previously.

"Very well. What are the terms?" the judge replied.

The other attorney spoke up at this point. "Your honor, in exchange for a guilty plea, we have dropped the breaking and entering charge but have retained the other charges. The Office of the Magistrate recommends two years."

"Leena Zhen, are you in agreement with these terms and what has been said on your behalf?" The judge looked straight at Leena to elicit a response.

"Yes, your honor," Leena said quietly into the microphone.

"Very well, then it is my duty to accept your guilty plea and sentence you to..."

The door to the courtroom opened, and a well-dressed young man entered. "One moment, your honor," he shouted as he made his way to the bench.

The bailiff jumped at the ready to block his access to the judge before the judge, recognizing the young man, waved her off.

"Mr. Martinez, you are interrupting my courtroom. Do you have an interest in this case?" the judge called out.

"Yes, your honor, I do. I am sorry to interrupt. May I approach the bench?"

"Granted," said the judge as Fernando Martinez and both attorneys met the judge at the base of his mighty desk. They spoke for more than five minutes as Leena held her breath. She did not know what he might tell the judge on her behalf and was not sure what he might be able to do with the judgment already rendered.

She looked for some consolation from Diego but saw he was clearly as confused as she was about the situation. Leena strained to hear the conversation at the front of the courtroom but to no avail. The judge whispered as the district attorney seemed to get angry but still spoke in a tone that was unrecognizable from that distance.

After what seemed like an eternity, the parties made their way back to their respective desks, and Fernando went to the back of the courtroom and sat next to Diego, giving him a quick pat on the arm as he sat down as some sort of nonverbal method of calming his anxiety.

"Ms. Leena Zhen, you have been found guilty by plea agreement. The magistrate accepts your plea and sentences you to two years, suspended, and releases you on your own recognizance to Fernando Martinez, who will see that you are placed under zone arrest. As a condition of this arrangement, you will not be permitted to leave Zone 6. Any failure to comply or further trouble you may get into will result in your immediate transfer to the magistrate prison to serve the two years. Is that understood?"

"Yes, your honor," Leena responded but didn't fully grasp what the judge had said. She thought she heard she was being released but did not understand the entire judgment.

The guard led Leena from her glass prison to the cell below once more and informed her that they would begin processing her release. As she entered the holding cell she began to weep. A wave of emotion swallowed her, and her body shook. Although she only faced a two-year sentence, she felt as if she was being saved from death row. She was incredibly thankful to Fernando Martinez and was thoroughly prepared to show her appreciation once she saw him again. *There is no way to repay the kindness* she thought. She thought about what she might offer. Live in gardener? Maybe she could volunteer to be his housekeeper? A chauffeur? She knew what he had done deserved a grandiose response and she was prepared to give it.

Within an hour, a guard released her from the cell, allowed her to change into her street clothes, and took her to the main lobby, where she was told to wait with a guard until Fernando Martinez could retrieve her.

She waited patiently in the lobby, watching people of all kinds cross the shiny marble floors. She heard many doors open and close, heard some shouts occasionally from rooms that contained other courtrooms, and heard the *click-click* of well-dressed Aberjay as they made their way to their business. It was quite a contrast to prison sounds. She felt more comfortable in her own clothes and could even don her pilot hat. She knew her clothes needed cleaning but could not help noticing the scent of Jordan resident on them. The long ride on the motorbike must have lingered.

About twenty minutes later, Fernando appeared, but he was not smiling. "I will take her from here, officer, thank you," he said to the guard, who then went back through the door down to the holding area.

"Are you okay, Leena?" Fernando asked with a moderate amount of empathy.

"I'm okay. Can you tell me what just happened in there?"

"They have sentenced you to two years, but they are going to allow you to serve it under my supervision. You must stay in Zone 6 for the next two years and obey all the laws. If you slip up at all or you are detained in any way, they will send you back to prison. Is that clear?"

"Yes," Leena said, "I understand."

"Let's go. I have limited time to get you back home."

Leena followed Fernando out of the courthouse and to the street, where he had a car waiting. His driver nodded and opened the door for him as he approached the car, but he motioned for Leena to go first. She slid into the back seat. This car was long and blue and nicer than anything Leena had ever been in. She marveled at how shiny and clean it was inside.

Looking around, she noticed that Diego was not anywhere to be seen. "What about your dad?" she asked with a worried look.

"He will get back on his own. I gave him a pass."

Once both of them were in the back seat, the driver drove off.

Leena wanted to show her gratitude, but she feared being too expressive with Fernando as he seemed upset by the prospect of having to rescue her.

"I used political capital to arrange this, Leena. I hope you realize you may have set back zone relations by this stunt. What were you even doing in the Aberjay zone after dark?"

Leena wondered at that moment how much Fernando knew. If he did not know about the pharmacy, she was certainly not going to fill him in. It would be best if he thought the CPU arrested her for a curfew violation.

"I was there to see Vincent Ryder; he's a friend of mine in the zone."

"You know the rules. You may not enter that zone without a work permit. When you do stuff like this, it makes it hard for me to convince the Aberjay that we are not a threat to their way of life."

Emboldened, Leena spoke her mind. "Why are you working so hard to accommodate them? *They* are the enemy! It is because of *them* we live in poverty and walls restrict our movements."

"They are not the enemy, Leena; we are all just trying to survive and do what is right for our families. Our very freedom is at risk here."

"We don't have any freedom," Leena said a little louder. "We live in poverty. while they eat well! We have no work, while they use MIRO to do their work for them! We have no access to medicine or healthcare, while they live twenty years longer than we do!" Leena was not sure about that statistic but thought it sounded good and helped her make her point. Right or wrong, she had always found hyperbole helpful to win an argument.

"We must learn to live together, Leena. It is more complicated than you are making it out to be. You are just a kid. When you get older, you will understand how things work." Fernando finished abruptly, signaling he was done discussing the topic.

The car slowed in traffic as it came to the wall. Leena looked out to the fence line that separated pedestrians from the roadway and saw a familiar face. Vincent was there looking through the fence, his hands held high, gripping the wire above his head. He had a sullen look and mouthed something to her as she drove by. She could not make out what he said, but it was likely an apology.

Leena turned her head away in protest. She did not think she could forgive such a betrayal. The authorities could have imprisoned her for years, or worse, and he turned her over without a tinge of regret. She wondered how bad his character must be to treat her in such a way and how her judgment could be so faulty in choosing to build a relationship with him.

The car motored through the tunnel to the gate entrance to Zone 6. The driver flashed a badge that the guard read with a scanner, and he was waved through. Leena had not been through the gate this way in years. She was shocked to witness so many heavily armed guards. At least thirty soldiers armed with tactical rifles guarded the first gate to prevent anyone from breaching the wall, and another twenty on the other side provided similar security at the second gate.

Once through the gate, the car pulled in front of Leena's building. She went for the handle, but Fernando stopped her.

"Wait. I need you to understand you are under my supervision. If you do anything that puts you within CPU radar, it will reflect badly on me. I could be held accountable for your behavior. I need you to promise me you will stay on this side of the wall and stay out of Aberjay business. They can make things extremely hard on all of us."

Leena gave a resistant nod, and he released her with a nonverbal swipe of the hand. Though she had agreed to Fernando's demand of compliance, deep down, she knew he did not do it for her. It was a favor for his father. Leena had always been good at understanding people, but Fernando was a challenge. She just could not get a read on him. Was he truly the savior of the Miniyar, fighting for their best interests? Or a charlatan only out to enrich himself. Her conclusion would have to wait until she had more time to think and investigate.

Running up the stairs to her third-floor apartment, Leena paused outside the door. She was not sure if her mom would be sleeping but wanted to enter quietly just in case. Slowly opening the door, she saw her mother sleeping, attended by a neighbor, Jun Lee. Jun was extremely helpful when Diego was away and would often sit with her mother for hours. Jun was well into her seventies, so she had little else to do during the day. Her son and daughter-in-law were working long days, which gave her plenty of time to be generous.

Leena quietly moved in behind Jun and asked, "did she eat anything today?"

"Leena! I am glad to see you home. No she has not eaten much." She pointed to a half-eaten bowl of soy okra. "She is very weak."

"Has the doctor been here?"

"Yes, he was here this morning to check on her and do her dialysis." Jun stood to allow Leena to come closer and sit with her mother. "Do you want me to stay?"

"Can you give me about an hour and then come back? I need to go to the market for a couple of things."

Jun nodded, smiling, and quietly left the room.

Leena sat with her mother for about twenty minutes, wondering what might become of her. She felt like a failure as she observed her mother's shallow breathing. She had tried to get the medicine but was thwarted by a half-baked plan and a friend's betrayal. She wondered if things could have gone differently. If they had, she would have given her mother lifesaving medicine a month ago. Even if she could figure out a way to obtain it, now it may be too late.

As she sat there recounting the events of the day, the power in her room shut down. The whiz of the oxygen machine was no more, and the few lights that were on were extinguished. This was a common occurrence in the building because of its age. It was always a breaker or an old cable shorting out the system.

"This damn building," Leena grumbled as she hopped up and headed out of the apartment and down the stairs to the main breaker box. Without someone to maintain the building, the electrical closet was left unlocked so that the inhabitants could repair any issues themselves.

Leena went into the closet on the first floor and opened the panels, looking for the thrown breaker. She got to the third box before she found the one that had tripped. Flipping it back on, it popped into place. "That should do it," she said as if she were talking to a helper.

She walked back up the stairs to her apartment and checked that her mom had working machines before she headed for the bathroom to take a much-needed shower.

Drying her hair while gazing through the window in the bathroom, Leena heard trucks. Peering through the broken glass of her window, she saw at least five CPU trucks full of soldiers heading south past her building. It was not uncommon to see a CPU truck, but when so many were in congress, it meant something big was happening.

She quickly put on clean clothes, and after checking on mom, slipped out the front door. She knocked lightly on the open door across the hall and motioned for Jun, who gladly put down her knitting and made her way over to the apartment to sit with Mei. Leena thanked her and then ran down the stairs.

Out on the street, she could see the dust that remained in the air from the trucks that had just rumbled through. She turned to look north and saw Diego coming toward her. She ran to him to see if he had any information.

"Did you see the trucks, Diego?"

"Yes, they are headed to the market most likely," Diego said while giving Leena a quick hug.

"Why would they be in the market? We have our own security."

"You have been gone several weeks, Leena. Since then, there have been no food shipments from outside," Diego explained.

"That is not abnormal, right? We go without shipments all the time."

"This time, it is different. Some say the Aberjay are holding back shipments on purpose. There is news that there is a warehouse full of food just outside the eastern wall, but I don't know if that is true." Diego stopped walking and motioned to Leena that he needed a break. He had walked from the courthouse where Leena was recently set free, and for a man of his age, that was quite a distance.

"There is a lot of anti-Aberjay sentiment right now. The troops are most likely here to keep the peace," Diego continued.

"Should we get some baskets down there to the market so folks have something to eat?"

Diego looked at Leena with sadness.

"You have not seen the garden yet?"

"No, what is wrong with the garden?" Leena asked as her eyes grew wide. Then, glancing toward the door of her apartment building, she took off in a flash across the street. Rushing up the stairs and bursting through the door to the roof, her heart sank at the sight of a garden in ruin. Someone had picked every vegetable clean. They had torn down all the supports. It looked as though a herd of elephants had stomped their way through.

Leena fell to her knees by her section of the garden and grabbed the soil with her hands. "No!" she cried out. This was more than a hobby for her as she knew this garden was the only thing that kept her and her neighbors alive during times of famine or drought. Leena's blood coursed with anger, but she was not sure who should be the target of her vehemence. Who would do such a thing to our garden?

She quickly took a mental inventory. In the apartment, they had a bag of rice, some canned veggies for emergencies, and several full jars of okra they had already opened in the refrigerator. This would not last long. Her survival instinct took over as she scoured the garden for remnants.

A light rain fell as she dug and dug for any remaining veggies that might be still in the soil. She found a few sweet potatoes and some radishes that she tossed into a basket, but eventually concluded that there was not much left. She had to replant. But where would she get seeds? They had some drying but not enough for the entire garden. They would need many supplies to get it going again. And then they would have to wait many months for new plants to produce anything edible—months they didn't have.

Leena washed her hands in a small pot that had filled with rainwater. She grabbed a towel from a rack and dried her hands before heading back downstairs. She had to compose a plan or they would be out of food within a couple of weeks.

She found Diego just inside the entrance to the building, peering out at the rain. It reminded her of when she was young. They used to sit together in lawn chairs in that same location, watching the rain. She loved the sound of rain hitting the ground and the smell it left behind as it moved on.

"How did this happen, Diego?"

"About a week after the shipments stopped, a bunch of residents started hitting all the gardens to stockpile. They were not locals. I didn't recognize any of them. I harvested what I could that was ready and did some canning, but the thieves took everything else: the unripe vegetables, the stalks, the potted herbs, and even some of the soil and fertilizer."

Diego rarely showed sadness. He took life as it came and tried to have a positive attitude in all things, but this was hitting him hard. He knew what the lack of food would mean for not only the apartment residents but for the people of the neighborhood. People get strange and desperate when the food runs out.

"We have to prepare for what comes next," Diego continued. "I know you are worried about your mom, but we need to make sure we have food to feed her and food to feed ourselves come spring. That must be the primary concern. I will work on rationing the canned goods when the time comes, but for now, we must replant the garden and make sure we get something started. How many seeds do you have?"

"I have some but not nearly enough," Leena said. "I think I need to go get more. Who might have them?"

"You might just have to try the other markets," Diego said in a defeated voice.

"Why don't we just go get the food outside the east wall?" Leena said with confidence.

"You know you can't get involved in anything like that. The moment you step outside of this zone, your bracelet will announce your location to the CPU."

Leena could hear the disappointment in Diego's voice, which was not normal. He was always supportive no matter what she got herself into, and to hear the disappointment was heartbreaking.

"Call your friend Jordan and ask him to run you around on that motorbike. It will be faster and probably safer. See if you can round up some seeds that we can get into the ground. And if you run across any food, get us what you can. Do you have credits?" Diego asked, pointing at her bracelet.

"Yes, I have enough. Let me go find a phone."

Leena had found a neighbor with a charged phone and called Jordan at home. She gave up her phone years ago because they couldn't afford it. Reception in the Miniyar zone had become shaky at best. Most people didn't even carry them anymore. The Aberjay had not maintained the towers, so the few people who still had phones worked in Zone 7 or had family there.

Jordan was planning to go to work later but had time to assist with her errands. He had avoided being caught when the CPU arrested Leena and returned to the park without issue. He was not even questioned when he passed through the gate with his work permit. They were both grateful for his good fortune.

Jordan pulled up on his motorbike at about four p.m. Because it was late in the day, they had little time to get to any markets. Some were open late, but during food shortages, many folks decided not to sell but to stockpile what they had for themselves. The Miniyar were communal. They enjoyed sharing and making sure everyone had what they needed. But when there was not enough to go around, a 'survival of the fittest' attitude prevailed.

Leena embraced Jordan for a long time, very thankful that he did not get caught. She told him her story so he would know what she went through. He seemed empathetic to her experience and even showed signs of guilt for not executing the plan he had developed.

"Let's go toward our market first to see what is going on," Leena said as she pointed down the street.

Jordan sped away with his female companion, making their way through the streets and turning frequently to avoid barricades and disabled vehicles in their path. They went past many abandoned shops. People filled the streets. They heard glass break as they passed a mob illegally entering a small breakfast shop that was still in operation but had closed earlier that day.

As they approached the market, they could see a large plume of smoke rising in the air. People were running in all directions and CPU soldiers were patrolling the streets, calling out threats as they attempted to control the crowd. Screams could be heard everywhere. Many of the booths that had become so familiar in Leena's life were burning. The booths were quiet and empty, with nothing left to buy. The air smelled of burning wood along with the heavy scent of diesel from trucks moving up and down the streets.

There was clear animosity toward the soldiers as residents screamed at the CPU and threw rocks. The CPU were not tolerant of this behavior and subdued residents in response to their protests. Many were already handcuffed with plastic ties in the back of the trucks. They had pushed them too far with their protest.

She glanced toward her own booth and was relieved to see it was still in one piece. Leena motioned for Jordan to speed past the market as it was clear there was nothing of value to be found there. Only violence. There was another market within a few miles.

Approaching the South City market was less of an adventure. Leena knew this market as there were many days when Diego would manage their booth while she would head to the South City market to sell her vegetables, usually in the summer when the harvest was at its peak.

This market was barely in operation. Most of the booths had been shut down for the day, leaving the air feeling still and heavy. Hardly any patrons were present, and the few staffed tables peddled only clothing and faux jewelry. No food.

Leena pointed to the left as Jordan drove slowly past the empty market and said, "Go that way."

"There are no markets that way, Leena," Jordan said, trying to be helpful.

"I know, just do it."

He turned to the left to satisfy his friend's desire and drove through a few streets lined with closed stores and then some residences.

"Where are we headed, Leena?" Jordan finally asked.

"Just keep going," she replied.

"But we're almost to the wall."

"Yes, I know," Leena said sheepishly.

Jordan pulled the bike over at that instant and stepped off the bike, shouting, "Have you lost your mind?"

"I don't think so," Leena said, still sitting on the back of the bike with her helmet on.

"If you go anywhere near the wall, you risk going back to jail. Is that what you want?"

"Of course not," Leena said, removing her helmet. "Jordan, we believe there is a warehouse full of food on the other side of that wall," Leena said, pointing to the towering structure in the distance. "If we can get over there and find it, we can bring food into the zone."

"Who is 'we'?" Jordan asked.

"Diego and I, as well as others, I'm sure," Leena replied in a high-pitched voice, clearly indicating she was making decisions based on less than reliable information.

"So, you don't really know there is food there?"

After a long pause, Leena continued, "No, I don't know there is food there, but you see, there is no food in the market and no seeds. We can spend days looking through closed markets or we can just go get the food that is right there."

"Leena, I know you don't think about yourself much, but you have to start considering what happens to *you*."

"Why?" Leena said, unsure of how to respond.

"Because there are those who love you and don't want to see you get hurt."

Leena smiled, blushing a little, and looked down at the ground.

"You love me?" she said with a smile on her face.

"Lots of people love you, Leena," Jordan said, backtracking.

"But out of those who love me, that includes you, right?" Leena said, reframing her question so that Jordan couldn't squirm out of answering her directly.

"Yes, okay, I love you—I can't stop thinking about you. I lost my mind when you were in jail. I was so worried, it hurt. I have loved you for years, Leena." Jordan turned around and moved closer to Leena, still sitting on the back of the bike.

Leena reached out and grabbed Jordan's shirt, pulling him to her lips. She kissed him long and deep, communicating clearly that she felt the same way. His lips were warm and inviting. She had always envisioned their first kiss would be awkward, but it wasn't. It felt like home. Jordan was her person. She knew that now. She knew he was always there for her, always risking his safety and even his life for her, always providing the foundation she needed to ground her. Waves of emotion flowed through her body as he wrapped his arms around her tightly.

As their lips parted, Leena glimpsed a sign a few stores down that read 'Pharmacy.' It was an old store and it was closed, but she thought maybe she could get lucky and find some meds that might help her mom.

"Look, Jordan!"

Leena dismounted and ran to the store. Jordan was surprised by the abrupt end to their intimacy and stood there confused.

Shaking the door, Leena got it to spring free, opening it and stepping into the beaten storefront. The glass in the door had broken in a past conflict and left the floor covered in dust, dirt, and broken ceiling tiles. There were empty shelves lining the store, and at the back, a counter where customers once waited for their medications.

In a flash, Leena jumped over the counter and began rummaging through the drawers behind the aging bench to see what she might find. Jordan followed her in but was more hesitant, knowing they were probably breaking some sort of law just being there.

She opened drawer after drawer, but finding nothing, her pace slowed. Once she had exhausted all options, she said quietly, "There is nothing left here."

"You didn't really think a pharmacy would leave a bunch of drugs behind, did you?" said Jordan, exhibiting his penchant for common sense.

"No, I guess not," Leena said, resigned to her failure.

They made their way back to the motorbike, and Jordan spun around with an idea.

"I have a work permit, so I can get through the east gate. But you cannot go anywhere near it, so you need to stay here. Let me go over and poke around and see if I find any useful information. And if I find out there is no food being stockpiled over there, we can hit a couple more markets. Sound good?"

"I don't love the idea of staying behind, but yes, go find out what's happening."

With his new plan in hand, Jordan gave Leena a last kiss, taking a moment to look into her eyes in a way that expressed his devotion, and then sped off toward the gate. Leena walked back to the pharmacy to find a good place to hide out from the chaos that seemed to be slowly engulfing the neighborhood. While it was likely illegal for her to be in the store, she felt safer than hanging out on the street. With a slight skip in her step and a tingle in her belly she carefully walked over the glass and debris. She had never been in love before but figured this euphoria she felt was most likely a symptom.

Leena sorted through shelves and boxes in the old pharmacy, hoping to find anything useful. Scavengers had looted the store for goods years before, so the attempt was probably futile. Kicking through the mess and turning over shelves in pursuit of hidden treasure was fun for her, but it was also sad. She thought about the people who once lived in this area, filling it with life, who depended on this pharmacy to meet their needs for medications. She could imagine the businessman picking up some cough syrup for his kids and the mom with twins looking for something to soothe their teething pain. Or maybe a retiree coming to get a vaccination or cough drops.

As she made her way to the back of the store, she noticed a steel door that was cracked slightly. Judging from the size of the store, this would be a door connecting it to the next business. She had not bothered to see which store was next to the pharmacy when she entered, so out of curiosity, she pushed the door to enter, but it only moved a little. Something had it wedged shut. She put her shoulder against the door and pushed with all her might until the door opened just enough for her thin frame to fit through. *There had better not be a body on the other side of this door*, she thought as she bent low and slithered through the opening.

On the other side was a large room with mirrors on the wall and old dusty mats on the floor. Fortunately, the weight blocking the door was not a body but a large duffel bag full of some sort of sparring gear.

"This is an old karate studio," she said out loud, not caring who was around to hear it.

She walked out into the center of the room and could see her reflection all the way down the wall. In some places, there were mirrors on the other side of the wall, too, so standing in the middle produced an infinity effect as she gazed into each one. Leena enjoyed this illusion for a few minutes and then realized it gave her a headache.

Pretending she was an actual karate student; she began practicing the art of kali that Clover had taught her. The movements were slow and intentional as she started in a fighting stance and then blocked on the right, then on the left, and attacked with a front kick, moving toward her fictional attackers. She remembered that Clover called these moves *katas*. Each set of moves went by a different name. It was like a dance, but with kicking and punching rather than swings and leaps.

She looked around the studio a little more but found nothing of value. The office was torn to pieces, and only an old rusty desk remained. Papers strewn about the floor indicated the last time this placed hosted real martial arts students was about eleven years ago. She figured she should go back outside in case Jordan returned earlier than expected.

Leena could not leave through the front entrance, however, as large workout equipment blocked it, so she headed toward the side door she used to enter the studio. As she made her way back to that door, she checked out the large bag that was blocking the door. She pulled several pieces of sparring gear out of the bag that were like boxing gloves for the hands and feet, made of a soft leather-type material that had several cuts in them from age. She also found a long, heavily-worn black belt and a smooth, two-foot-long stick. She swung it around like it was a weapon, using some moves her prison inmates had taught her, and decided this was not something she could leave behind.

She thought back to her time with Clover and believed she had called this an *escrima* stick. She took her backpack off and fashioned a loop on her pack to hold the escrima so it would be easily assessable while she was wearing it. She practiced a few times, grabbing the stick above her head and below from the bottom. If this weapon was going to be of any use, she needed to be able to access it in less than a second. This was an improvement on the toilet paper cardboard they practiced with in prison. She was proud of her find.

Once through the door, she hurried to the front of the pharmacy. She could see no one on the street, but looking in the wall's direction, she saw smoke. She could not determine the source. There were many factories in the area. As her curiosity got the best of her, she began walking toward the wall. She felt safe doing so as she was probably a mile away and not in any danger of crossing the invisible boundary that would alert the authorities of a violation.

As she walked toward the wall, block after block, she saw more people. Hundreds of people. She didn't really understand as it was unusual to see so many people together for no reason. It looked like a busy market day, but there was no market around here. As she came within about a hundred yards of the wall, she slowed, knowing she was getting close to the danger zone.

She saw hundreds of people milling around. Some in groups around a barrel fire, others in alleys huddling beside some sort of warming device. Many were just leaning against a storefront and others were on a cement wall at the end of the block. A familiar buzzing sound alerted her to Jordan's return. Jordan's bike emerged from the gate and came toward her. Recognizing her, he did a quick U-turn in the road, drove along beside her, and stopped.

"This is crazy," he said, removing his helmet and stepping off the bike. "Something is going on. There are hundreds of people near the gate taunting the soldiers. They keep throwing bottles and acting crazy. I made it through to the other side where it's quiet, but many guards seem to be forming some sort of blockade to ensure trucks don't make it to the gate. I saw them unloading some produce boxes, so I am fairly sure Diego is right about that warehouse. But I'm not sure which one because I saw many of them."

Leena was a bit stunned. Her curiosity and investigative skills had put them in this spot, but she was not sure it was the smartest place to be.

"The air is electric; I think something is about to happen," Jordan said.

"Hey, you two!" someone called out from behind them. "Did you just come from the other side?"

"I did," Jordan volunteered. "I have a work permit," he stated quickly just in case he was about to get in trouble.

"Come with me, you two," the man said as he placed his hand on Jordan and gestured for Leena to follow. This man was short and balding, with very few teeth. He wore army fatigues that looked like they had never been washed. He did not have a firearm, as you would expect of a soldier, but had a large knife at his side.

He guided them through a warehouse door that led into a small vestibule, then through another set of doors, then up some stairs leading into a large warehouse. The warehouse was filled with about seventy or eighty people, all dressed similarly to their guide, sitting quietly as if waiting for orders.

As Leena made her way down the stairs, she could see a few familiar faces. Right up front in discussion with what looked like several older soldiers of both genders were Liv, Julian, and Zoe.

"Leena!" Liv shouted, running over to give her a big hug. "It's good to see you here. How did you know we would be here?"

"I did not know you would be here; we just kind of found you," Leena said, realizing this was the first time Liv had ever greeted her without using the word *kid*.

"Well, this is great. We can use all the help we can get. Hi, Jordan."

"Hi, Liv," Jordan said, his tone revealing slight disdain. "I thought you were in jail."

"Ah, there is no jail that can hold me—right, crew?" she said while looking for confirmation from Julian and Zoe, who both just smiled and nodded.

"What is going on here, Liv?" Leena asked in a serious tone.

"We are thinking the Aberjay are hoarding our food on the other side of the wall in a warehouse to starve us out. We are going to attack the east gate and see if we can't get it back."

"It's true," Jordan chimed in. "I saw the warehouse and the food trucks."

"You were there?" Liv asked excitedly.

"Yes, I drove past it. I have a work permit." Jordan realized he was repeating himself and convinced himself it was nerves and not fear.

"Let me take you to the guy leading this little adventure. He is going to want to talk to you." Liv escorted Jordan to one of the men in fatigues who was talking with several other important-looking people in military uniforms. The leaders were gathered around a table full of maps and plans. Jordan briefed the soldier on what he knew and returned to the group.

"When is this happening?" Leena asked, hoping she could be long gone when it did.

"We're supposed to go at sundown, but there are so many people out there, I think this could kick off at any moment," Liv said, wrapping her hand in tape as if she were preparing for a boxing match.

The room was full of soldiers, many with handguns and some with rifles. There were also some with swords, clubs, and other street-fighting weapons. The presence of so many firearms surprised Leena as the CPU had outlawed guns in the Miniyar zones. Firearm possession in the zone got you a life sentence. Strangely enough, firearms were legal in Zone 7, and most residents had at least one.

An explosion shook the warehouse, breaking some of the windows on the east side. Everyone in the warehouse hit the ground and covered their heads as glass rained down from above. One of the soldiers in charge grabbed a radio and, after a minute of conversation, turned to the regiment and said, "The CPU has entered our zone and blown up a building just inside the gate. The time to attack is now. Team A, I want you at the gate. Other teams, I want you defending the citizens against the CPU to drive them back to their side. We will get the trucks moving as soon as we can secure the gate. Let's go!"

With the encouraging speech and rally call, the entire room erupted from the floor and headed to the exits. Within minutes, the room was empty save for Leena and Jordan. Liv was leaving, encouraging Leena and Jordan to join them. They followed the three familiar soldiers out into the street to watch the pandemonium. Several CPU trucks had already made their way inside the gates and were chasing down citizens, shooting them with phased weapons that stunned their victims and pulse rifles that were more lethal.

Leena looked to Jordan and asked, "What do we do?"

"I think we have to get out of here," Jordan said, heading toward his bike.

When they were within view of the bike, several CPU soldiers came around the corner wielding batons. The first one struck Jordan, and he fell to the ground while Leena charged with fury. She lunged forward to disarm the soldier and then threw him to the ground with such velocity that his helmet came flying off into the street. She quickly grabbed her new escrima from her pack.

Now surrounded by three other guards who paused to size up their diminutive enemy, Leena ran toward the closest one, hitting him hard with a running jump kick that knocked him on his back. Then, turning rapidly, she deflected a baton to the head and threw her second attacker on the ground next to her first victim with a swat to his temple.

The last remaining guard ran toward her with both hands on his baton. Leena grabbed the front of his vest and fell backward, using her weight to throw the soldier over her head and onto the same pile of guards, slamming his head against the brick wall.

She checked on Jordan and helped him to his feet. Jordan looked around, stunned, wondering what highly qualified soldier had put these four men on the ground to allow them to escape. He was confused, and Leena knew he probably could not drive as blood was pouring down his face from his injury. She looked around and ran with Jordan back toward home for a couple of blocks to get away from the action. Once they felt they were out of the chaos, they quietly slipped into an abandoned shoe store.

As she helped Jordan over to a chair, she grabbed her pack and retrieved a towel, dousing it in water from her bottle and then placing it on Jordan's head. "Hold this here," she said.

"Wow, this is crazy," Jordan said, only half-conscious. "Who was that scary guy who attacked those soldiers?"

Leena just smiled and kept quiet, thinking that the truth might further injure him.

Chapter 8

RESIST

The door to the shoe store flew open as about six Resistance fighters entered, including Liv. Zoe was also there, clutching a bullet wound in her shoulder. They all began stripping equipment from their bodies and checking their wounds, bandaging those who were bleeding heavily, drinking from their canteens, and then moving quickly to reload firearms.

One of them held a radio and listened intently to the garbled message coming through while tending to some leg wounds. Liv moved close to Leena and asked, "Are you hit?"

"No, I'm good, but Jordan took a baton to the head."

"Ouch, here, try this." Liv tossed her a cold pack and some bandages, an improvement on the towel that was now soaked in blood. Leena helped Jordan apply the bandage and secure it around his head.

"How was it out there?" Leena asked, hoping the worst of it was over.

"We are taking the fight to them, that's for sure." Liv stopped to tighten a holster on her hip, although she had no gun. "We put down the assault they attempted earlier and drove them back to the gate. Now we're trying to get through it so we can bring the trucks in."

"Trucks? What trucks?" Leena asked.

"We have about twenty trucks just down the block, lined up and waiting to enter once the Resistance fighters seize the gate. We're going to fill them with food and bring it back to the people." Liv wiped sweat and a little blood from her brow before continuing. "We will show them. They can't mess with us and expect us to stay quiet and die in our little holes as they starve us out."

A crackle on the radio came through, but the voice was unrecognizable. The soldier with the radio turned to the group and shouted, "We took the gate, let's go!"

Motioning for others to follow, the soldier dashed out of the shoe store as several large trucks started rolling past, slowing down momentarily as the soldiers jumped on.

"Jordan, you need to get out of here. You cannot do much more with your head like that," Leena told him.

Jordan nodded and realized he would not talk Leena out of helping Liv and the Resistance. He stood and moved toward the door, receiving assistance from Liv and Leena.

"Are you okay to drive your bike?" Leena asked.

"Yes, I'll be fine."

Leena and Liv helped Jordan get to his bike, which was a few blocks away, and turned to head back to the trucks that were still coming down the street in a roar. Leena gave Jordan a kiss and wished him well. Within seconds he was gone, choosing to go down a different street than the main vein that was littered with trucks.

Leena followed Liv closely as she strategized the best way to get onto the moving truck. Before she could think about it any longer, Liv shouted, "Run!" They sprinted fast enough to catch the back of an open-top supply truck. Climbing up on the back of the truck and throwing themselves over the tailgate, they secured a position in the truck's bed.

They traveled in the convoy toward the gate, filled with adrenaline. Leena had never heard of an occasion when the Miniyar had overpowered a gate. This was truly momentous. She held onto the truck and stood high like she was riding an ancient chariot into Rome with thousands cheering her name. She had never felt so powerful.

Leena descended slightly from her high as she realized her predicament. She was on a truck headed into Zone 7. She would be flagged and arrested if she entered Zone 7. But now she was in a truck that was not slowing for anything or anyone. She struggled to get Liv's attention, but the sound of the trucks and the excitement of the moment made her realize that any notion of having the truck stop for her was fruitless.

Leena knew there was only one solution. She stood on her toes to see above the truck cab, trying desperately to determine how close she was to the gate. She could see the red lights flashing at the top of the gate wall and knew that in seconds they would be under it. She swung her leg over the side of the truck and then, grabbing a handle on the side of the truck, leaned out until her face was inches from the ground. She closed her eyes and let go of the truck, hoping for a soft landing.

Her body hit the ground like a sack of cement dropped from the top of a building. She rolled over and over until slamming into a chain-link fence that caught her but failed to give. Lying there on the dirt at the base of the fence, her body cried out in pain. She struggled to catch her breath as the fall had knocked the wind out of her. She thought she might have internal injuries and just laid there to gather her strength.

Truck after truck after truck barreled past her, throwing dust and rock, and then there was silence save the gunfire and screams that were now in the distance. The fighting had moved past the gate and into the neighboring zone. Leena pulled herself up by the fence, brushing off the dust and checking her body for injuries. She could find no broken bones, and the abrasions on her arms and legs were negligible. She decided she didn't want to do that again—ever.

Leena felt as if she had gone AWOL. The rest of them were still in the fight, probably loading trucks with food right now, and she was spitting dirt and limping back to her safety. She wasn't sure if Liv or the others would understand, but she was resolved to explain the situation once they returned. She did not want them to take her actions the wrong way.

The area where the gate opened into her zone was a mess. Bodies from both sides of the skirmish were everywhere. Spent shell casings and broken swords and bats littered the street. Smoke still permeated the air as piles of smoke grenades had been used extensively during the battle. Fires burned everywhere, and one building was completely flattened. Leena saw several CPU trucks on their side or blown into pieces.

Leena had never experienced this type of rebellion. She had thrown in her lot with this band of rebels, but it was not in her nature to fight this way. She had no history of anger toward the Aberjay, but the events of the last few weeks had changed her. She saw the disparity between the Aberjay and the Miniyar in a new way.

What reason would the Aberjay have to withhold food? Longstanding agreements to purchase food from outside farms had been in place since the walls went up. No matter what their reason, Leena remained convinced that it was wrong to withhold food. *Some things are wrong just because they are wrong,* she thought as she limped back up the street toward the first warehouse they had stumbled upon.

As she stood outside the warehouse, she heard trucks again. A couple of trucks passed, filled to the brim with food containers, and then a few minutes later, another. And then another. She watched as no fewer than twenty-five trucks passed by carrying food and Resistance soldiers screaming in victory. Just when she thought the parade of trucks was over, one pulled in front of her and stopped. Liv was driving.

"Get in!" she shouted over the loud engine.

Leena ran to the other side and attempted to climb into the front cabin, which was filled with several fighters already. Seeing there was no place to sit, she just held onto the side of the truck at the door and signaled Liv to continue.

Within minutes, they were pulling into the South City market. Locals filled the place, surrounding the trucks with their hands in the air, waiting for their allotments of food. The fighters in the back of the truck handed out the food in the most equitable fashion they could muster considering the chaos. People took armfuls of squash, corn, and other vegetables. The trucks contained some items the citizens had not seen in ages like fresh oranges, apples, pineapples, and sugarcane.

Leena stood on top of one of the trucks and could see more people than she thought possible coming to retrieve provisions. Night had fallen, and the little light that was available in the market came from the trucks' headlights, which were shining in all directions. She looked down a street that led straight to the east gate, wondering why the CPU had not sent reinforcements yet. Certainly, there would be a price to pay for such an uprising. They would not let it go. She waited for some time, but no additional troops arrived.

As the crowd began to disperse, she grabbed a sack of provisions that she had collected and set aside. Taking to the sidewalk, she headed toward home. It was quite a walk from that market, close to three miles. She waved goodbye to Liv and Julian, and they waved back with a quick salute to show respect for her contribution. Leena crossed the street and began heading north as a cool wind began to blow.

Leena had gone about halfway home when she noticed the toppled CPU trucks. The revolt she was part of wasn't limited to the east gate. She saw several trucks smoldering on their side. There were no bodies, so she assumed the skirmish must have drifted to another part of the city. She needed to circumvent the rubble, so she took the alley closest to the trucks and headed east. She figured she would go over a block or two and then turn north to continue.

Once she was heading north again, she was on a smaller street. Barrel fires on every corner provided some light and a gathering place for residents. It was not long before she attracted attention.

Three people she walked past were suddenly behind her. She could feel she was being stalked. She had no way of knowing if they were trained soldiers or half-drunk scavengers, but she felt that avoiding conflict was the best choice.

She crossed the street to the other side and picked up the pace, but her shadows followed suit. She didn't want to veer away from the street as the alleys often led to dead ends. As she rounded a small bend in the road, however, it was clear she could not continue in the direction she was going. Vehicles stacked on top of each other created a barricade she could not pass.

She took the alley to the left of the barricade, hoping to make it back to the main street, which provided better visibility because of the streetlights and more residents. But as she increased her pace into the alley, her pursuers gathered speed as well. Before she knew it, she was running full speed and feeling them gain on her. She knew they would catch her as she was carrying a heavy bag filled with flour and cornmeal, dried beans, and vegetables. She decided she needed to face them.

Leena dropped the bag and grabbed her escrima, turning to face her attackers. There were two men and a woman, covered in what looked like coal dust, most likely from the barrel fire. They took an offensive stance and held out their arms as if to catch her if she ran.

"What you got in the bag there, girl," said one man.

"Why don't you come find out?" Leena replied boldly.

The man jumped at Leena, and she slid to the right and threw him to the ground next to her bag. Then the second man grabbed her from behind and turned her toward the woman, who grabbed a knife from her pocket and lunged toward Leena, intending to inflict fatal damage. Leena used her leg to kick the knife hand, sending the knife to the alley floor, and then threw her own head back to smash her captive's nose. Leena's captor dropped her with a scream, and she turned and hit him hard in the stomach with her stick. Then came another blow across the back of the head while she sidestepped a punch from the female, putting her on the ground.

By now, the first man had stood up again and came at her like a boxer. She took a defensive stance, and each time he would throw a punch, she would use her stick to crack his knuckles, likely breaking some bones. Crack, crack, and crack again. He threw four punches that she repelled before he gave up, holding his hands, then walked back from where he came, leaving the other two in the group writhing in pain from their injuries.

Leena picked up her food bag and continued on her way. She wondered how she had accomplished such a feat but was happy to be safe. Pride filled her head while sadness rested in her heart. She never cared for violence, and it made her sad, but she knew she did what she had to do to survive.

Leena arrived home at about nine p.m. Diego was sitting with her mother, so she used the time to clean up a little before getting ready for bed. She filled her old friend in on the events of the evening, and he showed little surprise. He went through the provisions she brought home and was pleased with the haul.

Once she settled into bed with a cup of green tea, she wound down. Her heart had been racing all evening from the day's events. She found it hard to shut it down when the activity subsided. The tea helped.

Diego poured some of it from her pot into his cup while taking a chair close to her bed. "I am worried about you, Turnip."

"I know, but I'm careful."

"Careful or not, the bug that lives in the garden of fire will eventually get burned." Diego often used ancient wisdom to convey a point.

"I don't try to get involved in these things. I just kind of fall into them."

Leena had convinced herself of many things over the years, but Diego could always see through to the truth.

"Uprisings are not new, you know. In my day, there was rebellion all over the city. There were many murders and a lot of destruction. Why do you think our neighborhoods look like they do?"

"Why do you think they want to take our food, Diego?" Leena asked sincerely. "It makes no sense."

"The one that controls the food controls everyone, wouldn't you agree?"

"I guess so," Leena replied, ruminating over the question. "But why now?"

"People negotiate with what they have. If what you have is valuable to your opponent, you are more likely to get what you want."

"What does that mean?" Leena asked.

"If a grasshopper and a butterfly are negotiating, the grasshopper has a better chance of winning if he steals the butterfly's wings first."

"So, the food is our wings?"

"Yes, young Turnip, you are an excellent student," Diego said with a chuckle.

"But what do they want so badly that they would want to steal our food?"

"That sounds like a question that is begging to be answered," Diego finished before going to the sink to clean out his cup.

"I bet Fernando would know!" Leena said.

"I think you need to steer clear of Fernando, little Turnip. He is quite upset with you right now."

"Yes, I guess you are right. I just hate not knowing why we all risked our lives tonight."

Diego sat up and took a sip of tea, wiping the remaining droplets from his scraggly beard. "Let me tell you a story that you probably didn't learn in school."

"After the Chinese invasion, Americans became afraid. Before then, they had an illusion of security that kept them sane. Once the Chinese revealed their illusion, they saw how vulnerable they really were. The leaders, intending to keep people safe, built walls. They installed security to control access in and out of buildings, and cameras to watch everyone. Because of their fear, many believe they built walls inside their hearts as well. They shut out those who were different. The leadership blamed their demise on those who did not share their values."

Diego continued, "most Americans think very short-term. They are only interested in today or tomorrow. Taking a longer-term view gives you a bit more perspective. Everything you see results from a decision made long ago that someone thought was a good idea. It isn't their fault. Most people think they are doing the right thing when they are doing it. We just get so wrapped up in our cause, we cannot look far enough ahead to see the result of our agenda years, decades, or even lifetimes later.

What you see around you now results from that inability to see across that great distance."

Diego paused for a moment to let her take it in and then continued. "We are all connected. And life, like a small pond, has a ripple effect. Everything we do affects everything we will be in the future."

"Like the MIRO," Leena interjected.

"Yes, the MIRO is a good example," Diego responded. "Someone decided long ago that it would be a good idea to create a machine to help humans do their jobs. What they failed to see was the consequence of that decision, or more accurately, the important decisions that would have to be made to prevent that one decision from causing pain and destruction."

Leena looked up, thinking for a minute, and then asked, "So the MIRO should have never been invented?"

"No, the MIRO are a gift, just as you are. We just failed to see it as a gift, and we let it become a monster." Diego stopped for a minute to let her process his words once again. "The MIRO could have been made available to everyone, improving everyone's lives, but they decided to profit from the invention instead. Do you see the distinction?"

"I think so," Leena replied.

"Maybe sleep will make it clearer for you, Leena," Diego said as he moved to turn out the light. "Sleep well."

Leena lay awake for several more hours thinking about the questions but eventually fell asleep.

Leena was up early to sort her provisions from her bag and look through the seeds she acquired. The seed collection included carrots, collards, turnips, potatoes, celery, and beets. Her mouth watered just sorting through the seed packs. She could certainly live on those vegetables.

On her way to the roof that morning she had contacted several residents to inform them of the planting she planned to complete that morning. Several neighbors followed her to the roof.

Once on the roof, she took to the soil, tilling and turning as she normally did during planting season. Adding just the right amount of fertilizer and continuing to turn the soil, she looked out from her roof on the bright morning and noticed the lights on top of the wall were still red. She wondered if the CPU had taken back control of the east gate.

Leena handed out seeds for her neighbors to rebuild the garden. There were seeds for all types of vegetables. They only hoped they had enough water for them to grow. After planting what she had, Leena grabbed a water can and filled it with rainwater. Then she slowly soaked the soil containing the seeds. Little by little, she moved from each section to the next until she had soaked the entire bed with water.

As she finished watering, she heard the familiar rumble of trucks. She went to the edge of the roof to look down and could see several CPU trucks stopped in front of her building. Her mind raced with ideas about why they were there. She looked down at her bracelet. They must have tracked her at the east gate the day before. As she was debating her next move, Jun Lee came through the steel door from below. She was way too old to be running but rushed up to Leena with a look of urgency.

"Ms. Zhen, you must go. Soldiers are here looking for you!"

Panic gripped Leena. She ran to the door and grabbed her backpack off the floor. Once it was on her back, she said, "Thank you, Jun" and made her way to the edge of the building. It was close enough to the building next door for her to hatch a solid escape plan. She took a running start and jumped across the gap, falling into a roll when she landed on the roof of the neighboring building.

She ran to the next building and completed a similar jump, this one much shorter. From there, she ran to a door leading below, but it appeared to be locked. There were no more buildings she could jump to, so she could either get the door open or find a place to hide and hope they wouldn't search the rooftops.

She remembered at that point that she still had Jordan's crowbar. She dug it out of her backpack and began prying the door with it, starting as high as she could. She heard the door two buildings away slam open as guards came through to search her garden. She pulled and pulled with all her strength to get the door opened on the building where she found herself, but it wouldn't budge. She was running out of time, so she moved the crowbar down closer to the lock on the door. She pulled hard once again with all the strength she had in her small arms, and the door opened. The force of the door threw her to the ground. She turned to see a guard looking in her direction when she slithered through the opening. She was not sure if the soldier had seen her but thought that if she was spotted, getting out of that building as quickly as possible would be essential.

She ran down the stairs as fast as she could, considering their condition. A putrid smell hit her like a wall as she descended. This building was not as filled with life as hers. The smell was something rotten. She hoped it was food, and not animals or people she was smelling. The stairs were riddled with trash, missing railings, and holes. She used her agility to maneuver past the obstacles and after an exhaustive trip down the long stairway she made it to the lobby.

Leena hesitated to continue until she had a good look around. She poked her head out of the entrance and looked one way and then another. She could see the CPU trucks in front of her building a couple of blocks away and knew it was their practice to leave guards stationed by their vehicles. But did they have any idea who they were looking for? Would they recognize her on sight?

She had to risk it. She pushed on the door leading to the street and nonchalantly turned left to walk away from the CPU presence. She remained casual, telling herself it was just another day. Nothing going on here. Just out for a walk.

She didn't want to look back but wanted to know if they were charging toward her, so she turned her head to the right just enough to see the reflection of the CPU trucks in the window of some stores. She saw no movement, so she believed she could elude them. Once down a block or two, she turned into an alley to get out of the sightline of the guards.

Now what do I do? she thought. She was in trouble. Was it her bracelet that gave her away? Maybe she should have used the aluminum foil on the bracelet the day before. Convincing herself that it probably worked, she pulled her bag from her shoulders and grabbed an old ball of aluminum foil she then used to cover her bracelet.

She had headed south but thought backtracking a bit to throw off anyone in pursuit was a good idea, so she headed west through an alley and then northwest toward Jordan's part of town. She wanted to check on Jordan anyway and make sure he had that head injury looked at by someone more skilled in medicine than a couple of untrained soldiers.

As she made her way north, near the train tracks, she could hear shouting. A crowd had gathered in the square on the edge of the rail yard. She could see Fernando Martinez, along with several unarmed Miniyar security on a flatbed train car, speaking to the crowd to calm them.

She could not make out his words, so she moved closer. At the back of the crowd, she could barely make out the speech. Fernando was speaking without a microphone. Orange signs posted on lampposts in front of the homes seemed out of place. She had never seen them before, so she figured it was related.

"Please calm down, people," Fernando said, speaking as much with his hands as he did with his mouth. "In order to do what is best for all, we need to accommodate the wishes of our neighbors."

"Those are not neighbors!" Someone in the crowd roared. "They're captors!"

"This is ludicrous," stated another.

"The government has offered vouchers for food and to provide trucks to help you with your belongings," Fernando shouted to deaf ears.

Leena moved closer to one spectator in the crowd, a middle-aged woman of Middle Eastern descent. "What is this all about?" Leena asked her.

"They are evicting us," the woman said sadly. "I have been here forty years, and they are moving us out to make room for a new factory."

"Who is 'us?'" Leena asked curiously.

"All of us," the lady replied as she motioned with her arm to ensure Leena understood that she meant the entire crowd.

"There must be more than a hundred people here. How can they do that?"

"Eminent domain, they call it," said the woman quietly. "Seems like just another term for robbery to me."

Fernando, frustrated by the crowd's unbending views, finally stepped off the train-car stage and into a waiting car that then drove away. Fortunately, he did not see Leena as he was preoccupied with the crowd. She did not want to have to explain to him that she was on the run from the CPU again.

The crowd slowly dispersed and formed small groups to discuss the situation, while some walked sullenly back to their homes. Leena eavesdropped to get more information.

"When do we have to be out, Cyrus?" one citizen asked a friend.

"They gave us ten days," he replied. "We can either be moved to a camp they set up down south or find another place."

"How is it possible they can just tell us to move?" a young man asked naively. "It doesn't make sense. Certainly, there is something that can be done. Are there no lawyers on our side who can stop this in court?"

The expressions of those around him made it clear that resistance was a fool's errand, and little could be done to thwart what was coming.

"We either have to fight or we have to move, I guess," Cyrus said. "Assault on the CPU is an act of treason, punishable by death. Does anyone here want to go down that road?" The crowd grunted and then quietly dispersed.

Leena made her way to Jordan's house feeling significant empathy for this group of people. She remembered hearing Clover tell a similar story, and she wondered if Fernando had given the speech multiple times. *How was he involved in all of this? Is he just the bearer of bad news?* She pondered these questions as she made her way across the tracks and back into a residential section.

The weather was getting warm. This time of year, it could be cold one day and hot the next. Leena's bomber jacket was great in the winter as it kept her warm, as if she were flying a jet at thirty thousand feet, but it became too much in warm weather. She stopped briefly to take it off, revealing her used-to-be-white sleeveless T-shirt. She stuffed the bomber jacket into her pack, filling it to maximum capacity.

She finally made it to Jordan's and found Liv and Jordan on the front porch, sitting on the stairs. Jordan still had a bandage around his head and a massive black eye. His hands and arms seemed to have many scratches that she didn't notice the day before but were likely from his fall to the pavement.

"Leena!" Jordan cried out in a guilty tone as if he had been caught with another woman.

Leena instantly felt jealousy. She knew her and Jordan had only recently become more than friends, but seeing Liv there with Jordan made her want to launch into attack mode. *Was Liv trying to get close to Jordan? Jordan didn't even like Liv? He called her a criminal.* Leena turned around to compose herself before addressing them, so she did not come across as angry. Once she had taken a few deep breaths, she turned to face them.

"Hello to the both of you. I came to check on your head, Jordan," Leena said. Then, looking at Liv, she continued, "And I did not expect to see *you* here. How did you even know where Jordan lived?"

"I asked around," Liv said. "I just wanted to make sure he was okay from that pounding he took yesterday."

"That soldier took me totally by surprise. If I had a moment to think, I would have put all of them down," Jordan said boldly.

"We were very lucky," Leena chimed in, hoping to change the subject so he would not ask about the stranger who saved them. "Any idea what happened after?"

"The CPU took control of the gate shortly after we came back through it, but we got what we needed," said Liv. "That warehouse had tons of food; we only got a small portion of it. We should hit it again." She paused to take a drink of water from her bottle. "I'm sure they have doubled their security presence there by now."

"Did you hear about the evictions along the train tracks?" Leena asked, again to change the subject.

"Yes," said Jordan, "they are happening all along that northern section near the wall. Not sure what they are up to, but they are building something."

"Fernando was up there trying to calm them..." Leena began before she was interrupted.

"Fernando? You mean Fernando Martinez, the zone advocate? You call him Fernando? What are you, like cousins or something?" Liv pressed.

"No, just a friend of the family," Leena responded, not wanting to get into too much detail as the zone advocate was disliked by many Miniyar.

"Wow, that guy is a total jerk," Liv said plainly, looking at Leena in judgment as if to question her loyalties. Noticing the aluminum foil wrapped around Leena's bracelet, she changed the subject on her own. "What is that for? You in trouble again?"

"The CPU raided my building this morning looking for me. I had to run and thought it was best to hide my location."

"You really need to go off-grid, Leena. The moment you turn that thing back on, they will be on you," Liv said in a helpful tone.

"Really?" Leena questioned. "How would I buy anything?"

"I think you are beyond that now, don't you? Your life is no longer controlled by that system. You make your own way. I know several people who have had them removed. You will have to become self-sufficient, but at least they couldn't track you anymore."

Leena thought about the ramifications. If she had no bracelet, they would never know her location, and breaking into the zone to get the medications her mother needed would be easier. She did not know how much tracking they were doing and knowing that they could do it was enough to make her want to rip the device off her arm.

The CPU surgically implanted bracelets around the age of ten. She had never even considered taking it off, nor did she know what would be involved in removing it.

"You are not actually considering this, are you, Leena?" Jordan said with derision. "You are not thinking clearly. This will ruin any future you might have imagined. No more school, no work permit, no groceries. How would you live?"

"I think Liv is right. The moment I turn it back on, I will be arrested and put in prison for two years, minimum. And what other charges do you think they might come up with if they can put me at the east gate yesterday? Insurrection? Treason? Assault on an officer? These are not minor crimes, Jordan." Leena turned her back on her friends and walked three or four steps into the yard. The weight of her situation was like a bus on her shoulders. She shook her head as if to throw off what had happened, but she knew she had to face it. She was not sitting down anymore. She had to fight.

"Okay, take this thing off, Liv," Leena said, now facing Liv and stretching out her arm. "It is the only way."

"Shit, I can't do it," Liv said with a giggle. "You need surgery and stuff. You need a doctor."

The light in Leena's eyes faded upon learning that getting the bracelet off would be harder than she'd thought. Of course, it wasn't simple, she then realized, or people would take them off all the time.

Noticing her disappointment, Liv offered a suggestion. "I think I know someone who can do it. Let me talk to a few people, and hopefully, I can get it set up. Are you sure you want to do this? This isn't like a tattoo, you know; this is for life."

"Yes, set it up."

"Okay, I need to run then," Liv agreed. "Leena, come to my place tomorrow, and I will hopefully have some news." Liv then flashed a quick goodbye to Jordan before heading off down the street toward her side of town.

Leena knew what she had agreed to but didn't see another way to save her mom. She cared little about what would happen to her if she could give her mother a chance at life. It was worth it in her mind. She just had to stay hidden until she could have the procedure done.

Jordan and Leena spent the morning on the front porch talking about the recent events and past adventures. While none of them had been as dangerous as the most recent incident, they felt a bond. They were entwined by the experiences they had been through together. Jordan did not understand what Leena was becoming, and she kept that secret from him so as not to bruise his ego. Leena was becoming a fighter. A renegade. An insurrectionist. The idea of it still made her anxieties soar.

By lunch, they had moved inside, and Jordan made Leena his famous cauliflower steak with mushroom gravy. He was a superb cook, although his affection for spices strayed a little outside of Leena's palate. Leena wondered why he was wasting his time in a factory when he should be a chef at a restaurant, but Jordan laughed it off as an unattainable dream.

As they sat on the couch, they were surprised to see that the uprising at the east gate did not make the news. If fact, there was nothing in the news about food being withheld or any type of violence apart from some thefts in the northern area of Zone 7, which they blamed on the unscrupulous Miniyar contingent.

Leena sat with her legs crossed, a position she was always taught as *crisscross applesauce*. Jordan lay with his head in her lap so she could investigate his wounds and change his bandage.

"Jordan, why was Liv here today?" Leena began after a long silence.

"You heard her. She wanted to check on me."

"But she doesn't even really know you," Leena said.

"She just showed up."

"Do you think she likes you?"

"I wouldn't know," Jordan replied.

"Of course you would. Does she touch your arm when she talks? Does she laugh at your jokes?" Leena pushed a little.

"Are you saying a woman would not laugh at my jokes unless she liked me? I think my jokes are quite funny."

"So, you don't really know when a girl likes you. Do they not teach that in boy school?"

"No, I guess not." Jordan was getting a little irritated.

"If you liked her better than me, you could tell me."

"Oh, stop it! I don't like Liv, so let it go."

"Okay, sorry I brought it up," Leena said, a little defeated but knowing she had received the reaction she expected. If there were feelings Liv had for Jordan, it was clear he did not reciprocate.

After a long silence accompanied by mindless gazing at the television, Leena asked, "Is it okay if I stay here tonight? I don't want to go home if they are waiting for me."

"My parents are gone for the night, so I don't see why not," Jordan said.

"Well, do you want me to stay?" Leena asked.

Jordan, obviously uncomfortable with what he perceived as a trap, acquiesced to the game. "I would very much enjoy it if you could spend the night with me," he said with his sarcasm only thinly veiled.

"Well, I guess I could," Leena said as if she had to be talked into the idea that was hers in the first place.

Chapter 9

PRESSURE

The previous day was like a dream to Leena. Apart from being chased from her home by soldiers, and being on the run, she spent most of the day with the man she loved. She spent the night with Jordan and, although she made every attempt to sleep on the floor, promising not to be a burden, ended up in his bed making love for most of the night. He was very gentle with her small body, as if he thought he might break her. It was her first time. She was not sure if it was Jordan's, as she knew he had other girlfriends. The nakedness was strange and at times awkward, but still enjoyable. She enjoyed being close to him. Her heart burst with feelings for Jordan and hoped that he felt the same way. She had not been saving herself for Jordan specifically, but she was glad her first time was with someone she had loved so long, even if it was only friendship for the first few years.

After breakfast, they headed back to Leena's house to check out the situation and see if it was safe. They left on the motorbike, but Jordan had forgotten to charge it, so the battery was less than half-full. They made their way through the streets and noticed the air was dense, as if fires were burning and consuming all the oxygen. Something just felt different about the day, but they both had trouble describing the source. They discussed it briefly as they rode, but reasoned it was most likely excess pollution. Nothing could dampen Leena's spirit anyway as she was basking in her newfound love affair.

The streets they rode through had an increased CPU presence, and Jordan made his best effort to avoid them. Sometimes they turned down alleys to turn around, while at other times, they just hid behind buildings or walked the bike down stairs and through narrow passages. The soldiers seemed to be at every major intersection in the northern part of the zone. There were one or two trucks in each location with armed guards outside the trucks, dressed for battle. Leena had never seen this many CPU in this zone.

Out of curiosity, Leena asked Jordan to travel along the north wall, which meant going northwest until they reached it and then driving east to ride along it all the way to her street and beyond. She wanted to determine if the evictions were a one-off project as Fernando seemed to insist, or was there something more sinister lurking?

As they reached the northwest wall and turned east, there was a heavy CPU presence and a lack of citizens on the streets. Leena again noticed several of the orange signs and asked Jordan to slow down so she could read one. The sign read:

> This area has been claimed by the Zone 7 magistrate based on the laws of eminent domain. All citizens on this block are commanded to vacate their homes within ten days or face penalties and/or imprisonment based on Magistrate Code 72, Subsection 4. For further information, contact your zone advocate.

As they continued, she could tell this was not isolated to this one area. Each area along the northern section of the zone had these signs. This was not a simple project but a clearing, as if they wanted to push the great wall a couple hundred feet south into Zone 6. Clearly, the CPU plan was coordinated to impact much more than one city block.

As they passed a couple of families packing their belongings into a small vehicle, Leena thought about how this might affect her ability to move freely in this area. She passed through here frequently, and the additional exposure would not be good for her clandestine movements.

The CPU heavily guarded the northern gate, just three blocks from her building. More than she had seen in the past. The lights on the tops of the walls were still red, indicating that the security profile was still high. This explained why there were few citizens on the streets. Even though it wasn't a violation to be out in public during a red Security Alert Profile (SAP), citizens were advised to stay inside. It was obvious the CPU expected more trouble from dissidents.

Jordan passed her street and drove another ten blocks to get an idea of the spread of the eviction notices. The pronouncements continued along the entire north end of the zone. After turning around and heading back, they turned onto her street and were shocked to see more orange signs that extended further into the zone than they had seen earlier on their ride.

Fortunately, as they reached her building, there was no sign of the CPU. They parked down the street from the building entrance in case they had to make a quick getaway. They trudged along the sidewalk to the front of the building and then cautiously went up the stairs.

"Jordan, look!" Leena cried.

Her stomach rose into her throat. More orange signs were on her street, her lamppost, and her front door. Her building was included in the mandatory eviction.

Panic gripped her body and mind as she thought through the ramifications. *She couldn't move! Her mother was in a hospital bed hooked up to fluids. Where would she go? How would they move her? What about the garden?* Thoughts flooded her brain until tears rolled down her face.

Jordan, sensing the moment, pulled her tight. "You can both stay with me," he said, trying to be helpful before realizing that his family really didn't have room for her mother.

"Jordan, what does this mean?" she said, ignoring his offer. "We have nowhere to go! The garden is how we feed ourselves."

Once inside, Leena closed the door behind them and marched up the stairs. She placed her hand on her escrima just in case there was trouble. She half-expected guards to jump out as soon as they entered and slap on cuffs, but they were able to make it up to her floor without incident.

Reaching her apartment, their entrance surprised Diego, who was tending to Mei. On previous visits, Jordan would wait outside to let Leena go in first, just in case her mother was dressing or indisposed. In this case, however, he felt it prudent to get inside and close the door as quickly as possible. Diego put down the tray he was holding and gave Leena a big hug.

"I was worried about you," Diego said.

"I know. They cornered me on the roof, and I had to jump down to Violet's building to escape," Leena replied.

"There was a whole patrol here looking for you, along with Sergeant McBride, who we met before. It seems odd to me they would send so much firepower to get one small girl for a zone violation."

Leena knew it was more than that but felt it would be better if Diego didn't know any details.

"Did you see the eviction notice?"

"Yes," Diego whispered. "They put those up right before they left."

"What will we do? We can't move," Leena said, beginning to tear up.

Diego comforted her. "Don't worry, Turnip, we will figure something out. Let me talk to Fernando."

"I don't think he can fix this; he seems powerless to help anyone. I just saw him giving speeches yesterday, and he had nothing but bad news." Leena moved to the other side of her mom's bed as she lay sleeping. She took her hand, although Mei did not stir or pay any notice to her touch.

"Diego, I am going to head south today to get some information that will help me get the meds I need for Mom. Are you okay staying with her?"

"You know I will, but are you sure you should spend time out there rather than spending time in here?" Diego finished, pointing to Mei.

"I don't have time to explain now, but if things go right, I will have the medicine to save her. She has plenty of life left, and I can give it to her. I just need a little more time." Leena feigned confidence even though she knew that any chance of success was a long shot.

"I know you will do the right thing, Turnip."

Leena spent some time with her mom as Jordan waited in the corner next to the window so he could keep an eye out for trucks. Leena knew that if she was cornered again, she could make the same escape as the day before, so she was mainly concerned about her mom and the rest of the building's residents. Mei was conscious and able to spend some quality time with Leena that seemed beyond her strength just hours earlier. She even laughed. It felt good to talk to her mother like she was a normal person. Not 'sick mom' but the mom who had always been her rock.

She didn't ask about what Leena had been up to. She likely did not want to know. Leena could remember many times growing up when she would sneak into the apartment past curfew, and her mother would pretend she was asleep. She always gave her the freedom to make her own choices. She could be strict, but in most cases, she let the little things slide.

Leena and Jordan made their way to Cabbagetown to find Liv. If Liv could provide a contact to remove the bracelet, it just might allow Leena to enter the Aberjay zone once again. She was determined to get the medication for her mother if she had to burn the entire zone to the ground.

The streets were teeming. This far from the wall, there was less CPU presence but, as a result, more people on the streets. When things get tough, people hoard supplies, which makes finding what you need more difficult. The people they saw were not warriors but desperate souls trying to survive. They were scouring the markets, the stores, and friends' homes in search of food.

As they made their way south, they noticed a checkpoint. The CPU had blocked the road ahead. There were probably thirty soldiers checking vehicles and waving them through.

"This is not good," Leena said, urging Jordan to take another route.

"Maybe this isn't about us. I have my work permit," Jordan said confidently.

"That isn't any help here. They might be looking for me. We have to go another way," Leena insisted.

Jordan didn't have much time to decide, and two lanes of cars packed the road. He moved the bike to the right and went around several waiting vehicles to reach the alley that would take them away from the danger. Turning into the alley, they could hear the escalated voices of soldiers shouting, "Hey, you" and "stop," so they knew they would not get away easily.

"Hit it!" Leena said while Jordan turned the throttle.

The bike accelerated, and they shot down the alley like a bullet. Leena attempted to turn around to check for a tail but could not do so at that speed without falling off the back. Jordan made a quick right onto a major street and then left to ward off any tails. He then slowed to go down another alley. He stopped and looked behind him, waiting to see if someone might be following him.

Leena could see ahead of them that the alley ended. If the CPU blocked them in, there would be nowhere to go.

"Jordan, we need to turn around!"

"Okay, jump off and I'll get us back to the other street," Jordan said, muscling the bike back and forth until it faced the entrance to the alley.

As Leena mounted the bike once again, a large CPU truck turned into the alley. It stopped abruptly, closing off any escape.

Leena was holding on tight to Jordan and could feel his heart beating through his shirt and jacket.

"They have us trapped," Jordan said.

"You can make it. Go!" Leena shouted.

Jordan sized up the size of the truck and the alley and determined they might fit on the left side. Just then, however, two soldiers exited the truck and stood in front of it. Brandishing their handguns, they taunted their victims.

"Stand down—you got nowhere to go!" yelled the soldier.

Leena strained to hear as she recognized the voice. Was it a prison guard? Someone she met in court? No, she knew that voice. It was Sgt. McBride.

"Hold on," Jordan said.

"I trust you," Leena said, most likely too softly for him to hear as he lay on the throttle and the bike took off, racing toward their adversaries.

Leena dropped her right hand off Jordan's stomach to reach for her escrima. She wanted to defend herself in case their attackers were to knock them off the bike. She gripped it in her right hand as Jordan raced toward the guards, then Sgt. McBride raised his right hand and fired in their direction.

At first, Jordan aimed the bike toward the right side of the truck to confuse the soldiers. At the last minute, he moved to the left side where Sgt. McBride was standing. Leena swung her escrima wildly before they went by and landed a strike on Sgt. McBride's face, throwing him back against the truck and onto the ground. The motorbike dashed through the opening, catching the right mirror slightly on the truck fender, which made a loud scraping noise and sprayed noticeable sparks.

Jordan maneuvered the bike back down the alley to reach a major road, turned left, and rocketed down the street to lose their predators once again. After a few minutes, while making multiple turns, they were certain they were safe.

Jordan brought the bike to a stop in front of an old bus station. They jumped off to regain their wits, and Jordan threw up in a nearby patch of grass. Leena was shaking, unsure of the events that had just occurred. She looked down at her escrima, which was dripping with blood. Shock overcame her as she dropped the stick and fell to the ground.

Jordan recovered, wiping his mouth, and moved back toward her, holding her while she was still on the ground. She turned and buried her face in his chest as tears rolled down. Suddenly, she let out a scream of exasperation, muffling it into Jordan's clothing so it would not attract attention. She then raised her face to look into his eyes.

"I know... I know," Jordan said, connecting his thoughts with hers. "We can't stay here. They will look for us all night now."

"Jordan, your bracelet," Leena said as she pointed out to Jordan that his tracker was not covered in foil. "They probably already know you were in that alley."

Leena took out more foil from her pack and covered his bracelet. She also checked hers to ensure it was covered. The CPU could not use the bracelets as evidence of a crime, but that did not stop them from using it for search-and-destroy missions. She knew they had to stay under their radar if they were to evade capture.

Jordan helped Leena to her feet, and after a few minutes of calm as they took deep breaths, they mounted the bike once more and rode toward Cabbagetown. They stayed on back roads as much as possible, thinking that the major arteries might have more roadblocks.

They pulled in front of Liv's warehouse apartment and made their way into the long hallway of doors. Leena did not know which one was Liv's, and as before, there was no receptionist, so she just headed for the common area to see if she might get lucky.

Liv was not in the gym or common area, but Zoe was working out and agreed to find her. Moments later, Liv arrived dressed in green fatigues and a black tank top, her short blonde hair still wet from a shower.

"Hello, you two," Liv said as she soaked up the water from her hair with a towel.

"Were you able to find someone who can help, Liv?" Leena asked, skirting any small talk.

"Well, this is one of those good news, bad news situations," Liv said. "I found someone who can remove your bracelet, but he doesn't take credits. You will need to bring something you can barter with to the meeting. Also, he is a Tullian."

Tullian was the word used to describe those who lived a nomadic lifestyle outside of the cities. They were survivors, often living on rats, snakes, and what they could steal from others. They were scavengers. They lived in such barren areas that anyone foolish enough to go out there rarely returned. They were a tribal people and had little use for the Miniyars' code of ethics and no desire for communal living. Each one was a killer.

"A Tullian?!" Jordan shouted.

"Calm down, Jordan," Leena said, attempting to lower the tension in the room. "Where does he live?"

"His name is Barren Chief—probably not his real name. He lives about sixty miles south of Zone 6. His place is not far off the highway, but getting there and getting back is quite dangerous. Zoe and I can go with you. I have a motorbike." Liv finished and headed toward the door back to the apartments. "Let me grab a few things, and we can go."

Leena then turned to Zoe and asked, "What can I give as payment?"

Zoe responded, "Do you still have the water we gave you?"

"Yes, I have one of them."

"That will probably do. Water is scarce out there. Here, take two more though, just in case." Zoe reached into the fridge and tossed two more bottles to her.

Leena and Jordan headed outside to wait. They were both quite nervous. Neither of them had ever been south of the city. Most people avoided the barren lands between cities unless they paid for secured travel: caravans of buses that were heavily armed to discourage pirates and other thieves. Going into the Tullian lands without security was suicidal.

Zoe pulled up beside them on a 'trike,' a motorcycle with two back wheels and one front wheel. It was a little larger and much wider than Jordan's small bike but still electric, so it traveled quietly. Liv sat on the back, and it was clear she was suited for travel, with heavy vests and a green backpack loaded with weapons and ammunition. She handed two-cylinder objects with pins in them to Leena.

"Smoke grenades," Liv explained. "Put them in your bag. May come in handy."

Leena took the munitions and dropped them into her bag. She did not know where Liv might get these types of munitions, but by this point in their relationship, she was sure she did not want to know. She was terrified to make this trip and knew based on the time of day that they would probably come back in the dark—but she had to go. She had to try.

Liv noticed Leena's wide-eyed look and gave further instructions. "They are simple, pull the pin and throw it within three seconds. They create a bunch of smoke, no explosion."

Leena nodded as if she were one of the soldiers in this army of four but inside, she felt as though she was not really cut out for this mission. She was glad she had an escort. She would not have wanted to do this with just Jordan.

The southern gate of Zone 6 was only a chain-link fence. There were no CPU down in that area as it could be dangerous without a large contingent. The CPU cared little about who entered the Miniyar zone on the south side. The four rebels rode through the gate and settled in for the long ride. It was only sixty miles, but travel on the highways was slow and treacherous. There were burned-out cars and tanks, as well as barricades created by the Tullian to trap unsecured travelers. They were certain to hit resistance.

It was very dark south of the city. The sun had not gone down, but storm clouds rumbled above, blocking natural light and making it feel a bit more sinister. They traveled only 15 miles per hour while having to dodge the highway's obstacles. At every overpass, Leena held her breath, hoping there was not a Tullian army of nomads on the other side, hiding and waiting to pounce.

She had heard stories in school about the Tullian. Not unlike ghost stories, they usually ended with someone losing their head or suffering a fate worse than death. She knew the stories were probably not real but desperately wanted to avoid contact with pirates and cannibals just to be safe.

Leena looked down at her bracelet as they traveled, still covered in foil, and wondered if she was making the right decision. Could she live the rest of her life without buying anything? She wondered if removing her bracelet would drive her out to these barren lands to scavenge for food and water for the rest of her days. She was willing if it meant saving her mother, but she also knew this was only the first step. She still did not know how she would get the medicine.

Leena had never seen so many miles go by without humans. There was no one. The lands were indeed barren. She knew people lived out here; she just never realized there was so much unused land. It was clear that no one had lived in even the few buildings that they passed for years.

Old billboards still stood along the route, although no one had updated them in more than twenty years. Most were unreadable anyway, but occasionally she could make out partial words and pictures. She wondered what a 'Cracker Barrel' was as she saw many of those signs along the journey.

They traveled for a couple of hours, and the sun went down. Darkness made travel even more difficult as Liv had suggested they not use headlights on the bikes. There was too much in the road and too little visibility to progress at almost any speed. Leena occasionally saw a light off in the distance, most likely a bonfire. She wondered what types of creatures were huddled around those fires. *Were they friendly? Or a band of pirates?* Her mind created some horrific pictures.

About two and a half hours into the trip, Leena was getting tired. Her posterior was sore, and she needed a good stretch. She knew that stopping was not an option, but she would have given anything for a break.

As she was dreaming of a hot shower, they crossed under an overpass and were stopped by a wall of cars and debris. Liv jumped off the back of the three-wheeled motorbike to see if there was a way around. Before her feet hit the ground, a large net fell from above as if unleashed from the clouds. It was thick and heavy, and it knocked Jordan and Leena to the ground, still straddling the motorbike.

Leena heard screaming sounds and knew she had to get out of this net before her hunters were on her. She struggled to push the motorbike off her left leg, which was pinned, and Jordan did the same. Once free of the bike, she crawled on her belly under the weight of the large net to get to the edge as she heard gunfire ring out. She didn't know if she was being fired on but knew her primary goal had to be escaping this trap that restrained her. She thought about Jordan but reasoned he would need to take care of himself.

Reaching the edge of the net, it got caught on her backpack. She had to let it go. Removing it from her shoulders, she slithered out and rolled outside of the confines of the net. She saw two unusual-looking humans come toward her who were covered in what looked like homemade shields of metal and rope. They had few teeth, long dirty looking hair and the remnants of homemade tattoos on their arms and face. Wielding bats, they came at her aggressively.

Leena sidestepped the first one and put him to the ground. She swung around just in time to meet the heavy end of a bat against her skull. The world went dark as she fell to the ground. The last thing she remembered before passing out was the taste of blood.

"Leena!"

Leena, wake up!"

"Leena!" She recognized this third voice as Liv's.

Opening her eyes, Leena tried to focus. She could see Liv speaking to her but could barely make her out at first. She was seated, but her hands were tightly tied together somehow behind her back—not with handcuffs but with some sort of plastic tie. She pulled them apart out of instinct to see if they would come free, but the band held fast. The taste of dried blood was in her mouth.

As her mind focused, she realized she was in a box truck. Liv, Jordan, and Zoe were there, all tied similarly. The only light was a small rusted-out hole in the top of the truck in the corner that cast moonlight.

"What happened?" Leena asked, tilting her head back and stretching her neck. Her head was pounding, and she tasted blood in her mouth. She vaguely remembered getting hit with something.

"We got jumped," Zoe said.

"They got us in a truck, heading south, I think," Liv said as she stretched to see out the hole.

"What do you think they want?" Leena asked.

"First, they want to take our weapons and water, which they did. And then they will probably carve us up and eat us," said Liv, only half-joking. "We must get out of here. Can anyone get their hands free?"

Leena looked over at Jordan, who was just regaining consciousness, so he must have been hit as well. She twisted and twisted her hands but couldn't escape her bonds.

"I can't get free," Leena said in defeat.

"If we can't get our hands free, we are finished," Liv said dramatically.

The truck stopped. They heard shouting and then gunshots, two of which ripped through the thin metal of the box truck, leaving two shafts of light behind. An explosion sent the truck onto its side. Liv and Zoe flew across the truck, landing on Jordan and Leena. All of them were then lying on their backs looking at the other side of the truck. They could smell fuel burning, gunpowder, and some other strange chemical they couldn't place.

A minute later, they heard a pounding on the back of the truck. It sounded like a hammer on metal, which resounded through the box of the truck as it made contact over and over. The pounding then stopped, and the door to the back of the truck opened. The position of the truck made it difficult to open the door, so a hammer was being used to beat it into submission. Once the door was opened wide enough for a human to slide through, a shadowy figure entered.

Stepping into the light was a young man of about twenty-five years of age. He had blond hair and bright blue eyes. He wore army fatigues and a bulletproof vest and was carrying a large rifle with ammunition tucked into loops in his belt. Grenades hung off his vest. He waved at the smoke in the truck and then spit to clear his palate.

"Hello, everyone," he said in a game show voice. "My name is Jesse, and I will be your rescuer today! Is everyone okay?"

Not knowing what to say, and a little stunned by the entrance, Leena just held out her hand to receive help getting to her feet. He grabbed her hand and pulled her up with such strength it startled her.

"Hello, Jesse, I am Leena," she said as she looked into his eyes.

Liv jumped up, and shaking off the fall she had just taken, thanked her hero. "Thanks for the rescue. I thought we were toast."

Jesse helped Jordan and Zoe to their feet and then, one by one, they each slid out of the small opening in the back of the truck. They were still on the highway, but it looked like a war zone. The two perpetrators who accosted Leena earlier were filled with bullet holes and lying face down on the pavement. Smoke was everywhere, and bits of the truck lay all over the road, smoldering.

A jeep with a large, mounted machine gun was nearby. Behind the bulky gun that was still smoking was a large man. Jesse guided the four to the jeep and pointed to the man. "This is Gus. Say hi, Gus."

Gus just grunted as he reached out to help the four get into the jeep. Leena was not sure why they were going with him so willingly except that he had just rescued them and they really didn't have a choice. The alternative was walking sixty miles back to the city.

Leena stepped into the back seat of the jeep and noticed her backpack, as well as Liv's, already in the jeep. She was thankful they were able to recover her belongings. She had grown fond of her escrima, and her backpack contained everything she needed. She could not imagine having to replace everything that was in it.

The jeep drove slowly across the median and then turned south. Leena wondered if they were going back to the city.

"What are you four doing out here?" Jesse asked as he drove. "Especially at night!"

"We're looking for someone," Leena said vaguely, not sure if she should share more information.

"Who exactly are you looking for?" Jesse asked, prying a little deeper. "Maybe I know them."

"Just a friend. You would not know them," Liv said quickly before Leena could answer.

"This is not the place you want to be at night. Those night crawlers would have had you all for breakfast."

"Where are you taking us?" Zoe asked.

"I need to get you off the road. Those guys who nabbed you were easy targets, but there are a lot more of them out here, and sometimes they're in greater numbers. You're lucky it was just a couple of numbskulls. I will take you to my place so you can get some rest. Then you can make your way in the morning when it's light." Jesse then turned onto a narrow road and drove into the darkness.

They had little choice but to trust him. They didn't know the location of their motorbikes or how to find them. They just hoped that this Jesse meant them no harm.

A few miles off the highway, Jesse pulled into a sprawling farm, the scent of freshly cut hay wafting through the air. Thick vegetation had taken over the fields, creating a dense, green landscape. It was difficult to tell in the dark, but Leena could make out some vegetables that made her think about her garden. At the end of the long dirt driveway, they arrived at a large farmhouse and barn. The farmhouse was dark and eerie, but the barn had a soft light coming from beneath its doors.

They exited the jeep and reaching in, grabbed their respective packs. There was no resistance to them reclaiming their possessions, so Leena thought this was a good sign that her new acquaintance meant no harm.

Jesse pulled back the sliding door to the barn, and the four entered, not knowing if they were about to receive salvation and rest, or more treachery. The interior was surprising. It looked less like a barn and more like a house. The stalls had been converted into rooms and the floors were packed dirt, but not dusty. The center of the barn was communal, with a long picnic table and a small fire burning for warmth. A hole drilled into the roof directly above the fire allowed the fumes to escape, and a sophisticated rainwater collection system directed rain to a waiting drum below.

Jesse directed them to a room just off the main area and pointed. "You can all bunk in there. There are four beds. We will have some breakfast at seven a.m., and you are welcome to join us. If you need water, there are buckets next to the drum there.

Don't worry, you are perfectly safe here, but don't venture off the farm. It can be dangerous out there."

And with those terse instructions, Jesse was gone. There was no one else in the barn they could see, but it was late, so maybe others were sleeping in the adjacent rooms. They decided to be quiet just in case they might disturb someone.

All four of them quietly located the bunk beds, their sleeping quarters, positioned on each side of the room. Leena threw her bag on top of one of them and pushed it to the foot of the bed, then used the rudimentary ladder to climb up. There was a mattress, but it was thin. Still, for being on the road in the barren lands, it was luxury accommodations.

Leena said good night to the others and lay back. Her head still hurt from the attack she suffered earlier. The bleeding had stopped, but her hair was sticky from the dried blood and asphalt. She thought about finding a shower but was too tired to pursue it. She was asleep within minutes as exhaustion overcame her.

Leena woke as light through a crack in the barn inched across her face. She immediately smelled something fragrant. Something amazing. An aroma she had not smelled since she was young. It was bacon. She sat straight up in bed and realized she was the only one in the room. Wondering if the others had been taken during the night made her quickly collect her belongings and run to the common area.

As she entered the makeshift dining room, she noticed all her companions seated at a picnic table. They were feasting on fresh eggs, toast, and yes, bacon.

"We were wondering when you would rise," Liv said cheerfully. "We were going to wake you but decided you needed your sleep."

Jordan dashed to her side. "Are you okay? Come sit with me. You won't believe this breakfast!"

Leena ate like she had not eaten in years. The saltiness of the bacon was like a dream. *Why does this taste so good?* she thought each time she put a piece in her mouth. Then there was toast with homemade butter, milk, and eggs. She had never in her life enjoyed such a meal. She had eaten each item individually before, but the meals she was used to eating didn't have so many courses.

As they ate and laughed and remarked on the quality of the food, Jesse came through the door with another plate. "Here are some stewed apples," he said as he placed the golden sweet morsels on the table.

"Jesse, this is amazing," Leena said. "How do you have all this?"

"We live off the land here," he replied. "We raise our own pigs and chickens, our own wheat, and many veggies. There is an apple orchard out back you probably couldn't see when we came in last night. And old Bessie gives us milk for butter."

"But how do you keep it secret from the others who live out here?" Liv asked.

"It's not really a secret, and we do have the occasional attack. We try to be generous with the local clans, and we have Gus to chase off the more violent elements. We make it work." Jesse piled some bacon onto a slice of toast and took several big bites.

"I may never go home," Zoe said.

The group laughed and finished their breakfast in silence. Everyone was enjoying the meal too much to spend much time in conversation. After the meal, Leena and Jordan were helping with dishes, and Leena thought back to something Jesse had said.

"Jesse, you said 'we' earlier. Did you mean you and Gus?"

"No," Jesse said, "I live here with my Uncle Bill. This is his place."

"Oh," Leena replied, her head still spinning with questions. "I hope I get to meet him before we go."

"You will," Jesse said. "He's in the house. He'll be over shortly."

As they were finishing the cleanup, Leena roamed through the barn. *Just one more slice of bacon,* she thought as she grabbed two morsels from the plate that had not yet been whisked away. She nibbled on the delectable salty goodness as she strolled around the common area, peering into each room to see what it might contain.

One looked like a barracks, like the room she slept in the night before. Another one was some sort of storage room with shelves of jarred food and bags of what looked like flour. The third room was dark, but the faint glimmer of light coming through the cracks of the boards revealed that it was used for medical procedures. It was probably not a sterile environment but clean enough for stitching wounds and bandaging minor injuries. There were no doctors among the Tullian as far as Leena knew. The last room she observed, as she ate the last piece of bacon, was full of communications equipment. A microphone and several stacks of radios and maps with circled coordinates on the walls offered evidence that this was used to connect to the outside world. She wondered who they could talk to way out here.

"It's to stay up to date with the other clans, enemy movements, and incoming threats," Jesse said as he came up behind her. "This is how I knew you were out there. The vermin who took you last night are from the Shilrag clan. Savages and cannibals who live further west."

Leena blushed a little as she swallowed the last bite of her breakfast and smiled like a schoolgirl with a crush. Jesse leaned forward to reach for the makeshift door. A curtain hung on a small spring rod. He pulled it closed. For a moment, their faces were only inches apart. Leena could not help but notice how handsome he was and wondered if he had a girlfriend. She realized how dirty she must be and hoped the odor was not too off-putting.

"Jesse, do you have a shower?" Leena asked.

"Sure, and hot water. Let me show you the way," Jesse replied. He guided Leena outside and then to the back side of the barn, where a door led into a bathroom with a full shower and plenty of space for dressing.

The prospect of hot water dazzled Leena. This was a foreign concept to her, and she took full advantage. She had taken lukewarm showers for years and had grown accustomed to it. Climbing into the shower stall that smelled clean and shone brightly, she washed her entire body. She flushed out weeks of dirt and dried blood from her hair. She had clean underwear and a shirt in her backpack. She was beyond excited to shed those smelly garments. Once dressed, she brushed her teeth before returning to the main area.

"If you want to get your stuff together, I will give you a ride out to the highway to see if your bikes are still there," Jesse told the group.

The four packed their things and walked out to the jeep. Leena saw the farm in the light of day, and it was impressive. There was another barn behind the house they had not seen before, along with a yard for chickens to roam. Apple trees lined the property, and she could see a fence in the distance that was quite high and covered in razor wire to ward off unwanted visitors. Large banks of solar panels were back by the fence next to a small building, which most likely held the battery system and components needed to provide power.

The layout of the homestead fascinated Leena. She knew that some people lived this way years ago but thought it was a thing of the past. She learned about the Tullian a little in school, but mostly through ghost stories. She and her classmates were always taught that it was the land of the uncivilized—that the people were only partially human, surviving like animals out on the plains and eating each other. But this was nothing like that storybook version, and she had yet to see a ghost. And the bacon! Oh, the bacon. She could get used to this uncivilized living.

As they were packing the jeep, the door to the farmhouse opened to reveal an old man with a long gray beard. He was heavyset, dressed in jeans and an old motorcycle vest. He sat on the porch and put on his leather boots before coming down the stairs and over to their location.

"Hello, visitors. My name is Bill."

Everyone greeted Bill politely, remarking on how lovely the farm was and how much they enjoyed breakfast. They also commented on the heroics of Jesse and how thankful they were to have been saved from the night crawlers.

The four loaded up in the jeep as Jesse took the driver's seat. With a quick wave, they headed away from the farmhouse.

"Bill is great, Jesse," Jordan said. "He reminds me of my uncle."

"Yes, he has been a father figure to me for as long as I can remember. But no one calls him Bill around here. They call him Barren."

Liv quickly grabbed the wheel of the jeep, signaling for Jesse to stop and then said, "Jesse, turn around!"

Bill, or Barren Chief as they called him, was a cybernetic engineer by trade. He had worked on the original MIRO project out west and was highly involved with many of the latest electronic advances over the previous forty years. Although he was retired, he still loved to tinker.

Upon the group's return to the farm after telling Jesse why they wanted to go back, they walked into the barn to find Barren eating breakfast. His eyes showed surprise as they walked in.

"Bill?" Leena began. "I am told you can remove this," she said as she pointed to her bracelet.

Bill nodded as he took another bite of his breakfast.

"Are you sure you want to do that?" He asked Leena.

"Yes. I cannot go into details, but I need to be able to move around without the CPU knowing my every step."

Bill finished his breakfast and showed them into the medical room in the barn. The shelves were lined with small bins containing cotton balls, bandages, and a fluid that was most likely alcohol.

Leena had never liked doctor's offices, and this room was no exception. The only thing she could remember about going to the doctor as a young child was Dr. Singh saying "this won't hurt" as he did something that hurt badly. She did not care for needles or the sight of blood.

"Leena," said Barren, looking deeply into her eyes, "if I remove this device, you will truly be off-grid. You cannot buy anything. You cannot sell anything. You cannot take part in the credit system of the Aberjay in any way. You will truly be without means in the world, and every meal you eat from this point until your death will be by your own bartering, grown by your own hand, or obtained through the generosity of others. Do you understand this?"

"Yes," Leena said emphatically.

"Do you also understand that no hospital in the country will provide services to you without this bracelet on? You will be without medical care until the day you die."

That ramification had not occurred to Leena, and the irony of her having to give up her healthcare to provide healthcare for her mother was not lost on her. "Yes, I understand."

Barren continued, "Do you also understand that by removing this, you are an enemy of the state? You can *never* be caught or questioned for any reason by the CPU, or you will go straight to jail for violating their citizen identification laws and may never see the light of day again."

Leena felt Barren was being dramatic with this line of questioning but understood it was to relay the gravity of the decision she was making. Although having another bracelet implanted was possible, off-grid folks were normally just executed as it was not worth the authorities' time and expense to re-implant someone who did not want to be a part of society. And the Aberjay were the only ones who could conduct the procedure as they maintained the database.

"I understand," Leena said as Barren motioned for her arm.

Laying her arm across the table, he covered it with a cloth that had a hole in it, positioning it over the bracelet. Barren took a long pointy instrument of steel and made a slight cut in Leena's wrist where the small electronic wire entered her body. Peeling the flesh back, Leena winced. It hurt worse than she could have imagined, but she knew her complaints would only slow the procedure. With a quick pull, Barren was able to remove the small chip that was tethered to the wire and freed it from her skin. The bracelet slid off her wrist, and he used a small surgical staple gun to seal her wound with four small stitches. He then wiped the wound with a cloth and sprayed an antiseptic, finally covering it with a bandage that wrapped around her wrist.

"There you go. All done," Barren said as he tossed the steel instrument into a metal tray of clear fluid. "Anyone else?"

"Me," Jordan said boldly.

"Jordan, no," Leena protested before remembering that he had most likely been identified in the alley. "I mean, are you sure?"

"You know I can't go back to the factory; they will be waiting to arrest me. I am certain my work permit has been voided by now. If you must go off-grid, then I want to be with you in this. We can take care of each other."

"That is very sweet, Jordan," Barren said, "but you cannot do this for her. This must be about you. You must make your own decision."

Jordan nodded in assent and put his arm on the table, preparing his mind for the procedure. "How do you know how to do this anyway?" he asked, trying to distract himself from the upcoming pain.

Barren picked up the instrument he had just used for Leena and after cleaning it with alcohol began the same procedure for Jordan. "I designed some of the first chips in this series," he answered belatedly. "It was never meant to be a control mechanism. I was just trying to make it easier for people to get better healthcare—to give doctors information about a patient's vitals in real time if they're having an emergency, or sometimes, *before* they have some sort of trauma. Imagine the ambulance showing up at your house twenty minutes before you go into cardiac arrest to tell you that you need treatment. It would have saved so many lives if they'd let me fulfill my vision."

"What happened?" Liv chimed in.

"What always happens. Money. Power. The Aberjay saw it could be used to track and control people, and they took my research from me for their people to develop. That was when I quit. I could not be a part of that."

Barren removed Jordan's bracelet and began the stitching before continuing. "You know, technology is supposed to help people. It's supposed to make it easier to live better and live longer. But those bastards have corrupted it like they do with the MIRO and everything else."

Jordan inspected his bandage and pulled his sleeve down to cover it.

"You two want to join the club?" Barren said directing his question to Liv and Zoe.

"Nah," Liv replied. "We are not wanted like these two," she said as she pointed to Leena and Jordan. "I will probably do it eventually; I cannot imagine it will be long before they have us on their list as well. Zoe? I don't want to speak for you."

Zoe shook her head to indicate she agreed with Liv and was not ready to take this step.

"We appreciate you helping us out with this. We have some water," Leena said as she reached into her bag for the bottles.

Barren took the water and looked at it as if studying the clear bottle. "It will be nice having something other than rainwater and whiskey to drink," Barren replied. "Thanks. You will get the hang of this bartering thing; it isn't all that hard. There are millions of folks who survive just fine out here."

The four went back outside to the jeep. Jesse handed Liv a bag. "Here are a couple of sandwiches for your journey. We better get moving. You need plenty of time to get back to the city by dark."

The four jumped back into the jeep and made their way to the highway.

Jesse drove them back to where they were first absconded. Fortunately, their bikes were still there. They moved their gear from the jeep to their bikes and thanked Jesse for all that he had done. Zoe took the lead and drove to the other side of the highway so she could head north toward the city. Once she hit the pavement, she picked up speed for the trip home. Jordan tried to stick close to Zoe as they drove in case they encountered any more trouble, but the three-wheeled motorbike was much faster than his and often left enormous distances between them as they traveled.

Leena clung to Jordan as they rode the empty highway. She felt free. Free from the eye of the Aberjay. Free from tracking. Free from control. She pulled off her pilot hat, threw her head back, and enjoyed the wind as Jordan drove. She gazed at the passing acres. She thought about Jesse and Barren. She wondered if they had not figured out something the Miniyar just failed to realize. They seemed to have everything they needed. *Why did people huddle in cities just scraping by when they could live out here and be more self-sufficient?*

Leena was deep in her daydream when the motorbike slowed. They lost track of Zoe in the distance as the bike came to an abrupt halt.

"What is it?" Leena asked.

"We're out of juice. I forgot to charge it, remember?" Jordan said, upset with himself over his absent-mindedness.

They dismounted the powerless motorbike and stared at it, hoping they might come up with a solution.

"I have solar panels," Jordan exclaimed as he reached into the saddle box and pulled out two small, folded panels. He laid them out on the ground near the bike and connected the panels to each other and then to the battery on the bike.

"Great, how long will that take to charge?" Leena asked.

"About twelve hours," Jordan said, knowing that he was disappointing Leena.

"Twelve hours? We can't sit out here for twelve hours!"

Zoe noticed they were not behind her and turned around to investigate. She pulled up to the team to get an understanding of the situation and seeing them looking at the bike and the solar panels, she deduced the problem.

"Let me head back and drop off Liv, and I will come back for one of you," Zoe said. "I will try to find a car, but if not, we might have to take turns or double up."

They all looked around for a meeting spot—something or someplace that would provide shelter and get them off this dangerous highway. They spotted a house about a mile ahead that was right off the highway.

"We will be there," Leena said, pointing to the house.

Zoe nodded and drove off.

Jordan and Leena made their way up the highway to the house. While it was likely abandoned, they secretly wished Jesse would be there with another wonderful meal, but both knew that was a fantasy.

Jordan took Leena's hand as they approached the door. The property looked abandoned. Old appliances, pieces of metal, and what looked like roofing material filled the yard in addition to some toys that looked as if they had not been played with in decades. Stepping onto the old wood porch made a snapping noise that made it clear that it needed repair. Reaching for the door, Jordan turned the knob and smiled when it opened.

He swung the door wide and gently stepped inside. The stench was musty and desperate, as if the air in the house had not been refreshed in some time. The hall opened into a small living space with an ugly couch, recliner, and antique television. From the hall, they could see a small kitchen decorated with an enormous amount of green.

The two released a sigh of relief that the home was empty. The dust alone showed that no one had been there in years. Leena searched the shelves for any type of canned food or water, but scavengers had picked it clean. They sat on the dusty couch to rest while they waited for Zoe to return. They sat in silence, both thinking about what their decision to go off-grid might mean for the rest of their lives. After what seemed like an hour, Leena broke the silence.

"Are you worried?"

"Worried? No, not really. Well, maybe a little worried—yes," Jordan stammered.

"We will figure this out. We're fugitives; we have no legal way out of this mess. We just have to accept that this is our life now," Leena counseled, though only half-believing her own words.

"But this wasn't supposed to be my life. I had a work permit. I was supposed to support my family. I thought I had a plan." Jordan had always kept up a wall of complacency with Leena, making her think that he liked to throw caution to the wind. But his wall was showing splinters. He was not as spontaneous and free-spirited as he led her to believe. Leena had always known Jordan to be the planner type, no matter how hard he tried to hide it. She speculated that he had his life planned by third grade. She felt responsible for derailing him.

"I'm sorry, Jordan. I know I got you into this, and I am truly sorry."

"Don't be sorry. You have made the last few weeks the best weeks of my life despite the messed-up situation. I don't regret my decisions. I am so in love with you. Nothing else matters," Jordan said with sincerity.

Professing his love for Leena took her by surprise. They had known each other for many years but only recently declared their feelings for one another. She leaned in and kissed him forcefully.

"I love you, too. And we will get through this. Maybe we will end up like Jesse and his uncle, running a farm as Tullians, growing our own food and fighting off the scourge."

"That sounds nice," Jordan responded without a hint of sarcasm.

They lay in each other's arms on the ugly couch for a couple of hours, enjoying a minor break in the drama that was now their lives to just cuddle with one another. Leena considered using the time to make love, but the cleanliness of the venue made that notion undesirable.

Upon hearing a vehicle and some rustling outside, they got up and moved toward the door, assuming that Zoe had returned for them. Jordan opened the front door and was hit with a pipe in the stomach that seemed to come out of thin air. He buckled and fell to the floor, and Leena took two steps backward, grabbing her escrima.

A man dressed in leather and wielding an iron pipe stepped into the doorway. Before he could get too far into the house, however, Leena charged him. She kicked him in the chest with both feet, pushing him backward with all her weight and sending him sprawling on the porch. The old boards gave way, and the porch collapsed. Leena, now on the ground rose, stumbling to regain her footing on the fallen boards and noticed there were two other men off the porch, one wielding a sword and the other a chain of some sort.

Leena rolled off the porch and jumped to her feet in front of one of the attackers. Not waiting for his first move, she kicked out one leg, making him unstable, but he kept his body upright, swinging his sword and making contact with Leena's arm. She turned into the attacker with her body, landing an elbow to his face then kicking his knee to bend it unnaturally. He fell to the ground screaming in pain, and she struck him with her escrima several times to stun him.

The other man then grabbed her from behind. She lifted her arms and slipped from his grasp, then landed a powerful kick to his groin that put him on the ground. He began making his way to his feet as Leena finished him off with her weapon, rendering him unconscious.

Jordan stumbled from the house watching the event, and his jaw dropped, eyes wide. He had never seen Leena act so aggressively. What his eyes were seeing shocked him.

"What the... How did you... How could..." Jordan stuttered.

Leena wiped the blood from her arm and grabbed her pack to get a bandage.

"Prison," Leena said in passing as she wiped more blood from her shoulder. "I learned in prison," she continued. "I had a cellmate who taught me kali."

"Kali? What is kali? Never heard of it."

"Kali is a Filipino fighting technique," Leena stated as she completed the bandaging of her arm. The sword had only grazed it.

"That is just amazing! I am riding around with a superhero and had no idea." Jordan's mind returned to the assault on the east gate and realized she was the savior. "And you saved us the other day at the east gate!"

"Yes, that was me," Leena said proudly. "But it isn't a big deal."

"It is a huge deal, Leena; you are good at it. I gotta admit it hurts my ego a little, but it is nice having my own personal bodyguard."

"Stop it," Leena said shyly.

Zoe pulled up as they were speaking.

"You guys ready to go?" Zoe said awkwardly, surveying the aftermath of Leena's war with the locals.

"Can we both fit?" Jordan asked, a little worried the girls might leave him behind to fend for himself.

"Yeah, I think so," Zoe said. "Let's try it."

Leena got on the bike behind Zoe and removed her backpack. She handed it to Jordan, and he put it on. It was small and looked ridiculous on him. He tried as best he could to sit behind Leena and could get his feet off the ground, but it was not too comfortable.

"What about my bike?" Jordan asked.

"I think I have a fix for that," Zoe said as she made her way to the highway, stopping in front of Jordan's bike. "Fortunately, these things are not that heavy."

Zoe grabbed a stretchy cable out of her motorbike's small trunk and was able to connect Jordan's bike to the back of the three-wheeler with the cable. "It isn't pretty, but it will work."

The three made the journey back to Liv's house without any further attack. Zoe dropped off Leena and Jordan at the door as she circled around to the back of the building to charge both bikes. All four of them congregated in Liv's quarters to decompress from the trip.

"What's next, Leena?" Jordan asked after they were able to rest and eat a snack.

"I need to check on my mom. Then we will figure out how to get back into Zone 7."

"Do you still think we can break into the pharmacy?"

"I don't see that we have a choice. My mom needs medication. And now that we are off-grid, they can't track us. If we can get in and get what we need quickly, we should be able to elude the CPU," Leena said with confidence.

Jordan was reclining on a couch, thinking it through. "I am not convinced this is the best approach, but I will go along."

Leena was not sure if Jordan's resistance indicated a poor plan or a bruised ego. Either way, she figured that was his issue. As they spoke, Liv got a call on the radio.

"Listen up, there is a food truck making its way through Zone 6 this evening. Its destination is the Aberjay. We are going to take it." Liv went back to her radio.

"Jordan?" Leena said to change the subject. "I want to go see Fernando."

"I am not sure he would be happy to see you now that you put McBride in the hospital."

"You think he went to the hospital?" Leena asked.

"I imagine you broke his nose, if not worse."

"Let's hope not. I want to question Fernando to see if we can get more info on what the Aberjay are up to in the northern part of the zone."

"Since when do you do investigations? Are you a sleuth now?"

"Fernando's behavior lately just doesn't seem right. I don't know him that well, but every time I am around him, it seems he is hiding something. I can't put my finger on it. It is like a sixth sense."

"Women's intuition?" Jordan said sarcastically.

"You don't believe women are intuitive?" Leena barked.

Jordan carefully considered his next words. He knew he was on shaky ground. Hoping to change the subject, he said, "Where does he live again?"

Leena got up from the couch to signal she was ready to go.

"What makes you think he will know anything?" Jordan said as he got up on his feet to join her.

"I have a sneaky suspicion he knows more than he tells us."

They bid farewell to Liv and Zoe, promising to meet up with them later to raid the food truck.

Chapter 10

CONFESSION

L eena had been to Fernando's house with Diego a few times when she was younger. She knew what area it was in but not the exact location. She figured if they got close to the house, she would recognize it. She remembered it was large, white, and colonial. There were large columns out front with a long driveway and a guard gate. It was south of Jordan's neighborhood, a little farther west. There were a lot of upscale homes in that area, most of which were occupied by people who worked for the Aberjay in some sort of administrative capacity. If their homes were any indication, these people were not afraid of flamboyance and were content with their avarice.

She used to believe these were the lucky ones. Somehow, they landed the best positions full of benefits and privilege. Her new perspective was more polarized. There were those who had power and those who didn't. Society was neither equal nor fair.

She pondered as they rode through homes in decay. *What made the wealthy different from the poor who labored just to survive? Was it intelligence? Luck? Or could it be opportunity?* The privilege of being born into a family that was already financially secure paved the way for young people to succeed. They had the freedom to study, excel in school, go on to college, and define

222 JOSEPH MICHAEL LAMB

what and who they wanted to be with no concern over survival. Others, born just a few blocks away, had no ability to complete school because their families needed to eat. Or they lacked the proper transportation. Or their parents didn't have any hope and figured schooling for their offspring was pointless.

Blocks and blocks of falling-down bungalows, burned-out trailers, and makeshift homes made of plastic and metal sheeting had given way to mansions—monstrous dwellings surrounded by gates and personal security forces. Leena no longer contemplated what it would be like to live there. She knew her conscience would never allow it. She couldn't live in such a place when she knew people were starving just a few streets over. Her mind was getting clear, free of a cloud that she felt hung over her from a young age. It was a story told to her for as long as she could remember: Those who work succeed, and those who work hard to complete a high level of education reap the rewards. And while those things might be true, she now understood it wasn't that simple. The Aberjay had access to good schools and jobs. They decided who had opportunities. And they took care of their own.

Turning onto a well-manicured street that looked more like a Zone 7 neighborhood than a street where Miniyar lived, Leena motioned for Jordan to slow down so she could look closely at each house. As each one went by, she became anxious, as they all looked quite similar. She was not sure if she could pick the right house. And if that was not difficult enough, her mind began contemplating the guard gate in front of each house, which spun off a whole new set of problems she knew they were about to encounter.

She had Jordan stop the motorbike at the end of the street. The wrought-iron gate directly across the street had a small white gatehouse in front. Leena could see the tip of the house popping up over the hill beyond the gate, but she couldn't see enough of it to establish whether there were columns in front. Her gut told her this was the house.

The guard in the gatehouse wore a white shirt and tie, but no jacket. Seated and with a pen in hand, he was writing something. Jordan put down his kickstand, and they cautiously dismounted.

"What is the plan here, Leena?" Jordan asked, feeling a bit out of his depth.

"We can ask to see if he'll let me in. But if he doesn't, I'm not sure what our next step is." Feeling bold and angry that this person she considered family was living in such luxury with little consideration for the surrounding blight compelled her to plot a devious course.

"Let's test their security, Jordan."

Jordan looked at her, puzzled, and replied, "Okay, but then you have to tell me who you are."

They smiled at each other. They had experienced adventures and crises in the last few weeks that had brought out something new in each of them.

Leena walked down the street outside the purview of the guard shack as Jordan moved the bike out of sight. Once together, they crossed the street to the wall that separated the residence from the sidewalk, looking for a vulnerability. As they made their way around a bend in the road, out of sight of the guard shack, they noticed a tree that was inside the gate but had a branch that extended above the wall. The wall was made of stone, and it felt rough and jagged against her fingertips. Though not designed for climbing, its jagged edges offered a foothold.

"There," Leena said, pointing to the tree. "I think I can make that work."

Leena asked Jordan for a boost and put one foot in his hands. With a quick look around to ensure no one was within sight, she launched herself up toward the wall and caught a foothold for her other foot just long enough to propel herself into the air—high enough to grab the tree branch. She pulled herself up and straddled the tree, laying on her stomach to extend her arm down to catch Jordan as he made the same move without the help of a boost. Jordan took a running start and hit the wall with one foot and launched up to Leena's waiting hand. Grabbing her hand with his and the branch with the other, he had just enough leverage to pull himself up.

The two scurried to the core of the tree and then made their way to a lower branch on the other side of the wall. Once perched on that branch, they could easily drop to the ground. They took a minute to survey their surroundings and catch their breath before moving closer to the house.

There were many trees in the yard to provide cover. The grass was a deep verdant hue, and the faint scent of freshly-mowed grass hung in the air. The house was down the hill from where they had crossed into the yard. Leena could now see the big white columns. This was Fernando's house. She also remembered the curving driveway and the fountain in front.

Leena motioned for Jordan to head around back. She thought it would be easier to get Fernando's attention, assuming he was home, if she was in the backyard. She remembered the pool the most. It was the first pool she had ever swam in. Diego taught her how to swim. She was not good at it, as she recalled, and didn't enjoy the experience. She was afraid of the water. As much as she had tried to follow every instruction, her fear of drowning paralyzed her. When the kids would play *how would you prefer to die* games in school, Leena always picked something other than drowning. In her mind, that was the worst way to go.

Once around the side of the house, she noticed the pool, and it was just as she had remembered it. Jordan and Leena took a position behind a tree and surveilled the home to determine their next steps.

There didn't seem to be any guards on the property other than the one at the front gate. They moved a little closer but remained hidden by the shade of the trees that covered the yard. As they came upon the pool deck, they could see movement in the house. Leena pointed out the car in the driveway that she always saw Fernando in and assumed he must be inside, along with his driver.

As they stalked the zone advocate's home, Leena daydreamed about her time here. She only remembered one or maybe two trips, but this visit brought back many memories that she had forgotten. Playing games in the yard. Drinking some sort of sweet cherry drink by the pool. Her mom laughing. There was a lot of laughing back then. Could the man she was remembering be the same man who's helping the Aberjay take away people's homes? It seemed so unlikely.

The rear sliding door to the home opened, and they could hear conversation. Fernando had stepped out onto the back cement portico, talking on the phone. They could barely make out the words, though his tone was elevated.

"Yes, sir, I understand. We are all set for Project Darwin." He was pacing back and forth. "I have taken care of that; I don't foresee any more complications. We will get it done."

After ending the call, Fernando stood outside, looking at the yard. He seemed to look straight through her. Leena stood and stepped away from the foliage that served as their hiding place.

Fernando saw her right away and made his way swiftly toward her.

"Leena, thank God." He put his arms out to hug her, and she moved toward him slowly, cautiously allowing the affection.

"Where have you been? You are in a lot of trouble."

Jordan stepped up behind her, and Fernando acknowledged he was there like a parent would greet his daughter's boyfriend.

"I was not sure you would want to see me," said Leena quietly.

"Of course I would want to see you. I think we need to talk about your situation, but I would never shut you out."

After a few awkward pleasantries, Leena said, "Fernando, I need some information."

The three of them made their way to the portico and then inside the residence. Fernando led them into an office illuminated by the sun beaming in through expansive windows. Everything was perfectly in its place. He sat behind a large desk and motioned for the two to sit in the chairs that faced his desk. Leena noticed a box open behind him on the credenza. It was a gun box in the shape of a gun, but no firearm occupied the foam cutout.

Fernando retrieved a few waters from the mini-fridge behind his desk and handed them to the young couple. After sitting down, he noticed the bracelet missing from Leena's wrist.

"Do you want to tell me about that?" Fernando said, pointing to her wrist.

"It was necessary. Do you want to tell me about that?" she said as she pointed to the empty gun case.

Fernando reached into his jacket and pulled out a small handgun. He proudly displayed his toy, which was about the size of his palm. He held it out for them to see. The surface of the firearm was a gleaming silver, and the handle was a deep, glossy black.

"This is an antique, a Walther PPK. This one was my grandfather's. I don't usually carry it around with me, but things have become very tense in the zone lately."

"I thought they were illegal in Zone 6," Leena said.

"They are, but this one is so old you can barely get bullets for it anymore. They have not manufactured .380-caliber bullets for forty years. I have them made special. The authorities know I have it and overlook my indiscretion. They know my job is dangerous. But let's talk about you. You need to turn yourself in. Both of you do. You attacked a CPU officer without provocation and broke his nose. They have the entire zone looking for you."

"That is not exactly how it happened, but it's the very reason I will not surrender. They will lock me away without the benefit of a fair trial, or worse, end my life." Leena was stoic. "But I am not here to talk about me. What is happening in the northern part of the zone?"

"Leena, what has gotten into you? That is not your concern," Fernando said.

"It is my concern because I want it to be my concern. They included my building in the evictions!" Leena raised her voice.

"I am sorry about that, Leena, but I can assure you the CPU will move everyone who cannot leave on their own."

"Why are you helping them, Fernando?"

"That is my job."

"No, your job is to advocate for the best interest of your people. How is this in their best interest?"

"The new factory will bring jobs to..." Fernando stopped, obviously revealing more than he desired.

"Factory?" Leena, now standing, interrupted him. "What factory?"

Fernando paused for a minute and took a long drink of water, appearing to stall. He got up and began pacing again.

"I am not supposed to tell you this, but it is likely the government will repeal the Drone Elimination Act because the CPU wants to build a drone factory. That is why they are clearing so many homes. They are going to complete demolitions within days to begin construction. But I made a deal that..."

"You mean weaponized drones, don't you?" Leena interjected. Fernando responded with a nod. "And what did *we* get out of the 'deal?'"

"They promised to free up supply chains to allow food to flow freely into the zone from now on. They have committed troops to ensure there are no shortages."

"The troops were holding back the food in the first place!" Leena shouted.

"That was just a rumor; there is no evidence..." Fernando began before Leena cut him off again.

"Liv stormed the warehouse beyond the east gate with Resistance forces. I was with her that day. It was a battle for food. The Aberjay are stockpiling it, letting it rot while they *negotiate*. Is that how negotiation works in your world? They steal something from us and then allow us to have it back only if we comply? Open your eyes, Fernando, you are either ignorant of their scheming, which I find hard to believe, or you are getting something out of this personally."

Fernando put his head in his hands to compose himself. His demeanor told Leena that she had hit a nerve.

"There is nothing I can do to fix this, Leena. They hold all the negotiating power. We have no army; we have no leverage. We must do what we can to ensure the survival of these people. Sometimes we must sacrifice the comfort of some for the survival of others."

"Comfort?" Leena shouted. "They are not sacrificing comfort, they are sacrificing their homes, their livelihoods, and their very lives. Quit buying into this story they have sold you. They are doing nothing to help these people; they are only taking from them to better their own position."

Leena signaled to Jordan that it was time to go. They both made their way outside to the side of the portico to make their escape, and Fernando followed closely behind.

"Fernando, I appreciate what you did for me growing up and helping me get out of that prison sentence. But I think we are done. I will tell you what someone recently told me. You need to pick a side. War is coming. You are with us, or you are with them."

Not waiting for an answer, Leena jumped down from the porch and made her way across the grass, back to the tree that had given them access to the yard. Within moments, they were up and over the wall, making their way back to the motorbike.

"Are you okay, Leena? That was pretty rough," Jordan said.

"I am perfect," she responded.

Jordan looked her in the eyes and half-expected tears. Instead, he saw indignation, strength, and a resoluteness he had never seen before in Leena. He saw the image of a warrior.

Jordan and Leena made their way to the south end of the zone. The gate they had passed through the day before while returning from their adventure in the south was the same gate that would provide passage for the food truck headed to Zone 7. This was not abnormal as food trucks had to travel from the south to the Aberjay zone several times a week. This truck was different because someone tipped off the Resistance fighters about the exact time it would travel through the city, allowing them the opportunity to strike a blow to the Aberjay food supply.

The rendezvous location for this operation was an old slaughterhouse on the south end of town near the train lines. It had been vacant for more than fifty years as the price of beef had become out of reach for all but the super-wealthy.

Jordan and Leena entered the building, which still displayed hanging hooks and conveyer belts designed to suspend meat and move it from station to station for butchering, wrapping, and shipping. They bypassed the processing area and made their way to the back, which had an open concrete floor and a large stage at the end. It might have been a makeshift concert venue at one time as some old cables and equipment were still visible on the stage.

Many folks were up on the stage who looked to be of some importance, and more than 150 people were mulling about on the floor, preparing for battle. They were loading weapons, sharpening blades, and checking their ammunition. This was a much bigger crowd than the hordes involved in the assault on the east gate. It was clear there was some planning involved in this mission.

One soldier on the stage called the room to order and slid an old whiteboard near the front of the stage to provide visuals. He sketched out his battle plan as he spoke.

"We have good intel that a food truck is coming through the south gate at precisely five p.m. today, about two hours from now. It is our intention to block that truck at this interchange, rain fire down on them to eliminate the drivers and guards, and if the truck is mobile after the gunfire, drive it to a warehouse here near Fifth Avenue. If it cannot be driven, it will be unloaded and the supplies taken directly to our depot. Everyone got it?"

After some specific assignments were made, everyone in the building made their way to their vehicles to prepare for the assault. Leena was concerned that Jordan lacked a weapon and made some inquiries, obtaining a small handgun and a few magazines of ammunition, along with a long blade and sheath that he could keep at his side for close combat.

"I don't know about this, Leena," Jordan said as he familiarized himself with the operation of the handgun. "I have never fired a weapon before, and I don't know how I feel about hurting people."

"Just keep it in case you need it. It's for defense. You can hang back and just provide support. You may not even fire it," Leena counseled.

Jordan eventually conceded and allowed her to show him a few moves with the knife as others loaded the trucks.

The makeshift army made their way to the south end of town, just a few miles inside the south gate. While the highway was mostly clear through this part of the city and vehicles traveled it daily, there were choke points. The Resistance planners had chosen an area for the assault with an overpass and buildings on each side of the highway to ensure they had the advantage of holding the high ground. Also present were several abandoned vehicles that could give cover under the overpass for the soldiers who would attack first. A large machine gun nest was already in place in each building that encompassed the choke point.

The officer in charge of the operation assigned Jordan and Leena to the highway with the first squad of soldiers responsible for stopping the truck and taking out the drivers. Leena's specific orders were to get into the truck's cockpit as quickly as possible to ensure control of the vehicle. Jordan would rush to the back of the truck with others to verify the cargo and eliminate any soldiers who might be guarding the provisions.

Leena could tell Jordan was quite nervous. She gave him a quick squeeze on the shoulder and patted his back to comfort him, but he remained disturbed by what was about to happen.

"Just breathe, Jordan."

"I think I'm having a panic attack. Are we deliberately about to take someone's life? Have we thought this through? Is this necessary?"

Leena said, "Look at me." She grabbed his face with her hand. "We must do this. There are lives that depend on getting that food. We have been docile long enough. Are you with me?"

"Yes," Jordan said with little enthusiasm.

"Are you with me?" Leena said again with more passion.

"Yes, I am with you. Let's get it over with."

They heard someone call out, "Here it comes." The soldier driving the Resisters' truck assigned to block the path of the food truck turned the key, starting the big diesel engine. Leena crouched behind an old burned-out SUV with no wheels, breathing deeply to calm her nerves, waiting for the food truck to come within sight.

The Resistance soldier pulled his truck into position, blocking the path before Leena could see the target. Her heart pounded loud and fast in her chest. She grabbed her escrima with both hands, twisting it in her grasp to cut the tension then tapping it on the ground as if keeping a beat to an invisible song. Then she saw the truck. The 30-foot-long gray beast shuddered to a halt in front of her, the sound of its big smokestacks producing a loud rumble as it pumped black smoke into the air.

Once stopped, the ten soldiers in her team revealed themselves from behind the barrier while Leena ran to open the door. Knowing the driver was likely armed, she jumped up to the door and grabbed the handle, hanging on it as it swung open for her comrades to fire on the driver. She opened her eyes when she did not hear the expected gunfire. She looked back to see the four Resistance soldiers with rifles preparing to engage but failing to fire. Something was wrong. She looked at their faces, and it was as if they had seen a ghost. Turning her head around the door to see what had bewitched them, she saw not a human pilot but a MIRO.

A MIRO driver was not uncommon in some circumstances. The MIRO often drove smaller vehicles but differing laws between the states made it unusual to see a MIRO driving a truck that crossed state lines. Leena's mind raced to understand why she was seeing a MIRO in this cab, and only one explanation came to mind. This was not a food truck but a decoy. Which meant the back of the truck was not full of food. This was an ambush.

Leena jumped down from the truck and began running toward the back to warn the soldiers. The four at the door registered what was happening as Leena ran by them and turned to yell, "Stop, don't open the..."

It was too late. The soldiers at the rear of the vehicle had unlatched the door and swung it open just in time to be greeted by gunfire. Like roaches escaping an old dusty couch, CPU soldiers began piling out of the truck and eliminating the Resistance fighters.

Leena had no time to think but only react and began taking them out with her escrima as quickly as she could make her limbs move. One, then two, then three were on the ground. Their proximity to Leena was the only way she survived as they were all equipped with long rifles that needed a bit of range to engage the enemy.

She was concerned about Jordan, who was in the initial crowd of soldiers, but didn't see him after the doors burst open. She realized she did not have enough strength to survive the fight if she stayed. There were too many soldiers. She ran back to the cover of her burned-out SUV and slid under it for cover. The sound of gunfire from one building was raining down on the highway with little regard for targets, friend or foe. The other building was quiet, so she assumed the enemy had already eliminated that position.

The CPU soldiers had fire shields. These large shields were a recent invention, made of clear aluminum and a thin layer of steel. You could see through them to target your enemy, but the strength of the shields held up to fire, gunshots from some of the most powerful weapons, and even explosives.

The CPU, fire shields in hand, lined up to create a barrier while many soldiers moved equipment off the truck to set up their own gun nest in the middle of the highway. Once assembled, they began destroying the remaining building's gun nest with more advanced weaponry than was available to the Resistance, quickly overpowering it and silencing the attack.

Many soldiers who were in reserve down below were making their way up to the highway to help, but they were no match for these large guns, and the CPU quickly dispatched them. Shell casings were littering the highway like raindrops as these large guns let loose their fury. The well-laid plan of the Aberjay resulted in a bloodbath for the Resistance. More than fifty Resistance fighters lay dead on the highway surrounding the truck.

Leena did not hear a retreat signal, but it was clear to anyone watching that this squad outmatched the Resistance fighters in skill and weaponry. She slid backward to get out from under the SUV and ran down the highway, hoping to avoid the gunfire. As she ran past the blocking vehicle, she noticed Jordan on the ground. She ran to him as quickly as she could and dropped quickly to shield herself with the truck.

"Jordan, get up!" she shouted. "We have to move!"

Leena helped him to his feet. She saw blood but knew she could not focus on his injury. Getting to safety had to be her priority. She pulled him toward the highway wall, and knowing the ground below this overpass was only about a ten foot drop, threw him over the low cement partition. She followed him with a jump, and they both landed hard on the ground.

They were out of the line of fire now but not out of danger. The CPU had started their push to eliminate any Resistance fighters that remained and were moving out in small teams to kill survivors. Leena turned to look out on the highway and saw Sgt. McBride with a bandage on his face, calling out orders and doing his own damage with his rifle. She knew they couldn't stay, or he would be on them in seconds.

"Keep moving!" she shouted as she helped Jordan to his feet. "There!" She pointed to a nearby building. She pulled Jordan along, barely walking to the building and then going inside. It was vacant and no longer had windows or doors.

"The first floor is too open. We need to go up higher," she said as she pushed Jordan upstairs. He seemed coherent, but she knew the blood loss would soon take its toll on his energy. She knew that pushing him to move was dangerous as he could bleed out, but the alternative was not an option.

They made it to the third floor and then collapsed near a window. They heard the gunfire clearly. It had slowed but was still constant as the CPU fired shots to end the lives of the wounded. Although they were on the third floor, their location was still too vulnerable. She did not want to take a stray bullet or a well-landed sniper shot. She thought about moving higher but looked at Jordan, and it was clear he needed to rest. She grabbed her bag and, remembering the smoke grenades, took one out. She pulled the pin and threw it out the window as hard as she could to provide cover without giving away their position.

Smoke billowed out where the grenade landed, shielding them momentarily from the enemy on the highway.

"Jordan, look at me. Where are you hurt?"

Jordan was hugging his stomach with a gun still in his hand. Leena gently removed the gun from his hand.

"Let me see your stomach, Jordan."

As she grabbed both arms and pried them open like a picnic basket, she could see blood gushing from his abdomen. Knowing it was a bullet wound, she went to her bag for bandages. Taking a stack out, she pushed them into the wound, and Jordan let out a groan. She placed his arms over the bandage.

"Keep pressure on this, Jordan. Do you hear me?"

Jordan nodded, but neither of them could hear very well, their ears ringing from the gunfire.

Leena scanned the empty building for an easy escape. "Stay here, Jordan. I will be right back." She ran up the stairs to get a vantage point above the smokescreen she had laid. Once at the top, she saw the gunfire had mostly subsided. The CPU were searching the area for survivors and moving the truck that blocked their path. This was not a food run but a coordinated ambush. The intelligence must have been a plant. She wondered briefly if Fernando was the culprit here, but as she thought about her afternoon at his house, she could not recall mentioning the plan to him.

She had to get medical care for Jordan. She was worried he would bleed out if she didn't get him to a hospital but knew that without a bracelet, no one would help him. They would let him die in the waiting room. She ran to the other side of the building, hoping something she saw would provide a solution. She scanned the rows of buildings and abandoned warehouses for something, anything, that would tell her what to do. Her eyes darted back and forth and then settled on a sign. "Veterinarian," she said out loud. "That will work."

After heading back down the stairs, she heard steps coming up. She stopped short of Jordan's floor and took cover as two soldiers and Sgt. McBride walked out onto Jordan's floor, heading toward his lifeless body. Leena knew that if they reached him, they would fire on him to finish him off.

She dashed down the stairs to get behind the three of them. She heard McBride say, "Kill him." That's all she needed to hear to launch into action, driving the sergeant to the floor with a strike of her escrima to his back leg. She then grabbed the handgun from his hip holster as the other two soldiers turned on her. With two quick shots, she put them on the floor. She then ran toward Jordan and fired another round into each of the soldiers before turning to finish off McBride.

Without a weapon, McBride knew the odds were not in his favor, so he ran toward the window. Leena got off two shots before he jumped through the opening. Following close behind, she looked down, expecting to see a body, but he had landed in an elevated construction dumpster that cushioned his fall enough to prevent injury. She fired again, emptying the gun, as he jumped out of the dumpster and ran for cover.

Leena grabbed a full magazine for the handgun from the downed soldier and reloaded it before running back to Jordan and helping him to his feet. He was alive but losing a lot of blood. She knew she had little time.

They made their way out of the building and through an abandoned industrial area, hoping to make it to the veterinarian's office before his injuries proved fatal.

Leena and Jordan entered the veterinarian's office through the back door. With Jordan's arm around her and another arm wielding a firearm, she pushed into the office and was ready to threaten anyone who got in her way. As she went into the hallway, a vet technician dressed in scrubs came from a small room and screamed, then retreated into the room. Leena then reached an open area where a couple of office personnel were working on computers.

In a threatening tone, she shouted, "Get the vet, get the vet!"

One technician ran off and returned with a vet in a white coat.

"Someone shot him. Help him," she yelled as she brandished her weapon.

The veterinarian and tech put up their hands as if to calm her and pointed where to lay Jordan on a table. The doctor grabbed one side of him to assist, and the two managed to get Jordan on his back. The doctor quickly placed bandages on the wound after removing the one that Leena had affixed earlier. Looking at the gushing blood, he stated emphatically, "I need to get the bullet out, or he will die."

Leena fell back against the wall in exhaustion. "Do what you need to do, but you keep him alive."

Leena watched helplessly as they went to work on her lover. She felt a tinge of pain in her heart as she thought about losing him but fought back tears. She found an office chair and slumped into it, resting her eyes. She thought about leaving just in case they were followed but did not want to abandon Jordan. She preferred to fight her way out than to leave him behind.

After a brief rest to catch her breath, she helped the few people who were there with their pets exit the building. She then locked the door behind them to prevent being surprised by any new customers. She pulled the phones from the wall to ensure no one would call for CPU assistance. She took a seat just outside the room where the vet's team was working on Jordan so she could monitor them but still rest her weary body.

As she thought through what had happened to her and the other soldiers, she was more resolute than ever to get justice for them. She knew she still had to come through for her mom, but the quest had changed. Her eyes were now opened to her oppressors. She now understood the control and barbaric nature of the Aberjay. She saw they had no mercy or respect for others' lives. She was determined to make them pay. This was not about revenge but justice.

Chapter 11

HUNTED

It was dark outside the veterinarian clinic when Leena woke. She had accidentally fallen asleep on the bench outside the entrance. The streets were quiet. She stood and stretched, looking down the street in both directions to ensure she was alone. Turning toward the clinic, she made her way inside to check on Jordan.

"How is he doing?" she asked the vet, who was at the sink washing blood from his hands.

"He will live, but he has lost a lot of blood, so he needs to rest. I am glad you brought him here as he would not have made it to a hospital. He can stay here for a couple hours, but you need to get him out of here once he wakes up. I don't have any love for the CPU, but if they caught me helping you, it would mean prison time."

"I appreciate your help, doctor," Leena said. "If I had any money, I would be happy to pay for your services."

"If you had any money, I would accept it. I am not really trained for this type of work. If you want to do something for me, just get him out of here soon, and don't let this blow back on me. I need to check on him."

The vet walked back toward the table Jordan was lying on and began taking his vital signs. Jordan was not moving. He was shirtless, with a large bandage over his stomach that wrapped all the way around his midsection. An IV was attached to his right arm with clear saline dripping slowly from the bag.

Leena worried about how she might get him home without a car and figured her best option was to head back toward the warehouse where they met with Resistance forces earlier to retrieve his motorbike. She did not know how to drive one but reasoned it couldn't be too difficult. She informed the doctor of her intention to return with transportation, gave a quick kiss to the sleeping patient, and exited the clinic.

It was late. After nine p.m. Leena estimated that she was about ten blocks from the warehouse. The weather had warmed a bit, but she still shivered as she walked through the dark streets, mostly due to a fear of losing Jordan, the weight of being a fugitive, and the exhaustion of the last few days. She was still carrying the handgun. She decided it was better hidden, so she placed it in her backpack before continuing her journey.

The area she walked through was industrial, but many of the factories had long since been torn down. The darkness enveloped her as she walked. This part of the city had no streetlights, no storefronts, and very few roadways. Leena left the pavement to take a more direct route and began walking on soft ground. She was confident she knew how to get to the warehouse, but the night was playing tricks on her ability to discern her location. She would walk about ten steps and then stop to look around to get her bearings.

The moon was just a sliver, so the farther she moved away from the scant light coming from the buildings, the darker it became. The ground went from soft dirt to hard rocks and what seemed like seashells. They would crack and split as she walked. She thought this was a strange place for seashells, and her mind raced to determine what could have moved these shells from the beach to this open field.

And then she realized: They were not seashells. They were bones. This was the *Bonefield*. It was used during the last conflict to pile up bodies left behind on the streets and inside the buildings. *The Uprising*, as the Aberjay called it, was put down by hordes of CPU who used a *blitzkrieg* approach to annihilate their enemy. They killed Resistance fighters, citizens, and even the homeless. They firebombed parts of the city that practically vaporized the residents in the buildings and on the streets. After the conflict, to eliminate the disease that would have surely followed, they used oversized bulldozers to push all the bodies to this field to rot. They didn't even bury them but dumped a thin layer of dirt and lye over the top and left the fragments for the birds.

Leena had never been here but had driven by it. The ghost stories of her youth crept into her mind. She didn't really believe in ghouls and monsters but knew that if they existed, this would be the logical place to find them. Her shivering went to an entirely new level as she slogged through the field, wincing every time there was a crunch, knowing it was a human bone or skull she was defiling. She thought about going back but by now felt she was already halfway through the field.

244   JOSEPH MICHAEL LAMB

In the darkness, she saw something flutter by. She hoped it was a large moth and not a killer bat or some other vicious creature from her books. She had never been hostile to insects or flying creatures, but she was fully prepared to destroy anything that would dare attack her.

Her next step into the blackness tripped her. Falling to her hands and knees, she could see an outline and concluded that the perpetrator was a large barrel partially buried in the dirt and bones. She tried hard not to think about what might be in the barrel as she peered into the darkness as far as she could see. She saw many barrels, and the silhouette of the other buried containers offered evidence that this went on for some distance. It was still walkable but required more skill. She lifted herself to her feet and rubbed the bone fragments from her hands.

Leena used her feet to guide her steps, slowly tapping the sides of the barrels that stuck out of the ground, groping for level ground. She finally worked her way to the end of the field and was again on the asphalt. She breathed deeply and shook her arms and legs to discard the repellent feeling of being among the dead.

She could see the outline of the warehouse from her vantage point as she walked the road that ran the length of the Bonefield. No lights were on, and she expected that if there were any Resistance fighters still alive, they would not risk coming back to this meeting place for fear of arrest. It was far enough from the battle site that the CPU was not likely to be wise to the significance, but there was no way to know what they knew or didn't know about the Resistance.

When Leena reached the motorbike, only a few other vehicles were still there. She strapped a helmet on and sat on the bike. She tried to figure out the controls, which were minimal. She understood the throttle and figured the brake was at her right foot. She located a start button and pressed it apprehensively. The lights on the display came on, as did the headlights. She slowly applied the throttle with her right hand and let her feet drag as the bike lunged forward.

Through trial and error, she determined that the right handle was also a brake, so she used it to start and then stop, start and then stop, and start and then stop again. Over and over, she repeated the sequence until she felt familiar with how it worked. Then she turned onto the road and increased her speed. She didn't know where the turn signals were but reasoned there were not enough people out this late to see them anyway.

Leena grew more and more connected to the machine as she made her way back to Jordan. It would only take a few minutes, even at her paltry speed. She made several shaky turns before coming to a red light that forced her to stop. There was no one around, so she knew she could press through it, but she didn't know if cameras were mounted on the stoplights and thought it would be better not to test the theory.

When the light turned green, she noticed lights behind her in her mirror. She pressed the throttle to go through the intersection and noticed the lights approaching fast. Turning in her seat, she looked behind her to see it was a CPU truck. Panic overtook her as she pushed hard on the accelerator pedal and drove the bike faster. She raced through intersections and bent over the handlebars to reduce the drag.

She could not turn around but heard the engine of the truck getting closer. She decided she could not stay on this road and slowed enough to take a left turn at the next major intersection. She barely maintained control as she righted the bike after the turn and then made a left turn to lead the truck away from her destination. She turned again and again, but the truck followed her trail. Each turn, however, placed the large truck a little farther behind because it lacked her bike's agility, so she kept changing her route to increase the distance.

Leena pushed the bike to its limits, which went far beyond her comfort zone as she raced toward her side of town. She reasoned that she knew the roads better there and might shake her pursuer. Racing past the market and approaching a bend in the road, she realized the CPU were far enough back that they had lost line of sight. She pivoted the bike into an alley and rode it behind a trash dumpster, pressing the stop button and turning off the headlights.

Shielded from view by the dumpster, she peeked over the top of the trash bin to see the CPU truck fly by at a high rate of speed. She felt relief but was not certain she was out of danger. She left the bike in the alley and made her way to the street. Looking both ways, she felt she could proceed toward home to lay low until the CPU stopped searching for her. She was only a couple of blocks away.

Leena was now walking along the street that she had grown to know so well. As she rounded an obstacle and passed a burning barrel, she could see the entrance to her building. It was flanked by two CPU trucks. Two guards stood at the entrance to her building, and she suspected more were waiting inside. She crouched by the entrance to a nearby building to mull over her next steps.

After a few moments of thought, she realized she was standing in the doorway of a building that would give her access to her residence via the rooftop. She had used it to escape the CPU. She knew that getting to her building from this one would be a challenge because it was slightly shorter than her own. Both jumps would be difficult. But she thought that if she could get a glimpse of her garden, she could tell whether anyone was there before going back for Jordan.

She made her way into the abandoned building and started up the stairs. It was too dark to see, so she rummaged in her backpack for a flashlight. Her light was one of her favorite belongings. It was very bright and had a flexible snake-like base that stretched a foot long so that she could adjust it to wrap around anything. A pipe, a shelf, a loop on her jacket or in this case her arm. Locating the light, she switched it on and wrapped the flexible base around her arm before continuing up the stairs. This gave her the ability to point towards anything in her path and it would light it up.

The stairs were in much worse shape than in her building. Only one out of every three steps were still intact, and the railing was similarly spotty. Fortunately, Leena could lean against the wall in the stairwell and slide to the top. The stench was worse than the danger. Leena attempted to cover her nose, but it was like the smell of death, and it penetrated the fabric of her coat.

Reaching the top of the building, Leena opened the door slowly. She slid through the opening and crept out onto the roof, two buildings away from her own. She paused only for a moment to wedge a small rock under the door so that it wouldn't close and lock automatically. This ensured she had an escape route if the roof was occupied by CPU. This was where she landed the other day, running from the CPU. She assumed that because they lost her before to her dangerous path over the roofs, they would be mindful of her using it as a stealth entrance. She proceeded covertly across the roof in the dark. Once she reached the edge, she looked over to the adjacent building's roof and saw no movement. She could not be certain of her safety as it was very dark, and there were plenty of places for the soldiers to hide.

The jump to the second building was a little over four feet, but it wasn't even with the rooftop she was on. She surmised she could make it, but only if she got a considerable lift. The ledge was a small step up from where she stood, so her plan was to get a running start. She stepped back from the edge about ten feet, and after taking a deep breath, ran toward the crevasse. After landing on the ledge with her left foot, she launched herself toward the other building and landed, not on her feet but on her side, a little below the waist, allowing her to roll onto the neighboring roof.

She took a moment to collect herself and then slowly made her way to the edge on the other side of the building to get a better look at her building. Her rooftop garden was dark and seemed empty, but to ensure her safety, she waited patiently to spend time observing it. She realized she had not eaten since breakfast, and it was fast approaching midnight. She reached into her bag to retrieve some oat bars she had picked up at Jordan's house. They were homemade and stale. Even fresh, they had little taste, but Leena enjoyed the crunch they made when she bit into them. After not eating for some time, they might as well be chocolate bars.

After her snack, she prepared to make the jump to her building. Like the last one, the height, not the distance, was the issue. If she did not land correctly, she would certainly bounce off the side and fall to her death. She felt strong and agile enough to make the jump, but the darkness added complexity. Stepping back to get a running start once again, she bent down to set up her run. As she was about to launch toward the building, she saw a flash. It was a reflection. A CPU soldier was standing guard atop her building. He was shielded by the darkness, so she had not seen him, but the reflection of the moon that flashed off his helmet made his presence clear.

She still had to go. She just needed to land on the roof and quickly make her way across the building to the soldier before he noticed her. It was not likely she could pull it off, but she had to try. She had to ensure that her mom and Diego were safe. She had come to know how immoral the CPU were and was worried her family might be in danger after her latest run-in with Sgt. McBride.

With another deep breath, Leena ran toward the building, this time with even more energy and strength than before. Launching off her left foot once again, she soared through the air and landed on the opposite side, not with her feet but by slamming into the side of the building, only keeping herself from falling by grabbing onto the ledge. She hung there, panicked that she had made a mistake and misjudged the length of the jump required. Slowly, she got a grip and pulled herself up onto the ledge. She glanced as she was rolling onto the roof to see if the noise had alerted the guard but could not tell if he was still in the same location.

Leena rose to her feet and crept slowly through the garden. The guard was still there. He could not see her in the darkness, but a large shaft of light from the moon would reveal her position within a couple more steps. She looked down to locate something she could throw that might distract him. Finding a medium-sized rock and an empty pot that was once the habitat for some sort of herb or small plant, she aggressively threw the rock to the right and beyond where the guard stood to ensure he turned his back to her. Once the rock landed, as suspected, the guard turned, and she ran toward him, stopping only momentarily to throw the pot as she charged. The pot crashed against the back of his head, sending him thudding into the door but failing to knock him off his feet.

By the time the guard turned around, he had dropped his rifle and likely did not see Leena when he felt the blow from her body landing on him, tossing him once again into the steel door. With one clean motion, she grabbed her escrima, knocked his helmet off, and leveled several strikes against his head, then two to his leg that put him on his back. The fall and the blows rendered him unconscious, and Leena turned him on his stomach, locating a small batch of twine nearby that she used to tie his hands behind his back. She fashioned a gag out of a dirt-covered rag and tightened it securely.

Leena next took two magazines of ammunition for her handgun and dropped them in her bag. She removed the magazine from the rifle and tossed it aside into the darkness. Locating a long knife on the belt of the soldier, she removed it too, along with its sheath, and fastened it to her waist. She wiped the sweat from her brow as she collected her wits and tried to slow her heart rate as her heart was now pounding out of her chest.

Prying open the door, she crept down the stairs. She knew there would be other guards, so she was on full alert. The stairway was dark. The only light came from below on the second floor, the only light still in operation. It was strangely quiet.

As she reached the fifth floor on her way to the third, a door to one apartment adjacent to the stairwell cracked open, and a shadowy figure grabbed her from behind and yanked her into the hallway. She flipped around with escrima in hand to face her attacker only to see Diego signaling for her to keep quiet. He motioned for her to follow, and they crept down the hall and entered apartment 5C. This was Diego's unit.

As Diego closed the door, he whispered, "What are you doing here? They have the building surrounded by soldiers waiting for you."

"I had to see if you were safe. Is mom okay?"

"I will take care of your mother, but you need to get out of here and run. Run far away."

Diego gave her a deep embrace before continuing his plea.

"I have heard you are CPU's most wanted. They are desperate to find you."

"Don't believe everything you hear," Leena whispered. "I am off-grid now and plan to enter Zone 7 to get medicine for Mom."

"I wish it was that easy, Leena," Diego said, resignation inhabiting his voice. "Your mom is not doing well. I am not sure medicine will help at this point."

"I have to try," Leena replied, fixated on the only sliver of hope she could muster as tears streamed down her cheeks.

Leena moved toward the window to see what her best escape route might be. Diego's apartment was at the front of the building, so looking down, she could see two CPU trucks parked outside and guards moving about. A larger presence existed than before. There were a few more trucks on the block, too, including two in front of the building she entered to make her roof jump. She knew her path was clear to the roof but was unsure how many soldiers were present in that building.

Diego handed Leena a couple of bottles of water and some crusty bread that he had on hand. She slipped them into her pack and walked toward the door to check the hallway.

"Leena," Diego said, "I know we are beyond asking you to be careful, but I want you to consider leaving this place. Your mom would not want you risking your life this way for her. She would want you to survive."

"I am tired of surviving, Diego. They don't get to treat us this way. Not anymore. I will save Mom if I have to kill them all."

"I really hope it doesn't come to that," Diego replied, knowing he had little control over her. "I have watched you grow up, Turnip, and I had hoped for a better life for you. I know I cannot get you to stand down, so just know that I love you. Your mom loves you. The best thing you can do for us is to survive this place."

"I'll be back soon, Diego," Leena said with tears in her eyes. She hugged him and went to the stairway.

"How will you get past the soldiers downstairs? There are several of them?" Diego asked.

"I have an idea," Leena yelled up to him as she descended the stairs.

Reaching the fourth floor, Leena could see through the opening to the third floor that there were guards outside of her apartment. They were using her mother as bait, and that brought fury to her heart and mind. She walked on the balls of her feet to be as stealthy as possible and went to 4A. She knew that apartment was above hers and vacant. She opened the door, which was never locked, and entered an apartment void of furniture and in much worse shape than her own. There were holes in the floor where she could see into her apartment below. She could see her mom, along with a caregiver she assumed was Jun Lee, but she couldn't make out her face.

She went to the first bedroom and, with a slight amount of pressure, opened the resistant window. She looked down to the alley below. It was clear of CPU as they were guarding the front of the building and the roof but obviously didn't believe an alley escape was likely.

Constructed of brick, the building had ledges on every level. They were not wide—a little wider than Leena's feet—but wide enough for someone to crawl on. She climbed out through the window, being careful not to cut herself on the broken glass, and stood on the ledge. She was four floors up, so a drop would inflict serious injury or death. She tried hard not to think about that, wrestling with the fear that often drove her. She shimmied her way toward the back of the building where there was an old fire escape. Rust had corroded the metal and broken many of the bolts securing it to the building. She had never used it, so she didn't know if it went all the way to the ground. In the darkness, it was difficult to tell. Even if it did, it was debatable if it would stay connected to the building if she attempted to use it.

Leena jumped from the ledge to the waiting fire escape and was able to grab onto the rusty railing and pull herself over to the stairs. She made her way slowly down the metal stairs as they creaked and cracked their protest, enduring a weight they had not supported in many years. She reached the second-floor landing and the ladder that was supposed to extend down to the ground, but the bottom part of the ladder was missing, and climbing down as far as she could still left her ten feet above the ground.

She hung down as low as she could, and after momentarily scanning the ground below to ensure there were no obstacles, she let go of the ladder, falling to the ground with a thud. She fell backward, so her backpack took the brunt of the impact. Once on the ground, she scurried to the side of the building to get out of sight and did a body check for injury. She felt some pain in one ankle but did not believe it was serious.

Leena crept to the end of the alley to survey her situation. The two trucks were still in front of the building, and the two guards were now at the bottom of the stairs, casually chatting with one another. Their rifles were on their backs, but she knew from their training that they could have them ready to fire within seconds.

As she was about to make a move toward the soldiers to attack, headlights approached from the opposite direction. Leena instantly aborted her plan and slunk back into the darkness of the alley. The headlights came from CPU trucks. Two soldiers from each truck got out and left the engines running in front of the alley. Words were exchanged by the four, and it became clear these new soldiers were there to relieve the team. One guard went into the building to notify the others. Leena knew that once they went to the roof for their colleague, they would search for her with even more ferocity.

Her mind raced for a solution. If she left the alley, she would be discovered, and a foot chase would certainly end in her capture. Climbing the wall was possible but probably not helpful as it would put her back into the building where they would focus their search.

One soldier showed signs of frustration over the time it took for his teammate to return and asked the others to go speed up the retrieval. Two of his cohorts accepted the command and ran into the building, leaving just one soldier and four trucks outside the building. The engines of two of the trucks were still running, billowing black smoke from tall stacks.

As the remaining soldier stepped toward the stairs, Leena crouched and then lay on her belly like a snake slithering across the entrance to the alley. She slid easily under the belly of one of the idling trucks. She scanned the bottom of the truck for a foothold or something to hold onto so she could hitch a ride away from the danger. She discovered toward the back of the vehicle a pocket meant for a spare tire, but the tire for this truck was missing, leaving a gap. She crawled over a painted metal bar and into the pocket, where she was hidden from anyone who might walk around the vehicle.

Her hiding place was uncomfortable but allowed just enough room so she could move her legs and stretch her arms to keep them from cramping. Within minutes, she heard the soldiers screaming and radios in the truck blaring, indicating they had discovered her handiwork. She lay perfectly still as she saw many boots run by the truck. She heard other trucks arrive and then many more start their engines and leave. There was quite a panic surrounding this area, and at times she could count more than twenty pairs of boots—but the guards attached to them had no way of knowing she was so close.

Leena lay quiet for hours, only moving to keep her body from hurting. Eventually, the truck she was in moved. It backed into the alley and then turned toward the north gate. She worried about inspections at the gate and whether they would discover her but knew she had little recourse at this point.

The truck rolled through the gate without inspection. Leena thought it was strange but then reasoned that the CPU posed no threat. The truck sped up once it reached Zone 7 as the streets were clear. The streets passed rapidly under her watchful eye. She had lost her sense of direction but felt they were still heading north. Habit caused her to look at her left hand, reassuring herself that the bracelet was gone.

Leena's body ached as the truck rumbled through the streets, each bump sending stabbing pains through her body as she bumped against the hard steel repeatedly. The dust from the street clogged her eyes and nose, making it difficult to resist sneezing, which might give away her position. She could feel the truck turning and passing through another gate, and then coming to a stop. The soldiers jumped from their perch and slammed the doors before walking away from the vehicle.

Leena lay still. She was unsure of her location or how many guards might have eyes on the truck. She could see it was getting light out as dawn burst onto the horizon. She knew she had to make her escape and risk being seen, or soon it would be full daylight.

She dropped to the ground, crawling from her hiding place, stretching madly to release the tension that had built up in her muscles. Creeping to the truck's front, she peered out. She recognized the building in front of her. It was the detainment center where she had attended court. The truck was one of many in a fenced yard. There was a guard gate by the fence entrance, but it appeared to be empty. It was early, and the sun was just coming up over the height of the building.

Leena crawled out from under the truck and ran to the back. Thinking the truck might contain ammunition or other resources, she lifted the back window and peered inside the bed. She saw no ammunition but located a box of grenades. Flipping the top, she grabbed a couple and put them in her bag, being careful not to jiggle the pins.

Looking around for cameras and soldiers, she ran toward the back of the yard and began scaling the wire fence. She paused on reaching the top to avoid the razor wire. She pulled the knife she had attached to her belt the night before and used the back of it to pull on the razor wire, cutting it by pressing it against the fence. She did this a few times until she had cut a space big enough for her to climb over. Once on the other side, she could drop to the ground.

She headed into the small forest that was behind the truck yard. With her knife in hand to cut away the vines as she walked, she made her way to the other side, ending at the edge of a road. Across the street, she could see homes, mostly small, with well-manicured lawns and streets that were standard in Zone 7. She knew that cameras were everywhere. She could not walk around in broad daylight.

Leena headed back into the solitude of her forest and, finding a small crevasse, situated herself out of sight. She used nearby foliage to cover her body and closed her eyes to get some rest.

Darkness was her ally, and even though she knew she had limited time, she surmised that her only chance of success was to complete her mission at night. She had totally failed Jordan and hoped that he had found a way home from the veterinarian. She was resolved to focus on her mom's needs.

Leena awoke startled, pulling her mind out of a nightmare. It was dusk. The humidity of the air had penetrated her jacket and gave her a chill. She sat up and looked around at the quiet forest. She could see the edges: the road, the fence, the houses in the distance. She rose from her sleeping fissure and searched her bag for provisions. Nibbling on an oat bar and hydrating, she slowly composed herself and prepared for her next task. She needed to get to the pharmacy.

There were most likely many pharmacies between her location and the north gate, but she was unaware of where they might be located and thought that staying close to the wall would be a better escape route once she found the medication. She pulled a scarf from her bag and wrapped it around her neck, leaving the front loose enough to cover her face when necessary. It was not cold out, but she thought that shielding her face from any cameras she encountered would confuse facial recognition.

Once darkness had fully descended, Leena left her safe spot in the woods and began walking through the neighborhood. She passed house after house, block after block, knowing cameras were on her. She wondered as she passed each streetlight whether the CPU were already on the way to her location.

Leena had walked through Aberjay neighborhoods for years. She never gave it much thought. Now she felt she was in the enemy's camp. She knew the citizens were mostly innocent but was beginning to believe that their lack of indignation over the injustice of their world made them responsible for at least a modicum of guilt. They had to see how the Aberjay bullied and oppressed those that were not like them.

Trucks broke the silence of the street. Leena looked around for a good hiding spot and discovered a home with a *For Sale* sign in the yard. She ran to the front porch and hid behind the front bushes. She heard the truck go by with its familiar rumble. She stood to continue but then heard another truck. She kneeled, waiting for that one to pass as well. It stopped close to where she was crouching. She slowly slid toward the front door of the house to get out of sight. She tried the door, but it was locked. She reached into her bag for the crowbar. Carefully, she eased the crowbar under the small opening of the door and, with a small amount of leverage, successfully freed the door.

The rooms were sparse, with only a few pieces of old furniture. It smelled musty as if no one had lived there for some time. The floors were hardwood stained a dark brown. There was still power in the house, though, evidenced by the ambient lighting that came on the moment she entered the room. Looking through the window, she could see the CPU truck still motionless in front of the house.

Moving to the small chair in the center of the room, she waited them out. As she sat down, a television wall activated a news program. It was common to have a television built into the wall of each room in the Aberjay zone. They thrived on convenience and, because they did little work, needed entertainment.

"Good morning, Zone 7," the news anchor said. "Here are the latest bulletins. Construction continues on the western wall that was damaged by a 200-year-old oak tree that fell during a recent storm. Repairs should be complete within a couple of weeks. Crowds gathered to celebrate the coming of spring in Vera Town Province with an outdoor festival and rides for the kids. And in further news, Governor Reynolds gave a speech to the Metropolitan Chamber of Commerce last night as he prepared for his reelection campaign, which is expected to kick off next week. Let's listen in."

The TV screen now showed a large room full of people at round tables. Up on the stage were dignitaries and CPU officials who all had their eyes fixed on the governor speaking at the podium.

"The latest uprisings have been put down. Law and order once again has triumphed over the outer zones that would seek to divide us and tear down our way of life. We must not be weak in our response to these attacks. Even last week, a truck full of food that was meant for our children was hijacked and destroyed by these murderers and thieves. Who steals food from the mouths of children? What sort of person believes it is their right to steal from hardworking people who only want to see their children thrive? My administration will continue to chase down and punish those guilty of these crimes."

The anchor came back on. "Some strong words from Governor Reynolds. In other news, federal agencies have repealed the Drone Elimination Act as of next Thursday based on repeated lobbying by the CPU and other law enforcement agencies that have determined that drones are the only way to ensure law and order in our neighborhoods. In anticipation of this event, the regional CPU, in coordination with Zone 6 leaders, has signed an agreement to acquire some land in the north end of Zone 6 for the construction of a drone factory and operations center. The factory will be the first of its kind to be built in more than twenty years and will bring more than one thousand jobs to the area."

Leena could barely stand to listen. She knew the factory was not meant to help her people but to enslave them. The jobs they spoke of would be filled by MIRO, not Miniyar, and the location of the factory made it clear that the impoverished areas around the factory were most likely the primary target for their killer drones.

She checked once more, and the truck that was directly outside had moved on. She raced through the house to determine if there was anything she could add to her spoils. Finding nothing of value in the house, she made her way to the front door and, with a glance to ensure there were no watching eyes, she fixed her scarf over her face and made her way outside.

Her mind rattled through an inventory of tasks she needed to complete as she walked through the darkness. She needed to break into a pharmacy, find the drug she needed, make it to the wall, and get back to her side. Once home, she would deliver the medications to Mom and then make her way to Jordan's house to ensure he made it home safely. Then there was that eviction notice to resolve.

Chapter 12

ASSAULT

Once Leena made it through the residential area, she breathed a little easier. The alleys that surrounded the commercial made hiding from view less challenging. She walked through alley after alley, wondering how they were kept so clean, before reaching the pharmacy that she and Jordan had intended to burgle many weeks before. She knew the crowbar would not work as they tried it last time. She had to think of a new plan.

She took up residence behind the same dumpster they had used before. She checked it to ensure it was empty so as not to be startled by the trash truck again. She kept her gaze on the pharmacy entrance as she formulated a plan. It was only about eight p.m., so an occasional car passed through the alley that she was careful to hide from. Leena could see that the light in the pharmacy was off through the narrow skylight window above the door. It reminded her of the window in her prison cell. It was about the same size and, for most people, would prevent access. But Leena was small, and she felt that if she could make it to that height, she could certainly fit.

She walked to the end of the alley on one side to look for cars and then walked back to the dumpster, which was on wheels. Looking for the locks on the wheels, she found two of them.

Kicking at the locks with her feet, she got the dumpster to move. She pushed it toward the back of the pharmacy. It was difficult to control, like a shopping cart with a broken wheel, so she had to go to one side or the other to push it back in line. The dumpster rolled until it was resting against the back door of the pharmacy.

Leena climbed on top of it to find that not only did it give her the perfect angle to reach the window, but it also gave her the reach to disable the camera. Using her crowbar, she smashed the camera until the red light dimmed and she was certain it was dead. While it was impossible to tell how the CPU monitored these cameras, a dead one was likely to send an alert. In any case, her action likely triggered an alarm somewhere in town, so she knew she needed to hurry.

Taking the crowbar in her hands, she slammed it against the window, which was double-paned and about three feet wide. She attacked the window repeatedly until it fell from its frame. Next, using the crowbar, she cleared all remaining glass from the window and then sat with her feet toward the opening. She removed her backpack and tied the loop on it to her arm where her bracelet used to be. Slowly, she shimmied her body into the gap so that she could slide through the opening. Barely a few inches of space separated her face from the window frame as she slid through and then dropped to the floor.

Once on the floor in the pharmacy, she pulled her backpack through the opening and was able to retrieve it. Putting her pack on her back, she surveyed her surroundings and explored. The door to the rear counter section of the store where she assumed the drugs would be located was locked, but this was not an external door and no match for her crowbar. She placed the tool next to the handle and, with a quick pull, sprung the door open.

As she entered the back room, a small white light flashed, lighting up the entire store. It was clear she had tripped the alarm. Her heart raced, and adrenaline flowed as she surveyed her surroundings.

There was ambient lighting from a security light that marked the exit, but it did little to light up the shelves, so she retrieved the flashlight from her pack and wrapped it around her arm as she did the day before in the dark stairway. Scanning the shelves of medications, she noticed they were in alphabetical order. Moving quickly to the last shelf, she looked up and then down the stacks until she reached the medications that started with an X. Then she found it. On the top shelf, a large white bottle of Xithraxin. She read the label to ensure it was the correct medication and then put it in her bag.

She thought about all the other medications she might want to take. Not only could they be useful for her family members and friends, but because many of them were not available in Zone 6, they were valuable as well. She could sell or barter them for provisions. Then she reasoned it might take too much time to collect them and would raise the risk of her being trapped in this store as the CPU descended. She decided to just grab a couple of bottles without looking and throw them in her bag before heading for the door.

She pushed the back door, but the dumpster blocked it. She was hoping the wheels would allow it to move when she applied pressure, but after trying repeatedly, it was apparent that something had stuck, and the door did not allow her enough room to sneak through. She ran to the front of the store to locate another exit.

When Leena reached the front door, she heard sirens. They were distant but getting louder. She attempted to open the door but didn't have a key for the bolt lock. She grabbed the crowbar and, like the window in the back, began slamming it against the glass door. This door was made similarly, with multiple glass panes, but it didn't give up as easily as the window. Leena frantically beat on the glass, envisioning being arrested and taken back to prison. She could not let that happen and worked feverishly to break free.

She eventually broke enough of the glass to crawl through just as a CPU truck rounded the corner, almost on top of her position. She rose to her feet on the sidewalk and took off running as fast as she could down the sidewalk to put some distance between her and the truck behind her, which was now gaining.

She crossed a street and then, a block later, turned down an alley. She knew that some of these alleys were dead ends. Sprinting to the end of the alley, it emptied onto another street that allowed her to take a right toward the park. As she crossed the street heading into the park, she could see two more trucks headed toward her, one from each direction. Added to the one behind her, she had three on her trail.

Almost out of breath, she ran into the woods in the park, around a small pond, and then toward the swings near the back of the park. She thought that the absence of roads in this part of the park would slow down the trucks, but they had driven directly into the park using the sidewalk and any space they could between trees to continue their pursuit. The truck behind her and the one to her right were closest, so she headed west along the wall as fast as she could, holding her side that had begun to burn as she gasped to get whatever air she could into her lungs.

Capture was imminent if she could not make it to her hole in the wall that would allow her to escape. She only hoped they had not called ahead to the other side of the wall. As she ran, she entered the back alley of the homes that were familiar and reached the area where she needed to climb. She had not eluded her pursuers. They were only moments behind her as they tried to navigate the neighborhood of residential streets.

Leena took a foothold and lifted herself onto the wall. She climbed faster than she had ever climbed the wall, using every stone for leverage to propel her upward. She was close to the top when she reached up to grab hold of the opening and felt something foreign. It was dark, and it took her eyes a second to adjust to what she was feeling. It was new stone. Why was she feeling new stone? As she pulled herself up further, she felt her mind was playing tricks on her until reality set in and she realized what she was observing. The hole was gone; the Aberjay had repaired it. What used to be a hole to freedom was now solid stone.

Panic struck her as she realized they had her trapped. She looked back and could see three sets of blue lights flashing and closing in on her position. They had turned off their sirens, but the lights were still flashing bright and blue. She knew she would never make it over the wall as razor wire and other obstacles made it practically impossible at the top, plus she did not know if there were rocks to climb on that high. She had never scaled the entire wall. The other option was to climb back down and try to make another run, but where would she go?

Leaning against the wall, with three points of contact with it, she used her free hand to reach into her bag for a smoke grenade. What her hand grabbed hold of was a regular grenade, and she figured that at this point, it might be her only way out. She grabbed the pin with her teeth and pulled it out of the grenade as two of the trucks were pulling up to the base of the wall. She strategically dropped the grenade so that it would fall under a truck as it came to a stop. She turned her head toward the wall to shield her face from the blast.

The explosion turned the CPU truck on its side and lit up the sky, sending shrapnel and truck parts not only against the wall but into the other truck, which sustained serious damage, as well as rendering unconscious two CPU soldiers who had already exited the vehicle. The fire roared as Leena made her way down the wall, hoping the confusion would provide an escape path. She hit the ground and turned around as four soldiers walked through the smoke and the fire with rifles drawn to corner her against the wall.

Leena put her hands up as she resigned herself to her fate. Adrenaline still pumping through her veins, she fought the compulsion to fight, knowing her opponent had her outgunned and outmatched.

"Turn around," she heard the guard shout.

Turning toward the wall, she placed her hands on it as the guards moved closer. Then she heard another sound that struck the wall. It sounded like someone had thrown a can or something metal against the stone. The area was now filled with smoke. She recognized the object as a smoke grenade and was curious why a guard would throw a smoke grenade when she was already surrendering.

As the smoke enveloped her, she heard a fight erupt along with several gunshots. She winced, knowing the next shot could be the one that would take her life. She moved her hands from the wall to cover her head, crouching on the ground and waiting for the end, when suddenly she was struck from behind and turned sideways. Two masked soldiers had picked up Leena and began carrying her. With all the smoke and fire, she could not tell what was happening but figured she was being taken into custody. She saw the bodies of CPU on the ground as her captors carried her through the smoke. Then she saw a mailbox, a lawn, and a concrete driveway. As she emerged from the smoke, she realized her abductors were taking her into a garage through a small door.

Once inside the garage, she noticed her attackers were dressed in green camo—military uniforms. They took her into the garage and then down a flight of stairs into darkness. There was little light and no way to see what was happening to her, but her captives held her tight. After guiding her for about fifty feet, they brought her into a room with a small light and dropped her gently onto what seemed to be a pile of old clothes.

As Leena turned to look at her captors, she recognized one of them. She had seen him before.

"Are you okay?" the man asked.

"Uh...I think so," Leena said, a bit rattled.

"I am Commander Johnson, and we are here to help. It won't take long for them to determine where we went, so we need to move. Can you walk?"

"Yes," Leena said, glad to be alive and dumbfounded by who this familiar face might be.

She stood as they motioned for her to follow them through another passageway and then down a ladder that went further underground. At the bottom of the short ladder was a makeshift tunnel carved out of the dirt that led south. The commander climbed into the tunnel, and Leena followed. The second man was behind her but took a moment to cover their tracks by closing a fake floor designed to hide the ladder they descended.

Hundreds of feet ahead, Leena could faintly make out a light. She crawled on her hands and knees in little to no light, so she didn't know what her hands were digging into. It was soft and wet. She hoped feverishly that it was just dirt, but often the dirt seemed to move, and at that moment she was glad there was no light in the tunnel.

Once she reached the end, she fell out onto the floor in a small, lighted room with a few makeshift benches. She pulled herself off the floor and sat on a bench, scraping the mud off her hands and feet. She looked up at the commander as she composed herself and remembered where she had seen him. He was on stage in the meat plant when they planned the attack on the food truck. She had determined that day that he was important but never knew his name.

"We should be safe now," Commander Johnson said as he cleaned his own hands with a towel.

"Where are we?" Leena asked, looking around the small room with dirt walls and only a small lantern to light the perimeter.

"You are in Zone 6 now. We finished this tunnel recently. It provides access in and out of the Aberjay zone. You must swear not to reveal this, Leena."

"Of course," Leena said boldly.

"I have been watching you. You know how to take care of yourself, and you were a big help in our last two campaigns—although that last one did not go well," the commander added with regret.

"How did you know I needed help? Were you following me?" Leena asked.

"No, the house we entered to get down here is a safe house. We have many in the Aberjay zones. We were having a meeting when we saw the lights and recognized you. We thought they were coming for us. Once we realized all that ruckus was just for you, we decided we had to risk showing our hand to get you to safety."

Leena was stunned. She didn't think anyone cared about her enough to risk their own lives, except maybe her mom and Diego. She did not know anyone even knew who she was, much less be willing to waste their resources and endanger their lives to save her.

"I am very thankful for the help, Commander. I hope I can repay the generosity someday."

"Oh, I am sure you will, Leena. You are a vital part of the Resistance now." The commander stood in the small room and extended a hand for her to shake.

"I am?" Leena said, quite stunned.

"I don't see that you have much choice, Leena. You know too much at this point. You are either in or…"

"No, I am definitely in," Leena said, not wanting to hear what the *or* of that sentence was going to be.

"Great, welcome aboard. Let's get out of this hole," the commander said, leading her to yet another ladder that took her up into a basement. Once there, the soldier guided her upstairs into a small, empty living room and then out the door of a townhouse that was right next to Banyan Park. She thanked the commander and his colleague once again, and they disappeared into the darkness.

Leena breathed deeply in relief. She had accomplished her mission of obtaining the medication her mom needed. She now had to deliver it to her. She walked through the dark streets cautiously, knowing that the CPU were still in this part of the zone often because of the eviction notices and protests.

She walked toward midtown for a few blocks before turning west and heading toward her building to avoid the outskirts. Within minutes, she was heading up the street that would lead to her building. As she turned the corner, she could see a large CPU presence. There were four CPU trucks and about twenty heavily-armed soldiers guarding the building entrance.

For a moment, she thought about going to the building she had entered before and jumping from the roof again, but when her hand brushed against her side, still aching from her near-death experience when she barely survived the jump between buildings, it made her realize she should not try that again. She also figured that sneaking in would probably not work a second time as the CPU presence was even greater now. She had to fight her way through. She wished she had some help, but at this point, she knew she was on her own.

Leena decided that an attack from the south was best, so she made her way back from where she came, walked south for several blocks, and then cut over so she could reach the CPU positions from the south side. She crept closer and closer until she was within a few yards of the first truck. She searched her bag for what might be helpful and inventoried one grenade, one smoke grenade, and a handgun with a few magazines.

The twenty-to-one odds were not encouraging, but Leena knew she needed to get into that building. With the handgun in one hand and the smoke grenade in the other, she pulled the pin with her teeth and threw the smoke grenade in the middle of the parked trucks. She quickly grabbed the other grenade and, after throwing it in the air toward the trucks, began firing the handgun. She hit two of the guards before they all lunged for cover behind the trucks.

The grenade hit the ground and rolled under the lead truck. The explosion rang out and put the truck on its side, crushing two of the soldiers and injuring several others. Leena began shooting from her position behind a barricade. Several soldiers ran out of the building to join in the fight and began firing on Leena's position in unison. She ducked as they sent rock and metal fragments flying with blasts from their pulse rifles.

This was too much. She had overestimated her chances. The CPU had her outgunned once again. She tried to get off a few rounds, but she could barely raise her head from behind the barricade without risking the CPU filling it with lead. She questioned what she should do as another explosion surprised her, destroying one truck and engulfing it in flames. She saw several Resistance fighters exiting a truck that had come from the south. They had come to her rescue!

Liv came toward Leena and grabbed her, pulling her toward the truck. "We've got some cover fire, but you gotta move now!" Liv said as she pulled Leena off her feet and toward the getaway car.

"No, wait," Leena said as she resisted Liv's pull.

"C'mon," shouted Liv as she holstered her gun and grabbed Leena with two hands, forcing her into the waiting truck.

The other fighters fell back and threw a couple more grenades before getting back in the truck and putting it in reverse. Within two blocks, they backed into an alley to make a U-turn and headed back toward the south.

"Why did you do that?" Leena shouted.

"Because you would not have made it. The CPU has an entire squad guarding your building. They want you badly. What did you do to get so much attention?"

"I kinda broke Sergeant McBride's nose."

"You what?" Liv said with a huge smile. "That is terrestrial."

"I have to get in there, Liv. My mom is counting on me."

"I know, Leena, and we will. Let's regroup, and we'll come back with more firepower." Liv grabbed a towel from the seat and wiped the sweat, along with gunpowder and dirt, off her neck.

"What were you doing at the building?" Leena asked.

"We were waiting for you. I met up with Jordan earlier. He told us you might come here, and he was worried when you didn't return to take him home from the clinic."

"How is he?" Leena asked with a tinge of guilt.

"He's fine. He took a bullet to the stomach, but the doc fixed him up real good. He will survive."

The truck drove toward the south end of the zone to an area where Leena had never been. They turned into a desolate warehouse and parked inside. Everyone exited the vehicle and headed to a small office in the back of the empty building. Once there, they entered a freight elevator, and one soldier pushed the lever down to force the elevator to lower. The elevator had no front or back, just flimsy, rusted fencing.

It moved down about thirty feet and then stopped, revealing a giant open area full of activity. Beds were stacked all over, and everything was draped in green camo: the blankets, the storage lockers, the cabinets, and the soldiers, who must have numbered three hundred in this room alone.

Leena walked through the sea of soldiers cleaning weapons, tending to wounds, and playing cards. Some were cooking on hotplates, while others were sleeping. She walked through the barracks to a room that was also painted green. The entrance was a flimsy door with a frosted glass window. It was a conference room, large enough for fifty people and full of tables, chairs, and whiteboards full of diagrams and battle plans.

As she approached a table full of maps, she recognized Commander Johnson.

"Leena, it's good to see you again so soon. What are you doing here?"

"We pulled her out of a firefight, Commander," said a nearby soldier. "We could not leave her there."

"Commander, I need to get back into my building," Leena said in a soft voice. "I have medicine my mom desperately needs."

The Commander turned and asked the soldier who was escorting her for a situation report.

"They have the building heavily guarded, sir, probably an entire squad, although Leena took out several before we pulled her out."

The Commander grimaced. "They probably have reinforcements by now. Leena, I would love to help, but the enemy has us spread too thin to be going on missions that don't have high strategic value."

"But my mom needs these medications, or she won't live," Leena pleaded.

"Commander, I told her we would help," Liv said boldly while realizing that she was speaking above her rank.

The commander walked to a coffeepot, clearly ruminating on the situation. He poured a cup and took a sip.

"I will give you two teams for a rescue mission," he said to Liv. Turning to a nearby soldier, he continued, "You get in and get out. I don't want another stack of body bags."

"Yes sir," the soldier said and then took off to relay the command to others.

"Thank you, Commander," Leena said.

The Commander sipped his coffee and placed it on the table. "Leena, you are a hero around here. What you did on the bridge saved lives, and tales of your valor are now being spun into legend. We don't mind that around here. Legends drive hope. We need more of that here. We have taken many losses lately. Go get your mother, and when you get back, we will have a conversation about where you fit in this ragtag bunch of soldiers."

Leena knew she could not retrieve her mother as she was too sick to move. She thought it best not to get into a discussion about this wrinkle as it might make the commander change his mind. She reasoned that if she could get the medications to her, that would be enough to put her on the road to recovery.

"Liv," Leena said, "take me to Jordan."

"Sure, I know right where he is," Liv replied as she took her by the hand.

Jordan was in another part of the facility, an area that looked like a medical clinic. Instead of green, the line of beds, tables, and walls were all white. Most of the beds were full of soldiers recovering from their wounds. Several nurses were tending to them.

Jordan was in the last bed at the end of the room and appeared to be sitting up.

"Jordan!" Leena said as she ran toward him and embraced him.

"It's good to see you are okay, Leena," Jordan started. "When I woke up in the clinic and they said you didn't return, I was worried."

"I'm sorry, Jordan. I tried desperately to get back to you, but I had some unforeseen run-ins with the CPU. But look," Leena exclaimed as she pulled the medicine out of her bag, "I got the meds I need for Mom. We are taking them to her right now."

"That is great, Leena. I am happy for you, and I hope your mom recovers quickly. Please be careful though. I don't want to lose you."

Leena moved closer to Jordan and kissed him. They sat in each other's embrace for the few minutes they had. Leena was eager to end this war, or at least her part in it, so she could spend more time with Jordan. She had never aspired to join an army. She only wanted to save her mother.

Leena looked toward the door and saw Liv waiting, knowing she had little time.

"I want you to know that I love you, Jordan. You have been supportive of me through all this madness, and I know you could have steered clear of it if you wanted. You are my rock, and when this is all done, I hope we can find someplace quiet like the Tullian farm and spend the rest of our days together. Let's get chickens and pigs!"

"I would like that," Jordan said, wiping her hair out of her face and clearing the tears from her cheeks. "Now go help your mom. We will have a room for her too, as well as Diego."

"Leena, we got to go," Liv called from the doorway.

"I love you, Jordan."

Leena pulled herself away from Jordan and headed toward the door, walking backward so she could see him as she moved farther and farther away. She blew him a kiss as she turned a corner, tears still flowing down her face.

Leena and Liv found their way to the latrine to clean up a bit. Leena was not fond of camouflage but forced herself to change clothes as hers smelled like the dead in that building near her house. She put the clean clothes on gladly but kept her bomber coat and pilot cap as these were as much a part of her as her fingers and toes.

They visited the supply room and were able to retrieve some ammunition and a few explosives for the operation. Leena found a collapsible baton. She fastened it to her belt. She preferred her wooden one but felt it would make a great backup or companion when she needed two during hand-to-hand combat. This one folded up nicely, but when grasped, it could be extended longer with a quick snap of the arm.

Leena's backpack was worn and dirty, but she could not give it up. She loved it and knew exactly where everything was located inside. She did find a tactical vest that allowed her to attach a few grenades and some backup magazines for her pistol.

The soldiers guided her to the staging area once she was fully armed. Each team included ten soldiers, a combination of men and women. She watched as they all put on their camos and felt overwhelmed with gratitude that these strangers would provide such accommodation for someone they didn't even know. She understood they were being ordered to do so, but she still felt appreciative.

"Let's rally at the trucks for a briefing," the commanding officer said as twenty soldiers plus Leena began moving out of the staging area and into the freight elevator. Once assembled, the leader began giving instructions.

"We will stop a few blocks from the south approach and drop one team here," he stated, pointing to a map of Leena's neighborhood. "Team One will ascend to the roof of this building and make their way across the rooftop to the target. Expect resistance on the rooftop. Once you eliminate targets, move down the stairways and rendezvous with Team Two on the third floor. Team Two, you will perform a direct assault on the CPU outside the building and, once cleared, proceed with caution into the building to eliminate any remaining targets. Watch for friendlies. Is that clear? Leena, you will ride with Team Two."

Leena was thankful she was placed with Team Two as she had no interest in making those jumps again. The teams nodded affirmatively and began piling into two trucks. These trucks looked like CPU but were stolen and repainted in dark green. When Leena climbed into the cab of the Team Two truck, she saw that the electronics had been ripped out, with wires littering the floor. The team of eight sat comfortably, four on each side. Once loaded, the two trucks pulled out of the warehouse and made their way north.

The trucks rumbled through the streets, headed for Leena's home. A month ago, she was gardening, reading books about life, and dreaming of what lay ahead for her. Now, she was embroiled in a war between good and evil, where the stakes were her life and the lives of her loved ones. She had always been a loner. Even in school, she had very few friends. Now she felt she had a family. Her Resistance family. She wished it was under better circumstances, but she was thankful she now had a group that gave her a voice in her future. Before, she felt she was playing a part in a play that she didn't write, just following the ebb and flow of the drama. Now, she felt empowered to create change. She felt liberated.

The drivers of the two trucks turned off their headlights so the enemy would not be warned of their arrival. It was two a.m. Stopping a few blocks from her building, all of the soldiers exited their vehicles. Team One entered the abandoned building and made their way upstairs. Team Two waited for them to get inside and then crept up the street. They wanted to ensure they were in position when the first gunfire rang out from the roof.

Moving closer and closer, Leena got nervous. So many things could go wrong with this assault. She wondered if this was putting Diego or her mom in danger. What about the other residents? Crouching behind a barricade, the soldiers took their positions. A signal from one soldier let the others know that the team on the roof was about to begin their assault.

Several gunshots rang out from the roof all at once to begin the attack. Leena could not see the Resistance soldiers on the roof but noticed how the gunfire lit up the sky and how the light from their weapons bounced off the nearby buildings. This was evidence they were receiving return fire from her building. Four soldiers at once threw grenades to begin the ground assault. With an explosion louder than she had ever heard, two of the CPU trucks flew into the air and flipped on their sides, landing next to the truck that Leena had destroyed earlier.

Gunshots rang out from both sides as the soldiers scrambled to their best positions. Unlike the earlier firefight, this one seemed more balanced as both sides gave fire and took fire. Leena waited patiently for the first wave of battle to conclude before she dared engage as she was armed with only a handgun, and these professional soldiers were armed with much more powerful rifles.

As the shooting died down, Leena chambered a round in her handgun and turned to look over the barricade. She began firing at anything that moved. She saw smoke, fire, and occasional flashes of light from weapons determined to destroy them. The Resistance fighters fought valiantly and were able to eliminate the soldiers in the street before giving the command to proceed further in this engagement.

As Team Two stood and walked toward the burning mess of bodies and metal, the stench of diesel fuel and blood hit Leena like a flood. She pulled her scarf up to shield her nose as she fell in behind the soldiers and made her way up the stairs of the building. She could hear that the sounds of battle had stopped on the roof and hoped that was a good sign.

Soldiers entered the building and immediately took several rounds in the chest as their comrades behind them returned fire to eliminate the few targets on the first floor. Everyone fell back to the doorway and then outside as gunfire rained down on the threshold and frame of the building. Two of the soldiers pulled pins on grenades and threw them into the nest of soldiers who were firing. The explosion seemed to blow fire from all the windows on the bottom floor, and shrapnel, glass, and brick flew on all sides.

The ground shook under Leena, and she knew what that meant. The building was not stable as many of the floors and stairs had rotted years ago. The walls were sound, but the explosions most likely removed any remaining stability they were providing. She had to hurry.

Rushing to the front, she cried out, "Let's go, let's go!" Now just behind the two lead soldiers, she leaned against them as they made their way up the stairs. The second floor was free of enemies, but once they were in view of the third, gunfire rained down on them once again. Stepping back to get out of harm's way, they returned fire. One grabbed a grenade, but Leena immediately put her hand on his and shook her head strongly to indicate it was a bad idea as her family was just on the other side of the wall.

Leena thought quickly and knew they needed a distraction. She reached down and grabbed a loose board that the earlier explosion had blown off the walls and threw it as hard as she could to land behind the soldiers who were firing at them. In the split second that it caught their attention as it flew over their heads, she took two steps up the stairs and took two shots to eliminate each solder.

"Great shooting!" one soldier cried out as they began their push again, heading toward Leena's apartment door.

Leena pushed past them as they came in contact with Team One coming down the stairs from the roof. She heard "all clear" on the radio as she burst into the apartment.

Diego was there along with Jun Lee, crouching on the floor as they had taken cover from the assault coming toward them. Leena saw that her mom was not injured and noticed that her bed covers were pulled over her head. She thought that maybe Diego had shielded her mom from debris falling from the ceiling until she looked into Diego's eyes and knew.

Horror filled her mind and body as she fell to the floor. Diego moved slowly toward her with one arm raised to comfort her.

"I am sorry, Leena," Diego said.

Leena cried out in pain as she lay on the floor, screaming at the top of her lungs, feeling the depth of pain that losing a loved one exacts on your insides. Over and over, she screamed "No!" as Diego attempted to comfort her. Liv came in behind her to lend support.

"What happened?" Liv asked, addressing anyone who might have an answer.

"Your mom died about an hour ago," Diego said, directing his reply to Leena.

As Leena continued to scream, the floor rumbled. Everyone but Leena stopped making noise and looked at each other, and a soldier behind them cried out what every one of them was thinking: "We need to exit the building immediately."

They all turned and headed toward the door, Liv dragging Leena up to her feet. She put her arm around her as everyone headed down the stairs. They could see the building breaking up as boards and stone and brick fell all around them. Liv practically carried Leena, who was still in shock from the news of her mother's passing.

The group flooded the stairs as wood and concrete began falling all around them. They reached the first floor when Leena seemed to come to her senses upon realizing that Diego and Jun Lee were far behind.

"Wait, where is Diego?" she asked as she turned. She saw Diego at the top of the stairs attempting to navigate the movement of the building, and after setting one foot on the top stair of the staircase, the entire structure gave way, falling to the ground with at least a ton of dirt and stone falling on top.

Leena screamed and lunged back toward the stairs, but Liv grabbed her along with another soldier and pulled her out the front door just as the building collapsed. As Liv continued to drag her across the street, the soldiers were all laid out on the sidewalk, coughing the dust out of their lungs while also trying to tend to several fellow soldiers injured by the falling bricks.

Liv struggled to keep Leena from going back into the building, shouting, "It's too late, we're too late!"

She was right; the building collapsed into a pile of debris. Smoke and dust filled the air as minor explosions were heard and a fire erupted.

Leena wept and wept. She had lost her mother and her adopted father. She felt lost, hopeless. Like there was no reason to continue. Her belly hurt from the heaving, and the loss hurt more deeply than the cuts and bruises she had all over her body from the building debris. Lying on that sidewalk, she did not know how she would go on. Wailing and wailing, there seemed to be no consolation for her pain.

The group heard sirens in the distance. The events of the evening had drawn attention to the neighborhood, and more than likely, the CPU was able to get a message to headquarters when the assault began and called for reinforcements. It was highly likely that the CPU were sending reinforcements.

The soldiers began to organize and head back toward their vehicles a few blocks away. "Let's move now!" shouted the acting commander.

Everyone moved toward the trucks except Liv and Leena. "Get up," Liv pleaded. "We need to get out of here or we'll be target practice for the CPU."

Liv helped Leena to her feet, and they started on their way toward the Resistance trucks. Once they were about a block from their destination, they glanced behind them to see blue lights. Picking up the pace, they limped their way to the trucks and clambered into the back of the second truck. Looking out the back window, Leena saw the CPU trucks reach the site of the building that was now just a pile of rubble. Many CPU soldiers exited the vehicles with their weapons ready, but the debris of the fallen building was enough to cover their escape.

The ride back to the base was surreal. Leena went numb. Like a dream, the streets and buildings passed by as she laid her head on the window, barely able to hold her head up. She felt dehydrated from the battle. The lack of water was the only thing keeping tears from forming again. She reached for a water bottle from her pack but barely had the strength to lift it to her lips.

The previous couple of hours were just a blur. She tried to bring more clarity to what had transpired, but her memory was fuzzy. As the trucks came to a stop at an intersection, a bird landed on the side mirror. It was blue with some red under its chest. It looked like the same bird she had seen at the coffee shop trying to penetrate the glass window. It seemed to look through her with black eyes that penetrated her soul. As the truck grumbled and moved forward, the bird flew away.

She made it to the barracks, which she assumed would be her new home. She collapsed into her assigned bed, a bottom bunk in the rear of the facility near the mess hall. She smelled potatoes cooking. The pain of her loss turned to deep remorse. If only she had been there sooner. If she had entered the building when she first attempted her assault, she might have saved her mother. She passed out as her mind punished her for failing to preserve her mother's life.

Something brought her out of her sleep. She looked down to see bandages on her arm and one on her leg, but only vaguely remembered someone tending to her wounds. Her whole body hurt, but she could not recall the source of the injuries. Exhaustion overcame her once again, and she fell back into a deep slumber.

Leena woke to the smell of eggs cooking. It was a pleasant smell. She knew they were not real eggs as they were a highly desirable commodity rarely available in Zone 6. They were made from mung beans and a combination of spices that made them taste like eggs. She had made them for her mother many times.

She sat up and put her feet on the floor. Rubbing her eyes, she tried to bring her mind into focus. Like assembling a puzzle, she slowly connected where she was to what had happened the day before. Sadness overwhelmed her as she remembered the details. She felt alone. All that she had known in the world was gone. Her mother, her adopted father. Jun Lee? Had Jun Lee made it out of the building? She struggled to think through who might now be dead. She had many neighbors.

She searched for motivation but had little success. She had resigned to lay back down and give herself to the grief when Liv showed up. She was out of uniform and wearing her normal street clothes.

"How you doin', kid?" she said.

Leena tried to speak, but no sounds came from her lips. She was too grief-stricken to respond to what she knew was just a courtesy.

"Let's get something to eat, Leena," Liv said as she helped her to her feet.

The two slowly walked to the mess hall, which fortunately was not that far away. They filled their plates with mung bean eggs, potatoes, and bacon made from pea proteins, and made their way to a metal table that was quite like the ones Leena remembered from prison.

"They are going out today," Liv said, "but in street clothes."

"I need to get my their bodies," Leena said quietly as she slowly moved food to mouth with her fork.

"I am sure there is someone who will take care of that. The CPU will be all over the place after what we did to that place last night," Liv said with a grin before realizing it was too soon to be jovial.

"Liv, that was my whole life. Those people were everyone and everything I have ever known."

Liv shook her head slowly, signifying she understood the weight of it.

"I need to get back to ensure the bodies are put to rest."

"I don't know how you are going to do that with the CPU crawling all over. Finish your breakfast, and we'll go see the commander for our orders," Liv said.

"Orders? Am I Resistance now?" Leena asked in a voice laced with both sadness and sarcasm.

"Actually, yes," Liv said as she dug into her pocket before placing two golden trinkets on the table. "They made you a corporal, if you accept. I demanded they let me tell you."

Leena picked up the trinkets, each one with two arrows pointing up. She was confused.

"Where did you get these?" Leena asked.

"Captain Lewis gave them to me this morning based on your efforts on that overpass, getting Jordan to medical care, and what you did yesterday to help save others. You are a hero around here now. You even outrank me."

"I never meant to be a hero," Leena said as she looked down at the trinkets. She traced the arrows with her fingers, not exactly sure if she should appreciate this promotion or loathe her involvement in the entire thing. Then her mind wandered back to grief and a feeling of loneliness.

"I'm scared, Liv."

"Scared of what?" Liv responded.

"Scared of being alone, I guess. My family is gone. I don't know what is next for me."

"You are not alone, Leena. Yeah, your world has changed, but you still have me and Jordan, Julian, and Zoe. We can be your new family. I know that doesn't help much, but it's all you got right now." Liv paused, knowing Leena was struggling. "You have a purpose here, Leena. The Resistance is about fighting tyranny. It's about changing this world for the better. What you are doing here matters."

"I was not fighting for the Resistance," Leena countered. "I was just trying to save my Mom."

"I know, but now you can focus on saving all of us," Liv said, standing from the table and moving toward the door. "I will meet you in the command room. I need to check on Zoe."

Leena finished her breakfast and felt a little better. Her conscience told her she shouldn't, but despite the injuries to her body and spirit, she felt she was regaining her strength. Maybe it was the mung bean?

She put on her street clothes as Liv had directed. She was not sure if she was going with the team that was headed out on a mission, but she knew that even if she didn't, she wanted to go by the ruins of her old building to scope out the activity. Somehow, she needed to bury her mom and Diego. It was not appropriate to leave the dead unburied. She was not sure where she learned that but knew it was part of her family history and culture.

She thought about what Liv said as she headed toward the command room. She had a family here. She had not known them for long, but when you put your lives at risk together, it forms a bond that is hard to understand or describe. It's like an ethereal connection, something beyond this world that locks you together, joining your spirits.

Leena wondered what the day might bring. Liv's words of encouragement were true but failed to lift her out of her despair. Within moments of processing her situation, her emotion turned to anger. Anger at the establishment that allowed these events to happen. Anger at the Aberjay for thinking they were better. Anger at the CPU for enforcing rules that were unjust. Someone needed to pay for these crimes.

Chapter 13

DAWN

L eena walked into the command room after being cleared by the sentry. She knew her new rank did not give her the privilege of access but felt she had a little more leverage than other corporals based on her connection to Commander Johnson. It was a large conference room with maps of the city on the walls and the table. Stainless steel coffee cups littered the room, along with communications equipment they used to talk to teams in the field. The equipment was old but still impressive.

Commander Johnson, Captain Lewis, and several others were discussing some sort of operation when they turned to notice her.

"Good morning, corporal," Commander Johnson said.

"Good morning," Leena said, unsure if she should address him as commander or sir.

"Congratulations on your promotion, Leena," Captain Lewis added. "You are an asset to our team."

"Thank you, captain," Leena responded.

"You are famous this morning, Leena," the commander added as he walked to the table and handed her a bulletin.

The blue sheet had her picture on it with the word "Wanted" beneath it, along with the instruction: "For crimes against the state, contact CPU at 911." The design was similar to the eviction posters that were plastered all over the northern part of the district.

"There is a reward as well," the commander added.

"Why do they want me so bad?" Leena asked.

"Because you make them look weak. You're dangerous to them because the Miniyar see themselves in you. Every win we achieve with you in our midst is another step closer to revolution. Even now, stories of your fight on the overpass and the assault on your building are gaining traction. We are adding more recruits than we have been able to muster in years." The commander walked to Leena and put a caring hand on her shoulder. "I know you lost loved ones. If you need to take a break for a bit, that's fine. You are dealing with tremendous loss."

"No, I want to make them pay," Leena said, more from emotion than thought.

The commander paused for a moment as if to gauge whether she was being honest about the request. "Okay then," he continued, "let's get you back in the game."

"Commander, what about my family?" she asked. "Their bodies, I mean."

"The CPU will be at the site today to clear out all their dead. They have equipment to move around the rubble and get their people out. They normally take all the bodies they can identify back to their coroners, but those who are Zone 6 residents they typically wrap and bury in the Bonefields."

"I would like to see for myself, commander," Leena said.

"Leena, your face is all over town. You can't go out there without being caught."

"I will disguise myself," she countered.

The commander put his hand to his chin, rubbing it as if the friction might help him think.

"I don't think it's a good idea, Leena, but we all grieve in our own ways. If you want to go, you can, but do it quietly and take someone with you. We can't always reallocate resources to rescue you if you get into trouble. Do you understand?"

"Yes, commander."

"You are dismissed," he said as he went back to his table of maps and plans.

Leena left the command room to find Liv. She needed a companion and someone to help with her disguise.

Liv and Zoe were in the medical area. Zoe was being worked on by a nurse who appeared to be inspecting the stitches that she had most likely received the night before. The medical area was filled with victims of last night's assault. Leena felt bad for the soldiers who didn't make it, but she was happy there was only a handful. It could have been much worse.

"Liv, the commander said we could go out today to do surveillance on my building—well, what's left of my building—but we need to be disguised."

"You mean *you* need to be disguised," Liv said as she held up one of the blue posters. "No one knows me."

"Yes, I guess you are right," Leena admitted. "Do you want to help me find one?"

"Sure, I am thinking a big bunny suit should do it."

"Hilarious," Leena said, cracking a smile.

Leena and Liv said goodbye to Zoe before stopping by to see Jordan, who was still on the mend. They made their way to a surplus area filled with old clothes, boots, and other articles. They were meant for those who normally wore a uniform but needed to dress down for clandestine missions. There were bins for pants, shirts, hats, coats, and scarves.

Both searched through the bins until they found a hat that would cover most of Leena's face, similar to the scarf she often wore but less prone to dropping and more of a neutral beige color. She swapped her bomber jacket for a long coat that almost dragged on the floor and swapped out her backpack with one that looked more upscale.

In her new outfit, she looked at herself in a half-broken mirror that had been hung on the wall. Turning around like a fashion model, she asked, "What do you think?"

"You don't look like you anymore if that's what you mean," Liv said.

"That is the idea, right?"

"Yes, but you don't want to look like Aberjay either," Liv said.

"Too much?" Leena questioned.

"Maybe. Let's try a different pack and swap out the hat. I like the coat though."

After multiple combinations, they both felt Leena looked adequately different from the girl on the poster. They were able to requisition a jeep from the transport officer. It was about thirty years old and in rough shape but had a top that gave them appropriate cover for their journey.

With Liv driving, they took off toward the north end of town. Something was odd about the city. There was little CPU presence. This might have been normal a few months ago, but in the last few weeks, the CPU presence had been increasing. As they drove through major intersections where they expected to see CPU trucks, there were none. Had the CPU pulled out of the zone?

Leena was thinking about Fernando as they pulled within a few blocks of her building and turned into an alley. She wondered if anyone had known to tell Fernando his father was gone. She felt it was her duty to do so and added it to her itinerary for the day as they exited the jeep.

She recognized the alley; this was where she stashed Jordan's motorbike. She walked a few yards into the alley and peered behind the dumpster where she had last seen the bike. It was still there. She wondered why it had not been stolen and broken up for parts by now, but she was glad she could return it to Jordan. Liv was confused when Leena walked back into the alley but understood once she saw the motorbike.

"What is the plan, Leena?"

"Let's just walk casually toward the building and see what we can see," Leena said.

As they walked cautiously, they could see that the CPU had cleared much of the rubble that had blocked the street. They had also removed the bodies. As she neared the building site, she noticed a car parked outside. It was familiar. It was Fernando's.

As she approached, Liv grabbed her hand to stop her and turned to face her.

"Do you see who is in front of the building?"

"Yes, I see him," Leena said.

"Do you think it's a good idea to have a conversation with the zone advocate right now? You know he knows both of us. What if he turns us in?"

"I have known him my whole life, Liv. It is not likely he would betray me that way. Plus his father was in that building."

Leena pushed past Liv toward Fernando, who was standing just outside the threshold that used to hold the doorway of the building. Fernando heard them approach and turned toward them. His eyes were tearing, but he was clearly trying to fight the flow.

"Leena, what happened here?"

Leena looked at him, not knowing what to say, but her eyes communicated clearly that they had both lost someone. She found it odd that he didn't embrace her but kept his distance.

"This was your doing, wasn't it?" Fernando said in an accusatory tone.

"What?" Leena said, disbelieving that he would place the blame on her.

"Your antics in Zone 7, your stealing, your lying... All of it led to this. And now my father is dead."

"And my mother is dead," Leena said, rebutting the attack.

Fernando turned to walk past Leena, heading to his car as his driver waited.

"Where did they take them?" Leena asked him.

Fernando stopped and turned slightly toward Leena. "My dad was taken to the Bonefields; I had him picked up by our coroner. Your mom is in Zone 7."

"Why did they take my mom and not Diego?"

"They are required to take all gunshot victims to Zone 7 for autopsy," Fernando finished before stepping inside the waiting car and driving away.

Leena and Liv walked back to the jeep in confusion.

"What did he mean by gunshot victim, Liv? My mom died of kidney failure."

"Maybe it was a mistake?" Liv speculated.

"You think they mistakenly saw a gunshot wound in the body? What the hell does this mean?"

"Random gunfire," Liv tried to rationalize. "There were a lot of bullets flying that night. Maybe she took a stray bullet after she had already passed."

Leena thought that scenario could be true but didn't feel it was likely. What was more likely is that Diego lied to her. He was dishonest about what killed her. Maybe he was going to tell her but really didn't have time. The building fell moments after she entered the room. But if it was a gunshot that killed her, wouldn't there have been blood on the sheet that covered her? *Was there blood?* Leena struggled to remember. She just could not recall.

Leena took the motorbike, while Liv drove the jeep back to the base. The news of her mother's cause of death stirred an ember in her mind that grew as she drove the motorbike through town. Like a fire taking over her thinking, she grew angry yet more confused. She had to figure this out. She thought through her options, wondering what she might find out on this side of the wall. Fernando mentioned an autopsy. If they were really doing an autopsy, there must be a report. She had to get her hands on that report.

She parked the motorbike in the warehouse before Liv arrived. She headed down the elevator to the communications area. As she entered an open area filled with tables clustered in a large rectangle, she saw that radios, computers, and machines she had never seen before occupied the tables. Several soldiers with headphones on were sitting in chairs. A tall man stood behind one of them with his arms crossed.

"Excuse me," Leena said.

"Yes?"

"I'm Leena... I mean, I am Corporal Zhen. Are you in charge here?"

"Yes, corporal, I'm Master Sergeant Williams, head of communications. What can I do for you?"

"My mother was killed yesterday," she began.

"I am sorry to hear that, corporal," the master sergeant said.

"Thank you. CPU took the body, and I was told they were going to do an autopsy."

"Was she shot? That is the standard operating procedure for gunshot wounds."

"I was wondering if we have access to the autopsy report here," Leena finished.

"No, I'm afraid we don't have access to CPU files here. We have no cooperation with their offices. It's part of the public record at some point. You could get it once it becomes public, but the way the CPU works, it will be years before it's available. I am very sorry."

"Is it possible for us to get it sooner? Can we access them before they're released?" Leena pleaded.

"Yes, if it's considered mission critical, we have spies in the zone who could locate it for us. Is this a mission-critical request?"

"Yes, definitely," Leena said, curious if he would just take her word for it.

"I will need a written request from Commander Johnson. Then we should be able to get it within a few hours of it being released."

Leena hung her head, knowing that the report would not have the same level of importance to the commander that it did for her. The master sergeant read her demeanor and understood she didn't think she would get approval.

"Is this really important?" he asked in a soft tone.

"It's important to *me*. I want to know how my mother died."

"Let me see what I can do," the master sergeant said as he gave her a wink.

"Thank you," Leena exclaimed, leaving the area as quickly as she had entered before he could change his mind.

Leena returned to her bunk and took off her boots. It was good to let her feet breathe. She had slept in her boots the night before, so they needed airing out. The news of the day put her off balance. Something didn't feel right. She was not sure why. It was like waking from a dream that you know was not real, but somehow you feel that some parts stuck with you. She really did not know what to make of this. Had soldiers killed her mother to draw her out? If so, why were Diego and Jun Lee still in the room? It didn't make any sense.

She was able to rest for a while and then, as she dozed off, a soldier woke her.

"Captain Lewis needs you in the command room right away, Zhen."

"Okay, thanks," she replied, only half awake.

Leena entered the command room to find Captain Lewis, Liv, and a few other officers sitting around the table.

"Leena, are you ready for another mission?" Captain Lewis asked.

"Sure—I mean, yes, captain," Leena replied, still not quite getting the hang of the proper military responses.

"They have begun relocation today in the northern part of the zone," began the captain.

"That makes sense. We saw little to no CPU activity on our last trip."

"Yes, they have moved their entire force to the northwest part of the zone to help with evictions."

"Do you want us to stop them, captain?" Leena asked.

"No, we would need a large force to stop the evictions. I'm afraid that boat has sailed. We need you to follow their buses to find out where they are taking the refugees. Anyone left in the buildings will be forced to evacuate. The CPU has offered them rides and lodging at an encampment, but we are not sure where it is as we have not noticed the construction of any such place in the zone. We need to find out where they are taking them."

"Yes, captain," Leena responded.

"I want you to take three others under your command and follow those buses. Report back here once you are done. Do *not* engage the enemy unless they fire upon you. Is that understood?"

"Yes, captain," Leena said as she headed out of the room.

She turned to Liv to get advice on which other two to bring with them, though she already knew what she would say.

"Zoe and Julian?"

"Yes," Liv replied. "Let me see if I can spring Zoe from medical."

They planned to rendezvous at the jeep in twenty minutes. This gave them time to collect belongings, restock any ammunition they might need, and put on their best disguises. Resistance uniforms were not the best idea for clandestine operations. Leena went by medical to check on Jordan, who was up and walking around. The medics said they were likely to discharge him from their care as early as the next morning. She spent a few minutes with Jordan and, after a quick but meaningful embrace, made her way to the jeep.

This was Leena's first command, and she was nervous. Her friends Zoe and Julian held the rank of private, while Liv was a private first class, so she outranked them. She was concerned about how they would manage that information, but once they all arrived at the jeep, it was clear the bunch was still the same. Soldiers adapt.

All of them were now armed with handguns and pulse rifles. They did not intend to cause trouble but certainly had the firepower to do so. They hid the guns in the back of the jeep and headed toward the northwest part of the zone.

Liv suggested they take a different route to the area to see if they might happen upon a makeshift camp they had set up for refugees. They went west until they hit the wall and then north to the area near the rail yard where the evictions were taking place.

Their trip was uneventful, and like everywhere else, until reaching their destination, there was no CPU activity. As they approached the western side of the rail yard, they paused to get a better look. Looking across the tracks, they could see the line of CPU trucks escorting folks out of their houses. There must have been more than two hundred soldiers going house to house, kicking in doors and dragging the unwilling out onto the sidewalks. Those who were ready to move with suitcases in hand were treated better.

From the jeep, their view was blocked by some of the old railcars. They decided to take to higher ground, finding a nearby tower in the rail yard and climbing it to get a better view. Atop the tower, it was easy to see what was happening in front of those homes. Soldiers were taking belongings and throwing them haphazardly into a truck while residents were being led onto waiting buses. These were prison buses. Leena was familiar with them.

They went house to house, either escorting folks to the buses or dragging them out by their hair. Every ten minutes, a gunshot would ring out, followed by screaming, and the CPU would dump a body on the sidewalk. The residents were unprepared for this assault. Those who were asked to move either did so or faced this firing squad of thugs.

"There are the buses," Liv pointed out. "Let's get ready to go. I think one is full."

They all climbed back down the tower and piled into the jeep. They turned around and headed south so they could find their way behind the bus once it got underway. Pulling behind an old train car, they waited patiently for the bus to begin its journey. Within minutes, it was on the move. The jeep fell in behind the target and followed it through the city streets. Eventually, the bus driver turned onto the highway, heading south.

"They must be bringing their luggage later," Zoe chimed in, "because the truck carrying all of their stuff is not following."

That seemed strange, but the CPU was not known to have much empathy for the Miniyar, so keeping track of luggage was not high on their list of concerns.

There were probably close to eighty people on the bus, including children. Liv was driving the jeep and kept her distance. She did not want to tip them off that they had a tail. They expected the bus to turn at any moment to a makeshift camp in the south part of the zone, but it didn't, so they kept following it through the zone.

"If they keep going, they will enter the southern gate," Leena said.

"Why would they do that? Is the camp outside the walls?" Zoe wondered.

"Just keep following," Leena said. "We will see where they go."

The bus went through the southern gate and kept going. There were no cars between their jeep and the bus any longer, so it was harder to keep out of sight. Liv hung back a little, but even at that distance, they could tell there was unrest among the passengers. None of them would have taken the ride if they knew their destination was outside the city walls. They feared what awaited them in the barren lands of the Tullian.

The bus drove about ten miles south of the gate before turning off onto a side road. Within another few miles, it crested a hill, and the team in the jeep could see a camp in the distance that was most likely the destination. Liv pulled to the side of the road to let the bus reach its destination, so they did not seem too eager. They were certain to draw CPU attention if they stayed on the heels of the bus. The bus made its way to the camp and stopped at the outer fence.

"Liv, pull over there," Leena said, pointing to a small patch of dirt off the road.

Liv pulled the jeep over and stopped. They debated which way they should go, though none of the options provided the cover they needed. Then Leena spotted a hill on the rear side of the camp and drove around to that side, where they could approach it on foot. This would also give them higher ground and allow them to look down on the camp, improving visibility.

It took more than ten minutes to drive the jeep through the field as Liv needed to stay far enough away not to be noticed, but they also needed to avoid the tree line. Once on the opposite side of the camp, they took off on foot, making their way up the hill.

Positioned on top of the hill, they all lay on their bellies to shield their silhouette from any eyes that might be watching from below, looking up at the hill. Leena grabbed a set of old binoculars from her bag so she could get a clear view and began scanning the camp.

The camp was full of barracks made of green canvas and surrounded by a chain-link fence. On each corner of the fence was a tall guard tower with a well-armed sentry. At the back of the camp was an enormous pile of dirt next to a giant hole. Excavators nearby were responsible for the big hole. The dirt from the hole was bright red and fresh. There didn't seem to be any activity in the camp, so she assumed this must be the first bus to arrive.

"This doesn't look like a camp," Leena said, "it looks more like a prison."

They watched as the bus made its way through the gate. It stopped in the center of the camp. As the residents started disembarking, CPU soldiers began appearing from the barracks' tents. Several made their way to the residents and directed them in single file to the back of the camp. They had set up a table at the end of the hole, and Leena saw several CPU soldiers there ready to check them into their new homes.

The line made its way to the table, and they began conversing. Leena's team was clearly not close enough to hear their words but assumed it was about name, family, previous address, etc. CPU soldiers lined up next to the residents, keeping order.

Suddenly, gunshots rang out. Screaming. Blood littered the ground as all the soldiers opened fire on the residents. The victims clutched their family members and fell backward into the hole that their hosts had fashioned for them. Shot after shot rang out until the entire group of eighty people lay in the hole. Men, women, children. All dead. The tower sentries shot those who ran from the slaughter.

Liv gasped, and Julian and Zoe got up to run down the hill, but Leena restrained them.

"No, we can't. It's too late. We would just draw fire," Leena said as she released her grip on both.

"I cannot believe what we just saw. They butchered all those people. Why?" Zoe said in unbelief.

"I don't know, but we have to get out of here if we don't want to join them," Liv said.

Soldiers started the engines of the excavators and pushed dirt on top of the dead residents to fill the hole. The soldiers walked back to their barracks. Leena thought she could hear laughing. This was beyond evil. A mass execution.

The team made their way down the hill to the jeep and rejoined the asphalt just before the bus they were following made its way back out of the gates toward the highway. They knew they had to get back to base and report what they had seen before the bus had any more time to collect more residents.

"Liv, drive fast," Leena said as they turned onto the highway headed north.

All four of them exited the jeep with haste, heading for the elevator to report their findings. Once in the command center, they recognized a few officers along with Captain Lewis.

"Captain Lewis, sir," Leena said.

"At ease, soldiers," the captain said. "Did you find the camp?"

"Yes, sir, we believe so," Leena reported. "First, the eviction is barbaric. They are dragging residents out onto the street and shooting them for noncompliance. We then followed a bus full of residents about ten miles south of the southern gate. They have a camp setup, but it isn't for the refugees."

"What do you mean? If it isn't for the refugees, who is it for?" the captain demanded.

"I believe it is a CPU camp, sir," Leena said.

"They executed the residents, captain," Liv blurted out, barely able to contain herself.

The captain just stared back and forth at both. "Executed them?"

"Yes sir," Leena said. "Liv is right. They executed about eighty, including children, and buried them in the back of their camp. And then went to get more."

The captain turned his attention to his aide. "Sergeant, locate Commander Johnson."

"Yes, captain," responded the soldier, who then ran out the door.

"Thank you for bringing this to our attention, corporal. You and your team did a great job."

"What's next, captain?" Leena asked. "We are going to attack the camp, right? We must do something; we don't have time to wait."

"Corporal, we will take it from here. Once we decide what action we need to take, we will let you know if we need you. You are dismissed," the captain said with finality.

Leena and the other three headed toward the mess hall to regroup over lunch, though none of them felt like eating after what they had just seen. They walked speechless toward the small hall and took seats together, none of them going through the line for a tray.

Jordan made it to the table shortly after they had sat down.

"Look everyone, I'm free!"

"How are you feeling, Jordan?" Leena asked.

"I'm good. Still a little sore in places, but I think I'll survive. What are you guys up to today?"

The team filled in Jordan on what they had seen, even though they knew he was not officially part of the Resistance, and it was policy not to share information about missions with civilians.

"This sounds horrific. What benefit would the CPU get from executing Miniyar?" Jordan reasoned.

"They did not need to do that for the land," Liv said, "They already had it."

"It can't be just the cost of housing them. That seems trivial," Julian chimed in.

"It has to be something else," Zoe added.

Leena thought intently, believing that she was missing something big. Then she lit up.

"Jordan, what was Fernando saying on the phone when we went to his house?" Leena asked while the rest of them looked at her, wondering why she was ever at the zone advocate's house.

Seeing their faces, she realized that not everyone knew the connection. "Yes, I know the zone advocate. He is a friend of the family. Can we move on?"

"Project Darwin," Jordan said. "He called it Project Darwin. Do you think that this is what Project Darwin is?"

"Anyone know what Darwin is? What it might mean?" Leena asked the group.

"I had an elementary school teacher named Darwin," Zoe said, realizing quickly that the information was not helpful.

"Isn't there a Darwin High School? Is it something about the school?" Liv wondered.

"Charles Darwin," Leena said.

"Who is that?" Julian asked.

"Charles Darwin is the father of the theory of evolution. He founded the evolutionary sciences. According to his theory, there is a natural selection or survival of the fittest among people. It says that a species that evolves and adapts to its environment is the one that will survive and thrive. I remember it from science class."

Liv gave Leena a smirk, as if recognizing that being an excellent student finally paid off for her.

"What does that have to do with the shooting of Miniyar?" Julian said.

"It's a code word, not something literal. Maybe the Aberjay see us as a *less fit* species," Leena explained.

"What happens to this 'less fit' species in his theory?" Julian continued.

"They die," Liv said, bringing the table to silence.

The lunch conversation rattled everyone. It seemed the Aberjay were not content with their fine neighborhoods and privileged position. They intended to eliminate the Miniyar from their view as well. Although conjecture, the thought of this genocide brought a sense of dread to all of them, fearing they were too small and ill-equipped to overcome their adversary.

Leena walked back to her bunk and changed back into her green fatigues. She pinned her corporal bars on her shirt as she saw the others wearing them and put her bomber jacket back on to replace the other clothes that felt so alien. As she sat on her bed to contemplate what was next, a courier arrived.

"Corporal Zhen?" she asked.

"Yes, I am Corporal Zhen," Leena said, still uncomfortable with the way it sounded.

"Sign here," the courier said as she pointed to a line on a clipboard.

She handed Leena an envelope that she opened, expecting to find orders. For a moment, she did not know what she was reading. The single sheet was full of words and phrases she had never heard before. It was the autopsy report. She read the entire document a couple of times but still could not make sense of it. She took the report and headed to the medical area.

Locating the nearest nurse, she grabbed him.

"Excuse me, can you read this and tell me what it means?" Leena asked.

The nurse scanned the report, flipped it over, and read the other side.

"It's an autopsy report."

"Yes, I know. I need to know what it means," Leena pleaded.

"Can you be more specific?" the nurse responded.

"How did my mother die?"

Scanning the document once again, the nurse looked up at her and said, "Gunshot wound."

"Does it say anything else about the weapon used? Was it a rifle?" Leena said, now begging.

"Well, that is strange."

"What?" Leena said, bursting out of her skin for a resolution to this conversation.

"The bullet used isn't even made anymore. It's an antique."

"How is that possible?" Leena responded.

"She was killed with a .380-caliber bullet. Don't make 'em anymore."

The nurse handed the paper back to Leena and walked away, just before she fell on the floor.

She knew now how her mother died and who had killed her.

Chapter 14

RETRIBUTION

Activity on the base had increased considerably since Leena entered the medical area. As she walked back through, the troops were preparing for an assault. She went back to her bunk to retrieve her rifle, her backpack, and her pilot cap, which she still believed was lucky. She plopped it on her head and tucked her dark hair up under the flaps that hung down. She headed for the command center to get her orders.

Leena entered the command center, which was filled with people. She found Captain Lewis, her commanding officer, and asked for her next orders. Upon receiving them, she left to locate the other members of her team.

Assembled in the warehouse above, she stood at attention, waiting to be dismissed to the field. By her side were Zoe and Julian, and Liv was on the other. She felt a strong sense of pride for her team and was certain in her mind that she was doing the right thing. Just a few months earlier, she had no perspective outside of her life of gardening and daily survival. Now she felt responsible for others. She didn't love the weight of the feeling but knew it was honorable. She thought her mom would be proud. She knew Diego would be her advocate if he were alive to see what she had become.

The commander entered the warehouse, which was now full of about five hundred men and women dressed for battle and armed for conflict. Resistance soldiers had moved the trucks and transport vehicles outside the warehouse to make room for the regiment. They were certainly ragtag, but Leena had yet to meet anyone who didn't have a caring heart and empathy for her people, which made her proud to stand with them.

"Listen up, troops," the commander began. "I will keep this brief because every minute we talk about it is a life we are not saving. The CPU has mobilized to move residents from the northern part of the zone to a camp in the Tullian zone. The camp is a farce, and they have been executing citizens all day. We don't know how many, but it is likely in the thousands by now. We must stop the CPU's relocation effort. We are waging an all-out war today, with only one directive: rescue our citizens and eliminate any CPU that get in the way. We are likely outnumbered and outgunned, but we have the element of surprise, and we have each other. That should be enough. We will catch a train at the southern station and fill the boxcars with soldiers. The train will head north and will not stop in the northern section, but it will slow down enough for us to get off. We will attack all at once. We are hoping this surprise attack will catch them off guard. We will immediately set up machine-gun nests to lie down cover fire while each team clears a section of the zone. There are civilians present, so watch your use of explosives and save as many as you can. Move out."

The troops began piling into trucks to take them to the train station. Leena and her troops, which included herself, her friends, and seven others, boarded a truck and began their brief journey. No one spoke a word. They just looked at each other.

They knew without words that this could be their last day alive, and despite the danger, they knew it was inevitable. Even if they chose not to go to war today, they would have to at some point. The CPU would not stop until they eliminated the Miniyar.

The trucks stopped in the train yard, about twenty miles south of the destination. The Resistance filled the cars and took their positions as the train rolled down the tracks. Leena took one last look at her team.

Liv, Zoe, and Julian had become family. Then there were Jim and Steve Sipher, twins who were not much older than Leena. Robert Shever was the communications officer equipped with a helmet that functioned as a radio to relay commands to and from the leaders. Vera Shelby was older and hardened by battle. She was probably twice their age, with scars on her arms and face. She spoke little, but it was rumored she fought the CPU with an unparalleled fury. David Cho and Victor Salmet were seasoned soldiers but didn't look the part. They were best friends. Both were from the same orphanage—they had grown up together. The two were recruited into the Resistance on their eighteenth birthdays. Last was Tina Redmont. She was crass, cursed regularly, and had a temper as flaming as her red hair.

Leena felt the weight of responsibility and knew they were counting on her. She wanted to throw up but knew it would not instill confidence. She wished they had time to get to know one another as she had only met most of her team recently. As she thought through it, though, she reasoned it might be better that she didn't know them very well. She may have to bury them.

She had been assigned a section of the zone that was a few streets over from where they would be dropped off. It was close to the building she grew up in, and she knew the area well. Her plan was to work south from the train yard and then over a few streets before heading north into the zone for the push. They would clear each building one at a time, leaving a few troops outside each one as they swept through to ensure runners don't get by them. This would keep their backs clear of forces while allowing them to move as far north as they could to meet up with other forces.

The training engineer hit the whistle twice, which was the signal to get ready to jump. The train had slowed and, looking out the door of the train car and down the track, Leena could already see troops jumping from the moving cars. Gunshots were also getting louder and louder as she approached, so she knew it was a hot zone.

"Ready, team!" she shouted over the sound of shots fired and the ringing sound of the train rolling on the iron rails.

Two at a time, her team jumped from the cars until she was the only one. She jumped out to follow them. Her team was south of the conflict intentionally. She had to get around the battle to reach the housing blocks so they could start sweeping the houses for friendlies. Her team crossed one block and then another as she heard gunfire and explosions from a few streets up near the train depot. Fear nearly paralyzed her as she moved building to building, looking for the enemy in the stores and up on the rooftops. She had to push herself to keep going. She could not let fear get a foothold or she would be of no use.

When they reached the street she had lived on as a child, they went north. As the plan prescribed, they came to the first building that was covered in eviction posters and stationed three soldiers outside as Leena and seven others ran into the building. Most of the apartments were empty in this building. Some citizens had remained to await their fate, but Leena convinced them to leave and go south before the CPU forces arrived.

Once cleared, they moved to the next building, and so on, until they reached the sixth one. It already had buses and CPU trucks outside. She ordered her team to take defensive positions and began firing on the CPU. About thirty soldiers took positions behind their trucks.

Leena could hear some of her team wasting ammo by firing too quickly and shouted at them to conserve. She knew this battle was likely to take a while, and the CPU had vast stockpiles of ammo compared to the Resistance, who only brought what they could carry.

David Cho took a bullet in the arm, falling over and crying out in pain. As they tried to dash away from the battle to find better cover, he was shot again as a bullet ripped through the back of his head, leaving what remained of him and a pool of blood on the street. Leena felt overwhelmed and used her radio to call for a backup team.

"One six, one six, this is Delta team. We are at rally point six and are taking fire," she called out. "Requesting backup team."

"Affirmative, one six, we will get someone to your location," the radio responded.

"Save your ammo and hold your ground, Delta, we will have backup soon," she shouted to her team. She turned around and lay against the fire barrel that had become her barricade and took a drink of water from her pack. The firing had lessened for the moment but would pick up once the enemy reloaded.

Noticing the citizens had cleared the area, either by going back into the building or taking cover on the bus, Leena took a grenade from her pack and called out to her team.

"Grenade!" she cried as she pulled the pin and threw it toward the first truck, far enough away from the bus that if citizens were taking shelter there, they would be outside the blast radius. The grenade went off and gave the truck some lift, landing it on its side.

"Go go, go!" she shouted as her team moved up to use the fallen truck as their new barricade.

Firing as she ran, the team was able to take out many soldiers in their path. As they took new positions, Leena could see her backup team coming up behind them, which would allow them to push even farther. Working together, they cleared the area of CPU by eliminating many and pushing the rest farther up the street toward the north gate.

They continued to clear buildings, most of which were empty at this point. Once they reached the bus, they convinced the citizens that they were not safe and evacuated them to the south. As they reached the north end of the street, they had been fighting for hours. They had taken many losses, including four from Leena's team: David, Victor, Jim, and Steve. But the enemy fared worse.

They had saved over a hundred citizens just on her street.

The radio operator called out for Leena's team to return to the train depot, where they were taking serious fire. Leena commanded her team to move south and then make their way west to the depot. As they got close, she could see lines had been drawn. The CPU had pushed the Resistance fighters back to the rail yard. The enemy had used the existing buildings and the buses to provide cover for them as they set up machine-gun nests high in the buildings, raining fire on the Resistance fighters.

Bullet casings littered the ground, which was perforated with many holes from the explosives. These holes provided suitable cover as her team moved from one section to another, trying to get closer to the battle. The smell of burning flesh and gunpowder overpowered their nose. Smoke from grenades and burning buildings provided some cover from the CPU's superior weaponry, but based on Leena's assessment of the situation, the Resistance fighters would not last long.

Leena took a position with her team behind a barricade at the south end of the street and began hammering their machine-gun nests in the windows to slow them down. She could hear the chatter on her radio as her commanders called every team back to the area to provide support. She knew retreat was probably the next step as the CPU were preventing the Resistance forces from moving outside the rail yard. The CPU were also still getting reinforcements from the north gate, which was still under their control.

Looking down the street, Leena could see a group of CPU soldiers pushing forward toward the train station—about twenty-five soldiers in all. Leading them was Sgt. McBride. She could tell it was him by the bandage on his nose. It gleamed through the smoke and reflected the sun's fading light when it hit it just right. She knew Sgt. McBride would eliminate the team in the train station if they made it to the platform. She ordered her team to change their focus and start firing on that position. It was a long shot, so accuracy was not likely, but she figured if enough bullets were fired on that area, a few were likely to hit their targets.

The attack of Leena's team drew their focus, and McBride's team seemed to split. About ten soldiers headed in their direction

318   JOSEPH MICHAEL LAMB

and took cover behind a CPU truck that was on its side. Leena called for explosives, and the team began pelting that truck with grenades. The distance proved too far, however, and none of them exploded close enough to do any damage.

Julian took fire and fell to the ground next to Leena. She looked down to see his skull shattered by a bullet, eyes wide open. She heard Liv scream and fall on the body. Julian's demise at close range affected Leena, but she knew she had to keep her mind in the fight. She stopped to reload her rifle and noted her ammunition was running low. She grabbed a magazine from Julian's vest and set it on the ground next to her.

Half of McBride's team was almost on the platform, which would be certain death for the Resistance fighters stuck there. Leena believed that not only was Captain Lewis in that building but also Commander Johnson and about fifty others. She wanted to save them but knew the enemy would cut her down with their machine guns if she even tried to run in that direction. Hope faded as she watched the scene unfold. This was certainly not ending as she had hoped. Her mind thought to retreat. Her commanding officers had not called for a retreat yet, but she was not ending her life and the lives of her team if she didn't have to do so. Her plan was to order a retreat and escape as soon as the CPU took the train station. There was no going back from there.

She looked south down the street, wondering how far they would get if they just took off. Just then, in the distance, she saw movement. Vehicles—lots of them. They somehow looked familiar. At least twenty jeeps with mounted machine guns were approaching their location. If these were CPU trucks, her team would certainly meet their demise.

Her mind played images of her life and what had brought her to this place. She felt sad, resigned to dying, and upset that she could not do more to save her group. She looked at her team, who had not seen the impending doom coming, and felt sorry for them. Sorry that they were stuck with a leader who let them down. She knew that in seconds, bullets would engulf them, ending their lives. There was nowhere to escape this enemy approaching from the south.

Then she recognized the jeep. It was Tullian. This wasn't the CPU; it was Jesse and a group of Tullian combatants. Jesse was in the first jeep with a machine gun in hand. He drove past without acknowledgment and spun to face the machine-gun nest positions. Several more jeeps followed him and laid down so much fire on those nests that the structure of the building gave up, causing the ceiling to collapse and come down on the CPU encampment.

Jeep after jeep drove past, firing on all positions and McBride's team, forcing them to fall back to the north. Leena lost sight of McBride as the Tullian pushed the CPU back toward the gate. The saviors eliminated the threat, and Resistance fighters surfaced from the train depot. They were not sure what to make of this army, and some of them showed some aggression, pointing their weapons at the apparent mercenaries.

Leena grabbed the radio helmet from Robert. "These Tullian are friends. They are not a threat to the Resistance. Stand down."

After circling several times, the Tullian troops drove behind some empty train cars and took positions they could defend. The firing from the machine-gun nests had stopped, but there were still CPU soldiers scattered about, attempting to defend themselves as they fell back toward the gate. Several of the jeeps pursued the enemy and began taking positions to eliminate the occupation of the north gate.

Leena emerged from her hiding space and leaned down to pick up a CPU fire shield just in case there were still snipers or other soldiers firing on the courtyard she was crossing. She walked slowly toward Jesse and some of his band of fighters while strategically keeping the shield on her right side to fend off any unwanted shots. Leena took two shots to the shield from the retreating CPU before Jesse targeted them with his weapon and ended their advance.

The battle was not over, but this area was becoming more secure as the CPU soldiers retreated. Jesse recognized Leena as she walked toward him, and his eyes grew wide. He jumped down out of the jeep and gave her a big hug.

"You have no idea how good it is to see you," said Leena.

"Yes, we were toast," Liv added.

"I am happy to be your rescuer today," Jesse responded in his jovial fashion.

"How did you know, Jesse?" Liv questioned.

"Zoe called us on the two-way radio this morning and told us you might need some extra hands. We were happy to lend a hand to our favorite city dwellers."

A quick look at Zoe, who shrugged her shoulders, indicated she was glad she did. Several patted her on the back or gave her hugs to show their appreciation.

Jesse looked around and continued sarcastically, "What a mess this place is—how do y'all live here?"

Several laughed as the captain and some of his troops made their way over to congratulate Jesse and his team on their victory. The captain dispatched several Resistance fighters into the building to secure the machine-gun nests while officers tended to the wounded and regrouped for any further combat that might be required.

"Leena Zhen!" It was a familiar voice.

"Leena Zhen, where are you?" she heard the voice demand in a harsh tone.

It was Sgt. McBride. He was calling to her from the train station platform. She looked behind the crowd of people and could see him with a pistol in his right hand, his left arm fixed around Commander Johnson's neck. The commander was taller than McBride, so he pulled him sideways, allowing him to be used as a human shield.

More than fifty soldiers in the area lifted their weapons immediately to threaten the sergeant, but he immediately responded: "Drop your weapons now, or I'll kill your leader."

The commander struggled but could not get free. McBride used the butt of the gun to beat on his chest and face each time he struggled. McBride walked down off the platform and then worked his way close to Leena, step by step. He dragged the commander around like a doll.

Leena moved toward McBride and waved others to get back. She faced him and gave an order to the Resistance fighters that she knew, based on her rank, they wouldn't have to obey.

"Drop your guns," Leena commanded as she dropped her rifle on the ground.

Still holding the shield, she confronted McBride.

"Let him go, McBride—you know it isn't him you want," Leena said with confidence.

The sergeant laughed in response. "Such a smart girl. You have a debt to pay, Leena Zhen. I am here to collect."

322   JOSEPH MICHAEL LAMB

Leena considered the possibilities and knew she could not put any more lives in danger. She could see that most of her team were without a weapon and not within proximity to take McBride. The Resistance outnumbered the CPU soldiers that were present, but she knew he could pull that trigger and end the commander in a microsecond.

"What do you want, McBride?" Leena asked him, attempting to negotiate.

"I want you to pay for your sins, Leena. You are guilty of crimes against the state. And I am going to render judgment right here and now."

"Let him go and I will go with you. You can do what you want to me, but let the commander go," Leena said, now begging.

"That is not how this works," McBride responded. "First, I am going to kill you because you are a scourge on this society—and because you broke my nose! And then I am going to kill your commander and all of your other friends lying about. And if you have any family left, I am going to hunt them down and kill them as well."

Leena grasped the shield tightly in her hand, trying to think of her next move. Her mind raced to determine what she might do with the shield in hand as it was her only tool. Then she looked down and realized she was still wearing a vest full of grenades.

"I was sorry to hear about your mother," McBride continued sarcastically.

Leena fumed. A wave of hatred washed over her, accompanied by a warmth that spread from within. Any hope of mercy was now distinguished by the sergeant's taunts.

"There is one thing you miscalculated, McBride."

"What is that, little girl?" McBride replied, clinging to the commander.

"I don't have anything else to lose," Leena said as she grabbed the grenade from her vest, pulling the pin with her mouth and, in one clean motion, threw it directly at McBride. He responded by pushing the commander away and jumping to the side while she lunged at them, falling on the commander with the shield over them to protect their lives from the blast.

Sgt. McBride, feeling he had lost control, turned to run but not before the grenade went off and tore him to pieces, splattering blood, shrapnel, and bone against the shield that Leena was holding while on the ground protecting her commander.

Smoke and gunpowder filled the air as many of the soldiers close to the blast coughed fervently. Leena pushed the shield off them and helped the commander to his feet, then walked over to retrieve the firearm she had left on the ground.

"Corporal, that was extremely dangerous and put my life and everyone's life here at risk," barked the commander. His feigned attempt at anger, however, turned to a smile as he continued. "Thank you," he finished, and gave her a wink.

Liv stood near Leena, picking pieces of Sgt. McBride off her uniform.

"Is that bone? Gross," she said as she flicked bloodstained bones and flesh on the ground.

"Let's find the wounded and get them some help, people," the captain called out.

Liv limped over to Leena, revealing an injury to one of her legs. She put her arm around her and slowly walked back with her to where their team was regrouping.

"It's over," Liv said as they looked toward the north gate where CPU soldiers had fallen back into their zone.

The wind blew fiercely, whirling dirt and gravel about while also stoking the fires that were burning, causing them to grow bigger.

"It's not over," Leena said as she looked back at the wall in the distance. "It's only the beginning."

The remaining soldiers did a sweep of the area for CPU and civilians before night descended. The smoke cleared as they called in the Resistance teams to clear the dead. The soldiers would take the bodies back to a facility that would cremate the remains and notify the next of kin. Funerals were uncommon in Zone 6 as too many people died on any given day. Poverty, famine, war—all were present in the lives of the Miniyar, and most of them could not afford the cost of a funeral anyway. Instead, communities had mass memorials to remember their dead.

Leena, Liv, and Zoe said their last goodbyes to their friend Julian and helped workers load his remains into a truck. The loss of life broke the team. Despite Leena and Julian only being acquainted for a short time, she felt the sadness of his departure profoundly and was aware that Liv and Zoe had been his friends for a long time.

The sun had set, but burning buildings and vehicles still cast a bright light on the streets. Leena walked farther looking for the dead and helped some others clear buildings. She felt good about the outcome of the battle. She knew she had saved lives, preventing more buses from reaching the camp south of the city. But she also had powerful emotions of guilt, pain, and loss knowing that these people would never return to their homes. The damage caused by war rendered many of the buildings uninhabitable, and although the battle may have ended in their favor, the war was far from over. CPU soldiers would regroup and come back to continue what they had started.

She looked over to see bulldozers already on site. She knew that once they cleared the area—maybe not tomorrow, and maybe not the next day, but someday soon—they would return and flatten all of these homes. They would not give up easily.

Her body hurt. Between shrapnel, scrapes, and the emotions of loss, she was spent. She knew she needed sleep but did not want to leave the field of battle until medics cared for every wound and honorably took every comrade off the streets. She didn't feel she should sleep until the work was done. Once teams cleared her street, she walked with Liv to the train depot, where the officers assembled an interim command office.

"Captain Lewis," Leena said to her commanding officer, "what about the camp?"

"We already have teams headed south to strike before dawn tomorrow, corporal. They will pay for their treachery."

"Good," Leena responded. "Permission to take my remaining team back to base, captain?"

"Yes, corporal. Tell them they did a great job today. I am sorry for their losses, but what they did today made an impact."

"I will, captain," Leena said as she turned and headed toward the transport vehicle.

"I'm beat. Let's hit the racks. I want to sleep for a week," Liv said as she climbed into the back of the truck.

"I can't rest yet. I have one more thing I need to do," Leena replied.

Sleep eluded Leena that night. The few times she did fall asleep ended in nightmares. She had never been one to dream, but these came in a flood. Blood, smoke, screaming. The death of loved ones. Strangers. Her slumber forced the demons to their surface.

As she lay awake for the third time trying to find some sleep, she thought about her mom, Diego, and all the people of her building who paid the ultimate price for the Aberjay avarice. She knew she would never be the same. The fury she felt earlier had not subsided, and she suspected it never would. Revenge does not heal hearts.

Thinking back to just a few months earlier, Leena did not understand the fight with the Aberjay. Her battle was over her mother's health. But now the war had become clearer. It wasn't rich versus poor. Or even Aberjay versus Miniyar. It was right versus wrong.

Every person should have the right to life, liberty, and the pursuit of happiness, as the United States had declared for centuries. Leena sat up in her bed. It was half past three a.m., and all she could hear in the bunkhouse was the sound of fans and the snoring of tired soldiers. She put on her boots and walked to the command center. She stepped inside the empty room and turned on a small light. Walking to the end of the room was a framed document that hung inconspicuously above a buffet table. It was *The Declaration of Independence.*

She had studied American history in school and had certainly read the document several times. She once had to do a report on its significance. She learned about the Revolutionary War and independence from Britain, but it had no real meaning to her. Now she read these words, and they felt life-giving:

> "We hold these truths to be self-evident, that all men are created equal, that they are endowed by their Creator with certain unalienable Rights, that among these are Life, Liberty and the pursuit of Happiness.—That to secure these rights, Governments are instituted among Men, deriving their just powers from the consent of the governed,— That whenever any Form of Government becomes destructive of these ends, it is the Right of the People to alter or to abolish it, and to institute new Government, laying its foundation on such principles and organizing its powers in such form, as to them shall seem most likely to effect their Safety and Happiness."

Leena let the words wash over her. She had always seen this document as the beginning of a nation, but the idea of throwing off an old nation or overthrowing a government was an insight that she had missed. For something new to begin, there had to be the dissolution of the old. The Americans abolished the British government because it destroyed their right to liberty.

This was the war she had been fighting all along. The Resistance was fighting to abolish a government that trampled on the rights of its people to restore the consent of the governed and to put right what had gone so terribly wrong. While there were still elections, the gerrymandering of districts and the dismantling of voting laws by the Aberjay had guaranteed victorious outcomes for the last century.

She walked back to her bunk slowly, processing what she had read and her new insight into American history, and how that was being played out in her life. She reasoned that if the Resistance could be successful, maybe it would give the nation another chance. A chance to get it right. A chance to give birth to something new—something that would provide liberty and justice for everyone equally.

Leena tried to sleep, but her thoughts and dreams kept slumber from her grasp. Each time she would doze off, the nightmares would return. She finally gave up at about five a.m. and got cleaned up. She had a new mission today. She had to visit the zone advocate.

Chapter 15

CLOSURE

Liv approached Leena's bunk as she was cleaning her firearm. Leena had made her bed, folded her clothes neatly, and laid out her belongings on the bed. Arranged on the floor were her weapons—escrima, rifle, knife, and several magazines of ammunition—that were ready to pack. Leena had a 9mm firearm in pieces in her hand, and she was cleaning the barrel with the precision of a soldier twice her age.

"Hey, where did you learn to do that?" Liv asked.

"I've picked up a few things watching all these soldiers," Leena responded.

"You look prepared for battle," Liv said, commenting on Leena's full fatigues, cap, jacket, belt, knife, and firearms.

"I may go to war."

"You need backup?" Liv asked.

"If you want, but it isn't really sanctioned," Leena said.

"That sounds about right. Do you want to give me a hint?"

"We are going to see the zone advocate today."

"Fernando Martinez? Why would you want to see him?" Liv said.

"I am going to kill him," Leena replied as she finished packing her things and hastened toward the door.

"Wait, wait, wait," Liv stopped her. "I know you and I like to do things off the reservation, but are you sure about this?"

"I'm sure," Leena said resolutely.

"Don't you want to think about this a little? You could be shot for that, and I don't mean by the CPU, I mean by Resistance forces. They don't take kindly to cold-blooded murder for no reason."

"I have a reason."

"What is that?" Liv asked, desperately trying to find a ribbon of logic to stop her friend from continuing with her plan.

"He killed my mother," Leena said before entering the elevator, followed closely by Liv.

"Sounds like a good enough reason. I'm in," Liv said as the elevator delivered them to the ground floor.

Leena and Liv were silent as they drove north. They could see the smoke from the previous day of battle in the distance, still smoldering. The CPU were still nowhere to be seen in the zone. Maybe they figured they had taken enough losses. Maybe they were regrouping beyond the wall and planning to come in with a mighty force. There was no way to know how they would respond to such a defeat.

She thought about the Bonefields—filled with the dead. The result of the last great uprising. She wondered if they were loading their jets to drop munitions of fire on them as they had done before. Leena had heard stories of the last conflict but didn't have a grasp of the big picture. She was not sure exactly how it started or how it ended, only that the Resistance took the biggest losses and the citizens of Zone 6 lost more than a third of their number in the bombs that pummeled the city.

Leena didn't really want to kill Fernando. She just couldn't wrap her head around how his bullet ended up in her mother's chest. She was already dying. Why would you shoot a dying woman? Maybe there was a scuffle, and the bullet was meant for someone else. Anything was possible, but the most likely answer was probably closer to the truth. But what was the simplest explanation? That there was another shooter with an antique firearm loaded with the same caliber bullets that Fernando showed off just days before?

Although she had just told Liv that she was going to kill him, secretly all she really wanted was the truth. She had to find out what really happened so she could get closure on her mother's death. As it played out, her mother would have died in the building's collapse, so the gunshot was not the only scenario that would have ended her life. If the building or the bullet didn't kill her, the disease would have killed her. There was no guarantee that the medicine she found would have worked. Either way, Leena felt the person who shot her killed her. It didn't matter what would have happened next. The intent to kill was still there.

Leena reminisced about her mother as they drove. Her mother pushing her on a swing, making dinner, teaching her to garden. Her mother laughing. The way she smirked at her daughter when she told a joke that wasn't that funny. The way she washed Leena's hair when she was too tired or sick. The way she would meet Leena outside the school to walk her home, even when she knew it embarrassed her. Mei Zhen was good and didn't deserve what happened to her. Anyone responsible for her death should be made to pay for their crime.

Liv stopped the jeep in front of the tree that had served as the entrance to Fernando's residence for Leena and Jordan. Both checked their weapons and gear to ensure they were prepared for any resistance.

"There were no guards present the last time we were here except for the old guy at the gate out front," Leena said.

"I am with you, Leena, but don't do anything stupid. I have grown quite fond of you," Liv said with a sincerity that Leena knew was a struggle for her.

Assisted by a boost from Liv, Leena launched up toward the tree and grabbed the branch. She swung her body up and, lying on her stomach, reached down to provide support for Liv. Liv jumped to catch her hand and, with the other hand, grabbed the branch after Leena pulled her up to it. Both straddled the tree and then inched their way toward the base.

As they arrived at the trunk and reached around to grab the other branch that would provide access to the yard, shots rang out, five in a row, and ate sizeable pieces out of the tree. They immediately reversed their movements to get back across the entry branch.

"Jump down," Liv said as she haphazardly dropped from the tree and back onto the sidewalk, Leena falling on the pavement just inches away.

"I think they have more guards, Liv," Leena said wryly.

"You think?" Liv responded, trying to be upbeat despite being shot at.

"Let's just walk through the front door. You got grenades?" Leena asked.

"Yes, I have five."

Leena started down the sidewalk with two grenades in hand. As she rounded the corner, the gate came into view. A guard stood outside of it looking bewildered, confused by the gunfire. Leena threw the first grenade at the guard gate, which sailed over the puzzled guard and landed inside the small sentry's station house. She threw the next one at the closed iron gate.

The first one exploded, lifting the gatehouse into the air in pieces and raining wood and paint chips down on the street. Liv and Leena took cover as the second one exploded, knocking half the gate off its hinge. Slowly, the gate fell to the ground, and through the smoke and gunpowder, Leena could see a path through.

Leena used her escrima to disable the old sentry, who went down without a fight. Both grabbed their rifles as CPU soldiers began running toward the gate. There was nowhere to take cover, so they pressed through what remained of the gate. Each bent down on one knee, carefully targeting the six guards running toward them. One by one, they eliminated the soldiers and then sauntered up the driveway.

"Look at the grass, Liv," Leena commented. "Isn't it nice?"

Liv looked back at her as if she had lost her mind and then hypothesized that she was using humor as a defense mechanism.

"Yeah, it's great. Can we stay focused here?" Liv replied.

Two more soldiers appeared near the front of the house, and Leena and Liv dropped to the ground. The angle was such that the soldiers had a hard time getting a shot as the two young women lay just below the horizon of the yard, but that didn't keep them from trying. They fired over their heads repeatedly while Liv took each one out with carefully calibrated shots with her rifle. They waited to see who else might charge out of the house before getting to their feet and continuing toward it.

Leena noticed the car in the driveway, indicating it was likely that the zone advocate was inside. She looked carefully for the driver to ensure she did not take an innocent life before tossing a grenade under the car. The explosion turned the car over and threw fire and car parts against the side of the house. The pile of metal, the yard, and the side of the house were now smoldering from the blast.

She knew that Fernando might not voluntarily give up information, so she felt that the intimidation of explosions shaking the home in which he was hiding, as well as the havoc of destruction she was inflicting on the property, would soften him up by the time she arrived to begin a line of questioning.

Weapons drawn, they moved closer to the fountain as two shots rang out from the front door. Carefully, the two took cover behind a plaster wall while Liv pulled a grenade from her vest, pulled the pin, and lobbed it through the front door. Fire erupted from the doorway and sent white paint chips flying. They swiftly entered the front door, firing on the three soldiers who were down as they struggled to regain control of their weapons.

Leena looked around the house and figured the most likely room where Fernando would be was his office, where they had conversations in the past. She also knew he would be armed, so she took a deep breath and gathered her courage before walking through the home to the office.

As she approached the closed office door, she called out to her prey: "Fernando Martinez, do I have your attention?"

She gave a wink to Liv, who was on the other side of the doorway and used her rifle to put two holes in the doorknob, freeing it from its lock. With a kick, the door swung open. Slowly, they both leaned into the doorway to peer in. They expected gunfire, so they were extremely cautious.

As expected, Fernando was standing behind his desk, holding his antique Walther PPK.

"Don't come in here," he shouted. "I have a gun."

"Yes, that is why I am here," Leena said. "We need to have a conversation."

A shot rang out, the bullet coming to rest in the wall across from the doorway.

"I would advise you not to shoot at us again, Fernando," Leena said calmly.

"Why are you attacking my home like this, Leena?" Fernando demanded. He was very agitated. "What have I done to deserve this?"

"I think you know, but if you drop the gun, we can talk about it," Leena replied. "I will give you ten seconds to drop that gun."

"What are you going to do?" Fernando replied.

"Ten," Leena began.

"I haven't done anything."

"Nine."

"Why are you doing this?"

"Eight."

"You will pay for this," Fernando shouted as he shook uncontrollably.

"Seven."

"Do you know what I have done for this community?"

"Six."

"Do you know what I have done for your family?"

"Five."

"Whatever it is you think I did, you are wrong."

"Four."

"Don't come in here, I beg you."

"Three."

"I don't want to kill you."

"Two."

"Stop!"

"One," Leena said with finality and threw a grenade into the room.

"Ahhhhh!" Fernando screamed as he dropped the gun and ran toward the door.

Leena hit him in the stomach with her rifle as he crossed the threshold of the doorway, sending him first into the wall and then to the floor. Liv took cover, expecting a blast, and Leena stepped directly into the room and straddled the zone advocate. Placing her rifle on her shoulder, she grabbed him with both hands and yelled, "Get up!"

She pushed him against the wall and, using some paracord she had in her pocket, tied his hands behind his back. Liv slowly took to her feet, looking at Leena in confusion because the grenade did not go off.

"I didn't pull the pin," Leena said with a smirk.

"What?" Fernando screamed, angry that he had been so easily fooled.

"Outstanding," Liv said.

Liv took point and walked out to the main living area. She kicked the back door open and then led the way onto the pool deck. Leena took her prisoner out near the pool and asked Liv to hold him. She grabbed a patio chair from the portico and dragged it over to the pool.

"What are you going to do, Leena?" Fernando asked again. "What is the meaning of this?"

Leena set the chair down at the edge of the pool, removed the paracord from her prisoner's wrists, and sat him down in the chair. Using several zip ties, she bound his arms and legs to the chair. Sweat poured from the zone advocate's head as his gaze darted between his two captors while continuing to plead for mercy. His suit, dress pants, and a blue button-up shirt and tie were soaked in perspiration.

Tying together the paracord and his tie, which she had removed from his neck, Leena tied one end to a light post nearby and the other to the chair as she leaned it back toward the pool. The tie was connected in a bowtie knot, so pulling on either end would undo the tension and jettison Fernando into the pool, causing him to drown. She placed a couple of patio blocks under the front legs of the chair to ensure he could not lean forward. Leena leaned in, putting her mouth next to his ear, and whispered.

"Try not to lean back."

Leaving him in this precarious position, Liv sat down on a lounge chair and began picking dirt and debris out of her nails with her knife, feigning complacency toward this violent affair. Leena slowly walked to the pool's edge, trying to stay calm while also driving up the suspense for Fernando to raise his stress level even more.

The zone advocate was unrelenting in his pleas for mercy, so Leena let him talk.

"It isn't my fault; I am only a servant. I cannot make decisions in this whole thing. I don't benefit at all. Why are you doing this? I will talk, I will tell you anything you want to know, just untie me. You have to listen to reason Leena, I am innocent. I lost my dad. Don't you remember that? I lost my dad in this whole mess. Let me go Leena!"

He continued for a bit until he was sweating profusely, drooling like a wild animal, and his face was as blood-red as a summer apple.

Leena took a chair and slowly dragged it across the pool deck, making a loud scraping sound. Fernando began to cry and sniffle, not knowing his fate. Liv looked around for guards to ensure they were alone. Leena took a seat in the chair right in front of her captive.

"Fernando, I am going to ask some questions, and you are going to answer them," Leena said slowly. "Let's start with why you shot my mother."

Fernando's eyes grew as big as saucers as he denied he had anything to do with her death. Leena let him finish his rant and then repeated the question.

"Why did you shoot my mother?"

"I didn't, I wouldn't," Fernando responded.

Leena took her rifle and set it down on the ground. She walked to Fernando's chair and pulled out her 9mm handgun, pointing it at Fernando's right knee.

"It is important that you understand how serious I am about this as I ask you once again: Why did you shoot my mother?"

Leena did not get an immediate response, so she placed her finger on the trigger to fire the weapon.

"Okay, okay, I will tell you, please don't," he said as Leena paused.

"I went there to check on your mom because I knew they were coming to evict her soon," Fernando began. "Your mom was awake and began saying strange things, things that didn't make any sense. She was delirious. My father tried to calm her."

"What things?" Leena demanded.

"Something about your family. She was ashamed. She wanted to end things. She knew she was dying. My dad wanted it to stop. She had been in pain for so long. We had to let her go. She begged us to let her go." Fernando trailed off, now sobbing.

Leena stepped away from Fernando, trying to think through what he told her. But something didn't add up. It didn't seem to fit the narrative. She knew Fernando was not really a man of mercy. If her mom really begged to die, she would have asked Diego to do it.

Leena walked back to the chair of death and fired a bullet into his knee.

Fernando cried out in pain, screaming.

"I told you the truth! I told you the truth!"

"No, you didn't. I will ask you again, and this time I will cut this rope and send you to your death if you don't answer me correctly. Why did you shoot my mom?"

Blood poured from the wound in his knee as he cried out in pain. The chair began inching toward the water as his movements struggling against the ties causing it to shimmy. His blood dripped from his knee to the chair and like food coloring, began staining the pool with red.

After he composed himself, he became resolute. "It's not my fault. The truth is... Project Darwin is the reason. It's not my fault."

Leena's eyes grew wide as this was not in her line of questioning. *What did Project Darwin have to do with her mother?* She grabbed the knife from her holster and placed it against the paracord as Fernando put up his hands in surrender.

"What is Project Darwin!" Leena shouted.

"Project Darwin is a campaign instituted by the government to eliminate all Chinese citizens from the zones. They believe the Chinese are planning another offensive. They ordered the zone authorities to eliminate all Chinese citizens and the families of Chinese citizens by any means necessary. The eviction notices are cover for Project Darwin." Fernando's head hung as the blood loss took a toll on his consciousness.

"Fernando, stay with me!" Leena shouted. She grabbed his belt, and after unhooking it and stabilizing the chair, pulled it from his body. She wrapped it around his leg and fastened it tightly to stop the bleeding.

"Why did you shoot her if you knew she was going to die? Fernando! Fernando, wake up!" she shouted and struck him across the face.

"She was talking crazy," Fernando said, barely coherent. "She would have told them about me."

"What about you?" Leena asked, grabbing his lapel and shaking him. "What about you?"

"She would have told them about our family," he said with little coherence or breath left in his lungs. He then passed out completely.

Liv looked toward Leena. "What did he say? Family? What did he mean by family?"

Leena turned and faced the house. Looking up at the sky, she said, "I get it now. It's been right in front of me this whole time. Why was I so blind to it?"

"Blind to what," Liv insisted.

"Fernando is my father. That is the secret he didn't want to get out. It would mean his death, or at least a prison term."

Liv and Leena left Fernando in his chair. She knew someone would come for him to revive him and treat his injury before he bled out, but if they didn't, she was okay with that as well. They walked through the house and out the front door without a word, and as they reached the fountain, Liv said, "Wait a second, I forgot something."

Leena was puzzled as Liv walked into the house and hurriedly came back out a minute later.

"What did you forget?" Leena asked.

"The pin in that grenade," Liv said as she handed her the pin and the side of the house exploded, followed by several larger explosions that caused the dwelling to burn with a violent intensity.

Miniyar authorities held the memorial service on a high school football field. They set up the stage below the goalposts. The chalk lines had faded as this school had not produced a football team in many years. The stands on both sides of the field were filled with spectators, and additional mourners occupied folding chairs that filled the entire field in front of the stage. The scene reminded Leena of her graduation ceremony.

The attendees were dressed in black. Photos of those who had lost their lives rested on three-legged easels placed side by side, encircling the entire field. Lines of family members walked past them as they wept, prayed, and paid tribute to their memory.

Flowers, mostly roses and carnations, littered the grass, honoring the loss of their loved ones.

A small orchestra on stage played somber music that kept the crowd in a mournful state. Conversations transpired in whispers, and many arms were grasped and backs patted. Families huddled together in pain, embracing one another, hoping the desperate feeling of loss might eventually pass.

Leena walked over to the wall of remembrance. Rows of blank sheets of paper allowed attendees to write the names of lost loved ones. She didn't have pictures of her family as everything she owned was now buried in rubble. This left her no choice but to write the names of those she loved on the wall.

The names were in alphabetical order. Leena found the Z section and, about ten down from the top, in her best handwriting, she wrote *Mei Li Zhen*. She wished she had better penmanship as these names were going to be transferred onto something permanent once the memorial service was over.

She cried as she thought back to handwriting lessons her mom gave her as a child. She would make her draw the letters over and over. She taught her in English and Chinese, as was the custom for young Chinese in America.

Walking toward the M section, which was already quite large, she read the names to determine if someone might have added Diego. She quickly glanced around to ensure Fernando was not nearby. She knew the state she left him in probably didn't give him good odds of survival, but if he pulled through, she didn't feel that this venue was the best place for their first meetup since their showdown weeks before. Not seeing Diego's name, she bent down to the bottom of the M names and wrote *Diego Rodriguez Martinez*.

She stood analyzing her work, thinking of Diego and what he had meant to her throughout her life. She could never remember a time when he was not there for her and her mother. Now she realized why. He was her grandfather. She was not even sure he knew it, but he probably did. As she thought about it more, it made sense that he would know. He could have lived anywhere but always chose to live in their building with them. He was around for all of her big events and never hesitated to take care of her mother, just like family. I guess he knew. But why did he never tell me?

A chime sounded from the stage, signaling that the service was about to begin. The authorities arranged these memorials quarterly because so much death had overtaken the zone. This one was quite large because of the recent battles. Leena learned shortly after the Train Depot Battle, as it came to be called, that more than 250 lost their lives that day, not including the more than one thousand residents who took their last breath in front of firing squads south of the city. Such a useless loss of life.

The crowd sat quietly as the volume of the string section rose when the orchestra played "Ave Maria", bringing many of the attendees to tears once again. A young man named Joshua Bennet then stepped to the microphone and read a poem he had composed for the occasion. Then another delivered a short homily, and then another sang a song of remembrance. This went on for at least an hour before the final speaker, Commander Johnson, took the stage.

His speech was not unlike the many talks he had given the troops before marching into battle. A little softer maybe. More respectful for the occasion, but still delivered with a force that only a man of the military can provide. He spoke of the desire for peace but followed with the idea that sometimes peace comes at a cost. He spoke of liberty but reminded the crowd that liberty is never granted without great sacrifice. His last words resonated with Leena:

> "The reward of liberty is often obtained through the toppling of nations. At times, and in every place that there is oppression of freedom, abuse of the poor, or the erosion of democracy, it is the duty of good people to stand up, throw off the chains that bind them, and demand a new world."

Leena let the words fill her with a passion for what might be next in her life. The crowd responded as one might expect and stood cheering. And after that brief burst of emotion, the crowd noise fell off, leaving only the sound of the orchestra performing a concluding march.

She walked out of the memorial with a feeling of loss. Jordan was there waiting for her. She took his hand and walked down the street toward the jeep in which she had come with her friends. As her party loaded into the jeep, she hesitated. She turned and walked toward the main street, about fifty feet from where they had parked.

As she walked out onto the main road, she looked north. In the distance, she could make out the wall that separated her home from the Aberjay. The wall that had cast a shadow over her world for as long as she could remember. The wall that was responsible for the death of her family and her friends.

"The wall must come down," she said, though no one was within earshot. It was a pledge she was making to herself. Wiping a tear from her face, she then walked back to rejoin her friends.

END OF BOOK 1

About The Author

Joseph Michael Lamb is an award-winning entrepreneur, business consultant, group facilitator, and author. He earned a B.A. and M.B.A from Southeastern University. Before beginning a career in writing, Joseph founded a technology firm in Atlanta, Georgia that he operated for nearly twenty years, selling the firm in 2018. From there, he founded a management consulting firm RedVine Operations where he provided business consulting and group facilitation services to small businesses.

Joseph writes in the science-fiction, thriller, and fantasy genre. His love of writing comes from his love for reading, which began in his early teens with the fantasy genre. While most of his writing has been technical non-fiction, including a book he co-wrote in 2000 and as well as his first full length non-fiction book in 2001. His latest work is his first fiction novel, Aberjay Rising, published in 2023 and is the first book in the three-part Aberjay series.

Joseph is married to Virginia Lamb and has three grown children: Jesse, Michael, and Emily. Keep in touch with Joseph or join the new publication notification list at www.josephmichaellamb.com

Also By

Enjoy other titles by Joseph Michael Lamb.
Be sure to visit josephmichaellamb.com for updated release dates.

Beyond the Miniyar (Scheduled for release January 2024) –
Book two in the Aberjay series, set two years after the first, Leena
must grow beyond her childish understanding of the world and
begin to navigate the politics and friction of a new government,
while contending with outside forces determined to destroy her.
Faced with the difficult choice of doing what is right for her
family or her country, she must be stronger than she has ever
been. At what point is treason justified?

Wellbeing (Scheduled for release late 2024) – A thriller that
follows John Lancaster, a stock broker that decides to change his
life and give up his career to become a writer, moving to the small
town of Fountain. John soon learns things are not what they
seem as his family begins to go through supernatural changes.
His investigation of these strange occurrences leads to a truth that
may destroy him and his family. Will he be strong enough to give
up his good fortune to save the ones he loves?

Made in the USA
Columbia, SC
01 August 2023

21121272R00209